This book is a work of fiction, whispered into my ears during the cold, dark nights of infinite exile from my native land.

ixysiin
Copyright © 2013 Eduardo Santiago
Cuban Heel Press
All rights reserved.

ISBN: 148275374X
ISBN-13: 9781482753745

For Mark Davis

and for my father

The music of the rumba fires the senses and transports you to the tropics. You feel the power of the waves, the warm wind and the whispering palms. The Rumba is the most sensual of Latin dances, but more than a dance, it is a veritable seduction as the lady attempts to dominate the man using her womanly charms, teasing, teasing and frequently withdrawing – and then teasing some more. It's no wonder they call it The Dance of Love!

Try to remain still while you listen to the Rumba – you won't succeed.

Learn To Rumba
Liner notes
RCA Victor – 78 RPM

Midnight Rumba

a novel

Eduardo Santiago

Eduardo Santiago

1

CUBA

1949

Every fall came the parade, after the carnavales and the circus had come and gone, just before the hot November rains made all the rivers overflow, flooding even the most joyous hearts and homes of eastern Cuba with despair.

They traveled in a beat-up canvas truck and a Model A that was so old and rusting it was a miracle that it ran at all. Inside the truck sat a motley and mostly disgruntled group of performers uncomfortably sharing the limited space with musical instruments, trunks filled with elaborate costumes, boxes of their personal belongings and the general sundries and detritus of an itinerant life. A collapsible plywood stage strapped to the sides of the truck with thick, fraying ropes pounded an unsteady, thumping beat in accordance with the condition of the road.

Estelita de la Cruz, the only passenger of the Model A, kept her eyes on the truck as it bounced and pounded its way from town to town. That was the whole parade, a truck followed by a car. To Estelita's constant amazement, they always drew an audience, deceived as the people were by their enthusiastic clatter and fanfare – the honking of horns, waving of arms, smiling of faces, lifting of dust off the road and the promise of something nuevo y espectacular.

As the truck and the car approached a new town, Estelita always rolled her window down and waved and smiled while the more agile passengers of the truck in front of her climbed on its roof and did their job, which was to make a spectacle of themselves. It was what she had always done, what her father, the man at the wheel of the Model A had taught her to do, "Smile pretty and wave."

They called themselves Sabrosuras, and every year they passed through to entertain, to help everyone forget a little of their lives, their hardships, the onset of bad weather and ruined crops. Just for a day. And like bad weather and ruined crops, the show was accepted with resignation.

Estelita de la Cruz was ten years old and Sabrosuras was her whole world. With age came the awareness that most of the performers were shabby, even by small town measure. The performers came and went, some joined other traveling shows, and the more confident and ambitious headed to big cities to try their luck at the luxurious casinos and theaters that reportedly existed in that faraway, exotic place called La Habana.

At the moment, Sabrosuras featured a trio of contortionists, a magician, and a short, fat woman who called herself a modern dancer but most people thought of as a clown. Her name was Aspirrina and she never, ever climbed on the roof of the car – she claimed she was too dignified but everyone knew the roof wouldn't hold her. The one exception in this meager group was the Rumba singer, Esteban de la Cruz. Estelita was as proud to be his daughter as she was of anything in her life. He was handsome and tall, funny and good-natured, and she adored him. He was the main attraction, the one with his picture on the posters, the one people came to see, the one whose gifts lifted Sabrosuras to a higher level.

"Tiene algo," she heard people in the audience exclaim. He's got something. She agreed, unlike the other performers he had something that came to light the moment he stepped on the stage and it thrilled her.

Not everybody was as enraptured by Esteban de la Cruz. Estelita heard it often enough from the ugly mouths of various people as they walked out. There were always a disgruntled few in every audience.

"A drunk," they said.

2

"Un loco."

"He thinks he's so special with his tight pants and his big...guitar."

"Chismes y envidia," her father said. Gossip and envy. And he was right. When she was smaller she had stood up to those people, even kicked one or two, bit a couple of others. But she was a big girl now. She knew to ignore the evil tongues, which were few compared to those who loved him, those who got up off their seats to dance when he shouted out to them, stretching the vowels, rolling his Rs.

"Vaaaamos, a bailar! Aqui esta la ruuumba!"

Night after night he satisfied them and they kept him smiling and bowing after the show to applause that continued long after he'd left the stage. In spite of what he did, what some people saw when he stumbled drunk around their towns at all hours, what they whispered about him behind his back, once on stage, with his silvery voice and well-worn guitar, Esteban never failed to dazzle.

Father and daughter had traveled with Sabrosuras since she was a baby, always on the go, moving from town to town. All year round she rode next to her father, following el camion, helping to set up their plywood stage in tiny towns that sprouted in the midst of sugarcane and tobacco fields. Sometimes not even towns, just clusters of bohíos, thatched-roofed huts with dirt floors and chicken coops, no running water, outhouses swarming with flies.

Estelita liked the coastal towns the best. Just before sunset, they often broke away from el camion and stopped at any of the thousand rocky beaches and coves for a swim. These were Estelita's happiest times, when she could plunge her little body into the warm, undulating sea. And she was free.

She'd swim in the clear, azure water, beneath a sky so blue it seemed painted by the angels, while her father tinkered with the engine of the car. The roads were so rough that the car was in constant need of repairs. In the water she felt safe, released into the blue, if only for a little while, borne away from the worries that tormented her on solid ground.

"Look papá, soy un delfín!" she'd shout over the gently breaking waves. I'm a dolphin.

Or she'd weave a sprig of fresh seaweed into her long, dark hair, "Look, papá, I'm a mermaid!"

Esteban always smiled and waved at her from underneath the car, his bright brown eyes reflecting the setting sun. She lived for those moments when his eyes were on her and no one else. He was her only constant as the towns changed from day to day and performers came and went, but those eyes looking at her with such sweetness, the mouth, when it curved with approval was all she ever needed.

They did not have a home, only the car and their tattered suitcases. There was no mother but they had each other. They were a family. From time to time she wondered what a mother would be like, what added comfort she might provide. She saw them everywhere, ladies with their children in all sorts of circumstances, sometimes crossing a road hand in hand, rushing them along, stopping on the sidewalk to wipe a runny nose with a handkerchief.

She saw the peasant women holding their newborns wrapped in blankets, holding them close to their bosom, or pushing toddlers in carriages. She envied those children and considered them lucky until she had taught herself to dismiss them. She comforted herself with just a look at her handsome father, letting her eyes linger along the planes of his face, the strong nose in profile, his whiskered jaw, his massive hands.

Night after night, town after town, she took her place in the audience to watch him perform in the bright, ruffle-sleeved shirts he tied with a knot at the waist. She loved the rough way he wiped the sweat from his neck with a scented handkerchief. The way his face, flush with power, broke into a big square smile, white teeth dripping with charm.

But her adoration of all that was good in him couldn't deny or conceal that there was some truth to the rumors, the ugly whispers. She had watched with mounting concern as his love for drink increased, as well as his love for gambling and for running off with a different woman at every opportunity. His luck with women was infinitely better than his luck with drinking or gambling. Estelita knew he liked all three, and combined them whenever possible. On stage he was the charming rumbero, but it was what he did after he came off the stage that frustrated her. She blamed las mujeres, the women who flocked to him to express their adoration, to offer a delicate handshake, throw their arms around him, beg him for a kiss.

There was a different one in every town. They weren't the

prettiest, these women, but they stood apart. Their hair was professionally coiffed, their makeup was brighter, their dresses were tighter than the others. The faces changed with every town, but the woman was basically the same. Every small town seemed to have one – just as every town had a shabby hotel, and every hotel room had a wooden crucifix hanging on the wall that her father took down and put away as soon as he walked in.

Estelita compared her looks to theirs and, in her estimation, she always came up short. But those women and their tight, sparkling dresses made a good match with Esteban who spent a good amount of his meager salary on himself.

"I have to keep up my image," he said.

Estelita wore the same three faded and wrinkled cotton dresses and the one pair of shoes until she grew out of them or they began to fall apart. Her hair was often dirty, rarely brushed, just a mass of brown curls pushed back from her face with a pink ribbon she'd found in a dresser drawer at one of the hotels. Her eyes, which she rarely showed, choosing instead to look at the ground, were brown, like her father's with an Asiatic slant, "Like your mother," Esteban said, a breath of sadness in his voice.

Her legs were long for a girl her age, and skinny and, as of late, so hairy that she sometimes thought she was turning into a spider and actually hoped she would so that she could join the performers. She imagined herself crawling onto the stage and spinning webs so beautiful that the audience would faint from awe.

She was used to watching Esteban preen in front of mirrors for hours, carefully shaving, trimming his mustache and sometimes just looking into his own eyes as if there was an important message in their depth.

Once he was showered and freshly shaved, he changed into one of his linen suits. He owned three: green, blue, magenta, and he wore them in regular rotation, a different suit for every night. Estelita didn't like those suits any more than she approved of his midnight prowling but said nothing. She knew that when he reached for the bottle of Baron Dandy cologne and splashed himself with it, he would be gone and she would be alone.

Sometimes her child's mind allowed itself the fantasy that he would return and one of the women would be at his side. She would be pretty and kind and she would stay. She would be her new mother and the three of them would move into a little house by the sea and she would go to school like other children and come home to the smells of cooking, to the sound of pots and pans banging in the kitchen. She would come home to open arms that she could run into and kisses and gentle words of welcome. She knew that world existed, she had seen it through windows and wide open doors, had occasionally locked eyes with a girl her own age, or a harried mother who would stop what she was doing just long enough to regard her with what Estelita would later learn was pity.

But Esteban always returned alone, and he would again the next time no matter how badly she wished and prayed for that perfect woman who would set them right.

Before he left for the night he always gave her the same instructions.

"Now lock the door and go to sleep, nena," he'd say as he planted a soft kiss on her forehead. "And don't open the door unless you smell smoke."

Estelita endured the lonely nights as best she could, but not having her father asleep next to her made her miserable.

When she was younger, just tall enough to reach his knee, just old enough to walk without falling, they'd had a different routine. After the show they would walk hand in hand through the crowd and he would always introduce her to men who stopped to shake his hand and congratulate him on his performance.

"This is my beautiful daughter, Estelita," he'd say and she'd shake the hand offered to her. The formal way she extended her little hand, palm down, fingers close together always drew gasps and chuckles.

"She's a little lady," the men sometimes said. And her father would caress her face or pat her head and say, "Papá's little princess."

She liked that, and she liked the way her father looked at her, so pleased and proud. After they had met everyone they needed to meet and he had stopped to swap stories and jokes with those he already knew they continued walking. Later they would stop at some late night diner for a bite to eat. On the way back to whatever hotel they were staying at, men who stood outside of bars, often the same ones who had called her *little lady* would offer to buy the singer a drink, which Esteban always accepted with great courtesy.

Inside it was dark and smoky and he'd lift her on the bar, setting her down among beer bottles and ashtrays, her feet dangling in the air. The men discussed topics she didn't understand and she entertained herself by watching those playing pool, cards or dominoes. She liked dominoes the best, the sounds of the tiles were familiar to her.

When she got too big to hoist up to the bar, and started asking questions, interrupting his conversations or running around and disturbing the domino players, Esteban stopped accepting those drink offers.

After eating they would walk back to the hotel, using back streets that did not have bars on them, just little homes that smelled of cooking and families.

"Why are we going this way?" she wanted to know.

Her father was thoughtful for a moment.

"To avoid temptation."

"What's that?"

"That," he said, smiling as he rumba danced around her, "is something men find hard to resist."

Whenever he danced around her, it made her laugh. She did not understand his answer but at least he wasn't answering her questions with a question, the way he usually did.

Back at the hotel, after he'd run her a bath and helped her into pajamas he let her play with his domino set until she got sleepy. She used the domino tiles to make little houses, build whole neighborhoods and make up stories about the people who lived there.

She was so little. He was her whole world and she was his whole world. She liked going to sleep with a kiss on the cheek and a smile on her face. The idea that she may not be safe all night long, or that things might change while she slept never occurred to her until that night in Cierro Gordo when, through a haze of sleep, she heard the door open and she sat up in bed as if she hadn't been sleeping at all.

"Where are you going?" she asked, searching the dark with wide-open eyes.

"To buy cigarettes," her father said. "Go back to sleep. I'll be right back."

She fought sleep until he returned. He was only gone for a few minutes.

Some nights later she heard the door again, and again he was only gone a little while. A few weeks later she woke up in the middle of the night and he wasn't there. Her throat was dry and she craved water but was afraid to get out of bed. She cried for a bit before deciding it was pointless to cry with no one watching. She forced herself to remain awake until he returned.

The sun was creeping through the shutters when she heard the doorknob turn. She kept her eyes closed and pretended to sleep. She heard him undress and get into bed and said nothing. She didn't want to upset him. In the long, dark hours while she waited for him, she had convinced herself that she'd done something bad to make him want to be away from her.

By morning she had resolved to be even more perfect for him. It wasn't long before he gave up on the pretense, came and went as he pleased. He bought her coloring books and coloring pencils, and small wind-up toys to keep her occupied. She accepted his gifts with joy and gratitude, and she never reproached him. Even at that age she knew it was not a daughter's place. If he felt that she was old enough to stay in the room alone, he must be right. But when did this begin? Did he also leave her alone when she was a baby? A toddler? How long had this been going on? She couldn't escape the sadness this line of thinking brought, the conclusion that she wasn't important to him, that all along she had been completely alone in the world and along with hot tears she began to miss her mother as she never had before.

The night of the hurricane was the only time she begged him to stay, fearing more for his safety than her own.

"It's just a little rain," he said as he changed into his magenta suit, "I'll be back before you know it."

"Lock the door after I leave and don't open it unless you smell smoke," he said as he kissed her head. "I'll just be a little while."

"But, there's a storm coming."

"What's a little wind?" he asked as he splashed on his cologne, the smell of Baron Dandy filled the room, a familiar smell, the smell of desertion.

"You're a big girl, you'll be alright for a couple of hours."

"I'm only ten," she said.

"*Only* ten," he laughed, "by the time I was ten I could drive a car."

Suddenly he became serious, sat next to her, looked her in the eyes.

"I have to see this person, just for a few minutes, then I'll be back. That storm is way out to sea, nothing to worry about, you know how people exaggerate."

She made him promise to teach her to drive and he agreed so she got under the covers, satisfied that something new was coming into her life.

She didn't see him again for three days.

Estelita de la Cruz would not remember the hurricane for what it did to the land and the people or for the howling winds that she feared would tear the hotel from its foundation and send it hurling into space. She would not remember the hurricane because it came shortly after her tenth birthday and struck with a force that she didn't think possible, or for the torrents of inky water that rushed down the street to meet the sea and flood the town.

She spent those long days watching through a crack in the wooden shutters as things floated down the street, cars, bicycles, bloated bodies, couches, dinner tables, chairs, wooden boxes and a million small objects she could not identify in the gray light. In her lifetime bigger and more destructive hurricanes would sweep through Cuba, storms of such unprecedented fury that they would be given the names of women: Flora, Hilda, Eloise. She would remember this particular hurricane because it changed the course of her life the way hurricanes were known to change the course of a river, the shape of the coastline.

She didn't expect anyone to look in on her, not Lúcido the Magician who was only a few doors down, or the triplets who were surely huddled in their room across the hall, not even Aspirrina Romagoza the dancer whose room shared a wall with hers. At the time, she kept her father's secret, an unspoken pact between them that excluded everyone else. She liked it that way, because she believed it strengthened her ties to him. No one needed to know that he left her alone when he went out, she made sure no one knew that she spent her nights by herself in hotel rooms. Not that anyone would have cared. She knew that most of the performers were like her father, unattached and unsentimental, they came and went with the seasons, had no family to speak of and if they did, they never spoke of them. They had traded domesticity for fleeting moments of glory in the dim limelight that Sabrosuras afforded them.

She would remember that it was November 11, 1949, a Thursday, when the storm hit shore and that she got into bed and pulled the covers over her head, and that when that didn't help she took her blanket and pillow and crawled under the bed. She remained under the bed imagining she was a puppy in a box safe and snug from harm. She would remember the darkness and the furious sound of the wind. Most of the time her mind was a jumble of indecision, should she get out and get help? She wondered if any of the other guests at the hotel would take her in, but she was too paralyzed with fear to risk getting out from under the bed, let alone leave the room.

The first time she wet herself she wept with quiet shame, the second time didn't matter, by then she was too exhausted and kept willing herself into a blank sleep, no thoughts, no fears, she was beyond fear.

Then all was just quiet, more than quiet, there was no sound at all. The storm had stopped as mysteriously as it had begun. She made her way to the window slowly looking for him in the dark. She saw the twisted trees lying helpless and uprooted, the wet and frightened people slogging through black mud looking for their loved ones. She felt a shuddering fear that wouldn't go away, and visions, ugly ones, much too ugly for any little girl. Whenever she closed her eyes she saw her father's nose and mouth filling with filthy water as his arms and legs flailed, the jerky movements of a drowning man only causing him to sink deeper.

She shook her head to dismiss the unpleasant thoughts and cleaned herself up, changed into a fresh dress, rinsed the soiled one, got ready for his return. She knew he would, he had to, and when he did she ran to him and he lifted her into his arms.

He held her tight. He smelled sour with booze, sweat, and smoke. But that was familiar and comoforting to her. It smelled like

10

papá.

"I was trapped on the other side of town," he said, his voice was choked and when she looked up to his eyes they were red and swollen, his whiskers, always meticulously trimmed, covered most of his face, his lips were dry.

"I was desperate to return, but there was no way possible. Did you see the rain? It was horizontal, not up and down but sideways, that's how strong those winds were. Oh, I'm such an idiot, I'm so glad you're all right."

"You're not an idiot, papá," she said stroking his face, "you didn't know it was going to be so bad."

He kissed her on the forehead and even though it was light out, they went to bed and she slept, for the first time in three days, with her arms around him.

After the hurricane, he started coming back to the hotel with her after the show and staying. She'd wake up in the middle of the night and he'd be there sleeping. This change made her happy at first. But she heard the whistles of the women, the ones who stood outside their window softly calling through the trees. Some even sent perfumed-scented notes up to their room. Estelita once believed that one of those women might make a good mother, but she had long given up that illusion. She had resolved that mothers were useless, she had gotten this far without one so they might as well continue as they were, just the two of them.

Her father became good at resisting temptation. She had figured out what the word meant. But the sight of him sitting by the window, staring at the moon, sipping a beer, smoking a cigar and absent-mindedly scratching himself was so pathetic, the time ticked by slowly, and the silence was just too uncomfortable. They were in Botones, a town they had been to many times before, a town known for its multitude of bars and clubs and particularly for its legion of beautiful women.

"Go on, I'll be fine," she finally said. "The skies are clear. I'm not scared anymore."

He resisted only slightly, he grumbled only once, and swiftly took her at her word.

"Solo un rato," he said as he kissed her good night. Before he

11

turned off the lights, she could see in his face that it had finally dawned on him that there might be something wrong with leaving a little girl alone in a strange hotel room, even if only for a little while.

She didn't care, she wasn't a little girl, not anymore, she was quite capable of taking care of herself and if another hurricane came, if an earthquake struck, if the whole world came crashing down on her, she'd survive somehow. Her feeling for her father hadn't changed, she still idolized him in spite of his shortcomings and perhaps because of them. The whistling women could have him all night long, she was content with the time they spent together in his car, traveling from town to town and sharing those magical sunsets at the beaches, then watching him perform, hearing the applause, enjoying it as if she'd been on that stage with him.

That night in Botones, as soon as Esteban was gone, she heard heavy footsteps in the hallway. The footsteps stopped at her door. She held her breath. There was a sharp knock. She did not move. She was glad the lights were off.

"Estelita, I know you're in there. Open the damn door." She recognized Aspirrina's voice. For a moment she regretted encouraging her father to go out, wanted to take it back. She waited until Aspirrina knocked again before she answered.

*

Aspirrina Ramagoza wasn't Sabrosuras's most popular performer, a fact that was evident to Estelita every time she watched her set foot on the stage. At 4'11" and 175 pounds, Aspirrina was no one's idea of a sophisticated or sexy dancer. But she tried to compensate for her lack of physical attributes and talent with yards and yards of flimsy fabric, tons of makeup and a serious attitude about her craft.

At every performance there would be a handful of insubordinate teenage boys who would take off their shirts and, waving them over their heads, run up and down the aisles in a mock-rendition of Aspirrina's dance routines; her incongruous tributes to her idol: Isadora Duncan. The crowds encouraged the boys with shouts and shrieking laughter.

If there was a part of Aspirrina that was hurt by this, she never let on.

"No te molesta?" Estelita asked her with the bluntness of a child. Doesn't it bother you?

"Not one bit," she said. "It is my mission to bring culture to the masses; to share a new art form with los mugrosos." Los mugrosos was Aspirrina's word for anyone she felt was beneath her – not filthy in the usual sense, but ignorant and lacking culture. Since Botones, Aspirrina had come to her room whenever her father "went out."

"I don't need a niñera," Estelita had complained, but her father didn't bother to respond.

Since the hurricane, Aspirrina would let herself in with the attitude that she was doing the world a favor, sit in a chair or the edge of the bed and not move. Only her mouth moved, and it never stopped as long as she could spit out another word.

"Those boys who mock me don't know it," she said with a well-studied sneer, "but they keep me on the road. Without them, my name would have been pulled from the bill a long time ago. In their stupid minds they're trying to ruin my performance, but they're actually perpetuating interest in me. Sure, people come to laugh but they go home enlightened."

Aspirrina took a deep breath, proudly puffing up her heavy bosom.

"It is the aspiration of every modern artist," she continued, "to awaken the primitive urges of the mugrosos, and to turn their inner impulses into outward expressions."

They were words Aspirrina repeated often, and no matter how often Estelita heard them, they never made any sense to her. Performing was what her father did – winning the adoration of the public, having people want to kiss you after the show, whistling through the window and sending perfumed notes to your room. Young as she was, Estelita knew that what Aspirrina did on stage night after night was simply insane. But most astonishingly, no matter how badly things went, how many men shouted insults at her, how many boys ridiculed her, Aspirrina always came off the stage looking triumphant.

"My only regret," she once said as she mopped the flop sweat from her face, "is that los mugrosos didn't rush the stage and beat me with sticks. I dream of the day when an angry crowd grabs hold of my hair and drags me through the muddy streets."

"You're such a martyr," Lúcido the Magician said, gently stroking his rabbit.

"I'm no martyr," she shot back. "I simply want to bring out the rebellious spirit I know lives in the hearts of each and every member of my audience. What I hate most are those who don't even bother to laugh, who suffer through my performance without reacting in any way. Those who are pleased as pigs to wait it out until the next performer comes on. I want riots started, rocks thrown, fires burning. I want to be run out of town. Confusion and rebellion are my ultimate goals."

And with that exhausted tirade out of her system, and much to everyone's relief, she took Estelita by the hand and led her back to the hotel.

Lúcido the Magician watched as the two walked away. Aspirrina had never before displayed an ounce of motherly instinct. He knew she had latched on to Esteban's little girl because it was the only way she could stay with Sabrosuras. That part was easy for him to understand. It was the words that spewed out of her mouth; and the things she did on stage that he could never, ever comprehend. All the performers averted their eyes or peered through shuttered fingers at the fat little woman's nightly catastrophes. They were mortified on her behalf and looked toward the day when she would finally come to her senses and leave the world of show business forever.

Even Isabel, Cascabel, and Mirabel, the deaf-mute contortionists, were aware of Aspirrina's disastrous performances. They weren't blind, after all. The three girls would gather in the wings and peek through the curtains. Their act followed Aspirrina's and they could see the sour displeasure in the eyes of the audiences, the scorn on their lips, the mocking dances of the boys, and dreaded facing the angry mob. But they soon discovered that following Aspirrina worked to their advantage.

A lovely silence would wash over the audience as the three girls entered the stage and began to gracefully twist and entwine their scrawny limbs around each other, until no one could tell where one triplet ended and another one began. Unlike Aspirrina, they held audiences in rapt attention because of their delicate artistry, as their movements, to everyone's amazement and delight, recreated the enlaced mess they once were inside their mother's womb. The triplets always received a big round of applause, one which they could never hear.

They also lacked the ability to hear Esteban's singing so they had always considered *themselves* the stars of Sabrosuras. They could almost appreciate the sorcerous, if bumbling, talents of Lúcido the Magician. Or at least, they could understand the audiences' fascination with him as he pulled a rabbit out of a hat or turned a dusty paper flower into a dove. But Esteban de la Cruz just looked like a big, prancing charlatan, and they were always annoyed that it was he who was surrounded by fans after the shows while they were shoved aside and pointedly ignored. They detested that Esteban drove his own car, like a dandy, while all the other performers had to cram into the covered truck that transported them from town to town.

At least, Mirabel thought more than once, he's never asked any of us to care for that cranky brat of his.

Mirabel was particularly resentful for, identical though they were, she considered herself the most attractive of the three sisters. Sometimes she would leave the other two behind and stroll the streets after the shows, hoping some handsome fellow would strike up a conversation or offer to buy her a drink. But it never happened. Together, they were a curiosity. Individually, they were insignificant, dismissible; as common as dirt.

They think we're freaks, was the bitter thought she couldn't escape. Mirabel was resigned to suffer in silence, her weak little heart shrinking and hardening with each passing day. But she couldn't communicate her thoughts to anyone. None of the triplets knew sign language. They talked to each other only with their eyes, which were big and bulgy and very expressive, but not in a pretty way. They were dark-skinned and skinny as twigs. It was as if God had been so busy, with His hands so full creating three little girls at once, that He had overlooked the essential characteristics that He magnanimously bestowed on others. They didn't posses pretty voices to seduce with, or luscious lips or full breasts or big, round asses with which to give and receive pleasure. They had nothing that would inspire lustful thoughts in men, draw admiration or inflame desire.

Nothing.

Even though they were always together, the triplets were lonely.

And at times each loathed the other two, wondering had they been born one at time, would they have been more complete? But all they really had in the world was each other. So any resentment or bad blood had to be set aside the minute they climbed aboard the truck and struck out for the next town. After all, without the other two, there would be no act. Without the other two, they would surely starve.

Cascabel was the only one who could see why women found Esteban de la Cruz attractive. When he had first joined Sabrosuras, she was taken by his good looks. She'd even looked down into the rattan box where he kept his baby and made funny faces at it. But either Esteban didn't get the message, or he pretended not to. After that incident, Cascabel kept him and his annoying child at a distance. Her sisters had followed her lead.

"Me miran con ojos de demonios," Esteban said to Lúcido the Magician. They look at me with demon eyes.

Lúcido the Magician didn't care. He had woman troubles of his own. Mostly, he had to fight off Aspirrina, who for years had been determined to become his assistant.

"I can help you, old man," she'd say to him. "You'll never be able to make me disappear for good. Look at me, I'm short, but I'm solid."

"Muy agradecido, pero no," he replied, thank you kindly, but no, and moved on.

His rejections were always so gentle, so infuriatingly placid, that they left her seething.

"*Muy agradecido*," she would mock behind his back, adding an obscene gesture.

Lúcido's problems were numerous and ongoing. His assistants, lovely and buxom, tended to disappear without a trace, leaving the poor man with half an act. No one knew what happened to these vivacious beauties. All anyone could see was Lúcido's black cape flying around backstage, looking in every nook and cranny, to know that yet another one of his assistants had vanished into thin air. Lúcido never lost his dove, Rubi, or his rabbit, Cero. They had been with him for years and years and performed flawlessly. But they were not enough to complete his act. He needed a woman. The audience demanded it. Who wanted to only see an old man in a tattered cape pulling a rabbit out of a hat?

No matter how many times he'd told her "no," Aspirrina always offered to step in, having seen the routine countless times. But Lúcido, although ashen-faced and shaking, chose always to go on stage alone. He would rather confront the blood-thirsty audience with no one to cut in half, no one to levitate or sail through a hoop. He'd rather have no one to hand his dove or his rabbit to, and no one to throw flaming knives at, than risk the mayhem that sharing a stage with Aspirrina was sure to inspire.

***

Sabrosuras had been Estelita's world for as long as she could remember. When she had confided in Aspirrina her desire for a family, a home, a mother, Aspirrina had turned to her with a hard look.

"Let me stop you right there," she said, "I come from a place like that, a mother, a father, sisters and brothers and let me tell you, it's all shit. What you think you want does not exist."

The performers treated Estelita as they would a gentle dog with a playful word here, a pat on the head there, then hurried off to catch up with their own lives. And since Esteban and Estelita traveled by car while the rest of them were crammed into the truck, there was little contact between them.

The triplets had been there quite a while and didn't seem to be going anywhere. Before Lúcido joined them there had been several other magicians, plus a team of crazy Puerto Rican acrobats, a brother and sister samba act who danced with such sensual precision they were rumored to be incestuous, a sword-swallower name El Gago, a snake enchantress called Serpentina, and many others. All of them had saved their money, packed up their dreams and hopped the bus for Havana.

"In La Habana," Serpentina told Estelita while she coiled ten feet of a sedated Boa constrictor into a wicker basket, "the new casinos are so desperate to entertain the tourists that they're hiring anybody with an act, anybody who can shake a maraca."

Estelita had no act. She was simply Esteban's unfortunate little girl. Only Lúcido, noting that Estelita, practically a young lady by now, was illiterate, took it upon himself to educate her. He'd sit down with her during the long, hot, dusty afternoons and patiently teach her how to read and write. Aspirrina, illiterate herself, always sat close by.

Not so close that she could be considered part of the lesson, but close enough to keep an eye on the magic man.

"Don't you dare make her disappear," she warned him while the girl frowned seriously over words Lúcido had written in the dust with his walking stick.

"I'm only trying to make her ignorance disappear," he answered in his usual mournful manner.

Now that Estelita was in Aspirrina's care, Esteban ran off after performing and no one knew when he'd return. More than once, the truck had to leave and Esteban was still missing. Estelita cried and screamed, but Aspirrina dragged her onto the truck.

"He'll find us," she said but Estelita wasn't convinced and promised herself she would not let that happen again.

But it continued to happen.

If he wasn't there by sunrise, Estelita tiptoed past a snoring Aspirrina and ran the town's muddy streets from end to end, had stopped at every bar that was still open, talked to anyone who was still awake.

"Have you seen Esteban de la Cruz?" she'd ask anyone she saw, and, if she received a blank stare, she would add, "the singer?"

She looked until she found him. And she always found him.

His face would light up each time he saw her.

"There's my nena," he would slur, taking her arm and letting her guide him back to the hotel room, where he would promptly fall asleep, filling the room with the comforting smells of rum and cigars until it was time for him to wake up and go on stage again.

Aspirrina would be furious the next day.

"If he finds out you're roaming the streets alone, you know who he's going to blame? Me, that's who. I am responsible for you while he's gone. Don't you ever go after him like that again." And so on.

Esteban would turn up at the next town and seemed to have no memory of it. He'd make it onstage at the last minute as if nothing had happened. Estelita quietly suffered Aspirrina's reprimands and did it again. Again she ran the muddy streets, again she shouted out his name, again she crouched on sidewalks weeping.

"Why do you get all worked up like that?" Aspirrina asked. "You know dogs always find their way home."

Estelita, with a voice tough and resolute beyond her years, surprised her with an unequivocal and defiant answer,

"He's my father."

2

The Rumba singer came from Pensamientos, on the Caribean coast of Oriente province. He was conspicuous in the small town– he played the guitar and sang on street corners, he rode a German motorcycle much too fast, and long before his beard had come in full, could be seen carousing with men twice his age, and with the unlucky sailors who sometimes had to take their shore leave there. From the older men Esteban learned how to hold hard liquor, from the sailors, how to say *hello* in many different languages, and from both he learned that the best way to make a new friend was to put your hand out first.

"Esteban de la Cruz is headed for a bad end," the wise women of Pensamientos predicted.

"Unless he finds a good woman," they often added. Most of them had good husbands at home who'd once been just as wild as Esteban, or worse.

To Esteban, Pensamientos was merely a nasty little village, a dinky blight at the edge of the beautiful Caribbean Sea. No tourists ever visited Pensamientos, and the only wharf whore was so old and demented that even the loneliest, most drunken sailors avoided her. There wasn't much for a young man like him to do there except dream of a way out.

Until he met her.

He was eighteen years old and ready to conquer the world when he first noticed Belquis Solano Martinez. In the beginning, he cursed the day he fell in love because he had seen it happen to other adventurous boys just like him, young men who'd had big dreams but had been tamed, at first by love, and then by the unexpected arrival of children and responsibilities. They were trapped in Pensamientos, never to venture farther than the edge of town, or for a day of fishing and beer at one of the barren, sandy cays that floated on the horizon.

Esteban had promised himself that this would never happen to him. He was going to see the world, and not just at the local movie theater. As a boy, he'd watched adventure movies whose titles promised to take him to faraway places, and beyond:

WEST OF ZANZIBAR
SOUTH OF PAGO PAGO
EAST OF BORNEO
NORTH OF THE RIO GRANDE.

That's me! That's where I'm going! he'd say to himself. But a sixteen-year old girl with teeth like pearls and magic in her eyes had changed all that. There had been the usual obstacles that such young and reckless love awakens in others.

"Es un loco," Belquis's mother, Eva, told her time and again. "He doesn't have a real job. He's crazy".

But Belquis wasn't listening. Eva's words of caution drifted through the air like particles of dust.

Eva was not oblivious to the changes this strange young man had caused in her only daughter. She was, in fact, embarrassed by Belquis' desire – her moist eyes reflected an indecent glimmer, her lips were always soft and parted, as if waiting for a kiss and then another. Eva knew that before long kissing would be insufficient and did everything she could think of to keep them apart. She banished Esteban from her doorsteps, she repeated threats and reprimands, and came close to tying Belquis to a bedpost. But Esteban kept showing up late at night with his guitar, sometimes with a friend who played the bongos, and he'd sing at the window.

"No te atrévas," Eva warned her daughter. Don't you dare.

One night while Belquis wailed and scratched at her, Eva threw a bedpan full of urine from the balcony to end his unwelcome serenades.

Nothing worked. The girl she had guarded como una prenda, like a precious jewel, became a stranger, someone feral who would not listen to sense or reason.

Eventually, much to Esteban's delight, all objections ceased, probably swept aside by the same saint who had first brought the young lovers together in the first place.

Shortly after the wedding, he accepted the news of his young bride's pregnancy with some misgiving. He knew this signaled the end of their romance. A romance that was still so new, so delicate. Another person was going to enter their little love nest and inevitably change their exceptional circumstances. Belquis would no longer live merely to love her husband. The love they had only for one another would now have to be shared, and would inevitably be diluted. Esteban was so deeply in love with his wife that he doubted if there would be enough love left for his child. All through the pregnancy, he felt a dark foreboding that increased as the time of delivery grew closer. They were misgivings that each member of his family in whom he confided dismissed as cold feet.

"Fucking is never free of charge," his father said to him as he had many times before. "One way or another, every man pays for the privilege."

For Esteban, though, there was something deeper at work within him. The uneasiness tormenting him wasn't the sort soon-to-be fathers were said to suffer. Something sinister and dagger sharp was prodding at his soul, as if trying to unearth something buried there. He was plagued by visions of fresh dirt. He smelled it, felt the pink earthworms weaving their tunnels deeper and deeper as if into his own flesh. To his horror, he would sometimes see the short, narrow graves of children, or torrential floods. The visions were not as easy to dismiss as the nightmares and always left him weak and shivering, even on the hottest nights.

He never told Belquis about the visions and later, after it was too late, he would wish that he had been man enough to share everything with her. For years to come, Esteban would spend daunting sums of energy denying what was undeniably a salient gift. He wanted no part of it. He knew that the ability to see matters beyond the range of ordinary perception wasn't so much a gift as a curse. He did not want to end up like those men he'd seen all his life, the Santeros, all dressed in white, their brown skin parchment thin, their eyes always hazy from looking too far into the future. Santeria wasn't for him and he did everything in his power to close those doors forever.

*

"There are very few living souls in this town that I haven't seen draw their first breath," Dorotéa, the midwife of Pensamientos was fond of saying.

And she was telling the truth. She had been the one who ushered both Esteban and Belquis into this world. Both without incident. Their births had been so uneventful that she hardly remembered any of the details. Dorotéa had been helping women deliver babies since she had been a skinny kid trailing along with her Aunt Clotilde, gawking wide-eyed at the miracle of birth. Her aunt had taught her well. Dorotéa had seen just about everything happen and was prepared to face any emergency, provided it ensued between the legs of a woman in labor.

"The birth canal is my field of expertise," she joked.

Now, as she prodded at Belquis' stubborn uterus, she sighed with exasperation.

Belquis Solano Martinez de la Cruz was not the first woman whose placenta was slow to emerge. The baby had been easy by comparison. She had slid onto Dorotéa's hands as slick as a jellyfish. The baby was healthy and strong – a screaming baby girl, tiny fists clenched in anger, mouth pursing in desperate need of her mother's milk, her pudgy legs running sprints in midair; all in frustration of not having the touch or feel of her mamá.

"Busca una teta para tu nieta." Find a breast for your granddaughter, Dorotéa whispered to Eva, who was hovering much too close, mouth trembling, eyes fretful. Eva didn't move.

"Go, go, go," Dorotéa hissed, beginning to lose what little patience she had left.

With a deep sigh, Eva did what she was told. She reluctantly scooped up the newborn and left the room, slamming the door. Dorotéa turned the lock with equal force. She felt insulted by Eva's worries. No need to worry, Dorotéa knew what to do, had watched her aunt triumph over just such a problem many times. She started gently massaging Belquis' distended abdomen with eucalyptus oil to loosen the clots. She made sure the girl's bladder and bowels remained empty, and, no matter how much Belquis moaned through parched lips, refused to give her even a sip of water. She massaged more vigorously and with mounting panic as she noted Belquis starting to drift into a languid agony. The placenta was now hours late in coming.

From the other room she could hear the newborn screaming and a chill, like a cold, blue finger, ran up her spine. Dorotéa closed her eyes, tilted her chin towards the ceiling and thanked La Virgen de la Caridad del Cobre that the baby was alive.

"The baby needs her mamá," she prayed to whomever was on duty up in heaven.

Dorotéa had lost mothers before, but not while she was still accountable. Usually, it was hours later when she was resting at home, too far away to be blamed. She continued massaging the flaccid abdomen. It now felt like a bag of lentils. That meant the clots had started to harden. Sweat dropped from her forehead onto Belquis's fading skin. She moved her hands up to the girl's breasts and gently stroked her cold, hard nipples; softly, the way her aunt had taught her.

A loud pounding at the door made her jump back.

"Open up," Esteban shouted. She ignored him.

Esteban started kicking at the door while Dorotéa continued to tease the nipples.

The door was groaning as if about to rip from its hinges. She heard male voices and Esteban shouting at them.

"That's my wife in there. That's my love."

A struggle and then all noise subsided as if Esteban had been forcefully dragged away from the door.

"Yes, keep him away," she thought and concentrated harder, remembering what she had learned so long ago.

Sometimes, her aunt had told her, *stimulating another sensitive part of a woman's body will beguile the mind, swindle the attention away from the contracting uterus, trick it into loosening up and expulsing whatever is lodged in there.*

Dorotéa was about to shout for the doctor when the ruse worked. A violent spasm lifted Belquis off the bed. Her body arched like an arrow's bow and when her back hit the mattress again, her legs sprang open and a blast of blood gushed into the air. The placenta and the hard clots flowed out of her like dark red molasses. Unfortunately, blood continued oozing as if the girl was being squeezed by invisible hands, wrung dry of all life.

It had all been so sudden and confusing – all that red blood, all that pain – that Dorotéa momentarily lost consciousness herself. Her vision went black and in a bright flash she saw through the entire universe and all the way to the gates of Heaven. When she finally gathered her wits about her, she was staring into Belquis's dead, beautiful eyes.

*

Esteban had been too young and heartbroken to understand what Dorotéa, in all the confusion, mumbled about death not necessarily being a punishment. He had rushed wild-eyed into the room and misunderstood her completely. He accused her of belittling his loss, called her a nigger, a witch and a whore. His anguish was such that Dorotéa cowered into a corner, so afraid was she that he might strike her.

He hit the wall instead. First with his fist, and then with his head. And then he threw himself on the floor next to the bed that held his wife's corpse and banged his head on the tiles until blood poured from a gash on his forehead. Eva remained impassive, holding tight to the newborn baby. She made no move to comfort the man screaming on the floor but stepped over him as one would the most minor of obstructions. It was Dorotéa who called in Esteban's brothers to pick him up and take him away,

"Before he does permanent damage to his brain," she told them in her most professional voice as she hurried out.

When his brothers came in, they were disgusted that no one had thought to cover the corpse. Belquis still lay in the bed, in a pool of bright red blood, a nude goddess flawlessly carved out of white marble.

*

Esteban did not attend his wife's funeral. It took him a very long time to truly understand his loss. What God had taken away, what He had granted. In fact, for two months he hardly thought about his daughter at all. He spent the first week locked in a room where his brothers consoled him with rum. At first, he'd spat it back at them. But later, as the pain in his heart gripped further, in his hurry to find oblivion, he started to swallow the harsh liquor as fast as they could pour it and stayed drunk for weeks.

Estelita, as the baby was named, did attend the funeral. She was at the grave cradled in her grandmother's arms, dressed in the embroidered baptismal gown her mother had once worn a scant sixteen years ago.

Eva tearfully insisted that Belquis be lowered into the ground in a light-pink coffin. It was her way of ensuring that her dearly departed daughter would luxuriate in the sweet, rosy dreams of innocence for all eternity. The baby she would keep and raise as her own.

"You owe her to me," Eva said to Esteban when he showed up drunk, belligerently demanding his daughter. "If you hadn't made Belquis pregnant she would be alive today."

She had him thrown out, banished him from the house. Esteban went away, but not for long. He returned time and again with increasing sobriety and better manners but every time she hid the child. He asked nicely, bargained, made promises, and pleaded. Eva would not accede.

He went home and waited. He hated himself for what he had to do and hated Eva even more for forcing his hand. He knew that stealing the baby was equal to cutting open Eva's chest and ripping out her heart, but there was no other way.

One sweltering afternoon, during one of those siestas that rendered the town unconscious, he walked through Eva's house like a shadow. Estelita came to him quietly and willingly. Tiny as she was, her nose made its way to his neck and found a scent there that soothed her. He felt her relax into his arms.

"He'll be back before nightfall," the people of Pensamientos whispered with complete certainty when news of what he'd done spread.

While Eva raged, wept, swore, and admonished God and all the saints, the people of Pensamientos waited patiently, went about their business, convinced that a single man, particularly a man like Esteban de la Cruz, was not capable of taking care of a baby. Not in Cuba in 1940, the year of our Lord.

*

It amazed him that the baby grew so quickly, that she learned to walk and talk with little help from him. He enjoyed her company, her constant presence. From early on he talked to her as he would to any adult. But she troubled him, sometimes he wanted her gone, wanted life to go back as it was. She was the best and the worst thing that had ever happened to him. Without the child he would have his cherished wife but without the child he would have nothing.

Estelita loved listening to her father relate the story of her life as they traveled from town to town, always avoiding Pensamientos and the eastern provinces.

She did not find her story sad at all.

"Otra vez," she'd beg.

"Again? You know that old story better than I do," Esteban would complain. But he'd tell her the story. At first he spun it into a fairy tale that began, "You were very, very small, the size of a dog's head, the size of a coconut, even smaller than a rat."

As she grew, he started to add more details, more information.

"I was very little, and I was bundled, right?"

"Yes," he'd sigh, bracing himself for her favorite moment and his least favorite. She'd kneel on the passenger seat of the car, her small hands on his arm, his arm on the wheel. She was four years old and her little face, turned up to him as it was, her eyes wide with joy and anticipation, so resembled Belquis's that it made his heart ache.

"In a pink blanket with little birds on it."

"That's right," he'd say, not taking his eyes off the road.

"What happened to that blanket?" she'd ask.

"You know what happened."

"Tell me again, papá."

"You had been up for days. Crying, crying. I was exhausted. I fell asleep rocking you and my cigarette fell from my lips and the blanket caught on fire."

"And you saved my life!" she'd trill, clapping her hands.

Esteban never confessed that that had been the day when he had almost returned her to Pensamiento. The day when he'd been so close to admitting defeat and handing her back to Eva. But something else had prevailed. He had felt Belquis's warm hand on his wet cheeks. He had felt it as clearly as if she'd been standing there, flesh and blood. The memory of her, who they had been to each other, what they had lost, and the little girl she had left behind was always there. Her memory was particularly strong when they stopped for a swim and he looked towards the water and saw his wife in his beautiful daughter's every move.

Look, papa, I'm a dolphin, I'm a mermaid.

Esteban told her stories in his sweet-potato voice as they drove along fields so full of sunshine that it seemed as if the trees, the grass, and the cows had never known night.

They drove past rain-flooded meadows where houses bobbed like giant beach toys. They drove through weather so perfect that it was as if the world had been created by the most gentle of deities.

She loved hearing stories of her life as a baby, as if the baby were another person, a character in a story, someone she'd love to meet someday. Esteban was careful not to dwell on the death of her mother. But he did keep her entertained with stories about his struggles to feed her and bathe her, laughing at the staggering amount of cloth diapers a baby would need in one day. How he dutifully washed them in bathroom sinks and hung them on hotel balconies like white flags of surrender.

He described for her the looks on the fleabag hotelkeepers' faces when he showed up with his crying bundle of joy. He told her about how he would stand at the front desk of the only hotel in town, or the only affordable one, and use all his considerable charms until he was reduced to begging and, finally, slipping them extra cash just so he could bring his baby daughter into the establishment. Meanwhile, prostitutes clicked their high heels past him, a miniature dog on one arm and a fervent customer on the other. He didn't tell her that there had been times when she had cried so much and for such a long time that these same prostitutes would stop by his room to offer their perfumed and bruised bosoms to his restless, unhappy child.

"Men don't like to hear a baby crying while they're screwing a whore," one of them told him with a weary eye.

During the day, Estelita had been a good baby, happy to lie in bed next to her father while he read racing forms and amused her with smoke rings from his cigarette. He proudly took her everywhere, to diners and bars, to cockfights and all-night card games. He noticed that Estelita had become so accustomed to the loud, deep voices of men that her face would scrunch up and squeeze out little tears whenever a woman's higher-pitched cooing voice praised her.

This posed quite a problem because, on the nights that Esteban had to perform, there were no men he could trust to watch his precious girl. At first, he would set her down in a rattan basket he got from a chicken farmer. He'd wrap her in soft, cottony little blankets, and place the box just outside the proscenium so he could keep an eye on her; and she could keep an eye on him. As long as he was visible, she was all right.

The small-town impresarios who hired him were not always comfortable with this arrangement, and they would stand near the baby, occasionally tapping her rattan box with the pointy edge of their shiny black shoes if she started to fidget. This was as close to a child as their repressed paternal instincts would allow them to get. The thought of picking up the infant and actually smelling her sweet head or feeling the warmth of her milky spittle running down the side of their necks never crossed their minds. That was a woman's job. Softly kicking her box to the beat of Esteban's music was as much as they were willing to do and more often than not, it worked.

Those first few years, after Esteban became a regular attraction with Sabrosuras, were excruciating. While half his mind was busy projecting the sexy rumba singer promised on the poster, the other half was spinning with anxiety over his baby. But he soon discovered these were to be the easier times. It didn't occur to Esteban, who at the time was determined not to look very far into the future, that, all too soon, the time would come when Estelita would learn how to crawl out of her rattan box and onto the stage. Nor could he have known that, later, she would be capable of show-stopping stunts such as running barefoot and naked through her father's act and falling off the stage, face-first into the crowd.

The other performers were horrified by the toddler's intrusions. But at the time, Esteban de la Cruz gave it no second thought.

"She's her father's daughter," he laughed, "always looking for the spotlight."

At the time, Esteban was not concerned. At the time, with a baby or without, he was at the top of his form.

A headliner.

*

Sabrosuras was like a gift from heaven. He no longer had to come into a town and charm his way into performing at whatever establishment would have him. Most nightclubs had steady entertainment already and he had to work hard to convince them to try someone new for a few nights. With Sabrosuras he became a featured attraction. The constant traveling was difficult, the roads were bad, the hotels cheap and dirty. But he always opened the second act. His romantic crooning had become as popular as Aspirrina's dancing was reviled, as Lúcido's magic was ignored, and the triplets were considered more suitable to a sideshow. Promoters knew that unless they saved Esteban for the second act, there wouldn't *be* a second act, and people would demand their money back.

Esteban was the main attraction. He was the one who smiled from yellowing posters pasted to the light posts all over town. The photograph was always the same: his mouth wide open in song, his ruffled shirt splayed to the navel, exposing a forest of dark chest hair. Some featured his guitar, others didn't. The ones that didn't revealed what the guitar was hiding. Tight white pants with silken white stripes running down the side and a bulging crotch.

He was well aware of his gifts, his good looks, and his charm. He knew it didn't matter much that he didn't have the greatest singing voice in the world. He sang all the popular songs of the day and played his guitar, danced a little when the rhythm moved him, and told jokes in between songs. He knew the women were there to see *him*. He could sense their heat when he stepped onto the stage. He was 27 years old and having the time of his life. Women threw themselves at him and he made enough money to drink himself into oblivion on any given night. It was the only way to forget, if only for a moment, the little town of Pensamientos and all that had happened there.

It wasn't until Estelita started making crazy demands, until the hurricane of 1949 when he'd returned to his room and found her curled up on the floor, shivering with fright, that he decided to approach

Aspirrina, a woman whose act he considered an embarrassment and whose acrid personality he could scarcely tolerate. He found her sitting in the truck, eating *pan de agua* and at a glance he knew she intended to eat the whole loaf. Who eats a whole loaf of bread, dry, without at least a beverage to wash it down? He set aside his revulsion, turned on the charm and laid out his plan.

"I'm nobody's nana," she said with her mouth full. "You made her, you watch her."

"I spend my whole life with her, a man needs to get out now and then."

"Not my problem."

He hadn't expected her resistance, but he was prepared. He knew that Aspirrina's time with Sabrosuras was coming to a close, and rightfully so. She was as ugly as she was untalented and worse than that, she made trouble wherever they went. As a caretaker, she was less than ideal, but it was better than trying to try and find someone new in every town they played. She was enough of what he needed, a woman who traveled with them and, if things went as he planned, would work for free. Women were easy to manipulate, to train. They wanted to be useful to men. Even Estelita, as little as she was, had learned to shine his shoes. She'd sit on the floor with a rag and polish them to a shine. It made her happy to do it.

"Everyone here wants you gone," he said, having honed his negotiating skills with hotel managers all over the province, "you keep my girl safe at night and I'll make sure you stay with the show for as long as you want."

He saw the rage build in her eyes as her mind quickly calculated the offer. She had no other alternative. He winked at her before he turned and walked away.

That wink, that was their contract.

3

Aspirrina Ramagosa had known many children and she disliked nearly everything about them. Watching Estelita sleep brought it all back with brutal force. She had been born in Bátey Oriénte, a place too small to qualify as a shanty town, just a one-room dirt-floor shack next to a barracks deep within the sugarcane fields. She remembered rain most mornings and the steaming heat that followed, and sugar cane everywhere. It had been a life lived in the scorching embrace of a green and sharp-skinned beast.

Her father was the overseer of the field hands at the Batéy - all of the workers were Haitians, brought over because they worked cheaper and harder than the locals.

Aspirrina helped her mother cook the meals that fed them every day. Twenty-eight stinking, exhausted men filed past the kitchen window to be handed a plate of yellow rice, black beans, and greasy fried plantains.

Theirs was the only home for miles around. The Haitians slept in barracks that had been built to accommodate ten, maybe fifteen men at the most, but all twenty-eight of them crammed in there every night; some slept on floor mats, others on the flat roof, under the stars.

The Haitians never complained, not about the heat or the

sameness of the food or the meager wages. They arrived every year when the canes were tall and green and left at the start of tiempo muerto, dead time, when every cane had been cut down and the last truck had departed. Her father prefered the Haitians.

"Cubans like to complain," he said, "nothing is ever good enough. And during their free time they drink too much and exhaust themselves. The Haitians work, eat and go to sleep and when the harvest is over, they go back to Haiti happy with a pocketful of pesos."

Her father didn't want to deal with troublesome workers. Fire and bugs were his main concerns.

"A spark from a cigar can wipe out an entire field."

Some days, when her brothers and sisters had taken everything out of her, Aspirrina wished the whole place *would* go up in flames.

"This little sliver of wood could be my salvation," she'd think, weaving a matchstick through her fingers.

She was the oldest of eight children and it was her responsibility to watch them, except watching them really meant *raising* them. For as long as she could remember she'd spent every waking hour with a child clinging to her. Every time she saw her mother begin to slow down, she knew that the woman's belly would soon start to swell and another newborn would be entrusted to her care.

"Why do you need another one?"

"This is what God wants."

She hated her mother's submissive acceptance of whatever scraps and hardships life threw at her. Late at night she heard her moaning beneath her father, and sometimes she heard the whispered pleas that he leave her alone. But he didn't much care that with each new baby, their poverty increased and Aspirrina was further enslaved.

In the area in back of the shack, her father raised chickens, pigs, and rabbits. The rabbits were kept in two cages; one for the females and one for the males. No sooner had one of the female rabbits weaned her litter than her father threw her in with the males. And, within hours, she would be pregnant again. That's how Aspirrina saw her mother, a big dumb rabbit.

She found herself hoping that the pregnancies would go wrong. And if she'd believed in God she would have prayed. Whenever her mother went into labor, she'd concentrate as hard as she could, wishing the baby the salvation of death. Unfortunately, her mother had a talent for delivering strong, healthy babies. But they didn't stay that way. The children got colds and fevers, cuts and bruises, broken bones. When one child got sick, they all got sick: measles, mumps, rubella, diphtheria. There was nowhere to isolate them from each other. There were months when the small house was like a hospital ward with sick children scattered on blankets all over the dirt floor. She got no sleep and her own temper flared until she couldn't stand herself, or them or anyone who came near. She nursed them back to health quickly and efficiently – although there were times when she'd just as soon let them die. But healing came easily to her and she learned that the sooner she got the child well, the sooner she could sleep again, get out of the house, regain a modicum of freedom.

Aspirrina hated every moment of it. She particularly hated the weekly treks to the river to wash, not just the mounds of diapers that collected every week along with her family's laundry, but also the clothes of the Haitians, who secretly paid her. She kept her earnings for herself, seeding her plan.

It was a long walk through trails so narrow she had to keep her arms close to her side to prevent the razor-sharp leaves of the sugarcane plants from slicing into her skin. Her brothers and sisters followed her, each entrusted with as big a bundle as they could carry. After hours of washing, she'd spread all the items out on the hot boulders to dry. While she waited, her brothers and sisters would swim. It was during this short respite that Aspirrina sat at the river's edge and dreamed of leaving it all behind.

The opportunity had always been there. After the harvest, huge camiones came in and went out. But year after year she missed her chance. At first because she didn't have enough money. Later, there was a bad storm coming, or one of her siblings was ill, or her mother was pregnant. Again.

Something. Always something. She felt cursed to be the smartest person in her family, the smartest person for miles around.

She was almost twenty-seven years old when she finally left. Without a word of goodbye she hid in the back of one of the sugarcane trucks. The stalks dug into her back for hours.

The leaves sliced into her skin.

No matter. She was free.

(Years later, when she heard that Bátey Oriente had been swept away by a great fire, Aspirrina accepted the news with a shrug and only wondered if, in the midst of the inferno, anyone had remembered to free the rabbits).

*

The truck stopped at a train station that was surprisingly close. She had imagined it all to be much farther away, another world. But it was right there, barely a whistle stop from home.

Beyond the station were enormous sugar mills. They were the largest buildings Aspirrina had ever seen. With smoke stacks the size of the world. The smell of molasses was so strong she felt she couldn't catch a full breath. It was a sweet, sulfurous smell that made the glands at the back of her throat tighten and her mouth water unpleasantly. She saw Cuban men and some Haitians sweating under the hot sun, unloading the sugarcane from los camiones and heavy bags of sugar onto freight trains.

And then she saw the others.

They were tall and white, these men, with chiseled jaws reddened by the sun and yellow, barbered hair. They sat on tall horses and chatted amicably with each other while the brown men worked.

Aspirrina walked down a wide, tree-lined road, and noticed large, beautiful wooden houses. They had perfect white fences around them. In yards full of flowering shrubs and fruit trees, honey-haired children played, shouting at each other in a foreign language. Americans! Just like the pictures she had seen in the newspapers the Haitians sometimes brought with them. She felt as if she'd stepped into a different country. So this was where all the money went! She'd always wondered why, harvest after harvest, her father and the Haitians continued to live in poverty. She looked through windows and saw beautiful white women wearing fresh cotton dresses and pretty aprons. She felt like a stranger, an intruder, and feared that unless she got out of there fast, they would notice her and send her back to where she came from.

That night, she hopped a freight train headed west, to Campechuela.

It was a small town, but to Aspirrina it seemed enormous. There were roads and shops and houses of different sizes crammed close together. And people! People of all ages and sizes, not all related to one another, or from Haiti. But brown-faced, fast-talking people just like herself. She asked around and found employment and a place to live in the home of Matilda Ortiz Infante. Aspirrina cooked and cleaned for the old woman, who taught piano to the scions of the local gentry.

Matilda's husband had been killed during the Spanish-American War, after the sinking of the battleship Maine in Havana harbor. An event Matilda could never forget or forgive. It was as if she still lived in that era so long ago.

"My husband was a caballero, a gentleman, as sweet a man as you could find in these parts," she'd tell Aspirrina, her clouded eyes drifting back to the past. "He had no business going to war. He was a man of words, beautiful words. Not violence. He was merely twenty-years-old when they killed him. "These are all his books." she said, turning towards the bookshelves that covered the walls. It was a house full of books, music and memories.

Aspirrina simply nodded; she had never learned to read.

*

Aspirrina was always in the kitchen when Matilda's students took their lessons, her body moving to the sounds coming from the grand piano. Sometimes, she would sneak into a doorway where she could watch Matilda's blue-veined hands gliding over the keys.

One student caught Aspirrina's attention. His name was Diego Cervantes Murillo. Diego was sixteen, much older than the others, and his relative maturity gave him confidence and a cocksure attitude.

"I don't want to play another stupid Bach sonata," he'd whine. "Can't we find something a little more modern. I'm growing gray hairs playing these musty old pieces."

And he'd bang loudly with clenched fists, while Matilda held her hands over her ears.

Intrigued by this unusual young man, Aspirrina determined to meet him, and one afternoon she circled his block until she did.

"I know you," he said once she was close enough, "you're that woman who skulks around Matilda's house."

"I don't skulk," she said, jabbing a finger into his chest, "I'm her maid."

He stepped back, grinning.

"I know that, you idiot."

She started walking away slowly. He followed, just as she hoped he would.

"Why are you here? Shouldn't you be sweeping or dusting or something?"

"It's my afternoon off," she said.

"And you've come to find me?"

"This is an accidental meeting," she said, trying desperately to match his arrogance.

"I've seen you watching me."

Diego kept his steely gaze on her, making her feel increasingly old and foolish.

"Take a good look," he said, "I don't think I'll be going back to that old witch's house. Not for lessons, not for anything."

"I don't blame you," Aspirrina said, "if I didn't need a place to live, I would never have set foot in that house."

Diego looked at her for a long time before he spoke.

"Do you mind if we walk a little?" he asked her.

They met regularly after that, mostly for walks around the shabbier neighborhoods, or out in the fields. Aspirrina longed to walk with him in the central plaza, like all other couples did every Sunday afternoon. It was a custom in Campechuela, as it was in most small Cuban towns. But Diego wouldn't hear of it.

"Someone might see us," he said.

Aspirrina understood. Not only was she many years older than he, she was of a different class –no class at all. Diego's father was the local doctor, and everyone in Campechuela knew him. She decided she would wait. She would wait until Diego began to feel for her the way she felt about him. Until neither age nor status mattered. She had never felt this way before. Suddenly, and for the first time, she understood her mother a little better.

Although younger, Diego had so much to teach her. From him she learned about music, theater and dance. He particularly detested Cuban music.

"It's so vulgar," he said. He talked about the eastern Europeans, classical composers who were breaking all the rules; his favorite was called Béla Bartók.

"He's Hungarian," Diego said, pawing at the air as if at a giant keyboard. "His music requires two pianos at once, can you imagine the glorious sound of that?"

Aspirrina nodded, not fully understanding, but willing to learn more. She wanted to know what he knew. She wanted to be moved by whatever moved him.

"And three kettle drums," he went on, growing more excited, "a xylophone, two-sided drums, cymbals, suspended cymbals, bass drums, even a triangle and tam-tam!"

He glanced at her blank expression.

"Don't you understand? It's simply not done by anyone else."

She didn't understand, but she promised herself she would. Diego loaned her books to read. She didn't tell him she couldn't read, that there were no schools near Bátey Oriente. She would look at the blurry photographs of serious men with crazy hair, waving batons over formal-dressed musicians, wondering what that music would sound like. One day, in one of the books she saw a photograph of a young woman with wild eyes dancing barefoot. She showed the photograph to Matilda.

"Oh, her," Matilda said with a sniff of displeasure, "that's Isadora La Loca."

"She must be a great dancer," Aspirrina said.

"A great dancer? Hardly!" Matilda replied in her reedy, quivering voice, "from what I understand she was crazy, regularly shouted off the stage. More of a spectacle than an artist; bound and determined to bring to ashes the sacred institution of dance."

Aspirrina wasn't put off by Matilda's scathing comments. During their next walk, she asked Diego about her.

"Oh, yes! Isadora Duncan," he said, wrapping the name sensuously around his tongue. "She personified everything I've been telling you about, Aspirrina. She danced like no one else. She skipped, ran, jumped, leaped, tossed. She was shocking. She was glorious."

Something in Aspirrina's heart was set free that afternoon.

She was shocking. She was glorious. Isadora Duncan had died tragically young, but that day, Aspirrina felt her true spirit come to life.

"I want to dance like that," she said to Diego, biting her lip as soon as the words had escaped, afraid that he would ridicule her.

But he surprised her.

"I think that's marvelous," he said, "I'm so sick of Cuban women who use dance to shake their tits and asses just to make men drool. Yes, Aspirrina, do what your heart tells you. Dance like the wind."

At that moment, hearing those words Aspirrina doubted that anyone in the history of the world had ever loved anyone as much as she loved Diego Cervantes Murillo.

That night, she searched through all the books in Matilda's library. In one of the newer books she found several photographs and drawings of Isadora Duncan in different artistic poses. In her mind, she could put them together, animate them, so that she could actually see this beautiful creature running across a stage, leaping and flapping and twirling. Dancing like the wind.

She began dreaming of Isadora. Isadora defiant, shocking and glorious. From her dreams, she put together a series of steps; and finally a whole routine. Aspirrina decided that she would dance alone and without music. She would express with her movements what she had kept locked in her heart. She would make Diego Cervantes Murillo proud. He would be so proud that he would beg her to walk with him on the plaza. He would take her to parties and introduce her to his friends, even to his family. She would become like one of the daring artists he admired.

On their next walk, she planned to talk to Diego only about Isadora Duncan. Just Isadora. Diego would understand. But Diego was in a strange mood. He led her deep into the forest, deeper than usual. It was getting dark and Aspirrina was growing tired.

"We should start back," she suggested.

Diego looked at her seriously.

"Aspirrina, have you ever been with a man?"

He stepped closer to her.

"No tengas miedo," Don't be afraid, he said unbuttoning his trousers, "put your hand in here."

Aspirrina's heart started to beat fast; too fast. She felt like a little girl with him, their chronology somehow reversed. He had the power, she could see it in his eyes. He was close to her, closer than anyone had ever been. Suddenly she realized how lonely it was to walk through life with no one close. As if she'd been starving without knowing it, believing hunger to be a natural state. So when he took her hand in his, she let him guide her. She felt his hardness.

"Take it out," he whispered.

His voice was strange, deep.

She wanted to do what he wanted, but the feelings were jumbling up inside of her. She was familiar with sex, it brought hungry children into the world.

"You're too young," she whispered.

"Does this look too young?" he whispered back.

Aspirrina didn't know how to answer, so she remained quiet. She had seen all her brothers naked, but not like this, hard and strangely beautiful. Some of the Haitian men had trailed after her, but she had been too smart for them. At the moment she did not feel so smart.

"Besalo." Kiss it, Diego said, pushing her head down.

"No," she said, a playful giggle escaping her lips. She wanted to refuse but didn't want to disappoint him.

"Come on, do it. It's what girls like to do."

He pushed her down even more until she was kneeling before him, her resistance melting.

"Come on," he insisted, his voice growing more urgent, as if he were in pain.

And so she did. To her surprise, a warm feeling washed over her. As he writhed his hips and moaned with pleasure she felt connected to him in a way that she couldn't have imagined. She had heard women at the river talk about this act.

"*It's the only way to please a man without getting pregnant,*" she remembered one saying.

Was she pleasing him? From the sounds he was making, she was. She felt a broken twig cut into her bare knee. No matter, it was only a twig. When he groaned with pleasure and she felt his fluid flow into her mouth she, at last, and instantly, understood love.

On the walk back, she kept thinking: He's my lover. He belongs to me now. Not until she got home did she notice the thin trickle of blood flowing from a small, dirty wound in her knee. No matter. She would kneel on broken glass if Diego asked her.

Those afternoons with Diego made her fearless, and when the opportunity to dance presented itself she grabbed it.

"I'm going to perform next Saturday night," she said to Diego during one of their silent walks back to town. "At the talent competition."

"What are you talking about?" He was only half listening. It was getting more and more difficult to talk to him. Once she had done what he wanted, he seemed to want to distance himself from her completely.

"I'm going to dance. Like Isadora Duncan."

This he heard. He stopped and grabbed her shoulders. For the first time in weeks, he looked her in the eyes.

"Aspirrina, don't do it," he said with unfamiliar compassion in his voice, "they'll throw tomates at you."

"I don't think so," she said, breaking away from his grip.

"This is Campechuela," he laughed, "they like *young* girls in rumba dresses, flowers in their hair, shaking their asses. Trust me, I know these people."

"I'm going to be shocking and glorious," she said, walking away. Diego could say whatever he wished; nothing was going to stop her. She'd show him. She'd show them all.

On the day of the event, Aspirrina arrived at the park where the stage had been set up wearing a toga she made out of a bed sheet and a crown of white flowers –just as Isadora had worn in a photo. While she waited her turn, she breathed in the excitement.

The air that day was different, it was wonderful and for the first time in her life she felt she was home. No matter that the area behind the stage was crowded with young, pretty girls in rumba dresses. Girls half her age with large breasts, thick thighs exposed, feet lifted and curved by high heels of their shoes. Next to them she felt like a big potato bug. No matter. She watched the others perform while she waited. She took a peek at the audience, everyone in town was there and they seemed nice enough. From shopkeepers and servants to the town's elite, they were all there, eating greasy churros, sipping beer or lemonade. A grouping of trees provided shade from the afternoon sun, she could feel a soft, encouraging breeze on her face.

She waited and waited as other contestants sang, played instruments, told jokes, danced or recited poetry. Her turn came soon enough. As if in a dream, she was on the stage. She looked at the expectant faces of her audience. *Her audience!* Soon to be friends, fans! She gathered her courage and for the first time in her life, she spoke in public.

"This dance I dedicate to the two people I love most in this world, the great Isadora Duncan..."

A murmur shot through the crowd: "Who?" "What?"

"And," she continued, "Diego Cervantes Murillo."

With that said and blood pumping into her head, she clenched her fists and struck her first pose. A fierce warrior, just like the photo of Isadora. Then, possessed by the spirit of her muse, she jumped and hopped, skipped and twisted. She felt as lithe as the sugarcane of Bátey Oriente. As fluid as the river where she had pounded laundry, as wild as the wind that soared through the fields and the birds that rode its currents with complete abandon. She was lost in a dream when she heard the first shout.

"Get off the stage," someone growled. A waterfall of laughter followed.

Another called her a pig. Then they all started to make the sounds of pigs.

"Oink," they shouted in unison. "Oiiinnk..."

She ignored them until something sailed past her face and struck the stage with a sharp crack. They will throw tomatoes at you, Diego had said. But it wasn't a tomato it was a rock. Other rocks followed. Aspirrina continued dancing as rocks landed all around her. She stepped on one, hard. The pain shot through her foot, and she lost her balance. She landed on the floor with a thud. The dance had ended. Someone rushed out and helped her to her feet, dragged her from the stage – the audience continued shouting, laughing.

She limped away quickly, shamed and shocked, but strangely exhilarated. She limped all the way home; her eyes bright with tears. Matilda was sleeping. Aspirrina slunk past her bedroom and into her own. She sat on her bed, wondering what had gone wrong. What would Isadora do? She wouldn't back down. No she wouldn't.

Ungrateful bastards, she thought furiously, they just don't appreciate culture. If I had put on a rumba dress and shaken my ass for five minutes, they would be eating out of my hand now."

A rapping at her window made her heart jump. She heard Diego's deep voice.

"Aspirrina, are you there? Open up."

She sprang to the window. Who cared what others thought? Diego had been there, he had seen her, he knew modern dance and music, he understood, he was proud. He had rushed to congratulate her. She threw open the window with a radiant smile. Diego's hand caught her hard across her face. The slap resonated a harsh new consciousness into her.

"How dare you, you slut! How dare you embarrass my family like that!"

"But mi amor..." she said, dropping to her knees before him. He pushed her and she fell back. The shock of it all left her without the will to get up. Through eyes flooded with tears she saw his face. She had never seen such hatred.

Diego was reaching into his pocket, pulling out a wad of money.

"This should get you far from here," he said. "I never want to see you again in these parts. If I do, I will kill you."

And just like the harsh and fleeting sound of the slap, he evaporated into the night, leaving only a burning pain behind. She remained on the floor for hours, staring at the ceiling. She knew that with time his memory would fade to a tolerable murmur. She would never love again, but she would dance even if to do so meant she had to sit night after night with Esteban's melancholic daughter.

"Let me look at you," Aspirrina said as Estelita came in from a shower. The girl was wrapped in a towel, her dark hair wet and framing her freshly scrubbed face. La Perdida. The lost girl, as she had taken to calling her, was no longer a child. She was fourteen years old now. The baby fat was melting from her rosy cheeks, her legs, once Aspirrina (over Esteban's objections) had taught her how to shave them, emerged long and shapely. Her youthful bosom was firm and perfect. In spite of her faded dresses, tangled hair and obstinate disposition, it was becoming clear to Aspirrina that a true and luminous beauty was coming to light.

"What's there to look at?" Estelita said as she began dressing.

"I could write a book about the things you don't know," Aspirrina said.

"Go ahead, but stop bothering me, I have to get ready."

Aspirrina knew very well what Estelita was getting ready for. Esteban had promised her a night on the town, a nice dinner and a movie. Aspirrina also knew that Esteban would let the girl down, that he would return to the hotel room drunk, broke and apologetic. And that Estelita, after waiting for hours dressed and eager, would forgive him.

It irked Aspirrina to no end, but when it came to Esteban, Estelita was absolutely helpless. A girl as pretty as that could snap her fingers and get a husband, get away from Sabrosuras and her father, leave the whole mess behind. But Estelita wouldn't dream of it. Plenty of young men had approached her, but she ignored them and eagerly moved on to the next town. Still, there were things that most people couldn't see just by looking at her. Aspirrina had been at her side for years and nothing escaped her. She had witnessed Estelita's desperation slowly turning into mature determination. By the time she was fifteen, Estelita no longer became angry or frightened or despondent. She no longer burst into tears at the slightest provocation. She even stopped running through the streets at all hours looking for him.

They had been in the remote town of Grandes Pasos the first time Aspirrina had truly believed they would never see him again. Everyone had looked everywhere countless times with no success. They were all ready to give up and move on, but not Estelita.

"Stop fretting," Aspirrina said, "you're going to get wrinkles on your face. He'll return, he always does, unfortunately."

As soon as she said the final word, she regretted it. Estelita turned to her and the look was cold and powerful. No words were necessary.

"Have you tried the police station?" Lúcido, an inveterate searcher himself, calmly suggested.

They found Esteban behind bars, wearing the magenta suit and curled up like a baby on the filthy floor. His face was caked with dry mucus and blood. His nose had been shattered one more time. Estelita held her father's hand through the iron bars of the cell while Aspirrina took the necessary steps to obtain his release.

It was the first time Estelita had found Esteban in such deplorable conditions, but Aspirrina knew it would not be the last.

4

Estelita had to learn how best to speak to the jailers who held her father. At first they treated her like a child, but she was older now and carried herself with all the dignity her father willfully squandered. She learned that it worked to her advantage if she stopped at the local diner and ordered a big hot breakfast to go. She'd enter the police station carrying a greasy paper bag, well aware that after they ate the *huevos fritos con chorizo* and drank the *café con leche* she brought them, they would be much more receptive to her requests.

"Your father will never change," Aspirrina said, "if you don't let him face the consequences."

Aspirrina's words were meaningless to her. She didn't set out to become his keeper, it had all been so gradual, his decline so imperceptible. Now she blamed herself, she should have seen, she should have known, she should have done something. But what could a little girl do to stop her father from doing as he wished? It was at times like these that she missed her mother the most, imagined how the woman she never met would have handled the situation.

Would Belquis have known that Esteban wasn't just going out for drinks with friends? Would Belquis have noticed before it was too late that Esteban was slowly walking towards an abyss? She pushed the

45

thoughts away, questions with no answers were of no use to her, they left her feeling stupid. All she could do was rush to his side, make sure he was safe, hope that it was the last time, be kind to him. She hoped that her kindness would be rewarded, that he would come to understand how much she needed him to be strong. But until that moment came she had to be strong enough for the two of them.

At first, the charges against Esteban were nothing more than public intoxication or disturbing the peace and could easily be dismissed as the eccentric behavior of an artist. But as the frequency and violence of his outbursts increased, the charges were not so easy for officials to ignore.

Only thirty-four, her father often looked much older, particularly after a hard night – his belly was bloated, his eyes bleary, he ended each performance disgustingly sopped with sweat. Women no longer flocked to him after the show. His prowling had long been relegated to the cheapest brothels, and even those had started to close their doors to him because he had, over the years, developed a taste for the unusual.

Frightening hard-faced men came to her, one hand outstretched, the other in a coat pocket, more likely than not, fingering a loaded weapon.

"I don't care what he does to them," they said with voices too tired for an argument. "But las muchachas have to be compensated according to the damage he inflicts."

Estelita was afraid but found the strength to face them down. Time and again she dismissed them with a practiced sneer and the slam of her hotel room door. It wasn't until she found Esteban in the dark and rank ward of a hospital, his big, beautiful teeth knocked out by someone's angry fists, bruises like the wings of a purple butterfly adorning the area under his eyes, that she started to reconsider Aspirrina's words. Would her father mend his ways if she were to turn her back on him? Not that she ever could, the mere thought of it made her stomach churn, as if she was were being pulled inside out. So, time and again, she diligently visited him in the various hospitals, waited until he was better and, time and again, was released to her care.

Esteban would be shamed into silence for the first few days, until he performed again. But his work was no longer the same, he no longer thrilled an audience. He no longer opened the second act. But

46

still he went on night after night.

"I can't face them," he said to her. He was lying face down on the bed. "I'm too tired, I'm sick. Have pity."

With each excuse her heart broke a bit more but she persisted.

"We need the money, Papá," Estelita told him repeatedly.

"Ah, money," he mumbled as if it were a new concept, a foreign sound.

It had become routine. She allowed him to wallow for as long as possible, but minutes before he was due on stage, she created a commotion, once again she summed up her energies and his, she forced him up, brought him glass after glass of water, then black coffee and finally, a shot of rum. Eventually enough of his energy returned to stand upright, find his balance. He smelled awful, as if something had died inside him. They stood toe to toe while she combed his hair, smoothed out his mustache, she held her breath as she fumbled to tie the shirt knot at his thick waist. The days of washer women were long gone. It was now Estelita who looked after his costumes, shined his shoes, washed and ironed his shirts. It had been years since they could afford new costumes. All of them were many times mended, and tight, the ruffles limp and faded. He dressed slowly as if the garments had grown heavy. Before he set out for the stage they avoided each other's eyes. She did not want him to see her disappointment.

On stage she watched him return to life and from a distance he could still charm the audience. But now it was the charm of a trained bear. He went through the motions but without understanding why.

After the show, his demons would be unleashed – out came the suits – now a faded green, blue and magenta. By sunrise he'd be in some sort of trouble again. He was no longer welcomed, like a star as he'd once been, at the many gaming tables and poker games that went on until morning. He'd knock on hotel doors, use the secret passwords that had granted him access for years, to no avail. All privileges had been revoked.

"You come around here again," he was told, "and we cut off your cojónes."

Estelita never nagged him, in fact she never talked to him about it. She knew her place, she was his daughter, and daughters don't have the right to reproach their fathers, particularly one who was, when not drunk, still a wonderful, magical man. Yes, her father was the same inside; it was she who was changing. She could feel it deep in her heart, a hardening. This toughness of spirit, though disturbing, became essential when his incarcerations could no longer be shortened by a hot breakfast, when his behavior was not to be dismissed by a leering policeman's crooked smile.

Despite his promises, Esteban continued to get more complicated and expensive –his stays in small town jails were longer. She learned to cut deals with bail bondsmen. She would sit anxiously through quick trials while country judges shook their heads sternly, wondering how the charming singer they had enjoyed a few years before had turned into the bloated mess that quivered before them.

She learned to tolerate a lawyer's sweaty hand on her knee and how to charmingly stop it from creeping too far up her thighs. By the time she was sixteen, she learned she could get her way by quietly weeping into the nicely ironed and perfumed handkerchiefs of public defendants, bail bondsmen, lawyers, police officers, psychiatrists and internists.

"Tan bonita," they all said with a mixture of admiration and compassion. Such a pretty girl.

Esteban de la Cruz now spent less time on stage and more time strapped to hospital beds. He received soothing shots of morphine and long talks from well-intentioned nurses. Afterwards, he would only talk about their white, starched uniforms and how their breasts pushed against the fabric.

The latest doctor looked too old to still be practicing, his gaze was weary as if he'd seen too many cases like this. She appreciated that his desk was tidy as was the rest of the small office. He did not stand up to greet her but leaned back in his chair and entwined his hands at the back of his neck.

"You're the wife?" he asked.

It was the first time Estelita had been taken for an adult and it took her a moment to answer. Shocking, considering how old and worn Esteban looked, and she again she questioned the man's abilities but chose to simply answer but remain alert.

"No, señor, I am his daughter."

"And your mother, where is she?"

"Dead," she answered quickly, the word like broken glass in her mouth, and braced herself for more questions. He seemed only to speak in questions and now she questioned his interest in her situation. He doesn't really care about us, she thought, he thinks we're trash.

"How old are you?"

"Sixteen."

"Sixteen," he repeated.

"I can look after him, I've done it all my life," she added quickly.

"He's a very sick man, un borracho," the doctor said, his hands still behind his neck, his eyes fixed strongly on hers. His words were an insult yet there was nothing derogatory in his tone, but neither was it compassionate.

"I know," she said lowering her eyes. This man, this doctor, was trying to make her cry and she wasn't going to let him. She took a step forward.

"You've heard this all before," the man said. "But perhaps no one has told you that your father is playing a very dangerous game."

She nodded and kept her breathing even, steady.

"You have to prepare yourself for the worst."

Her tears came, hot and angry because she did not need a doctor to tell her this, she knew. She could sense it, she could smell it, she could see the shadows gathering around him. She knew the doctor was still looking at her so she dried her eyes and faced him once again.

"He's not going to die," she said, "I won't let him."

And with those words, more a promise to herself than anything else, she excused herself from the room. Aspirrina and Lúcido sat up with her that night, the air was warm and clean and the night was full of stars. The three sat on folded tarps by the truck.

"You don't have to get to the end of the line," Lúcido the Magician said, "to know the destination of the train."

"I can't give up on him," Estelita said, "I just have to be more vigilant, stronger somehow, stronger than him."

"You're just a child," Lúcido said, "he should be taking care of you."

Exhausted, Estelita rested her head on Aspirrina's thick lap. The woman shifted slightly to accommodate her.

"He's a wonderful father," Estelita said, her voice heavy with sleep, "he's just, sick, the doctor said so."

As she drifted off she felt Aspirrina's hand tenderly brush her hair as she said,

"A girl looking like this," Aspirrina said, "without the protection of a father, is like a bowl of candy left in the town square, anyone can grab a handful."

Once again, her father was released to her care. He was fine for a while, then he began to run off again.

*

It was broad daylight, hot and dry. Three men wrestled Esteban to the dusty ground, held him down while they punished him for resisting. They pummeled his face, swollen and transformed by alcohol and bar fights. Estelita screamed as one of the men kicked his ribs, she heard the low cracking sound that made her father stop struggling.

"Estelita!" he cried out. Her name echoed upwards, high into the painfully blue sky. His call carried a sorrow like she'd never heard. It had been just three months since she'd made herself the promise that she would protect her father, keep him alive, but he continued to slip away from her, it had become a sort of game to him, disappearing into the night, worrying her into a froth.

As they dragged him away he whispered a single word, as if in prayer.

"Belquis."

She shuddered, thinking of the many times she had invoked her mother's name in prayer, begging her for the divine intervention the dead were said to provide.

The straight-jacket was firmly tied. His arms, which she would always remember wrapped in colorful, ruffled, sleeves, were now encased in dirty, white canvas sleeves and fastened behind his back. His body vacillated between rage and resignation. He was raised to his feet and pushed into the van that would take him to the psychiatric hospital.

"Only for six months," Aspirrina had assured her. "Time will pass quickly. He will return healed."

Estelita looked at her through eyes that seemed to desire nothing now but to cry forever. She saw Lúcido, his black cape tightly wrapped as if he meant to make himself invisible. Not far from him stood Cascabel, Mirabel and Isabel. The triplets were so closely huddled, they

seemed one body, three heads, as they slowly walked away.
Only Aspirrina had stayed by her side.

A month later, when they visited La Casa De Locos, the crazy
house, as the psychiatric hospital had been nicknamed, Esteban looked
past her no matter how often she touched his face or repeated her own
name.

"Look papá, I'm a dolphin, I'm a mermaid." But there was no
response. Aspirrina held her up as she stumbled into the sunlight.

"Forget six months," Aspirrina said. "It's going to take a lot of
time."

"You're right," Estelita said, "he needs to be here for as long at
it takes. At least here he is safe. Clearly, I'm not strong enough to make
him well."

"He's too much for you," Aspirrina said, "he'd be too much for
anyone."

Estelita nodded in agreement but as she walked away she
determined that her father would not be forgotten even if he had
forgotten her. He would never feel abandoned even though he had
abandoned her.

*

"What will you have to offer him if you stay here? Nothing."
Aspirrina asked and answered herself. "He has nothing to offer you. No
one will hire him. If you stay you'll both end up living in the dirt."

Estelita knew Aspirrina was right. Other girls in her position had
to take in washing, sell goods at open markets, or beg outside the
churches; clutching dirty infants born of loneliness and despair. She'd
seen them all her life; their faces drawn and aged before their time,
their eyes hollow with disappointment. She had also seen the
prostitutes, girls her own age or even younger; dozens in every town.
She'd admired them for their colorful way of dressing, their carefree
way of walking, talking, laughing; their casual camaraderie.

Until Aspirrina pointed out the others.

They were older and emerged as if from shadows. She saw them
trembling in rainstorms, or being kicked by men in bright daylight.

She saw them chided by groups of women who walked past
them. She saw them running down crowded streets bloodied and

stumbling, talking crazy through cracked lips; knees scabby, clothes torn.

"Your father will be useless when he gets out," Aspirrina said. "You want to take care of him, you want the house with the cooking smells and the comfort of your own bedroom, you need money, and there's only one place to go for money right now."

So, when Aspirrina finally left Sabrosuras (much to everyone's relief), Estelita went with her. Not without some misgivings. She'd heard Havana described as a cesspool of sin and violence by some, and paradise on earth by others. No matter. She knew there were more casinos scheduled to open, that opportunity was unlimited if you knocked on the right door, met the right people, took a chance.

"The new casinos are going to be bigger and more glamorous than anything anyone on the island has ever seen," Aspirrina said. "Havana will be the Monte Carlo of the Caribbean."

Estelita listened as Aspirrina droned on, as she had on those nights when she'd watched over her. She had no idea what or where Monte Carlo was but she made it sound desirable.

"Maybe it's too late for me," Aspirrina continued, "but not for you. I couldn't let you get trapped in that horrible traveling troupe. That life leads nowhere. In Havana you won't have any trouble finding a job. Anyplace where you can be seen."

"I guess I could be a waitress or a cigarette girl," Estelita said.

Aspirrina looked at her for a long time. Estelita had never thought of herself as anything special. She was the singer's daughter, the lost girl. That was all. She was stupid and useless. She couldn't save her father.

"You have no idea, do you?" Aspirrina said slowly. "You are a gold mine. And just like a gold mine, you must be discovered."

"You're talking crazy."

"Maybe. Or maybe you just need to set your sights a little higher. In Havana you will meet wealthy men." Aspirrina said, "either a husband or un amante acaudalado. A wealthy lover."

"A lover! Are you out of your mind?"

"Chica, it doesn't matter," Aspirrina said with a serious face. "In this country only money matters now and a lover means money. Money matters to you in particular. If you ever want to see your father again, take care of him properly, you're going to need a lot of it."

Estelita kept silent, this did not need to be decided yet. Whether she took a job or a lover would have to be seen. She had always imagined that falling in love would be like the story her father told her over and over, about meeting Belquis, about fighting to be together, about that one special person, but with a happier ending. In her story, Belquis lived, at least long enough to raise her. Her father had done that for her, brought her into the world and taken good care of her for as long as he was able. Now he was a sick man and it was her turn. For now he was safe, at least from himself, and she found herself anxious for a new life to begin. In her new life, she would be the one who took care of him. She didn't know exactly how that shift would take place but she had no doubt that it would.

A week later when they boarded the train at Palma Soriano, Estelita had stopped crying every time she thought about her father, had accepted her fate with Aspirrina; had even come to see it as a welcome change. Perhaps this adventure in Havana *was* the best way to help him. Six months would pass quickly. She would write him frequently and once she and Aspirrina were settled, he'd have no trouble finding her.

As they made their way through the first compartment, she felt the eyes of the female passengers on her. They were looking at her differently than cops and lawyers had. Suddenly she felt shabby in her cotton dress. It was starched and ironed, but faded. And fit tight around her bosom, perhaps too tight. Or maybe too short. Unlike the women on the train she wore no makeup although Aspirrina had tried to force some on her. Her hair was clean and she had tied it back with a ribbon.

They continued to the back of the train and as they walked she noticed that it was mostly men and animals and that the few women there were dressed even more humbly than she. But even they were staring at her.

"What are you looking at?" Aspirrina sassed as they took their seats. No one said a word back to her.

The train was full and unbearably hot. Everyone was too tired to speak, and what could have been a joyful crowd full of laughter and chatter was just a silent ride with people sweating and drifting into restless, uncomfortable sleep.

There were campesinos, farmers, carrying groups of hens tied by the leg, like big feathery bouquets. They were taking the birds to the city markets to sell for Noche Buena, the Christmas Eve celebration. But the hens, not used to traveling, were nervous and making quite a mess on the floor. Every so often, a uniformed conductor would walk by, mopping his forehead with a sopping handkerchief.

"Clean it up," the conductor said sternly, "or you'll be taken off the train at the next stop!"

The campesino would make a feeble attempt to wipe up the mess with newspapers, but no sooner had they done so than another high-strung hen would relieve herself in almost the exact same spot. There was no way to escape from the stench.

At every stop, throngs were allowed into the cars to sell their wares: cups of lukewarm lemonade they called raspa, burnt coconut pastries, little ceramic toys, embroidered napkins. Among them, beggars limped through, some hopping on one leg, or with one arm or an eye missing, all asking for alms. Aspirrina had no trouble waving them away or just pointedly ignoring them until they went away. She had a flagrant disdain for beggars. On the other hand, she was much more charitable to the strolling musicians. They were artists like herself; they were contributing something, working for their handouts. But her generosity had its limits. The first time a guitar player came down the aisle, she immediately fished into her purse for a coin, which she offered with a wide smile. She even tried to get the man engaged in conversation. But the man had no time for small talk. He still had several more cars to serenade before the train took off again. But as the train continued to make more and more stops, and more and more artists strolled by for a handout, they started to annoy her. She was equally disdainful, but distant and polite to the women who carried dirty babies and sang religious hymns.

When they stopped at Cienfuegos, a group of university students came through the car selling Fidel Castro dolls. These dolls, basically converted baby dolls from the five-and-dime store adorned with a black beard, olive green fatigues, and the famous cap, were the height of contraband. They were being used to raise funds for the rebels in the mountains that everyone was talking about. More often than not, the students had to run through the cars, the angry conductor nearly at their heels. They stopped, their voices rushed, eyes wild, waving the forbidden dolls above their heads and shouting that they wanted "just three pesos" or "isn't three pesos a small price to pay for freedom?"

The conductor shouted words like "traitors" and "thieves" at them. Some of the passengers strategically stood up or moved a bag to block and slow down the fuming conductor once the students had passed.

Estelita watched the students with admiration and envy. She wondered what it had been like to have a normal childhood, with schools and rules and to grow up with passion for a cause. She knew nothing of politics other than Aspirrina's rants and raves. When the last of the students were gone she leaned against Aspirrina's beefy shoulders and tried to sleep.

Night fell quickly, without a moon but full of stars, as if the train itself was pulling along a massive black, diamond-studded cloak, shrouding the sky, darkening the countryside.

Estelita kept her eyes closed, but hard as she tried she couldn't fall asleep. She felt the train taking her hundreds of miles away from Esteban. Farther than she ever thought possible. Even in their endless travels around the country, neither one had ever considered visiting Havana, any more than they had considered visiting the moon.

"Havana is the heart and soul of everything," Aspirrina said. "Only very special people get to go there and we may not be very special people now, but we will be by the time we get there."

How Aspirrina was going to make this happen Estelita did not know, couldn't fathom. But she was well aware that this was her big chance. Sure, she could be a special person. Why not? No one knew her except Aspirrina, so she could be anyone she wanted. With her father she had always felt special, even as things turned bad, she was the singer's daughter, his one and only precious girl, his light. She would be that for him again and now that she was older she'd know how to better accomplish that, to guide him to a better life.

As the train screeched and slid to a stop she had made up her mind. She'd become a real Habanera – a true lady of Havana, someone worthy of living amidst the beauty and glamour of the big city. The great capital. She felt too young for a husband and had no use for a lover. But she would make her way, there were undreamed of opportunities in Havana. When her father came, she would be ready. She would have a nice apartment with two bedrooms, one bedroom just for him. Far from the small towns and the cheap bars he would flourish again, get a job singing at one of the casinos. She would help him, before long he would open the second act once more.

Maybe even headline. Why not?

Anything was possible in Havana.

They'll hire anybody who can shake a maraca, as Serpentina once said. And her father was capable of so much more.

Havana.

A good place to start the new year. In just a few days it would be 1957, and in just two short weeks, she would be seventeen-years old. The flower of her life was just about to bloom. After all, the absolutely worst thing that could have happened, already had.

5

HAVANA

1957

El Convento de la Santa Caterina was not as large as El Convento de Belén, nor as elegant as El Convento de Santa Clara. Those ancient and respected Havana institutions were like million-dollar mansions compared to the humid, crumbling house that housed more than a dozen women from the Catholic Order of the Nazarenes. Las Monjas, as the nuns were known, were overseen by Sor Maria, the Mother Superior, although she forbade anyone from addressing her that way.

"You must call me sister. I am just one of you, a humble servant of our Lord," she'd admonish. Although only twenty five years old, she ruled the convent with the tyrannical force of a much older woman. Many women came to her in their darkest hour to seek shelter and salvation – few were taken in and even fewer were allowed to stay.

The Nazarenes were the most self-sacrificing of all the cloistered orders. Their devotion to humility, poverty, and atonement was clearly evident in their cold, dark, cockroach-infested retreat.

The sisters starved themselves and concentrated on their acts of charity, which were numerous and performed in such a way that even those who benefited from their generosity hardly knew that the sisters existed. Needy families often found bags of food at their doorsteps, or discovered that their overdue rents had been paid. Hospital rooms were mysteriously filled with fresh flowers. During the Christmas holidays, toys appeared in the cramped living rooms of humble families as if benevolent shadows had been listening to the hushed prayers of the children who lived there.

The nuns received a minute stipend from the archdiocese, which they proudly repaid by cleaning the altars and sanctuaries of the many churches of the city. All proceeds were immediately invested in the needy of Havana. Sor Maria Quintana detested the accumulation of wealth. Their work began as soon as the sun had set, it was performed in secrecy and in absolute silence. Silencio, the sisters believed, helped them walk on spiritual, interior paths, and it was an unwavering rule of the Nazarenes.

They were rarely seen in public, few saw the sisters enter or depart, no one heard their dainty footsteps as they crept through the dark and narrow alleys and backways of the city. Their silence, their black habits and the heavy wooden crucifixes that hung from their slender necks protected them from criminals. They were never accosted, harassed or propositioned by drunks or accosted by any of the numerous sinners that abounded in the city. They came and went with ease.

Come morning, the faithful, the penitent, the mournful and the fanatical never wondered who was responsible for the sparkling, stained glass windows, the gleaming altars, the polished pews, or the immaculate marble floors. The churches were always as they should be.

Once all the churches were spotless and ready for early services, by 10 p.m. they were back in the convent, and in complete silence, without so much as a "good night" or a "God bless" they retired to their cells until the following day.

Mornings found them in the basement chapel where they prayed for those who did not pray for themselves. After prayers they retired to an adjacent work room and engaged their delicate hands in the moneymaking endeavor of manufacturing rosaries, chaplets, scapulars, badges, medals and calendars.

Having renounced all material goods in order to be more like

Jesus Christ, the proceeds from these popular sacramentals funded their inconspicuous acts of charity. The work filled their hearts with a joy that completely vanquished any mortification, any doubt, or any anguish that might disquiet their mortal souls.

Every night they humbly thanked God for bestowing on them such a beautiful vocation, for the privilege to live and work in His presence, and for the grace to perform small quiet miracles in His name.

The nuns avoided the outside world; they lived in complete seclusion, seldom venturing outside the crumbling cement walls of the Convento de Santa Caterina in daylight. Men were never allowed inside except for extreme emergencies: a fire, a flood, an earthquake. Exceptions were made for doctors and priests, but their visits were rare and those men were usually too old to pose a threat.

Convento de Santa Caterina was at the edge of El Fanguito, a bustling, impoverished neighborhood, populated with lottery vendors calling out numbers, offering strokes of luck, women who yelled at each other from one house to another, vegetable carts pulled by mules, their wooden wheels and clomping hooves resounding off the cobblestone streets. Meat markets displayed everything edible in a beast – big cow heads looked sullenly through fly-covered eyes. Ragtag beggars stopped everyone who passed, petty thieves slithered through looking for opportunity. Police and ambulance sirens competed with the bell-shaped amplifiers of political candidates and religious proselytizers who circled in little white cars promising every sort of solution and salvation.

In spite of its central location, it was as if the convent and its inhabitants didn't exist. The only indication that something sacred was working behind those walls was the pious neighborhood ladies who stopped briefly and crossed themselves. They made the sign of the cross silently, from forehead to navel and from shoulder to shoulder, as they walked past the convent's front door, the same way they did whenever they walked past a funeral home, a church, a bar, or a brothel.

The sisters prided themselves on their self-sufficiency and had become quite adept at hauling their own water from the well in the courtyard, mending their own walls and repairing the roof. It was the little things they couldn't fit into their daily schedule. Someone was needed to shop for groceries, cook their meals, wash and iron their clothes and help keep the place from filling up with spider webs and rodents, but so far everyone had failed them. Whomever they took in soon became so lonely and sick of the silences and demands, that once out at the market, they couldn't help but engage in conversations and gossip.

Sor Maria Quintana always knew because suddenly there would be people at her door asking questions that they did not need answered, and begging for favors that she found extremely inappropriate. The night when she reluctantly answered an insistent knock at the front door, she had known at a glance that the woman standing before her was an expert hustler. She would have slammed the door in her vulgar face if it hadn't been for the look on the young girl that stood at her side. Sor Maria would never admit this to anyone, but the girl, in spite of her modest dress and dime store shoes, reminded her of the girl she herself had been not long ago.

*

She had been born into what most people would consider enviable circumstances, the only daughter of the social and profuse Calixto Betancourt and his glamorous wife, the former Isela Castillo y Plana. She had been the sought-after heiress to the popular Minerva Soft Drink fortune. Her family fortune was second only to the Bacardi's and that never would have happened if it wasn't for the increasing popularity of Coca Cola.

The fortune had been amassed by her paternal grandfather, a crafty curandero. He had called himself an herbalist but was better known as The Witch Doctor, the man who magically turned a common weed known as Yerba Mate into a golden bubbly soft drink many called the "Cuban ginger ale."

Maria's early life had been spent floating distractedly from the beautifully decorated drawing room in her parents' great country estate and beach front residence to the equally breathtaking homes of the friends in their circle. The talk was always of servants, schools, and who was going to host the next lavish coming out party for their daughters.

Maria attended the best private schools, always under the

instructions of strict Catholic nuns. She never gave the nuns much thought; they had always been there, like the servants. They were people who got paid to do things for her. The nuns were paid to teach (or try to teach) her and her wealthy friends. She saw them as sad and bitter women in shapeless cotton dresses, thick black tights and uncomfortable looking shoes.

But slowly, almost imperceptibly, as her body started to change, something inside her had started to change as well. After a lifetime of luxury, she began to believe that luxury was not enough, and the thought of it frightened her. A terrible emptiness started to gnaw at her and she could not understand, define, or explain it. Then the headaches began.

The throbbing behind her eyes started late at night and continued until dawn. In her spacious bedroom, alone in a four-poster bed big enough for three people, deep in layers of fresh, pink-flowered sheets and ruffled pillows, surrounded by her dolls and stuffed animals, her thoughts echoed like shouts in a canyon. As she took stock of what the day had been like, and what awaited her the next morning, a strange sadness invaded her, a sorrow she had never felt before, and could not have anticipated.

She tried everything, counting sheep; reading heavy and boring books on subjects that had never appealed to her, and sipping warm chamomile tea sweetened with brown sugar. Nothing soothed her. She began to notice, much to her aggravation and confusion, that when she whispered the word "meaningless," the headaches would subside. She found this alarmingly odd and feared she was losing her mind. The more she did it, the more it worked. Soon she began chanting the word to herself before she went to bed every night and discovered that it appeased the pain. She started to play with it, to spell it out and rhyme it with other words or to imagine the letters writing themselves across her ceiling. It amused her that she was going mad and that nobody noticed.

Grateful as she was to catch up on her sleep, she was left with a horrible feeling that seemed embedded into her flesh and bones. If everything is meaningless, she wondered, how does one find meaning?

Most women in her social circle seemed to find it in the hunt for a husband and plans for a family, but Maria shuddered at the thought. When she looked around her at the older generation, all she saw was pampered ladies who hardly ever saw their husband or children, who kept busy with art or jewelry design classes, or fancy luncheons and other obligations that just seemed silly to her. Even their philanthropic projects looked like more creative and amusing ways to spend money, not unlike their shopping trips to New York City every spring and fall. There was only one person she knew who might understand. His name was Leonardo Delfino.

Leonardo was a strange boy she had known all of her life. They had birthdays exactly two days apart, and although he was three years older, their families celebrated them together. Their mothers had been best friends since they were schoolgirls and through the children had developed an even stronger bond. Year after year, their families came together in one place or another to enjoy pony rides or carnivals. Once the candles had been blown out, the cake cut and distributed, the opulent presents opened, she and Leonardo would huddle together like two shell-shocked refugees. They often escaped to one of the many empty, well-appointed rooms, their only desire to get away from the noise and unsolicited attention of distant relatives and their fathers' business associates.

Like her, Leonardo was an only child, which was unusual in a country where couples had many children. But the better families, and families didn't get any better than Leonardo's, often stopped at one. Maria's mother did everything Leonardo's mother did, even if it meant leaving the family without a male heir.

Leonardo's family owned land, lots of land all over Cuba. Hundreds of farmers depended on them. They grew everything of worth on the island: coffee, sugar cane, pineapples. Unlike Maria's family, whose fortune was relatively new, Leonardo's family always had money and were used to it. Maria's parents worshipped Leonardo's parents' money and social ease. Maria was attracted to Leonardo for his sweet nature. The boy was so withdrawn that he made Maria appear gregarious.

Although he could have been spoiled and arrogant like the other rich boys and girls they knew, Leonardo was shy and humble, almost ashamed of his aristocratic background. But what really stole her heart was that he was constantly teased and tormented by other children. He was born with a great big shock of white hair sprouting from his widow's peak. He had a beautiful, angelic face but that shock of white, like a crescent moon in the center of his head, gave him an ancient, almost demonic look. He was constantly under attack. Classmates called him ugly names. They accused him of dying his hair, of being "like a girl."

The boy did not know how to defend himself because unlike the other burly, vicious boys, he lacked the killer instinct. Instead of fighting, he would run away, and he didn't run very well, so they always caught him. One time a group of children tied him to a tree and left him crying until Maria found him and untied him.

His parents seemed oblivious to their son's suffering. But Maria, who was loved by everyone, and had never known a day of unhappiness in her life, made Leonardo her best friend. She would invite him to her house to play. He liked to do the things she enjoyed. They read together, often lying on adjacent sofas, not speaking for hours, both lost in a book and happy to be in each other's company. Or, if they were feeling more energetic, they dressed up in costumes. Leonardo liked to dress up like a girl and insisted that Maria dress like a boy, sometimes they both dressed like girls and he let her pour the tea while he pretended to cool himself with a feathered fan.

Her parents, if they were home, stayed downstairs while they played. The only people who saw them were the servants, who shook their heads and clacked their tongues disapprovingly. But they never said a word. More could not be expected of spoiled, rich children.

When Leonardo was thirteen-years old he had been sent away, unexpectedly and without notice, to a military academy. Maria did not get a chance to say goodbye to him and missed him terribly. She wrote to him often, but the letters from him were infrequent and as time went by they stopped altogether. Over the years, she thought about him often. From her mother, she heard that he had graduated from the Academy and taken a trip to Spain. She thought he was just on vacation, but it would be several years before she saw him again.

*

"*Leonardo ha regresado*," her mother said during a rare occasions when she joined her parents for Sunday breakfast. Leonardo has returned.

"He's in Havana?" Maria asked unable to hide the excitement she felt.

"Yes, and his parents are mortified," her mother said.

"If that young man had any sense," her father added, "he would have stayed away. What their eyes don't see, their hearts won't feel."

"He has taken his own apartment in Vedado," her mother continued as if her husband hadn't spoken at all. "Why he would do that I have no idea. He has three lovely houses to choose from and he's living down there. But of course, as I always suspected, he's living a life of absolute degeneracy, if you know what I mean."

"What did they expect?" her father said, "sending a boy like that to Europe. They can expect no less."

"He now calls himself only Delfino," her mother said, "even though he has turned his back on his parents' business and is determined to drag their name through the mud. He's sells ladies' hats that he designs himself. I hear they're quite chic."

Maria continued to move the food about on her plate, but she was no longer listening. She had heard enough. She couldn't wait until breakfast was over. She had to see Leonardo Delfino.

She just had to.

*

Standing outside of the shop, Maria could see that Leonardo was an undisputed success. It was on one of the most elegant blocks in Havana. His customers, no doubt, were the rich wives of the men who, when they were children, had made him so miserable. She approached the door with some trepidation, not sure what kind of welcome to expect from her childhood friend. Her anxiety vanished the moment he saw her. His eyes grew wide as he ran to embrace her.

He was tall and thin now, and his face was no longer pale but had burnt into a dark deep tan. He was dressed in black slacks and a black silk shirt and the shock of white that had been a curse during his childhood was now an elegant asset. With a few words he turned his customer over to an assistant and whisked her into the back of the store. He led her into a small sitting room. Three of the walls were shelved and on the shelves rested dozens of beautiful hats, on the fourth wall were photographs of Delfino and famous clients. There he was with

Tongolele, the singing legend, and Maria Felix, Mexico's biggest movie star, and the singer Sarita Montiel, Spain's national treasure, as well as other elegant women she did not recognize but who looked extremely important. Next to the photographs hung a large oval mirror. In the center of the room were two French antique chairs and a round coffee table. He led her to a chair and sat across from her. He lit a cigarette and offered her one. She declined.

They talked about everything, as comfortably as if no time had passed since they had last seen each other. She did not mention the unanswered letters, the years of wondering. He was with her now. Looking into his eyes, hearing his voice, that was all that mattered.

He told her about a man he had met while living in Madrid who had taught him about hats.

"Well, you're certainly doing well," she said.

"Success runs in the family," he responded. "I can't help ascending."

There was a brief silence and then she heard herself ask the question she had told herself not to ask.

"Is it true, what they say."

He smiled gently.

"That I am a flamboyant homosexual?"

She nodded, blushing. He took a deep breath.

"It's none of my business," she said quickly, regretting her intrusion.

"I will say this," he said waving his cigarette, "on the rare occasion when I succumb to my carnal desires, yes, it is, with a man."

Her face was on fire. What could she say now?

"Is there someone special?" she asked, trying for a sophistication that felt disingenuous. Her mind was racing. She wondered how his parents must feel, never to see a grandchild, an heir. But wasn't she in fact considering the same?

Delfino sucked on his cigarette and with a mouth full of smoke, said.

"There was, in Madrid, but that's all over." He waved his hand to disperse the smoke. "Let's talk about you, I'm sick of me, is there someone special?"

He sat quietly smoking while she revealed her own secret.

"A nun?" he whispered seriously when she was finished.

"A nun," she repeated and tried to smile, but tears were welling up in her eyes.

He smiled back, his own eyes sparkling. "Well, why not? Considering the genetic pool of savages you get to choose your husband from, I can't say I blame you for wanting to remain celibate. My advice, and I assume that's why you're here, is go live with the sisters. And if you don't like it, you can always leave, you can always try something else. The worst that could happen is that you'll learn something."

He stood up and paced around the room small room. She remained seated, quiet, wondering if this visit had been a mistake. Now someone knew.

"Try it," he said, "I'm all for trying new things, and if it doesn't work out, you can come work for me."

"Selling hats?"

"No darling, modeling them, you are gorgeous."

And with that he took a plumed hat off a shelf and placed it firmly on her head.

He took her hand and brought her to her feet. Then he took another hat and set it on his own head and turned her towards the mirror.

Leonardo wrapped an arm gently around her shoulders. She looked at their image in the mirror and their eyes met and he smiled sadly and it was as if they were children again. Except for one significant exception: he had experienced so much, she had experienced nothing.

*

Maria Quintana spent the weekend of her graduation from Sacred Heart High School dancing until dawn with every boy who asked her. There were parties twice a day for two days, the last one of which was celebrating her eighteenth birthday was held at the Havana Yacht Club (her father was a founding member). Leonardo Delfino was invited, but he declined. In his stead, the hat she had tried on at his shop arrived by special messenger.

She played along with the girls, showed off her brand new

dresses, and much was made of her new hat. She made silly, giggling promises to several ardent suitors. An heiress always has plenty of young men around who are ready to drop to one knee and offer her the world and Maria was no exception. But she already owned the world, or as much of it as anyone could possibly want; she didn't need a man to provide for her.

The following morning, a clear, cloudless Monday, she had awakened feeling fresh and determined. She had dressed in the pale pink linen dress her mother had bought for her on one of her trips. She had walked the familiar hallways of the palatial house, seen herself reflected in the hallway mirrors, the polished marble floors, the abundant crystal vases and taken her place at the breakfast table. Then gently but firmly, she had announced her decision.

They objected, but she was determined. They offered her complete freedom, her own apartment, cars, servants. She declined.

"This is not the sort of decision *una señorita* makes abruptly," her father said.

"Think about it a bit longer, take a trip and see the world before making such an enormous resolution."

Maria remained firm.

"We can go together," her mother said in her gayest tone. "Italy! We'll see the Vatican in Rome, perhaps that will satisfy this sudden need for religion, and while we're there, the Spring collections in Milan."

But Maria could not be swayed. She also could not give them a good reason. As the weeks passed, their loving patience, their paternal indulgence for their only daughter diminished and finally vanished altogether.

"You're throwing your life away," her father shouted.

But his shouts did not intimidate her.

"This is what I wish to do with my life," she said, "if I cannot have your support, I will settle for your respect."

He had no answer for this and retreated into his study to weep unobserved. Maria could hear his suffering through the thick wooden door and it was at this moment, just when she was about to run to him, throw open those doors, put her arms around him and kiss his tear stained face that she felt God enter her heart. It was as if the marble floor had vanished beneath her feet and she was suspended in midair.

Although all windows were closed and the draperies drawn, she felt the warmth of the sun on her face. She stood there a long time and would have remained there forever. Such was her joy.

Her father eventually emerged from his study, clear eyed and as stoic as ever. But her mother was inconsolable and relentless.

"I know you better than anyone, Maria, better than you know yourself. I remember clearly how many times I had to plead, bargain and finally force you to attend mass. This does not feel to me like a calling, it's just a rebellion. You may as well have declared that you are becoming a prostitute and joining a brothel! It's just not done. What will I tell people?"

While her mother watched, she calmly picked out her smallest valise and dropped a few items into it: a toothbrush, a hair comb, a plain brown skirt and a blue cotton blouse.

"That's all you're taking? Out of all the wonderful things you have? At least take some decent shoes!"

Maria zipped her valise and walked out of her bedroom. Her mother followed down the long hallway, down the stairs, through the sitting room, the anteroom, the living room, the foyer, the veranda, out the front door and to the waiting car.

"No," her mother screamed and grabbed her hand, knocking the valise to the ground. Maria's tears matched her mother's. She looked back to the house where her father stood at the doorway.

"Help me, father," Maria said. But he didn't come running as she'd hoped, instead he lifted a hand and waved goodbye. It was a small, simple gesture. Maria stopped struggling and wrapped her arms around her mother. Her mother returned the embrace and they held on so tight that for a moment Maria felt they would crush each other and fall to the ground in pieces.

Her mother let go first and took a step back. Maria picked up her valise and opened the car door.

"After one night in that dimly lit, horribly decorated cell," her mother said, "you'll come running."

Maria was aware of the pain she had caused. She rode in her father's car for the last time, and entered the convent. The instant she sat alone in the dimly lit, horribly decorated cell, she knew she was ready for a life of poverty, obedience and chastity. That very same night, the word Sor, archaic for Sister, was placed in front of her name. The next day her headaches had disappeared forever.

For months after she received long impassioned letters from her mother luring her with everything that she was missing. They contained detailed descriptions of the new yacht, or of someone's fancy wedding. She included photographs of newborn babies and the latest Paris fashions. It saddened her that her mother had never known her at all.

Beautiful young men, terrified that an enormous fortune was slipping through their fingers, sent large bouquets of roses, the engraved cards bearing their names stuck among the leaves and thorns. She kept the roses at the altar in the basement chapel as an offering to Jesus Christ until they dried up and turned a deeper color.

She hardly noticed when the flowers stopped coming.

Delfino sent her a beautiful rosary made of rosewood, and its fragrance always reminded her that somewhere in the world she had a true friend. She prayed for him every day, hoping that God, who only saw good in people, would one day cast a loving glance in his direction.

Although the convent was in the center of the city, as time passed the distances between her old life and the new, the past and the present became longer and longer until her former life became a delicate, transparent, almost invisible impression, like the scent left behind by a lace trimmed handkerchief as it drops slowly to the floor.

Like Delfino had said, success ran in her family as well. She couldn't help but ascend. It wasn't long before Sor Maria became Mother Maria Quintana. She did nothing to deserve it, it simply came to be. Mother Superior swallowed a box of rat poison and a succession had to happen quickly, lest the others also become suicidally despondent. Sor Maria accepted the responsibilities with equal measure of fear and courage.

She simply did what God ordained.

Years had passed before she realized how long it had been since anyone had come to see her or had sent her anything. Sometimes she wondered how often her mother or her father glided silently past the convent door in one of their shiny and air-conditioned cars and if they said a prayer or sent a curse or if they even gave her a second thought anymore. It was not the kind of musings she allowed herself very often, but she was made of flesh and blood.

In her dream that night, the night that would change everything, nails were being hammered into a living hand. Whether it was the hand of the Christ or some random hand was not clear to her. But the pounding wore her and she realized with irritation, that someone was pounding on the front door. It had been years since anyone had knocked at the front door and it had been forever since anyone had knocked so late in the night. She was going to ignore it but decided to see who it was before the knocking woke everyone up.

She opened the door a crack and it was flung open by an unseen hand and the force of it almost knocked her off her feet.

6

The first weeks in the convent were awful for Estelita. Sor Maria Quintana took her aside every afternoon to talk to her about Jesus Christ. She spoke softly and repeated herself again and again until Estelita strongly and fearfully believed that everything she had done since she arrived in Havana was a sin.

"Are you a Catholic? Aspirrina asked her?

They were huddled in the tiny cell they shared, their voices less than a whisper, just a breath. Estelita shook her head remembering the countless times her father had taken the crucifix off the wall and put it in a drawer, proclaiming it, "Esta mierda." This is shit.

"Well, then, you've got nothing to worry about."

"But Sor Maria said..."

"Listen, Sor Maria is a nun, I could tell you stories about nuns," Aspirrina countered, her voice dangerously rising.

"Shhh," Estelita warned.

Aspirrina lowered her voice, but her tone remained firm.

"You don't know what she did before she came here, you don't know. The only thing you know for sure is that we've got to get out of here and the only way to do that is to get a job. You have to stick to the plan."

So far the plan had been one lie after another to the good woman who had taken them in. Taken them in because of the enormous lie Aspirrina had told her at the door.

Aspirrina did all of the lying but Estelita had learned during the afternoons with Sor Maria that there was something called lying by omission. She was just as guilty if not more so than Aspirrina. But the plan had worked, Estelita got a job. Aspirrina had guided her to the artist's entrance to the casino. She had told her what to say, who to ask for. She had been nervous but determined and when she had been asked to disrobe she almost left, but she remembered those nice ladies who worked for Lúcido. They had worn even less. She had crossed herself as Sor Maria Quintana had taught her and it seemed to her that it was that gesture, a gesture she didn't entirely understand that had earned her the job. She had seen the expression on the man's face, the choreographer whose name was Chucho.

"You're very beautiful," Chucho said, "and very sweet."

He'd left the room while she dressed and was waiting outside the door.

"You start tomorrow, Estelita de la Cruz," he said. "Is that your real name?"

The question had puzzled her, it had never occurred to her that anyone would change their given name.

"Yes."

She left in a swoon, convinced that it was the sign of the cross, that somehow Jesus Christ was behind her good fortune. Once she had enough money to leave the convent she would make up for it. At the earliest opportunity, she was going to give some of her money to the Nazarenes. And having made that promise to herself, lying to Sor Maria became a lot easier.

Two weeks later she was ready for her debut. There were butterflies in her stomach, but she was only days away from her first paycheck. That was all that mattered.

She took a deep breath, stretched her long legs and tried to stand up straight. She was wearing the highest heels she had ever seen in her life. All the showgirls wore them. They took some getting used to, what with all the others rushing past her; all just as statuesque in their own higher-than-high heels, each still in various stages of undress. The wide, light-trimmed mirror reflected a storm of black corsets, pale breasts distinguished by uniquely shaded nipples, red panties, bare tummies dotted with perfect navels, embroidered girdles, lovely young faces all talking at once, diaphanous streams of red, yellow, and purple tulle, vigorous legs and arms bending and stretching this way and that, pink satin head-dresses cascading multicolor ribbons and white feathers, bare, smooth shoulders, long slender necks. The chaos was overseen by a team of stern-faced dressers in light blue smocks who communicated with each other through pursed, unpainted lips firmly holding bobby and safety-pins. It was their nightly task to prepare 22 gorgeous but often clumsy and thoughtless girls as they struggled through thirteen costume changes in the span of one frantic, exhilarating hour.

The new shoes pinched her feet but she didn't care. They were the most beautiful shoes she had ever worn. Everything about the small, cramped room had been beautiful to her that night, even the smell of face powder, lipstick, less then efficient deodorant, too strong French perfume, sticky hairspray and layer upon layer of cigarette smoke; a smell she would associate for the rest of her life with this first night, the first of many in the dressing rooms of the Riviera. She caught sight of herself in the mirror as one of the dressers turned her around and expertly fastened all the tiny hooks up the back that held her costume together. Her new platinum blonde hair still surprised her. It had been Aspirrina's idea.

"With your light brown eyes and creamy complexion," she insisted, "you should seriously consider bleaching your hair blonde. The blonder the better. The impresarios want American looking girls."

"If they want American girls, why don't they go to America to get them?"

Aspirrina shook her head at her at her stupidity.

"They want girls who look American, yes, but everything else," she said shaking her shoulders and swaying her hips, "they want it to be caliente. The American girls are good at being pretty but they don't have the fire."

It took three bottles of hydrogen peroxide before her hair stopped looking like copper wire. But in the end, she looked as if she'd been born that way, or so she thought until she met the others.

Aspirrina had ben right, Estelita was not the only blonde in the chorus, even the mulata showgirls at the Riviera had lightened their hair, there was even a redhead. Not that it mattered, the blonde hair got her the job, but the headdresses that accompanied every costume covered most of it.

The frantic pace took getting used to. She almost fell over as quick hands flashed around her waist, cinching a frill and tail, making her look for all the world like a sparkling, sequined version of the peacocks she'd seen all over the countryside during her life with her father. A life now as distant as they were from each other. A rhinestone and feather skullcap tightly placed just so atop her hair, completed the first costume. She looked identical to all the other girls. She would simply be one of many. The routines had been easy enough to learn and while the others chattered endlessly about nervous stomachs and trembling hands, Estelita felt no anxiety whatsoever. This was simply a job, the best she could get in the only profession she knew and the temporary means to an end.

She had never desired the limelight and had been perfectly content to travel with her father and the troupe, to watch them night after night vying for the audience's approval. It seemed silly to her. Not for one moment had she ever considered the absurd life of a performer for herself.

She had gone on stage before and found being in front of an audience as easy as walking into an empty room. And that was only to rescue her father. Esteban had been missing since the night before and shown up just seconds before he was due on stage. Estelita had been standing in the wings in what had become her customary place, next to Aspirrina. From the moment he greeted the audience they knew he was in trouble. She followed Aspirrina to the edge of the stage. Esteban had been singing a popular lovelorn ballad and suddenly he stopped, the lyrics lost inside his addled brain. And they both knew he wouldn't get them back.

"*Coño,*" Aspirrina whispered.

The audience started to make that unmistakable sound, like a cloud of locust closing in, louder and louder.

"Someone's got to do something," Aspirrina said with a concern in her voice that Estelita never heard before. Aspirrina started resolutely towards him, but Estelita knew that would only compound

74

the disaster.

"No, I'll do it," she said with unquestionable determination, and taking a long breath, and after moving Aspirrina aside she strolled casually onto the stage, as if her entrance had been planned and rehearsed a hundred times.

The wolf whistles and cat-calls began the moment she stepped into the spotlight. She felt ridiculous in her faded cotton dress, flat-heeled shoes, her hair pulled back with a rubber band. But from the audience's reaction you'd think she was in satin and emeralds. Esteban looked at her slack-jawed. She gave him a friendly wink, gently prying the microphone from his frozen hand, and she picked up the song exactly where he had left off. It was called, "Me Conoces" (in English, "You Know Me"). A song so loved it had already been recorded many times all over the world. A surprisingly upbeat song considering it was a letter from a mistress to her lover's wife.

"Me Conoces" was making waves at the time because it had been banned by the Catholic League of Decency, as they declared that it justified the woman's indecent life.

That specific song, emanating from the lips of such a young and beautiful girl, was truly a sin, and the audience ate it up. For the troupe, it was a saving grace, but Estelita felt no sense of accomplishment, she simply did it to rescue her father, as she always had.

Show business was not for her. In her daydreams she saw herself married to a nice man, living in a stable home surrounded by children. She imagined Esteban as a doting grandfather entertaining them with his guitar. But it was a dream that had become more and more unattainable.

She felt the pinch of hairpins digging into her scalp as the dresser attached the head-dress that now towered above her, she was relieved that it no longer wobbled as it had during rehearsals.

The dressing room had reached a fever pitch as more head-dresses went on more heads, more pins dug into scalps and a chorus of girls yelped in pain. She looked around the colorful disarray. No one knew her here. They didn't know anything about her father or Aspirrina. They didn't know where she lived or where she came from. The rest of the showgirls seemed to know each other well, they grouped around mirrors, shoving each other out of the way as they added another layer of lipstick, painted on another beauty mark next to the eyes where it would draw the most attention. Although hired to look and move identically, each showgirl wanted to stand out in her own small way. Anything to break the monotony, to catch the eye of that special man in the audience who would get them out of the chorus forever, bring the magic of romance to their lives.

"Places, girls!" the stage manager hollered.

Estelita stood up, her top feathers brushed the ceiling. The dressers gave them a final inspection and they began walking towards the stage. To get there, they walked up a steep flight of stairs and when she reached the top and stepped onto a platform twenty-five feet in the air. The applause thickened and the music quickened. The theater, she'd heard, had room for 550 guests and every seat was filled.

Suddenly, the nerves she'd been able to abate came rushing through. Her whole body was trembling and her legs had locked in place. Her breath was gone and in its stead there was only nausea. She felt the hand of the girl behind her pushing between her shoulder blades and a strong whisper, "Estelita, move."

But she couldn't take a step. Her rushing thoughts contradicted each other: You must go on I can't go on I think I'm dying. Her mouth was dry and her lips were numb. How had her father done this? This was his realm, this is what he lived for, those moments in the limelight with all eyes fixed on him. She realized she'd forgotten the steps and her panic deepened. There hadn't been enough rehearsals, she should have demanded more practice, she should have worked harder. She thought it was going to be easy, she was Esteban's daughter, the only progeny of the best rumbero in all of Cuba. But suddenly she felt small and separate from him, a pale imitation, an inferior replica. No one will notice you, you're only one of many, she told herself, grateful that a part of her mind was still rational. Suddenly she began to understand why he drank, how a drink or a dozen drinks, would make this easier. The hand at her back pushed her harder, a shove that sent her stumbling forward on those damn high heels. Oh, God, help me. She slammed against the girl ahead of her and suddenly she was there.

She regained her balance as she entered the pink spotlight and her mind quieted down, the voices in her head were soothed by the music. In unison with the others she raised her lovely arms and the multicolor gossamer wings that were part of her costume opened up. Her crimson lips parted to reveal a perfect smile; her eyes caught the light and reflected it tenfold. Her shoes still pinched but she didn't feel it, that minor discomfort had been replaced by an unexpected current of excitement as her body moved to the rhythm of the music, basked in the preternatural light, felt her heart pump as if a capacious new one had replaced her old, inexorable little heart. The choreography came back to her, every step, every turn. She felt powerful, invincible. Beautiful. No one could see that under the costume and makeup there was a lost, penniless girl. She loved the illusion, it filled her completely and for the first time she also understood the rapturous magic Aspirrina and her father talked about, she danced and smiled with the brash assurance of a young woman who had fortuitously touched the white hot center within her that, until that very moment, she did not know existed.

7

Three handsome black waiters, impeccably dressed in white dinner jackets, filled the champagne glasses at table one, but none of the men seated there paid any attention. They were the most powerful men in Havana at the moment. They were the men who had dreamed up and financed the very room they were sitting in. There were whistles, shouts and applause all around them in anticipation of the floor show, but none of the men at table one was applauding. It would be unbecoming – after all, the glittering girls who were about to magically appear on the stage were their personal property.

At table one was the President of Cuba, Fulgencio Batista, his trusted partner in the casino business, Mr. Lansky, and George Raft and Errol Flynn. The two American actors had joined forces to convince Ginger Rogers, the famous American actress, to fly to Havana for a limited engagement. Rogers was the reason the room was full to capacity, the reason the event had made the international papers. The success of the venture was certain.

Also present at table one was a much younger man, with eyes like a fox: Juan Carlos Talente. Talente sat at the edge of his seat because he knew he couldn't quite yet relax in this high-powered coterie. He worried one of the men would talk to him, ask him questions, inquire about his past, ask for his credentials. He had none.

His place at that table was unexpected and confounding. No one looked in his direction but his foot kept bouncing, his knee kept shaking and his neck felt stiff under the starched collar.

*

Ten years before he had left the orphanage in Guanabacoa and set out for the capital. He was tall for a twelve year old and had finally given up all hope that his parents were going to realize their mistake and come back for him, or that some lonely, childless couple would want him for their own. Alone among dozens of other boys, in the dark dormitory he knew so well, he had finally admitted to himself, in a brave little voice that only he could hear, that no one in the world would adopt a boy as big and sad as he. So, without telling a soul, and knowing from experience that there would be no attempt to bring him back (over the years he had seen older boys do the same), he escaped from the only home he had ever known to try his luck shining shoes in Havana.

Every boy in the orphanage dreamed of one day breaking away and joining the ranks of limpiabotas, the self-motivated, industrious, shoeshine boys that populated Havana sidewalks. The legend of black-fingered boys who made money, saved money, and eventually got themselves a stand selling fruit, magazines or cigars, had kept him awake nights. Juan Carlos couldn't wait to get out of that hot, overcrowded orphanage and try his luck. After some careful planning, he was able to make his dream come true. With the contents of the local church's collection box jingling in his pocket, he set out to meet his future.

His first stand was on a dirty corner of Old Havana where people looked down on him, their noses turned up in disgust as he smiled and flashed his eyes at them. He wasn't making the kind of money he needed. He was sleeping in an alley just around the corner and, although he had heard that Havana was large and beautiful, he hadn't had time to see very much of it. He felt as if any minute spent away from his corner was a missed opportunity to make one centavo, which is what he charged to shine two shoes.

On the day that he finally ventured to another part of the city, he knew where he'd gone wrong. He realized why he wasn't making any money: he was at the wrong corner. He set his sights on one particular intersection and although he had to fight for it with lots of shoving and yelling amongst the other boys who worked the neighborhood, he got the corner he knew would bring him luck.

It was at the junction of Barrio and Prado Boulevard, one of the most elegant and well-traveled intersections in the city. It was at that corner that Juan Carlos Talente became a star.

Well-heeled men became his friends, his curious chatter amused them. Juan Carlos wanted to know everything. What's that building called, who owns it, who lives there? Who is the President, does he have a wife, where does he live? Who's in charge of the armed forces, the police, the airport? Who is the most powerful judge, lawyer? Who is the most feared criminal? What do those signs on the walls mean? Is Fidel Castro really a threat to the President? His clients answered the endless barrage of questions until Juan Carlos became one of the most erudite shoeshine boys on the street.

He learned to read by glancing up at the front page of the newspapers his customers held while sitting at his bench. The same headlines all day long. He asked his customers more questions as well as their help with unfamiliar words.

Those men who became regular customers were glad to assist, and mumbled their answers through clouds of cigar smoke. Others didn't like it at all, they just wanted their shoes shined and some peace and quiet. They went to other corners, where less annoying boys could do the job just as well.

Before long Juan Carlos could not only read the big black headlines, but could actually anticipate what the next day's headlines were going to be. Politics, he learned, was cause and effect and often repeated itself. He started to take the discarded newspapers with him, to read beyond the headlines.

This newfound trove of knowledge, combined with the respect and admiration of his clients, who now made it part of their daily routine to discuss current events with him, and the nickel a shine he was now earning, made Juan Carlos feel like a real success, a man of the world.

He picked up flashy gimmicks from other shoeshine boys, like the spit-shine and the flaming dye. He affiliated himself with local shoe repair shops that brought their most expensive shoes to him for special detailed attention.

Juan Carlos bought a new shirt and started to take Mondays off. By the time he was sixteen years old, he had become accustomed to a few of the good things in life and the time spent in the orphanage became distant memory. He made enough money to rent a room in a run-down boarding house, ate regular meals, and frequented the movies and the dog races.

He bought a suit and tie, new shoes – he was becoming a true gentleman of Havana. But he was still a shoeshine boy and, in spite of his attractive appearance and respectful manners, even the girls from the most humble families didn't give him a second look. That all changed the day Jose Garcia Orozco planted his dainty shoes in front of him.

Jose Garcia Orozco, whom everybody called Orozco, was a big, tall man with tiny little feet that he pampered with custom made, two-tone leather shoes. His shoes were black and white, brown and white, brown and beige, beige and black. Never just one color. Even at a time when the dandies of Havana, men of means, style, and position, were sporting fine, imported, outstanding footwear, Jose Orozco Garcia's tiny shoe collection was without equal.

Juan Carlos knew that Orozco liked, almost to a fetishistic degree, the care he took with the tiny shoes, that Orozco appreciated the cardboard flaps he had devised to prevent sock stains, the minute brushes he used to keep the dark polish from bleeding into the lighter panels. Juan Carlos sometimes spent fifteen minutes or more hunched over each shoe until he could feel his shoulder blades starting to separate from his spine.

Orozco was never in a hurry and he always rewarded the young man he called his favorite shoeshine in Havana with a peso. As Juan Carlos grew older, Orozco started to add an invitation to his establishment, the Shanghai Theater, a small but wildly popular tourist trap nestled within the narrow, winding streets of Barrio Chino, Havana's Chinatown.

Juan Carlos gladly accepted the peso but had never taken him up on his other offer because the Shanghai was no ordinary theater. It was the world's rawest burlesque house, and everyone knew it. Havana, known as the sexiest city in the Western Hemisphere, was famous for its girlie reviews, raunchy bars, and government-sanctioned red light districts. But the Shanghai's reputation surpassed all others.

On his 17th birthday, Juan Carlos filled himself with enough courage to walk down the steamy streets of Old Havana, past the fat-assed hookers who whistled at him, the white-clad sailors who stumbled by, the wide-eyed American tourists who took one step forward and one back (for this was a mean, frightening, part of town) and found himself at the brightly-lit door of the Shanghai Theater.

Orozco was not there that night, so Juan Carlos had to pay to go inside. That amounted to a lot of shoes but he wasn't about to turn back once he had gone that far. The next day, he mentioned it to Orozco, who felt so bad that he returned the money and offered Juan Carlos a job as the usher.

It was a great job. Just on tips and bribes, he could make as much money in one night as he would shining shoes for a week. Tourists were willing to slip him fifty centavos, sometimes even an American dollar, to get a front-row seat. After a while, the spectacle, which was so shocking to him that first night, no longer intrigued him. But best of all, his black fingers were returning to their natural color.

The show itself consisted of a comedic play that utilized a marginally talented group of performers. The action took place on a proscenium stage with thick, red velvet curtains. The plays dealt with the usual themes of burlesque – a young bride, for example, trying to dodge the advances of her so-old-he's-falling-over husband and still manage to make love to the younger, dashing lovers stashed behind the drapes, beneath the bed, inside the closet. Every time the overheated young bride, now completely naked, was to consummate her passion with one of the young lovers, she would make a baby face at the audience, freeze her pose and the curtain would close to the disappointed groans and knowing laughter of the audience.

During these intermissions, strippers of all shapes and sizes, and with varying degrees of attractiveness (from sort of pretty to downright ugly and apparently chosen only for their willingness to strip down to nothing) would come on stage and do an exuberant routine to live music from a drummer concealed in the wings. Complete and absolute female nudity was the Shanghai's specialty.

While the strippers performed, the theater would be almost entirely in a blackout except for a weak blue spotlight that followed the dancer from one side of the stage to the other. Throwing the room into shadows was the management's courteous way of allowing some of the men to quietly masturbate into their scented handkerchiefs if they so desired.

Part of Juan Carlos's job was to keep an eye on the errant homosexual who would crawl through the shadows from row to row and offer to orally service the more adventurous patrons. Sometimes there would be a misunderstanding and it was up to Juan Carlos to break up the fight and toss out the miscreant. When the violence was more than he could handle, he was the one who performed the worst horror of all – switching on bright flourescent lights and exposing not just the culprit but decades of sin clinging to the walls and the curtains.

The Shanghai had a side door entrance for VIPs who sometimes tired of the glitzy shows at the casino, the way rich people get tired of eating steak every night. The VIPs could sit in the balcony, undetected by the commoners below. Often they were local entrepreneurs entertaining foreign investors who wanted to sample the low-life of Havana, sometimes they even brought women with them, North American girls who giggled at anything.

Juan Carlos was eager to accommodate these big shots, running to the corner store to get them anything they wanted, a bottle of booze, a box of cigars, candy for the girls. They liked to ask questions, fascinated by the personal lives of the naked performers.

"Is Concha her real name?"

"Where is she from?"

"How old...?"

"How much?"

Juan Carlos answered politely but accurately to the amusement of his guests. Before long they started to ask him to sit with them, poured him a drink.

One night Orozco told him that a couple of the men wanted to see him at the office for the new casino being built. He dressed in his best suit and impatiently shifted from one foot to the other while Orozco briefed him on how to act, what to say, but Juan Carlos was hardly listening. He knew exactly where he was going.

"My name is Lansky," the man said. And those four words, said in an even tone that revealed nothing, placed Juan Carlos's life on a completely new course.

Juan Carlos had assumed they wanted a waiter, or a busboy, or some other lowly job that would require that he wear a uniform and scrape and serve. Not so. Juan Carlos was recruited to smoke out the hole-in-the-wall gambling traps that still specialized in fleecing unsuspecting Americanos. A recent article in *The New York Times* had caused a serious panic –and tourism had started to decline.

"They cruise through the casinos offering bigger action, better odds, and the suckers fall for it." Lansky said. He was a surprisingly short man given to wearing custom-made bow ties and a battered straw hat; he was at once easy to overlook and absolutely impossible to ignore.

The meeting was brief and to the point. As Juan Carlos walked out of the casino he eyed the waiters, busboys and doormen, all Cubans and all scurrying through as if they wanted to be invisible and he thanked God for his own good fortune. His future was set! It was a job Juan Carlos knew he could do better than anyone else. After three years at the Shanghai Theater, he knew everybody and everything immoral, illegal and clandestine that went on in Havana. He knew where the cockfights were held, where the all-night poker games took place, what bail bondsmen worked the red light districts, where the high class brothels and low class cribs were located, how the gambling boats operated, and the seven perfect street corners to roll a drunk.

Lansky liked him right away and once he started seeing how useful his new employee could be, he encouraged Juan Carlos to follow him around and learn how he ran his business.

"A smart, handsome Cuban kid on our team is priceless," Lansky said.

"Hungry, too."

Juan Carlos liked this world. Gorgeous women, fancy cars, breathtaking penthouses. He started to dress like them, walk like them, talk like them. Before long, he was receiving discreet white envelopes containing more money than he had ever thought possible. The money was never discussed. The envelopes appeared, he took them, placed them in the breast pocket of his navy blue suit, and went on with his work.

For the average customer, the door to the Shanghai Theater was just a passage to sleazy entertainment. But to Juan Carlos it had been the gateway into the rumba-thumping heart of Havana.

Now, looking at the lovely chorus girls from his favored chair at the President's table, Juan Carlos couldn't help but smile when he thought back to his days at the orphanage. A lucky star must have been watching over him the night he ran away. He was just about to relax and enjoy the headlining talent, who just happened to be one of his favorite leading ladies, the American song and dance queen Ginger Rogers, when one of the casino's doormen came running, red-faced, to his table.

A sharp glance from Lansky let him know that he'd better take care of whatever it was before anyone noticed. Nothing could go wrong on opening night; nothing. Millions of personal dollars belonging to the men seated at table one were invested, and a good deal more the President had "borrowed" from the National Treasury. If it failed, the whole island could sink into the ocean. And as much as everyone was trying to enjoy the show – the gorgeous girls, the choreography, the spectacle – they also were aware that Fidel Castro and his rebels cast a shadow across every table.

The students at the university continued protesting; there had been ongoing disturbances, even bloodshed. Some had been killed while others awaited their fates in jails. Batista, in his all-or-nothing attitude, closed down the university until further notice. Two female medical students committed suicide and their parents were paid off in exchange for silence. But word got out as word in Havana always did. The whole city was quiet for a few days and then signs had appeared on the walls of prominent buildings faster than the police could get them painted over. The signs read:

THIS IS THE YEAR

Everyone knew what that meant. A change was on the horizon; there was no doubt about it. How that change would come about no one knew. But the question remained, could the President and his friends make their money back before it was too late? And could they do it without cheating?

Lansky was a famously cagey operator, brought to Cuba, ironically enough, to clean up the casinos. After word spread that

Cuban games were crooked and tourists started to stay away in droves, Batista had invited the mob in to change that perception, and they had done an incredible job. The games were squeaky clean, and the houses were making money. Everyone was happy.

As he walked through the nightclub towards the casino lobby, Juan Carlos wondered what trouble was waiting for him there. He had never been much of a fighter, and he hoped that he would be able to take care of the problem without too much of a ruckus. Lansky detested a ruckus and Juan Carlos couldn't afford to look incompetent.

8

As the applause subsided, the stage darkened and the house lights rose to a warm, white glow. Silver trays shimmered as waiters rushed to refresh empty cocktail glasses. Groups of women in gossamer gowns chattered gaily all the way to the powder rooms. Estelita heard the joyful din, it was the sound of a satisfied audience, of a successful opening night. The first act had gone well. Once she had overcome her panic she had made no major mistakes, none that anyone would have noticed. The costume changes had been timed to the second and clothes came off and went on without a hitch.

Estelita took her bows and walked off the stage in perfect unison with the others, she had countless and delicious emotions rushing through her, feelings so new to her she didn't know if she had room in her heart to hold them all.

"Smile, smile, smile," Chucho had screamed at the chorines again and again during rehearsals. He was wasting his breath on her. Estelita couldn't stop smiling. Aspirrina would have been proud, and probably envious. She never had an opportunity like this. Her whole life had been spent on creaky, wooden stages decorated with cheap balloons, streamers and faded paper lanterns.

Estelita's only regret was that her father wasn't there to see her with Ginger Rogers, not on a plywood stage but on a solid one with revolving ramps and descending scenery, and the vibrant sounds of the huge orchestra. Yes, that was she, Estelita de la Cruz, the singer's daughter, la perdida, smiling and dancing among all the beautiful girls in their glittering costumes.

Esteban would have been so happy he'd have insisted on a party that lasted all night and well into morning.

"What will it be like?" Estelita had asked Rosario, a baby-voiced chorine, at one of their first rehearsals.

"It will be like going to the most wonderful fiesta in the world every night,"

Rosario had said while brushing her eyelashes, "only it's your fiesta, every one is here solo para ti." Only for you.

Backstage it was madness once again. The dressers were anxiously waiting and as soon as she was in the door they undressed her – off came her headdress, her necklace, her gloves. All would be tagged and sent to the cleaners, to be ready for the following night's performance.

Estelita kicked off her shoes, the cool tile floor felt good on her bare feet. All the girls were talking and laughing. They each had their own version of what had just happened, whom they had spotted in the audience.

"George Raft is at table one," Barbarita said. Barbarita was one of those girls who looked even younger than Estelita, but under the makeup lurked the eyes of a much older woman. Estelita studied her own face in the mirror and was pleased with the reflection. She was pretty, prettier than the others. She did not resemble Esteban, handsome as he'd once been. No, her looks she got from her mother, Esteban had told her so enough times but it wasn't until now that she finally believed him.

"Es un sueño!" He's a dream, added Rosario, who was dusting herself with rose-scented talcum powder. Rosario's baby-voice was a breathless whisper.

"Did you see Errol?" a dresser asked.

"No, but I will later," Barbarita answered with a dirty wink.

George Raft! Errol Flynn! It had been fantastic enough that afternoon during their first rehearsal with Ginger Rogers. Estelita was shocked to see how short the movie star actually was, but that face and the way she danced had been unmistakable.

When they filed onto the stage for their first rehearsal, in leotards and high heels, Ginger Rogers had whistled at them like a sailor, a loud wolf whistle that made everybody laugh.

"Hello ladies," she'd shouted with a big wave of the hand. Then she'd turned her back on them and did not pay attention to anyone but the musical director for the remainder of the rehearsal.

The chorus girls took their places, struck their poses.

"Tan profesional!" Such a professional Rosario said with an admiring smile.

"She's a legend," another one added.

"She's a bitch," Barbarita said.

Estelita had no opinion to offer. Just to be on that same stage with Ginger Rogers had been almost more than she could stand. Again her thoughts drifted to her father and how much he would have enjoyed meeting the show business legend. But she quickly swept those sad thoughts of him from her mind. She would bring him to Havana soon enough. Now, getting him a job at the casino would be a cinch – not in the big show, only top recording artists performed there – but perhaps in one of the smaller lounges. There were plenty of those sprinkled throughout. For now all she could do was follow the rules, work hard and pave the way for him. Rule number one was no sadness. This was a place for joy and laughter. Later, if she so desired, she could be sad. Later, she could pray for him.

The intermission would only last twenty minutes, then they would join Miss Rogers for the grand finale. It was amazing how easy this was. All she had to do was enter and circle around while Miss Rogers sang her final song, then line up with her arms stretched up to the ceiling looking lovely. How could she not, her face was thick with makeup and the rest of her was decorated with everything that sparkled.

"Ten minutes," a stagehand shouted into the room.

Time passed quickly in the dressing room. Estelita was practically naked, wrapped only in one of the silk kimonos while the girls were being tended to. Girls who required more time, such as a change of makeup to look like zebras or tigers went first. She was about to slip into her next costume, a gold and silver cat-suit, when a man walked into the room. He hadn't even knocked.

The others reacted with mock outrage and flirtatious giggles. Estelita instinctively stepped behind a screen. It was one thing to expose herself on stage along with the others wearing no more or less than she would at a beach. But the way this man barged in, the way he looked at them as one would animals at a zoo felt disdainful not just of her privacy but the others as well. Some of the others were, at the moment, completely nude.

The intruder, an ugly mountain of a man, stepped up to one of the dressers and whispered something in her ear. The dresser pointed a finger   all heads turned to follow the finger. It was pointed at Estelita. "Venga conmigo." Come with me.

Estelita felt herself reddening. Maybe someone *had* noticed her delayed entrance or the one or two steps she had missed.

"But I'm not dressed," she said, wrapping the kimono tighter. She was certain she was being fired and considered dressing and leaving.

"You better do what he says, cariño," Rosario whispered, her baby voice taking an ominous tone.

Estelita looked around, the other girls were nodding in agreement. Only Barbarita appeared uninvolved in her decision.

The big man was already out the door. Estelita stood up, her legs felt like water. She tied her kimono tightly with its sash, and stepped back into her shoes. She took one last look in the mirror before she rushed out the door. Her hair was a mess, matted down from the headdress. She ran her fingers through it and moved quickly, following the big man down a long, white corridor. Chorus girls were not allowed to wander around the hotel and could only enter the casino floor if escorted by a gentleman. They stopped at a service elevator and he pressed the call button.

"What's wrong? Where are we going?" she asked him.

"To see the boss."

"Did I do something wrong?"

"He didn't say," the man answered and tried to smile, but the effort resulted in a frightening grimace.

Her mind was racing as the elevator climbed and climbed telling her what she should have done differently, what the boss was going to say, what she'd have to say to him. Maybe they had found out about the convent. Maybe Sor Maria had noticed she was missing and had reported her. Her heart raced as she tried to come up with reasonable explanations but her mind had locked into a screaming match with itself. The numbers above the door read six, seven, eight, nine. She had never been in an elevator that went further than three or four floors. She tried not to panic but she caught her face reflected on the polished aluminum wall of the service elevator and she could only see complete and absolute terror. Could she get fired on the first night? She couldn't let it happen. She had to calm down.

They got off the elevator and entered a wide, pink hallway. Everything was in different and subtle shades of the softest pink –the walls, the fluffy carpet, the ceiling, even the framed art hanging on the walls was in hues of white and pink – pink sunsets, beaches, gardens.

She was not accustomed to walking on such thick, lush carpet, and she almost toppled over. The man expertly held her elbow as if he'd been waiting for this to happen. He stood patiently while she regained her composure.

"Gracias," she murmured, but he kept going. They stopped in front of yet another elevator. The doors opened immediately when he pushed the button. This elevator was even more elegant than the last. The walls were polished wood and everything else was a golden metal; maybe it *was* gold. She kept her sweating hands from touching anything.

The elevator doors opened directly onto a large suite with a row of floor-to-ceiling windows that overlooked the city. Estelita had never seen Havana from so high above; she was lost in the twinkling lights. She was not giving this up. She took a deep breath and stepped into the room. A man stood waiting. He was tall and at a glance she saw that he was also young and very well dressed.

And next to him stood Aspirrina, in a beige dress and no makeup. She seemed particularly small and round next to this tall and slender man.

"Here she is, boss," the big man said and stepped back into the elevator.

"Is your name Estelita de la Cruz?" the man asked before she'd had a chance to acknowledge Aspirrina's presence. Was that really Aspirrina? What on earth? Her mind started working very fast. She looked into the man's face before answering. Not a pretty face like the men in the chorus. His eyes were dark and slightly slanted with eyelashes that all the girls back in the dressing room would kill for. His nose small, narrow, his jaw wide, with a dimpled chin. It was the very essence of a handsome, masculine face. In some small way reminiscent of her father, back in the day when just a look from him could make a woman lose her balance.

Estelita looked at Aspirrina for a moment before she answered. Aspirrina's eyes were sending not-so-subtle signals she could not read. But there was no mistaking that they were both in some sort of trouble. Something about the man's face calmed her, maybe it was the resemblance to Esteban, or the way he stood back, or the easy way he spoke. She did not feel threatened.

"A gentleman would introduce himself first," she answered keeping her voice soft, careful – but her eyes were firmly on his.

"I'm very sorry, you must think I am very rude." The man said with a smile. "I am Juan Carlos Talente, with hotel security."

He stepped up and offered his hand, she shook it gently and immediately withdrew.

"Why am I here, Señor Talente?" She kept her tone even, as she had with lawyers, judges and jailers.

"Well, this is rather awkward but this woman–"

He signaled to Aspirrina with his eyes. Aspirrina didn't let him finish.

"Estelita" she screamed, jumping forward, "tell this person who I am, he's been–"

The man froze her with a look.

"I will do the talking," he said. "I think you have already said more than enough for one night."

There was not so much menace as authority in his tone.

"This woman," he continued, "claims that you are her daughter, and insisted to be let into the show free of charge. When denied, she tried to sneak in past the guards."

"They wanted fifty pesos to watch you!" Aspirrina said, "They might as well ask for fifty million!"

Estelita knew she had to answer this man right away or he wouldn't believe her.

"This woman?" she asked, looking Aspirrina up and down as if she were an exotic animal.

"Yes, this woman."

Estelita smiled at her sweetly.

"I'm sorry, señor, but I have never seen this woman before in my life."

Aspirrina looked at her with disbelieving eyes. "Estelita," she said again, this time an outraged reprimand, and took a step towards her, but Estelita took two quick steps back.

"Stay where you are," Juan Carlos cautioned, "you're frightening the girl."

"Estelita." Aspirrina now whispered as if feeling her heart breaking. But it was too late, Estelita had turned and pushed the call button on the elevator.

"If that is all you need to know, now you know it. If you will excuse me, Señor Talente, intermission is almost over, and I have a show to do."

"You are sure you don't know her, she insists..."

Estelita turned around, avoiding Aspirrina's eyes.

"Señor," she challenged, "do I look like that woman's daughter?"

Now that Estelita had brought attention to herself, the man looked her up and down, brazenly assessing her from head to toe.

"Don't leave me with this monster," Aspirrina shouted as the golden elevator doors opened and Estelita stepped inside.

"Just as I thought," Juan Carlos said with a sharp glance at Aspirrina as the elevator doors begin to close, "but she was making such a racket...you understand?"

Before either could say another word, the golden doors sealed tight and all that was left of her was a subtle and sweet perfume.

Estelita's hand was shaking with fury as she pushed the elevator button. Aspirrina had left her no choice. What else could she have done? They had made an agreement. Aspirrina was to wait until Estelita felt more established in the show, then she would go through the proper channels, get her admitted. Why had she turned up on opening night? Why did Aspirrina always insist on having it her way? Aspirrina had left her no alternative.

The elevator doors opened and she was relieved that the big man who had brought her was still waiting in the pink hallway. Her head was spinning and jumbled with thoughts and she didn't know if she could find her way back alone.

"Take me back to the dressing rooms as fast as you can or I'll miss curtain," she said sharply, as if he had been responsible for the whole unpleasant scene.

Soon they were retracing their steps, her mind spinning with emotions. Why had Aspirrina taken such a risk? Surely, at the convent, without Aspirrina to cover for her, they would be missed, found out and outsted. She wondered what would happen to Aspirrina at the hands of Juan Carlos Talente. The man didn't seem particularly upset, hopefully he would have her escorted to the street and banned from the establishment forever. Her stomach churned at the thought of something awful happening to Aspirrina. Would they strike a woman for trying to sneak into a show? Turn her over to the police? No, nothing as drastic as that, Señor Talente surely saw Aspirrina for what she was, a crazy lady, one of the many eccentrics that populated the streets of Havana. One thing was certain: Aspirrina would never get to see the show even if she offered a stack of pesos.

This was not the time to think about such things. Not about Aspirrina, and not about Juan Carlos Talente. She would ask the girls about him later. Aside from his obvious good looks there had been a sweetness about him. Maybe she could see him again, and in calmer circumstances tell him the truth about Aspirrina and why she had lied, get Aspirrina a ticket to the show. No, she could never admit having lied to security. They would never trust her again – and she knew only too well what happened to liars in the world of gambling. Her father had the scars to prove it, inside and out. She decided then and there to do all she could to avoid Juan Carlos Talente. It would be best.

The moment she was out of the second elevator she began running towards the dressing rooms, her heels making quite a clatter. Inside, all heads turned to her, every face a question mark. She ignored them. She had only moments to calm down and get ready to join the line-up and smile. As soon as she was in the door, hands were tearing at her robe. On went the cat suit, the jeweled collar, the gloves.

"What was that about?" Rosario whispered.

"Later," Estelita replied with finality. Through the mirror she could see Barbarita staring at her and Estelita stared back, her face hard and inscrutable until Barbarita looked away.

Moments later she was on stage, a vast glittering space. She dared not look into the audience. This wasn't the provincial crowd she was used to, this was Havana. And they were loving the show; the frequent waves of applause told her so.

No one can tell, she said to herself as Ginger Rogers took the stage. No one knows me here. I'm just another body in a sparkling costume and a face with a ridiculous amount of makeup. On the outside I look just like all the others. But how many chorus girls, she wondered as she undulated in unison with the others, spent their days in a convent and their nights in a nearly naked review? Who would ever guess that just a few weeks ago she had been at Aspirrina's mercy – two women in the big city without a centavo in their pockets, a friend in the world, or a place to call home. Again, her mind pulsed with guilt. She owed Aspirrina so much.

When the lights hit her face, Estelita smiled, a big chorus girl smile, but inside, scenes from that first horrible night in Havana careened through her mind, a barrage of memories too recent to obstruct. From the moment they stepped off the train and onto the crowded platform, it was clear they didn't belong. Everyone had someone there to meet them. There were shrieks of bienvenidos, welcome, hugs and kisses. Everyone was talking at once, it was Spanish, but the accent was different, more melodious than the Spanish she was used to. Aspirrina took her hand and rushed her through the throngs and into the street.

She had stayed close to Aspirrina as they slammed into a world she had never dared imagine. People everywhere, rushing in all directions and traffic. Cars, buses, trolleys, trucks, bicycles, pushcarts and their drivers honking a horn or shouting. All over the walls and on top of buildings, bright signs advertised everything under the sun – soft drinks, rum, beer, beach vacations. And the biggest signs of all were for the casinos: The Riviera, The Tropicana, The Nacional. The words, Win! Win! Win! Flashed everywhere.

This is the place you come to win, Estelita thought. What am I doing here with Aspirrina without a centavo to our name? She was sure they would have to spend the night on the streets, at the mercy of anyone who passed.

"The worst that can happen," Aspirrina said, "is we break the law in some minor way, nothing serious, and spend a night or two in jail. That way we can at least get some sleep and a few hot meals."

"I'd rather die." Estelita said, "I have seen the inside of too many jails.

"Relax, girl, it's just a joke."

Estelita had not been amused. She knew that the things that Aspirrina said in jest, she was sometimes seriously considering.

"You think I don't have a plan?" Aspirrina said, cutting into a side street. "I know exactly where I'm going."

A few moments later Estelita watched as Aspirrina knocked on the unassuming wooden door of Convento Santa Catarina.

Her memory of that door opening and the subsequent exchange threatened to erase her smile, and this time she was able to send all bad thoughts away and allow herself to get lost in the choreography, the lights, the extraordinarily talented star, and all the beautiful girls in high heels and colorful, spangled costumes who, she was convinced, lived a much less complicated life than she did.

Beautiful music...
Dangerous rhythm...

Ginger Rogers sang the signature song that closed the show and bowed to thunderous applause. Then, and only then, did Estelita allow herself a lingering glance into the audience, to lower her eyes and peer beyond the footlights. Was Errol Flynn really at table one? She let her gaze surreptitiously travel from man to man. Someone who resembled Errol Flynn was there, indeed. And next to him, exhaling a long plume of smoke was that man who'd almost made her miss her entrance. Señor Talente.

Juan Carlos.

9

On the sidewalk outside of the casino Aspirrina did a little dance. It was not a joyful dance. She struck the pose of a warrior and with clenched fists she cursed the casino and the sky. Groups of tourists giggled as they walked past her wearing dark fur stoles even in the Havana heat, their ears sparkling with sapphires and rubies, and she cursed them too.

She cursed the balding white men who dabbed at their foreheads and necks with perfumed handkerchiefs. Stupid tourists. She could always tell the tourists, they were the only ones who could break into a sweat merely by walking from an air-conditioned car to an air-conditioned lobby. She wanted to kick them.

The anger she always felt towards the world she now felt for herself along with a deep, gnawing shame for the matronly dress she had chosen to wear only to be rejected, humiliated and stripped of all dignity by Estelita de la Cruz, that mindless, selfish girl. Aspirrina was used to being jeered by audiences, but this insult, from a girl who wouldn't be in those fancy shoes if it hadn't been for all her sacrifices, had her boiling mad.

I should have left that idiot in the middle of nowhere without a second thought, thrown her to the wolves. I should have known better, she muttered to the balmy night.

It had been Aspirrina who had knocked on the heavy oak door of the Convento de Santa Catarina. She was the one who had secured a place for them to live. It had been a very quiet night, the kind of night that usually signals an earthquake, an electrical storm, a cyclone or some other disastrous act of God.

"Just let me do the talking," Aspirrina cautioned as a nun reluctantly opened the door a crack. She saw the nun gasp at the sight of her. Suddenly she was aware of her looks: a travel-weary woman whose round, fleshy face was painted as brightly as a circus performer with a young girl who was staring down at her own scuffed shoes.

"I'm a widow alone with my daughter," Aspirrina said, fast and much too loud, "we just arrived in this big city. We're frightened and hungry, just like Mary and Joseph, you know."

"I'm terribly sorry, but this is not a hotel," the nun said and began to close the door. Aspirrina stuck her foot in, preventing the closing of anything.

"Have mercy, sister," Aspirrina implored, still too loud. If a representative of God on Earth was going to turn her away, she wanted all of Havana to hear it. "Not for me, for the girl. I don't care about my self, no one will bother me, but I'm not strong enough to protect my girl from all the evil out there."

Aspirrina made an exaggerated gesture that emcompassed the whole city. The nun looked at Estelita, then at Aspirrina with a quick movement of the head.

"Men," Aspirrina hissed, her eyes wild. "Everywhere we go they want to touch her and who knows what else? In the short walk from the train station to this holy house, at least a dozen men offered to buy her from me."

Aspirrina could see the nun developing an interest, she had her just where she wanted her.

"And the money they offered was an insult." She continued. "Look at my angel, she's priceless. Oh sister, have mercy before she falls into bad ways. You should have heard the offers they made, what they wanted her to do. They wanted to-"

"That's enough," the nun said, cutting her off before she went into further details.

With a sigh she took Estelita by the hand and quickly pulled her into the foyer, as if wanting to keep Aspirrina out. Aspirrina barely slipped in before the door was closed and triple locked.

"Ah, this place is beautiful," Aspirrina said, her voice echoing in the dark hall. "How many of you live here?"

"Silencio, por favor," the nun said, "Others are sleeping."

Aspirrina dropped her voice to a whisper.

"It's very nice of you to take us in. I will cook, clean, I'll do anything you nuns don't want to do. You can spend more time with God. It is such a big and scary city out there, just me and my innocent girl. Who knows what could happen to us. I don't worry so much about myself, you know how us mothers are. But my little girl. She's still a virgin, you know. A rarity these days."

The nun signaled for silence again, this time by placing a finger to her lips. Aspirrina closed her mouth and kept it that way. Moments later, suitcases in hand, they were following the flapping black and white folds of the nun's habit to the back of the house and into a small dark cubicle.

"You can't stay here long," the nun whispered, "we will talk in the morning."

After the nun had retired, Aspirrina sniffed the air, the room was small and it smelled of mildew, but it was free. At the moment they couldn't afford a room in even the most run down of hotels in Havana. They had started the journey with some money, but Aspirrina had spent most of it on train tickets, and what was left on a new dress for Estelita. The dress was so beautiful that Estelita had been reluctant to try it on.

"That dress," Aspirrina had shouted, much to the elegant shopkeeper's dismay, "is going to open doors for you all over Havana. You don't want to go there looking like a guajirita."

"It's too expensive," Estelita gasped

Estelita had never bought a dress that wasn't second-hand before. Let alone at an elegant shop. The one Aspirrina picked out was beautiful, bright yellow satin with orange and green ruffles along the scoop neck and at the hem of the skirt. She knew Estelita would look like a delicious tropical fruit in it. She wanted it, couldn't wait to see it on her, send her out into Havana in it.

"It's an investment," Aspirrina sighed as she emptied her purse into the shopkeeper's pale hand.

Now, the dress was carefully packed in her suitcase and they were no longer without a home even if they were at the mercy of a rigid, unfriendly nun who hadn't even bothered to introduce herself.

Aspirrina had trouble falling asleep that night. She watched Estelita's pretty face in the moonlight and wished her pleasant dreams. The convent would do for now, living among these crazy, pale-faced penguins wouldn't be easy, but they wouldn't be here long. She had plans for their new lives, plans so big that they threatened to keep her awake forever. None of the other performers who left for Havana had returned. If El Gago and Serpentina can make it here, so can we.

In Estelita she had an untapped gold mine. The girl had beauty and talent. Months before, Aspirrina had seen the reaction of the public on the night when Esteban had been too drunk to finish his set. Estelita had closed his act to the loud acclaim of the crowd. Aspirrina had stood in awe of Estelita's emotional force, the finesse, the masterful control. There was no way to define talent, it was something you either have or you don't. Years of practice had given her nothing, and yet this girl effortlessly had it all.

That was the night, the moment when the idea had been born. If she could get Estelita away from Sabrosuras and to the glittering show rooms of Havana, the world would be at their feet. Now, she had another challenge – how to get Estelita away from the watchful eyes of the nuns and out into the real world. She had seen how the nun had looked at Estelita. Here was an easy convert, an innocent young girl they could offer to Christ as a bride.

"Over my dead body," was Aspirrina's last thought as she finally drifted into restless sleep.

*

Aspirrina's appraisal had been correct. In just a few days Estelita, in her new dress, landed one of the most coveted jobs in the city. But now as she walked on her swollen and aching feet over the cobblestone streets, all she could think about was how tightly she could wring the stupid girl's neck without actually killing her.

She couldn't believe the way Estelita had treated her in front of that greasy buffoon, Juan Carlos Talente. The image of the beautiful girl, in those fancy shoes, with her platinum hair complementing her creamy complexion, and perfect makeup, looking as classy as Aspirrina always knew she could, had almost brought tears to her eyes. But the way those lovely lips had denied knowing her, and the cold, distant look in her eyes, as if she was looking down on her from a great height. This, from a girl she practically had raised as her own. Did Estelita forget that if it hadn't been for her she would be walking the streets of Holguin begging, or renting her body to satisfy the lust of sailors? The girl's ingratitude damaged her spirit, clouded her optimism. And that she could never forgive, because lacking conventional beauty and talent, Aspirrina had always relied on her boundless enthusiasm to get her through. It was all she had.

Mostly, she feared that this chorus job would be sufficient for Estelita, that she would be satisfied just to be a chorus girl, a decoration. Was a little intelligence too much to ask of a beautiful girl?

There had been a time when Aspirrina would have traded all her intelligence and intuition to be taller, thinner, prettier. But she stopped feeling that way a long time ago. Why couldn't Estelita understand that this was only the beginning? Together they could go so much further. She would deal with her later.

Aspirrina soundlessly let herself back into the convent. Estelita would have to return eventually, and she would be waiting in the shadows, as she had every night since Estelita started working. The nuns never slept for long. At ten at night they all filed out to clean churches, returning after midnight. That window of opportunity for Estelita to come home undetected was narrow. They always locked the doors like the convent housed the national treasure, making it impossible for Estelita to get in. So Aspirrina kept watch every night and at the sound of Estelita's approaching heels she quietly unlocked the door. It was an exhausting routine that robbed her of her sleep time.

The night after Estelita blatantly insulted her in front of Juan Carlos Talente, Aspirrina was going to let Estelita spend the night in the streets, teach her a lesson. But what if Estelita, in all her stupidity, decided to knock? No, she couldn't risk being evicted, so she took her place by the back door of the convent. She still couldn't believe she had been so foolish, giving her heart to such an ungrateful girl. How did it happen? How had she become so weak, so sentimental? She had always been perfectly content with her practical, independent life, and she had thrown it all away on Esteban and Estelita de la Cruz, the most selfish and undeserving people she had ever met. Aspirrina enjoyed a long, deep yawn. She was tired. The Convent of Santa Caterina was not a place for idle hands.

*

"You will cook, clean and run errands in exchange for room and board." Sor Maria, as the nun was called, said to her the morning after their arrival.

So she was back where she started, where she had always been, cooking and cleaning, as she had done for her family and the Haitians and later for Matilda. But she worked without a word of complaint, and agreed to follow all the nun's senseless rules: no visitors of any kind, no smoking or alcohol (not even a drop of sacramental wine), no trips into the city alone, no talking or even whispering unless absolutely necessary, and the final indignity of all, no makeup. Fortunately, there were no mirrors in the convent, and she learned to avoid her reflection in the buckets of water that she carried every day.

Estelita had it much easier. She was kept busy in a workroom where the sisters insisted on teaching her to sew, crochet and embroider all sorts of religious boberias. From the first morning, the nuns had taken her under their dark wings, separating her from Aspirrina, keeping her downstairs with them, making her sing hymns; they even gave her a small, white, leather-bound Bible to read at night and a delicate silver cross to wear around her neck.

Estelita, who was not of a disrespectful nature, went along with the charade. She spoke only when spoken to, never disagreed nor refused their requests, appeared to do her best to learn and excel at her chores and even read from her bible every night so she could answer questions about it the following day. At night, once the nuns had retired to their cells, she would steal into the night, to the bright lights of Havana. She would return just before dawn, before the nuns woke up – and Aspirrina would be waiting by the back door, listening for the sound of the stilettos, opening the door before Estelita had a chance to knock. Night after night she kept vigil so that Estelita could make her way. Was a little gratitude, a little consideration, too much to ask? Apparently so.

No matter, soon the money would start rolling in. There was so much of it in Havana. She would force Señor Talente to kiss her feet. She would walk through those casino doors in furs and jewels after arriving in a car too damn big for the driveway. Aspirrina Cerrogordo would show them all.

10

In the three months since Estelita had joined the show, on her
walks back to the convent, she had been whistled at almost every night,
loud, sensual and uniquely masculine whistles that sliced through the
cacophonous air.

At first, Havana had been so new to her that time passed quickly
as she traveled the avenues, marveled at all the life on the street, the
music that poured from every bar and restaurant, the peanut vendors,
and the constant whistling of young men who gathered at street corners
solely for that reason, to let women know they found them pretty. She
had enjoyed their attention, found their brazen, naked desire amusing,
thrilling, even.

But on this night they grated on her and, abruptly, she took to
the smaller side street that wound a longer, darker path to her dreaded
destination. In the labyrinthine callejones of Havana, at this late hour,
she felt remarkably safe. She knew that every corner she reached and
every shadow she passed concealed a potential danger but she was not
afraid. She had covered much more dangerous terrain in search of
Esteban, who always picked the most sinister bars in the darkest, most
dangerous parts of any town. And on this particular night, Estelita was

well aware that her real threat lay in wait, coiled and furious within the thick, damp walls of the Convento de la Santa Caterina.

It was during this walk, away from any distraction, the only time she spent truly alone, away from the hubbub of the dressing room and the stage and the prying eyes of the convent, away from the loud crowds of the teeming streets, that Estelita began to plan her escape. In the still darkness she started to get a glimpse of her future, as she walked her vision took shape until she saw it clearly laid out as a map no cartographer had ever touched, a route that she would create as she went, and she would go it alone.

Up to now, Aspirrina had been in charge, but that had to change – she would figure out a way to gently cut her loose, to gently disengage. A chill ran through her in the balmy night and she knew it was fear, a thread of fear that ran through her, but it was just a thread, most of her was resolute, she just had to be patient with herself, formulate her plan until it was solid and she found the fortitude to move forward. As she neared the convent, saw its somber walls looming before her, she stopped, remembering what her father often said as they left one town and set off for another.

"Detrás, nada, delánte, todo." Behind us nothing, ahead of us everything. He lived by those words before it all turned bad and what lay ahead was worse than what was left behind until he too got left behind. If she was going to get him back, make it all good, she needed to forge forward, take his words to heart and make sure that her map avoided the pitfalls he could not. Estelita was convinced that if her father did not have her to hold him back, he would have been more focused, would have seen the coming dangers, but she had been a distraction as Aspirrina was a distraction now. She would have to handle it all very carefully, every journey and every dance begins with the first step, a carefully calculated, crucial step.

The encounter with Juan Carlos Talente on that first night, had been awful and she knew it would only get worse. She was right.

The instant Estelita set foot inside the convent, Aspirrina grabbed her by the arm and dragged her roughly up the stairs. Estelita fought back.

"Suelteme," she said, let me go, her voice rising unexpectedly.

Aspirrina placed a hand over her mouth and shoved her up the rickety stairs two steps at a time.

"Shh, you want to wake up the penguins?" she hissed roughly letting go of her arm.

"I'm so sorry, Aspi," Estelita whispered. She knew that with Aspirrina it was best to affect docility. Aspirrina was moving fast, she had already reached the top landing. Estelita followed slowly. Once inside their room, Aspirrina closed the door and in a hushed tone unleashed a torrent of every conceivable emotion. She reproached her like a betrayed lover, cried like an abandoned little girl, whimpered like a wounded animal. The room could hardly contain her short, corpulent body as it trembled with rage.

Estelita sat on her bed and kept her head down but with every insult Aspirrina hurled at her, with every recrimination she repeated, her resolve became stronger. She had to get away from her and stay away.

Aspirrina was bad news and bad luck, her father had often said. Everyone at Sabrosuras said so too. Even on the eve of their departure, Lúcido had taken Estelita aside and questioned her decision.

"She makes a mess wherever she goes," Lúcido warned her. Estelita had nodded thoughtfully.

"Then you take me, Lúcido, I would make a good assistant, I'll work hard to learn."

Lúcido took his time before answering, and his voice, when it came, was raspy with regret.

"It wouldn't look right," he said, "we're not blood. I have too much respect for your father."

"Then I'm stuck with her, you see?" she said.

"Our destiny is never in our own hands," he replied.

Now, it was so clear to her. In his effort to protect her reputation, the magician had linked her fate to Aspirrina. And she had accepted his decision. She didn't push hard enough, she should've begged, pleaded, bargained. Instead she had accepted defeat as if defeat was her legacy. But, tonight, on the big glittering stage she got a taste of what life could truly be, what was available to her and very possibly how to get it. But it was going to take smarts; and Aspirrina was wily but she was stupid, ignorant of how the world really functioned. She overstepped boundaries, overreacted to any situation and defied authority with such tempestuous force that it kept her in constant conflict with everyone everywhere.

Estelita knew she had a lot to learn, but she also knew she could. Aspirrina had had a long time to make her life work out and she'd done nothing but fail.

Even her father had been a success once, before the devil brought him down, but Aspirrina didn't even have that in her past, just a confounding series of wrong turns and misjudgments.

Aspirrina's words had continued, collecting within the walls of the cell like a sour smell, invisible but potent. Estelita realized she hadn't really been listening when she noticed a length of silence and looked up to see Aspirrina's red-rimmed eyes waiting for a response. She had to think fast.

"I realize that what I did was wrong and hurtful," Estelita said.

Only more silence, and that look, those eyes, the mouth closed tight, her lips pinched and bloodless. "But you of all people should have known better," Estelita continued, careful to keep her voice low, controlled, "There was no possible way I was going to allow you to get me fired on my first night. We can't stay here forever, sooner or later they're going to find us out and throw us back into the street, they're not as stupid as you think just because they're nuns. My God, you almost ruined everything before I received my first paycheck."

"Ruined everything?" Aspirrina sniffed, "without me you'd be in a dirty shack in some backwater town selling your ass for centavos instead of living your dream life in Havana. You *owe* me everything."

Estelita knew that in order to initiate the plan, take that first step, she had to handle Aspirrina with delicacy. She went to her, kneeled at her feet, placed a hand gently on Aspirrina's forearm.

"That is exactly my point," she said softly. "You went against your own plan. You have worked so hard, sacrificed so much. Why would you risk it? We had agreed that once I was established I would arrange for you to see the show, but on opening night? What I did, ugly as it was, I did for us."

"Clearly," Aspirrina said, calmer now, and with a voice still quivering with emotion, "you are too selfish and stupid to understand why I needed to be there last night."

"You're right," Estelita said. "I'm stupid and selfish. I should have been able to handle the situation differently and if I could do it over, I would. But you caught me completely off-guard, I had just come off the stage, my brain was scrambled. I had just made a series of stupid mistakes, nerves got me as I made my entrance and I almost brought the whole show down. Oh, it was horrible and to see you standing there, with that man..."

Aspirrina looked at her with a smirk, her mouth opened, her lips curled, but what she was about to say she never did. Footsteps outside their door ended the conversation.

Estelita blew out the candle with a silent prayer for her father's soul. The following morning they returned to their routine. The incident was never mentioned again, but it was not forgotten.

*

Estelita was not entirely without gratitude. On the contrary, she knew how crucial a role Aspirrina had played in her life. Just the same, Estelita felt entitled to her freedom. Night after night, while all the other girls went out for drinks with fellows and enjoyed the pleasures that Havana offered, she had to run back to the convent and knock on the back door, only to be greeted by a groggy and increasingly unpleasant Aspirrina.

Night after night she hurried through the back streets of the city, feeling as she had all those dawns she had spent looking for her father. Would she ever stop running, searching, hiding? She had to work hard to keep the truth from the other performers and just as hard to keep from being unmasked at the convent. She had thought all this would end once they got to Havana, where everyone was free, where everything was out in the open. But here she was, in the most exciting city in the world, running, lying and hiding as she always had – a fugitive.

So far they had been able to get away with it. The nuns didn't seem to suspect a thing. Aspirrina and Estelita joined them for almuerzo at noon, the only meal of the day.

Mornings and nights, everyone fasted. Estelita was always

careful to conceal her platinum hair under a scarf. She was sure the nuns would be horrified and certainly throw both of them out if they knew that she had changed her hair color and was sneaking off every night while they slept. But the nuns also concealed their hair, so it was never questioned. Rather, they saw it a sign of respect, an indication that Estelita might one day join their ranks. And although she was often tired, she always helped wash dishes after the meal, while Aspirrina cleaned up everyone else retired to their cells to read the bible or pray or whatever it was the nuns did. Estelita used the time to catch up on her sleep.

Some of the girls backstage had commented on Estelita's hands. All the girls had long, polished nails. Estelita did not.

"Do you spend your days peeling potatoes?" Barbarita asked her.

Estelita didn't respond, she knew that with Barbarita it was better not to engage in conversation. The girl, although very young, was smart, maybe too smart. If Estelita was in danger of being found out by anyone, it would be by her.

Besides, Estelita knew the audience couldn't see her nails from afar. She was just one of many. There had also been comments about her clothes. Showgirls wore the latest fashions, something Estelita knew very little about. But she learned. Her first paycheck went to new dresses and shoes. She was quickly becoming the young lady of Havana she wanted to be, clad to the nines without a centavo in her expensive purse.

But every morning she met the nuns in the same old dress and flat-heeled shoes she had arrived in. Sor Maria always motioned for her to sit at her side in the chapel. The nun would smile at her gently, turning her missal to the day's prayer. And while the others prayed, Estelita planned. It was equally important to her that she remain in good graces with the sisters because she wanted Aspirrina to have a home and a job when the day came and she finally could break away. That was an essential component of her plan, of the map she was creating. Her independence had to be complete, she didn't want to spend the rest of her life wondering if Aspirrina was all right, if she had a place to live, food to eat, companionship. At the convent she would be safe. So she observed silences, mended clothing for the poor. Every morning she allowed Aspirrina to inspect her for traces of makeup and sniff her like a police dog for any hint of perfume.

Soon she would get a place of her own, but first she had to think of the best way to get away from Aspirrina, who had yet to find a modicum of gratitude or considerations for the nuns.

"Me, they treat like a slave, you they pamper," she said, "and you know why? That Sor Maria wants to trap you. The Catholics nowadays are as bad as the Jehovah's Witnesses."

"I'm not worried," Estelita replied. "I enjoy praying and I'm glad I learned to sew. At least now I feel I know how to do something."

"Sure, it's easy to spend a day sitting on your ass while I scrub floors. What you should be doing is looking for a man to get us out of here before they have completely finished me off and brained-washed you. I don't know how much more of this I can take."

Estelita nodded as if taking the words to heart when in fact she was adding it to the list of preposterous decision and suggestions Aspirrina, growing more desperate with each passing day, repeated with alarming regularity.

Estelita had stopped listening, there was neither room nor need for a man. She was done shopping for now, she had enough dresses and shoes, and pretty underwear, she no longer got shaming looks in the dressing room. The next few paychecks she would save and soon she'd have the money she needed to strike out on her own. She directed a smile at Aspirrina, the light of all that's possible illuminating her pretty eyes.

Aspirrina, not without enormous effort, returned the smile. It was a closed-lipped smile, more of a grimace, really, and in it Estelita could see all the fear, pain, resentment and envy that surely devoured a bit of Aspirrina's soul every moment of every day, and she knew that from that moment on, she would have to carefully weigh every step she took, every decision she made, every single word she uttered.

11

Juan Carlos Talente knew that a man in his position had to be careful. He had learned that lesson at the Shanghai Theater where the girls back stage constantly made themselves available to him. They always were giddy after their performances, bubbling over with lust. It was not forbidden, but the management discouraged sexual activity between the girls and the patrons. There had been times when some of the girls had been approached by men as they were walking home from the theater, and when the advances had been refused, the stimulated men often turned belligerent, aggressive. As one dancer had said,

"They show less respect for us than they would a common, streetwalking whore."

Perhaps the men had been right on some level. Girls who were willing to take off their clothes and dance suggestively onstage for a male audience were not exactly paragons of lady-like virtue. But none of them considered themselves professional prostitutes, either.

"There are plenty of those to choose from in Havana," one said. "Why don't they go after them?"

But the patrons of the Shanghai simply wanted to sample what had been so vividly displayed for them. It became part of Juan Carlos's job to escort the girls after the midnight show. He walked with them through the dark maze of Chinatown and Havana Vieja until they reached the brighter, and relatively safer avenues of the city center. The system worked well, but it also made it easy for the girls to slyly suggest a drink at a bar. And after a few drinks, they tried to entice the young man to their rooms for a sweaty round of the horizontal mambo. Juan Carlos succumbed on more than one occasion, losing his innocence in the arms of one of the better-looking strippers. But this caused problems.

"Why not me, mi amor?"

After a while, Juan Carlos began to feel as if he had more wives tugging at him than he could handle. The girls had never been mean-spirited, mostly they razzed and teased him, as they would a younger brother or cousin, brushing their tasseled breasts too close as they passed him backstage, or telling him dirty jokes and using his name for a punch line.

Even Orozco Garcia, who had appointed himself his unofficial guardian, teased him by putting an index finger to an eye as if to say, "I'm watching you."

But it was all done with a great deal of playfulness. In fact, only a sense of humor kept the Shanghai from sinking into complete depravity. Serafin, the man who dreamed up the skits, was not interested in women in a romantic manner. So he brought a light, almost childlike tone to what could have been a dark and dismal atmosphere. The same with the two male actors who performed with the girls in the roles of cuckolded husbands or lascivious villains; or whatever else the scene called for. They were easy-going guys who were well-known at the local precinct for their participation in the unsavory business of marijuana smoking or petty burglaries. But in spite of their criminal tendencies they were always well-behaved backstage. They showed up for rehearsals without fail, and while onstage worked hard to get the audience to laugh. They were clowns to the very essence of the word, and while killing time between acts, played cards in their undershirts, drank frequently from a bottle of rum, and made the girls squeal by pinching their round bottoms.

The time Juan Carlos spent at the Shanghai had been a valuable experience. By the time he started working at the Riviera, he knew how to handle temptation. He was no longer the curious colt he had been two years before, when sex had been so new that every night he walked to work with an erection. But in spite of his self-control and sophistication, the encounter with Estelita had affected him. Now, when he watched the showgirls from his prominent place at table one, he couldn't take his eyes off her. She was a beacon, her platinum hair shining like a halo, her creamy skin glowing almost as brightly as her spangled costumes. For months he watched her. Night after night, show after show he watched her. He was glad to see she had been given more to do than parade around and look enchanting. Now she participated in the set piece that opened the second act. It was a daring, sultry dance inspired by the ritual movements of Santeria, the venerated Afro-Cuban religion.

The Santeria number featured the dark-skinned women in the company. Dressed in sheer white dresses and elaborate white turbans, they writhed and wriggled on the vast stage to the violent beat of six tumbadora drums, as if possessed by demons. Muscular black men, wearing colorful African masks and little else, tried to tame and possess them while rings of real fire burst on the stage. In the midst of this mad choreography, Estelita, dressed in white sequins, her platinum hair teased straight up like smoke, would appear out of a blast of lights. At this point, the drums went silent, and all the other dancers stopped moving, freezing into rigid and uncomfortable poses, as she surveyed the situation with arrogant eyes.

Now, only the violins could be heard, swelling and swirling; the melodious music wrapping itself around her. She was White Magic, a sorceress, and she had the stage all to herself. As she danced, the violins receded while the single line of a lilting, melancholy flute wove a blistering, romantic passage that pierced through the heart of the audience. Her hips and arms swayed, her crimson lips parted into a bewitching smile, her feet hardly touched the floor, she moved from one frozen figure to another and purified them with the touch of her slender hand.

The chorus dancers, one by one, would come to life again, encircling her, lifting her high above their heads and onto a golden throne. It was an audacious performance, her lithe and sensuous physique gracefully accomplishing what Aspirrina, with her awkward, stocky body, could only dream.

At the end of the scene, there was thunder and lightning as the entire orchestra stood up for an electrifying blast. And then, without warning a surprising blackout left everyone gasping in the dark. But even in that darkness, Estelita's radiant image remained seared into the collective mind of the enraptured audience; but particularly into his.

Juan Carlos also knew that the more powerful men often wandered around backstage spreading compliments and expensive cigar smoke. And could frequently be seen walking through the casino, arm in arm with a stunning showgirl or two. He wondered if he should ask his bosses where the line was drawn, if they would allow him to escort a chorus girl for one night. Not just any girl.

Estelita.

But he resisted temptation. He didn't want to jeopardize his position in any way, and he comforted himself with the knowledge that he could have his pick of the dozens of cigarette girls or cocktail waitresses who populated the casino floor. They were always available to him. But none of them captured his imagination like Estelita did. He had gone as far as casually strolling through the backstage area, his heart pounding, his eyes sparkling with anticipation of a chance encounter. But she was nowhere to be found.

He had imagined the encounter many times, the look of surprise and recognition on her pretty face. He planned to flash her his most winning smile, and compliment her on something. There were so many things they could talk about: her beauty, her talent, her performances. He wanted to know all about her. Where did she come from? Where did she live? He wanted to meet her family, to smoke a cigar with her father, compliment her mother on her fine cooking. He considered summoning her up to his suite under one pretext or another, but he couldn't come up with a reason that didn't seem too obvious. He certainly didn't want to upset her again. Once had been enough. As unpleasant as the business with that crazy woman had been, it remained a pleasant memory for him because it had brought Estelita into the center of his life, to the forefront of his thoughts. But he was smart enough to realize that most likely, the haughty showgirl didn't remember it the same way. And he was determined to make a much better impression on her next time they met.

Lansky, who never missed a thing, who was rumored to read minds, shouted to him across the table. "Whaddaya think of the new girl?" Lansky asked in English.

Juan Carlos felt the blood drain from him face. He thought he'd been so careful but someone had noticed, and not just anybody, Lansky. He wanted to pretend he didn't hear the question but he knew Lansky was waiting for an answer. Lansky always wanted his questions answered no matter what.

"She's magnificent," Juan Carlos said.

Lansky- smiled, a rarity for him.

"Yeah, I think so too. I think so too."

Juan Carlos watched as all the men at table number one fixed their eyes on Estelita de la Cruz and he became very worried, furiously so.

12

There were times when Estelita felt she would go mad with envy when she heard the other girls talk about what they had done the previous day, hours spent by someone's aquamarine swimming pool or at a secluded beach, or breezy drives in the countryside in luxurious convertible cars, even clandestine outings with married or difficult men. And sex, which they spoke about freely and seemed to enjoy in a wide variety of locations and positions. The more outrageous the position, the more loudly they bragged. She struggled against her resolve to remain single until she could bring her father home, to keep her life uncomplicated, focused.

No man had ever approached her after the show, while the other girls constantly received notes and messages, flowers, candy, jewelry, even lewd invitations, which were fanfared and laughed about throughout the dressing room, there were never any for her.

"It's you," Barbarita said, "you have a wall of ice or something, it's invisible but any man can feel it just from looking at you."

"Barbarita, the things you say," cautioned Rosario with a look of pity that Estelita did not appreciate.

But Barbarita was right, even if Estelita had not meant to build an ice wall or any sort of wall, it was just as well. She had no time in her schedule for such adventures. She always made sure to be the first one out of the dressing room, and by the time the other girls were merrily slipping into sparkling, air-conditioned cars driven by rich and handsome men in crisp summer shirts, she was blocks away.

Sometimes she would slow down her pace a little, just enough to lose herself for one delicious moment in the crowded streets of the central city, prolonging the moment when she would arrive at the convent, her prison. Luisa the dresser, who had overheard what Barbarita and Rosario said, took Estelita aside.

"If you want flowers," Luisa said "you have to make friends after the show."

"I don't care about flowers," Estelita insisted.

"I saw you looking at them," Luisa said with a compassionate smile, "you can have all of it if you want it. Just go sit at the bar after the show, let them know you exist. Up on the stage they can't tell you apart from the rest of them. There are men in Havana who live to pamper pretty girls. And all you have to do is everything they tell you to."

Estelita nodded as if considering the option, but she wasn't. Not for a second. Flowers, gifts and invitations would have to wait, she had no time for that. And she was definitely not interested in doing whatever any man told her to do. That could be just about anything, and the mere thought of the infinite possibilities frightened her.

She knew she was attractive, certainly just as attractive as any of the other girls in the chorus. This was confirmed out on the streets, where even the men who'd seen her before (she was beginning to recognize faces) tried to engage her every time she walked by. She always gave them a friendly smile for she had learned that if she acted like she was above them, it might provoke them to try harder, follow her, try to engage her in conversation. She had seen it happen to other girls whose haughty attitude provoked a scene and they would be followed for blocks on end by packs of taunting men. It was smarter to seem friendly and hurry on past them, to leave them hoping that the next time she walked by she might have a moment for them. To accept their piropos – whispered compliments – without stopping or slowing her pace.

117

Some nights, keyed up from performing, she took longer strolls along the avenues, delaying her return to the convent, drifting past bars and cafés, drinking in the laughter and the chatter, the honking horns, the different languages. She admired the New York-style fashions of the tourists, and the music spilling out of the nightclubs thrilled her. She began noticing the seductive titles of the movies on the marquees, and above the titles, the stars of the moment: Kim Novak, Marilyn Monroe, Lana Turner, ladies with hair like hers.

Havana was just as she had imagined that day on the train, but so far she had tasted very little of it. She felt about Havana the way she did about the jewelry behind the glass windows, she could enjoy their sparkle but there was a barrier between them.

She couldn't complain - her life was exciting beyond her wildest dreams, especially now that she had a featured solo. How the stars had aligned so that she, the newest (and by her estimation, clumsiest) of all the girls had been chosen for this honor she would never know. Chucho had simply swept into the dressing room and made the announcement.

"Estelita," he called out like a Roman emperor choosing the next slave for the lions. Her throat had gone dry. What had Aspirrina done now? All eyes were on her again. But this time the news had been good, very good. He did not take her aside but spoke in front of everyone while she felt her face reddening, something that a glance at the mirror confirmed.

"You're dancing solo, second act. Think you can handle it?"

She barely heard the words but definitely grasped their meaning. She wanted to question him, why her, why so soon, but instead she nodded in silent agreement. She could feel the other girls in the room looking at her, but she couldn't look back. She was elated and embarrassed and wondered why Chucho would tell her this in front of the others who had been there longer and had more experience. But Chucho, she had noticed, cared very little about anyone else. During rehearsals he felt free to shout at anyone for any infraction. He was not known for his courtly manners.

"This calls for extra rehearsals, you understand," he said just before he left. Again, she nodded in agreement. His face looked as if he had been expecting a much bigger reaction from her. Any other girl would have been jumping up and down screaming with gratitude. But

Estelita could only nod because extra rehearsals meant extra time away from the convent and her mind was already busy trying to figure out how she was going to make that happen. But make it happen she would, she had to.

She had stopped confiding in Aspirrina, hadn't talked to her for weeks except for routine communications. She had grown particularly protective about anything to do with the show. Aspirrina was always eager for any kind of backstage gossip and Estelita was willing to give her that, little tidbits now and then about the girls. But made sure to keep any progress she made to herself.

Instead of telling her about the new rehearsal schedule, she told her that Sor Maria had insisted that she attend afternoon mass at the cathedral. The lie flowed easily from her pretty lips, so easily that to Estelita it felt like the truth.

"The penguins are going to trap you," Aspirrina said. "You'll end up married to Jesus Christ instead of a rich man like you're supposed to, and cooped up in this home for dried up women."

"You worry too much for my soul," Estelita said. "Is it so wrong for a girl to want to say a prayer for her father?"

"Prayers aren't going to help him, what you need is money."

She ignored Aspirrina's comment and went off to see Sor Maria. She took her aside and whispered in all seriousness that she wanted to start attending afternoon mass, "to truly hear the words of God."

She felt a pang of guilt, the nun had been so kind to her, but Estelita saw no other way. She feared the nun would see right through her lie, that she would corner her, sit her down under a crucifix and question her until Estelita to confessed the truth. Nothing so dramatic transpired. Sor Maria accepted the news with her usual serene smile, a smile that said she approved, that she was proud, that there was progress. But as she walked away Estelita thought she noticed something else, maybe it was just her own guilt reflected back at her; but it was definitely there, a shadow of suspicion in the eyes of the nun.

Every afternoon as Estelita entered the back door of the casino, she could hear the cathedral bells ringing in the hour – as if to alert Sor Maria and all the others back at the convent.

119

"You're being deceived," the bells sounded, "you're being deceived."

Rehearsals were severe, Chucho would settle for nothing short of perfection. They always began by warming up her toes and arches and hip joints, which was painful enough. They worked in a small, mirrored room, and by the time they were done the mirrors were steamed. To see her efforts manifested in the mirror was exhausting and exhilarating. Even after she learned the steps and could perform them with agility, he demanded even more.

"Now, infuse your moves with personality," he said, "always put your best face forward."

He wanted more from her than she believed she had, and in turn she demanded more of her body. He wanted her to be in pain but appear serene, he wanted her heart pounding and her lungs pumping beyond what she thought humanly possible. Her dance was only three minutes of a two-hour show, but it was an intense three minutes. The walks home at night were torturous, every inch of her body ached, and for a few days she walked with a slight limp that she thought would never go away. But day after day she showed up for rehearsal as the cathedral bells chimed. She worked as hard as Chucho exacted, especially after she saw her next paycheck. No one had bothered to tell her that the solo came with money, it was only a bit more, but it was getting her closer to her goal.

She concealed the raise from Aspirrina, the money was for her emancipation. She did anonymously drop some pesos into the poor box at the convent, whether to assuage her guilt or out of gratitude she couldn't decide, a bit of both, she concluded, shrugging off all questioning thoughts as she stuffed the narrow slot with her hard-earned cash.

When the big night came she was nervous but felt prepared. She had learned how to perform the routine without her heart beating out of her chest, she could control her breath, she even began adding her own intricacies to the number, effortlessly shifting from fluid to staccato movements, she'd learned to let the music guide her.

Her costume was simple, but beautiful, a sparkling red cat suit that was custom made to enhance every curve of her body. And a new headdress to match, created just for her by a man reputed to be the top designer in the city.

"Estelita, I want you to meet someone very special," Chucho said one afternoon.

Out of the glare of the rehearsal lights stepped a tall, thin man with shoulder length hair, a thick strand of white running down the center and casually swept back.

"Hello," she said. He did not reply, instead he turned to Chucho, as if she wasn't there.

"You are right," the man said, his voice measured and proper, "You were absolutely right to choose her. She's the one."

Chucho looked as if he'd just received the biggest compliment of his life, when in fact, the compliment was all about her.

The man had quickly taken her measurements and left, vanished as easily as he had appeared.

A few days later, the headdress was waiting at her vanity when she arrived. It was the most beautiful thing she had ever seen. Unlike the headdresses they all wore, which were beautiful from afar, but not up-close due to overuse and hasty repairs, this one was a delicate work of art. It was simple but elaborate at the same time, it spiraled magically towards the heavens and rather than the cheap feathers and glued-on sequins of the others, this one was stitched and embroidered as if by magic hands. She picked it up, it was so light.

Enclosed was a small note, it simply said, *Delfino.*

Estelita dreaded what the reaction in the dressing room would be. After all she was the newest member of the chorus and suddenly she'd been catapulted over their heads and onto center stage. Their reaction was not what she anticipated.

"You think you got something special?" Barbarita said. "You don't. We've all been pulled into the so-called spotlight by Señor Chucho."

Estelita knew to not take anything Barbarita said personally. Of all the girls she was the most bitter, the one who looked at the dark side of everything, someone Estelita knew to avoid. But this revelation had the ring of truth, particularly as the others nodded in agreement.

"Yes," added Rosario, "we've all been pushed to be Chucho's dancing doll, and you know what, it's not worth it. Who wants to work that hard for a few extra pesos?"

There was such a clamor of so many in agreement that Estelita didn't know where to look, who to listen to. All she could see were brightly made up lips spitting out reasons and excuses as they started and finshed each other's sentences.

"He works you half to death!"

"…by the time you leave you don't have the energy to do anything…"

"…you just want to go home and get into a hot bath…"

"…alone…"

"…what's the point, right girls?"

"…if they want a martyr they should bring over one of the ballerinas from the Teatro Nacional…"

"…he treated me like an animal.."

It was Luisa, the dresser, who put a stop to the chatter.

"Maybe Estelita is enjoying the opportunity," she said, a hairpin as usual dangling from her lips. "Maybe she's different from the whole lazy lot of you."

"That's right, honey," Barbarita said, "maybe you're better than the rest of us."

"Not better," Luisa said, "just a bit different." And she winked at Estelita.

Estelita was used to being different, had not grown up with friends her own age and in spite of Barbarita's taunts, she enjoyed the dressing room, so different from the convent. She wanted to stay there forever, she wanted to learn the best way to respond to Barbarita's sarcasm as she saw others doing, just words that came and went while they tended to their faces, applied layers of makeup, brushed their hair, adjusted their spangled brassieres. She loved how free the girls were to express their opinions, she even admired Barbarita for her tenacity, her ability to air her hostilities openly.

Estelita wanted to stop hiding. This was her world, it was her father's world. A world of costumes and music, dance, spectacle. Unlike the convent, there was no silence in the dressing room – although sometimes the chatter could get filthy. The girls loved to compare their lovers' equipment and sexual technique out loud, relishing and divulging the most intimate details.

From what they said, Estelita was led to believe that all men had sensuous lips just made for deep, hard kisses; warm, well-muscled, hairy chests; long, thick, brutal penises, and an insatiable need to use them all night long.

"I took one look at that huge, black thing," this from a pretty young girl who barely weighed one hundred pounds, "and I said to myself, I can't take that, but I did!"

Her comment was greeted by cheers.

"Darling," another one said, "last week I was on my hands and knees and I turned to him and I screamed 'do you think you could do it to me with a little more affection?' You should have seen the look on his face!"

"Oh, I've seen that look!"

"I know that look."

"Once the pounding begins, there's no mercy."

Estelita had never heard such words before. So far, she had managed to conceal the shameful fact that she was the only virgin in the show. Again she found herself in her father's world, first a show then sex with whoever happened to be next in line. That seemed to be the way for performers but in her father's case it had led to a dark place.

She studied their young, pretty faces and wondered which ones would survive all the indulgences and which ones would be dragged down. She remained quiet, furiously working at removing every speck of makeup from her face while listening intently. She had so much to learn.

"This one is so mysterious," Barbarita said, pointing at Estelita with her lipstick,

"We know what that's all about, don't we girls?"

"Who are you protecting?" Rosario asked, a dirty whisper.

"He must be married!" several chimed in at once prompting peals of dark, knowing laughter.

"We know all about married men, don't we, girls?" another said.

Estelita only smiled as she wrapped a scarf around her bright hair. Let them think what they wanted. If they only knew her closely guarded secret was that she lived with a short, fat, dancer with a penchant for making loud embarrassing scenes, in a convent overseen by a gaggle of silent, celibate nuns.

"You're all crazy," Estelita said as she reached for her hairbrush, "There's no one, no one at all."

But while she brushed her hair she was thinking about Juan Carlos Talente. His handsome face crossed her mind frequently, but she was quick to dismiss such thoughts.

The last thing she needed was one more complication. She barely had time each night to jump out of her costume and run back to the convent before it became too late. She had no time to entertain thoughts of a lover.

Not Juan Carlos Talente, not anyone.

13

Aspirrina took her usual seat near the back door of the convent. Estelita would be knocking soon. She would much rather be tucked away in her bed even if the mattress was hard and the room hot. She found it exasperating that the nuns voluntarily lived this way. She was always irritable nowadays, more than usual. Most of all she missed her old energy. She was always dead tired by the evening.

It wasn't so much the chores or the stifling heat, but the silence that exhausted her. Day in and day out she communicated with the nuns through nods, hand signals and sighs. Sometimes she wanted to jump on top of the heavy kitchen table and do one of her dances – something wild, with lots of gyrations and fierce looks, something that would symbolize the end of tyranny. Maybe she could get the nuns to dance, that's what the old girls needed, freedom of expression.

It was well past midnight and Estelita had not arrived. This was the latest she had ever been out and Aspirrina was worried. She knew that, sooner or later, Estelita was going to fall under the influence of the other, more experienced girls in the show. She knew what those girls could be like, angel-faced tarantulas. Aspirrina had been around long enough to know about the collective euphoria that follows a successful performance.

The applause, the adulation, it all inevitably led to debauchery. She was grateful she never had to struggle with any of that. Look what it had done to the great Esteban de la Cruz. It could happen again. How long before Estelita got swept into the garish glamour of Havana's nightlife? And who could blame her? It wasn't as if the dark den full of sour-faces they currently were living in was a proper place for a young girl.

So far, Estelita had returned every night and Aspirrina was always there waiting, wishing she could smoke a cigarette to pass the time but afraid that the smell would wake up the penguins. Stealth was crucial, they need only keep their cover a bit longer – soon they would have enough money saved to check into a cheap hotel in the nice part of town, or find a small apartment in the bad part of town. They just had to keep the nuns happy and in the dark a few more weeks.

Aspirrina stretched, yawned and checked the clock again. Time was dragging, her ass ached from sitting on the hard chair. She felt she just might fall asleep right then and there. Her mind had started to go into that strange, nodding state where she would start to imagine things when she heard footsteps in the pitch-black hallway. Were they real, or was her mind playing tricks? Her eyes felt gummy, she opened them as wide as she could, peering in the direction of the sounds. And slowly, out of the gloom, like a ghostly vision, emerged the daunting figure of Sor Maria.

There was no point in running or trying to hide - there was no place to go. Aspirrina was completely cornered. Sor Maria Quintana didn't walk, but seemed to float into a pool of moonlight that provided the only illumination in the place. She continued to move forward until she towered above Aspirrina.

"What are you doing out of bed?" she said, a look of severe displeasure on her face. Although she had her answer ready, Aspirrina took a moment to respond. Too many things were going through her mind, mostly that she had never seen Sor Maria not wearing her veil and noticed how strange and lovely she looked in the moonlight, rather like a life-size version of one of the icons on the altar. She seemed much younger too, with her light brown hair loose and falling to her shoulders. Not much older than Estelita, Aspirrina estimated. But so

126

much more confident, and in daytime, with her pale face and black clothing, almost threatening. How did a such a young woman get to run a place like Santa Catalina?

"I can't sleep," Aspirrina whispered and with an exaggerated gesture of extreme pain reached back to massage her spine. "It's my back, it's in spasms."

The nun remained unmoved.

"Where is Estelita?" she demanded.

"Oh, she's in bed, Sister," Aspirrina answered, the lie easily rolling off the tip of her tongue. "I left the room because I didn't want to wake her up with my tossing and turning."

Aspirrina continued massaging her back, giving the nun a pitiful look. Sor Maria Quintana suddenly stood in alert, cocking an ear. Outside the door, heavy footsteps could be heard. She froze as the footsteps grew closer, but did not relax when they vanished.

"Go back to bed now and try to sleep," she said, her eyes cutting into Aspirrina. "I don't want to find you roaming around like this at all hours ever again. Do you understand me?"

"Yes, Sister." Aspirrina said, straining for a humble tone. She walked slowly into the shadows, knowing that before she made it to the stairs, there might be a knock on the door, and both she and Estelita would be out on the street before morning, all her plans destroyed. Once inside her room, she paced up and down, wishing she had a window, some way to warn Estelita who was surely about to step into a nightmare.

*

As soon as Aspirrina was out of sight, Sor Maria unlatched the door and waited. Her heart was beating so fast that she could hardly hear the prayer she was repeating in her own mind. Her stomach was in knots. She had felt safe until she heard the men running by. Police? Soldiers? Rebels? She was sure they were coming to break down the door to the convent, and God only knew what would happen then. She must have been insane to get involved in this crazy business. But it was too late to back out now. They had been so persuasive, and it had seemed like such a good cause, the kind of deed for which she had taken her vows.

But now she felt selfish for placing the others at risk. They could lose their freedom, their home. No one else knew, and no one would ever know. She had almost fainted when she had come face to face with Aspirrina. But she was satisfied with the way she had handled her. What was that woman doing up at these hours? She despised having to treat Aspirrina so harshly but she knew that a woman like that could turn a convent into a madhouse if given half a chance. Sor Maria had often wondered why the woman continued to stay with them. From the start she had made Aspirrina's life as difficult as possible, adding more chores and duties.

"There are other places," Sor Maria had told her that first night, "cheap hotels abound in Havana, other places where people with few resources can receive asylum."

"Look at her," Aspirrina had replied, pointing at Estelita, "would you take her to a cheap hotel? Do you know what happens to young girls in cheap hotels? I'm not strong enough to protect her."

Aspirrina was doing an excellent job cooking and cleaning. It had been weeks since Sor Maria had seen a spider web whereas before they could be found in every corner. Rats, ants, even cockroaches, had all vanished from the convent. For that, she was grateful. But just the same, she could not risk having her walking around at all hours, groaning and moaning like a restless spirit in an ancient graveyard.

Tomorrow morning she would explain the rules to her once again. She would be very specific about what areas of the convent were off limits. She had to be very definite because Aspirrina had a tendency to interpret rules to suit herself. Also, she was taking much more time than necessary to do the daily shopping. She was certain the woman, in reaction to the silence in the convent, was stopping to chat with anyone who would lend an ear. Sor Maria did not approve. The people outside did not need to know what was happening behind the convent walls. This is the way she wanted it, the way it had always been. Yes, she would take care of this woman in the morning. She would explain the rules once more. But now she had a much bigger concern.

They were late.

Sor Maria sat in the chair by the door, in the same spot where she had found Aspirrina, and waited. A few minutes later, she heard a car pull up, and she knew the moment had come. She heard a car door open and then another, then both car doors were closed. The soft clack of metal on metal made her cringe. How much could the neighbors hear? She clasped her hands together to keep them from shaking, they felt ice cold. And then they were there, at her doorstep. The wooden door squeaked open, and in spite of her current apprehensions, she made a mental note to have Aspirrina apply oil in the morning. And then, for the first time in years, men were inside the convent after dark.

A half-block away, Estelita stood in the shadows. She had been running fast. She had almost reached the convent when she saw a white car with darkened headlights crawl around the corner and stop in front of the very door she was trying so desperately to reach.

Earlier, she had been enjoying her walk so much that she had stopped for a cold drink. Aspirrina was waiting for her but she didn't care. Let her wait. She stopped at a brightly-lit corner bodega. She was the only customer at the moment and was happy to spend a few minutes collecting her thoughts, taking in the balmy night air, feeling, even for a few minutes, like the independent city girl she longed to be.

The couple who ran the bodega had been arguing and when she sat on the stool, they did not stop simply because they had a customer. The man was young and attractive. The top buttons of his shirt were undone and she could see the muscled chest beneath. He was the kind of man the girls talked about in the dressing room. The woman, probably his wife, was much older, all lumps and curves, large breasts, wide hips all squeezed into a tight, low-cut dress. The woman set the drink in front of Estelita and returned to bickering.

"And I tell you it's a stupid idea," the man said.

"Are we supposed to stand around and let them steal the bread out of our mouths again?" the woman asked, slamming the worn wooden counter with the palm of her hand.

"That depends on who you listen to, Luisa. Open your eyes. There wouldn't be any bread to steal if it wasn't for them." His tone turned to disgust. "You're listening to the wrong people, and as usual, you won't listen to me."

Estelita was enjoying herself, sipping the sweet coconut water, noisily crunching the ice cubes and eavesdropping on the couple. But she soon lost interest when she realized that the argument wasn't an isolated event; this was probably the way they always talked to each other. How she longed to have someone to bicker with, someone she loved, someone other than Aspirrina. She wondered if her mother and her father had ever argued. Their love story had always been presented to her as sublime, harmonious, and cut short by death. A death she had caused. What she wouldn't give to have two parents arguing.

She had been daydreaming and searching in her purse for a coin to pay for her beverage when she heard loud voices, hundreds of them, singing "La Bayamesa," the Cuban national anthem. She stopped to listen to the beautiful, powerful voices and wondered where they were coming from. The booming chorus seemed to fill the night. She looked up, the sky was clear, black and dotted with tiny silver stars. When she looked down again she saw the somber, singing crowd, as wide as the street itself, moving in her direction with the strong, steady pace of an enormous steamroller.

"Otra protesta!" said the woman behind the counter. Another protest.

"And at this hour," the man added. "These people have no respect."

He took Estelita's money and, without another word, closed down the establishment and turned out the lights. Windows slammed shut all around her. She stood up to leave and found herself squeezed between the marching crowd and the wall. Young and old, men and women marched past her. Women in modest summer dresses, arms linked, hands holding purses and flags. College students in their austere uniforms, strong and defiant, carried signs and shouted for liberty. Fear gripped her, she knocked desperately on the bodega's door, but it was like knocking on a tomb. She tried inching her way towards the corner when she heard the sting of police sirens; they were getting closer, louder. The crowd broke apart, running in every direction. Men picked up rocks and threw them at the approaching squad cars. A fire engine rammed through and people jumped out of its way. It was obvious that either they stepped aside or they would be run down. It was all happening so fast. Commanding voices were amplified through loud-speakers calling for order, but no one was listening. Two women next to her set the tablecloth of one of the bodega tables on fire. And then another, until all the tables were burning.

Estelita continued to edge past the crowd. If she could just reach the corner...if she could just go one more step without being trampled. More people poured onto the sidewalk. Policemen ran in all directions. People rushed past her with such force that she was being buffeted back and forth. She continued inching along the wall; the burning tables had led to burning awnings, the flames lapping up the side of the buildings.

Men and women tumbled down the street like rolling barrels. For a moment, Estelita was on the opposite side, behind the fire engine, in the clear just long enough to reach the corner, and when she did, she took off her shoes and ran. She ran blindly over the cobblestone streets. The rough surface burned the soles of her feet, but she continued running. She feared that if she slowed down someone would mistake her for one of the demonstrators, grab her by the arm, and throw her kicking and screaming into a patrol wagon.

The people of the neighborhood, alerted by the sirens, stepped onto the sidewalk in groups of threes and fours, asking one another what was happening in that slow "I don't really care" way that the people of Havana have of talking. She ran past them, even pushed one or two out of her way, not caring that they were shouting curses at her.

Suddenly she looked forward to seeing Aspirrina's face, wanted to feel the cloistered safety of the convent's thick walls. Her heart was pounding, her side ached, it was an eternity between breaths, sweat poured from her head and down the back of her neck. Finally, the convent was in sight. As she rounded the corner a car approached and she quickly ducked out of sight. But instead of passing her, the car slowed down and stopped at the back entrance to the convent. Two men got out. She watched as Sor Maria opened the convent's door. She could hear quick, whispered greetings and then the two men opened the trunk and carried two large wooden crates inside. Sor Maria remained at the door as if keeping guard until the men returned to the car and drove off.

Estelita pressed herself further into the shadows as the car passed. She could not see their faces clearly, but she noticed that the driver had black hair, and a big white shock in the center.

"Delfino!" Her hand went instinctively to her head, as if expecting to find the now familiar and much admired headdress he had designed just for her.

She waited but it wasn't until the early morning sunlight colored the sidewalks a soft pink that she saw the door of the convent crack open. Aspirrina stuck her head out, saw Estelita crouching and waved for her to hurry. Estelita crossed the street, her shoes in her hand, and together, quiet as church mice, they scurried up to their room.

14

It was one of those nights when the north winds blew with such force that the Malecón seawall couldn't hold back the unrelenting assailment. Giant, white-crested waves smashed against the rocks and concrete, spewing eight, ten, sometimes even twenty feet into the air then slapping down full-force onto the already flooded highway.

On nights such as these, the people of Havana stayed away. The Malecón area, usually crowded with festive tourists, illicit lovers, peanut vendors, lotto peddlers, guitar players and roaming packs of prostitutes, was deserted in every direction. And it wasn't just the weather – an unexpected demonstration, held late at night, had awakened the city leaving it frightened and unsure.

High above the Malecón, in the Presidential suite of the Riviera, Lansky could feel the effects of the general unrest spreading throughout the country. His anxiety was understandable. In the United States, he was an outlaw, but in Cuba, through hard work and at great personal risk, he had established himself as a respected figure, the man who had put things right.

He had been hand-picked by President Batista and neither man was about to let a mob of political dissidents trample what they had accomplished. Lansky picked up the phone and got immediate attention.

"Yes, sir," the voice said.

"Get me that Cuban kid," Lansky said, sounding distracted although he wasn't. Sounding distracted was one of his many tactics. Lansky always knew exactly what he was doing, he even knew the Cuban kid's name, it was Juan Carlos Talente.

*

Juan Carlos had been sitting in one of the comfortable shoeshine stands outside of the Riviera Hotel and Casino, enjoying a cigarette and getting what he considered a decent but in no way outstanding shine from a ten-year-old boy when a uniformed page informed him that Lansky wanted to see him.

"He wants you now," the page urged.

Juan Carlos tipped the shoeshine boy a peso, in spite of his mediocre performance, mindful of the days when he had performed such a service himself. He strolled leisurely through the hotel lobby, was greeted respectfully by the elevator guards, and entered the small, private lift up to Lansky's office with the confidence of a man who knew his way around. When the brass door closed, he admired his reflection on the shiny surface which was kept aglow by the busy hands of Cuban maids and janitors. He liked what he saw. Smooth, very smooth. He was wearing a dark gray suit just picked up from his tailor. His white shirt was immaculate and starched to a shine. The Windsor knot of his blue silk tie projecting all he aspired to – polished, professional elegance. Juan Carlos was proud of the man he was becoming. Self-assured, good at his job, undeniably a success. There had been a time when, upon entering this elevator, he'd calmed himself down by repeating "you can do this, you can do this."

Now he approached every meeting with Lansky with the certainty that nothing could be asked of him that he couldn't execute to perfection.

Juan Carlos was becoming well-known in Havana. People respected him, even those who just a few months before didn't know he existed. His dealings with Lansky had been few, but each time they'd met, he had been impressed by the man's soft-spoken, relaxed style. He commanded any room he walked into, and forced taller men to meet his piercing brown eyes, which could go from warm and compassionate to ice cold in a flash.

Lansky was used to wielding great power, and there was a humble, almost fatherly side to him. But Juan Carlos instinctively knew that this side was not to be trusted. Lansky reminded him of a big snake that wraps itself around you and smiles sweetly as it squeezes.

As the elevator reached the penthouse, Juan Carlos gave himself a final check, the doors slid open, dividing his image in two. He had come a long way, but he wanted more.

Not as much as Lansky had, but certainly more than he was getting. He wanted to move out of his room and get a spacious flat, big enough for a wife and some children. He wanted smart, beautiful children who would grow up with a mother and a father and the safety and certainty of belonging to a family. He would give them everything he had been denied at the orphanage. He was satisfied for now, particularly when he saw the shoeshine boys he'd known years ago still shining shoes, still waiting for coins to drop into their blackened hands. But Juan Carlos Talente wanted more and he knew Lansky was the only one who could make it happen. After the Riviera, there would be other hotels, casinos, and theaters, bigger and better. The country was completely surrounded by beautiful coastline, it was a treasure trove for developers – and someone had to attend to them. For now he had to do the dirty work, but he knew that in time, he'd have others do the dirty work for him.

Lansky was alone in his office. It was a large room furnished with elegant antiques, built-in shelves full of neatly aligned old books covered every wall. There were framed photographs of his family everywhere, as if Lansky couldn't decide which one he liked best. From all corners of the room, the sweet faces of his wife and children, trapped behind flawless glass, bestowed soothing smiles upon nervous visitors.

Juan Carlos tapped lightly on the door frame and Lansky looked up, concern clouding his face.

"Juan Carlos," he said, "come in."

He entered and Lansky directed him to a couch. He took a seat and Lansky sat across from him.

"I'm a little concerned," he started. "What the hell," he added with a weary sigh, "I'm a lot concerned. It's about this business in Jaimanitas."

Juan Carlos quickly nodded in agreement.

"So you know about them," Lansky said. "Why haven't we done anything about it?"

Yes. Juan Carlos knew all about them. Jaimanitas was an impoverished fishing port on the north side of the city where the local gambling boats docked. Until recently Jaimanitas could only be reached by boat or by taking the long way around on the Guanabacoa Highway. Now it could be reached in minutes through a recently completed concrete tunnel, an engineering marvel commissioned by Batista that took you under Havana harbor and spit you out on the other side on to a narrow, sandy road full of potholes and sharp rocks.

The gambling boats that operated out of Jaimanitas couldn't compete with the big casinos. Their owners had watched bitterly as multitudes of tourists poured into Havana, and they were getting more greedy and desperate by the minute for a piece of the action. Most of them were old sailors who had managed to stash away some cash and bought themselves a small vessel. They had resigned themselves to a lifetime of misery, fishing their fingers raw all day long and drinking away their meager earnings at night. But all that had changed when they had been recruited and united by a man named Felipe Arjuna. Arjuna, a smart, even-tempered man, had explained to them, using words they could easily understand, that by converting their fishing vessels into gambling dens, they could make a lot more money, and have a hell of a lot more fun.

Their success had become the stuff of legend. Everyone in Havana knew how in the privacy of the old boathouse that now served as their headquarters, Arjuna had knelt before the group of skeptical and hardened sailors, and using broken pieces of white chalk on the dirty concrete floor, had drawn out a business plan. It had not been very difficult to make them see the advantages of his proposal.

"No one will touch them," Juan Carlos told Lansky, "they think because they're operating in the open sea, they're above the law."

Lansky stood up, clearly upset, but as always, keeping a cool head.

"Nobody's above the law here," he hissed, shaking his head from side to side like an annoyed schoolmaster. "Not anymore. They're like goddamn pirates, those guys."

Juan Carlos nodded in agreement. "But the Cubans need a place to go," he offered in defense of his people, "your casinos and nightclubs are too expensive for us."

"I know that," Lansky replied. "That's why I've stayed away from Jaimanitas. But what's really going on over there, it's disgusting. Sure, they're making money, but along with that comes a load of trouble they don't know how to handle."

Lansky returned to the couch and sat down again. He softened his tone a little, but passion still quivered in his voice. Juan Carlos had heard plenty of talk about Lansky, about his brilliant business instinct -- instead of incriminating account books, he was able to keep complicated figures and deals in his head; his handshake was worth a million signatures; if he had chosen to go legit, he could be running General Motors.

"They're playing Razzle and Cubolo, for chrissakes. You have any idea what it took to clean up the games in this town? Frankly, and I mean no offense by this, I don't care what the Cubans do. But they're recruiting my people, offering them more for less, offering them a true Cuban experience. If they're going to share my business, they're going to have to share the profits. You understand?"

They're doing a lot more than cheating you out of a few pesos, Juan Carlos thought, but didn't say. He'd heard that they were using the gambling boats to smuggle in munitions from dissidents in the States to aid the so-called rebels, those dreamers and lunatics up in the mountains hiding among the trees like the rats that they were.

These were only rumors, but in Havana rumors, particularly nasty ones, had a way of proving true. But he didn't want to complicate the conversation with Lansky- until he knew more, until he had hard facts.

"We have to talk some sense into these guys." Lansky said, raising a warning finger, "they're shooting themselves in the foot and they're shooting my foot right along with it. I didn't come all the way down here to clean up this mess just to have a bunch of amateurs spoil it."

"I agree," said Juan Carlos thoughtfully. "How do you want to handle it?"

"Very carefully," Lansky said. "I trust as a Cuban you will know best. But you have to be very careful. So far the uprisings have stayed clear of the casinos. The last thing I need is to give anybody an excuse. You understand?"

Juan Carlos understood perfectly. Lansky, if he wanted, could sink every ship in Jaimanitas simply by snapping his fingers. But he couldn't risk it now. Havana was a pressure-cooker. That's why Lansky made sure he hired Cubans in all the hotels and casinos. Waiters, cooks, maids and janitors, were all making a living from him. But these same people, if provoked, could cause a lot of damage. A riot inside one of the casinos would be the end of everything. Tourists wanted to feel protected while they gambled, and Lansky wanted them to feel as safe as they would in Las Vegas or Monte Carlo. In fact, it was Lansky who had started calling Havana the Monte Carlo of the Caribbean. He'd even named his hotel the Riviera to perpetuate the illusion. There was no end to the man's genius.

Just the same, Havana couldn't afford one more scandal. Just one would be enough to set back the gaming industry twenty years. And if anybody had the power and the backing of the Cubans, it was the people from Jaimanitas. To them, the gambling boats were more than a good time. It was the one thing left on the island that belonged to them. One wrong move and the pressure-cooker could explode.

"So you're thinking this would be more of a goodwill visit?" Juan Carlos asked, hoping he was right.

Lansky smiled. "Not quite, my friend," he said. "I need you to squeeze them, but with soft gloves. You know what I mean?"

"Yes." Juan Carlos said. The snake's embrace, squeeze, smile, squeeze.

"I trust you know what to do." He said with finality. The meeting was clearly over. Lansky returned to his desk. Juan Carlos walked to the elevator and pushed the call button. He was excited by his new mission. He'd been waiting for a moment like this.

Suddenly the elevator doors slid open in that silent, expensive way. Inside, in the soft, golden light, stood Estelita. Her eyes seemed to flicker with recognition when she saw him, but he couldn't be sure, maybe it was the moisture welling up in his own eyes.

He stepped back to let her through.

"Hello," she said as she walked past him. She was so close he could smell her talcum-powdered skin.

"Hello," he said.

Time stopped, the moment froze. All of Havana was silent, as if the entire city was suddenly holding its breath.

"Estelita, my star," Lansky shouted, shattering the moment like a mirror, the shards falling at his feet.

Estelita turned her beautiful face towards Lansky, a smile played on her ruby red lips. She extended a graceful hand, which Lansky took and held. He pulled her gently into the office. The showgirl, in her stiletto heels, towered over him. As she followed the little man into his great room, she turned to look at Juan Carlos once more.

"Good bye," she whispered with a voice so soft it was almost as if he had imagined the words. Then she turned her full attention back to Lansky..

Before the door became a solid barrier between them, he heard Lansky say, "Let me look at you, yes, you are as young and lovely up close as you are up on that stage. My darling, you are...Cuba."

Juan Carlos did not hear her reply, but he was sure it had been quite modest. He wondered what the meeting was about. Was the old man trying to get her into bed? Those guys were notorious for banging chorus girls two and three at a time. But not Lansky. Lansky was a devoted husband and father. But why was Estelita summoned to his office, and why did he call her his star? He chased away the ugly, nagging thoughts. Lansky, he convinced himself, was not a rival.

The elevator continued its slow descent, past floor after boring floor filled with people in rented rooms who had no idea that Juan Carlos Talente had just been in the presence of an angel.

Juan Carlos commanded a great deal of influence over the small-time gamblers of Havana, but he suspected that a man like Felipe Arjuna would prove challenging. His suspicions were confirmed when he was partnered with Marino Seveces. Juan Carlos was used to going on these inspections alone, in a cranky old Ford Fairlane borrowed from the casino. But on this night Lansky must have felt he needed the additional weight of one more man on the job. Seveces was one of Lansky's favorite strong-arms. Now in his sixties, Seveces had been around a long time and his savage reputation was legendary.

His quarrelsome approach to even the tiniest infraction had grown more brutal as he got older. People said he would do anything to maintain the fearsome reputation he had worked so long to build.

Thunder and lightning played havoc with the sky, and every few seconds the darkened city became illuminated by a flash that penetrated deep into darkened homes along the Malecón. Juan Carlos sat in the passenger seat of a brand new Cadillac Eldorado Biarritz. He was trying to act casually, but it was hard for him to hold back his excitement. He had never been inside such a magnificent car; the casino recently purchased a fleet of twenty in every color available.

They were riding in one of his favorites, an elegant, midnight blue, and every inch of it, from the leather upholstery to the electric door-locks, exuded success. It always took his breath away when he saw one of the gigantic cars rolling through Havana's narrow streets, its wide, sharp-winged rear-end competing for space with donkey carts, ancient trucks and rusting buses.

Now they traveled along the deserted road with sheets of sea water pounding on the unjustifiably long hood. Seveces had insisted on driving and Juan Carlos knew better than to argue. He kept his eyes on the drenched highway, that had turned into a wet funhouse mirror, reflecting back, in ever-changing patterns, the multicolor buildings that lined the world-famous avenue.

Juan Carlos watched the robust winds bend the royal palm trees towards the ground. He liked storms and sank back into the soft, leather seat and stretched his legs to their full length to relax and enjoy the spectacle.

"This fellow, Arjuna," Seveces said, drawing Juan Carlos out of his reverie, "has one very important item missing from his calculations."

Juan Carlos didn't answer, his eyes on the windshield wipers. Wondering what Estelita was doing this very moment. Was she on her hands and knees? He stopped his train of thought, this was the way a

140

fellow from the Shanghai Theater would think. He had to believe that he was above those thoughts and that Estelita was above those deeds.

"The power of the American dollar, my friend," Seveces continued. "He hasn't stopped to think that Lansky, Batista and their friends didn't dump tons of their own money into cleaning up the games just to let a bunch of floating whorehouses ruin it all."

"We'll see what we can do," Juan Carlos answered.

"Yeah, we'll see." Seveces said as a bolt of lightning split a palm tree in half.

Juan Carlos didn't want to get on Seveces's bad side, and the man didn't seem to have a good side, so he chose to remain quiet. Again he wished he was going to Jaimanitas alone. Seveces was just one more dangerous element to contend with, one more opportunity for things to go wrong.

As the car started to descend into the tunnel, he felt the full weight of the waters of Havana Harbor overhead. As the car emerged from the tunnel, the cannon from Morro Castle shot off its nightly boom. Both men instinctively checked their watches. The cannon was fired promptly every night at nine o'clock. For centuries, Havana had been attacked by pirates. To protect it, the governor had built a stone wall around the city, lorded over by an imposing fortress, the majestic Morro Castle. The opening and closing of the wall's main entrance was announced with a resounding blast from the mighty cannon. And, although the wall no longer existed, the cannon-shot tradition continued.

The residents of Havana set their clocks and watches by it. Some people said a quick prayer, others placed dinner on the table or sent the younger children to bed. The nine o'clock boom was always received with a smile – what had been put off all day could be finished at this time: bets were settled, decisions made, compromises reached, chores completed, and Havana emerged from the sluggish stupor characteristic of tropical islands.

Only after the cannon fired did young couples step out in their fine clothes for a movie or a café, music in bars was turned up louder, the pace on the street picked-up speed, chairs and tables were brought outside, and groups of neighbors, freshly showered, gathered on sidewalks for games of checkers, chess, canasta, or just to watch strangers walk by and then gossip about them. Laughter filled the night like an intoxicating perfume.

Juan Carlos tried to be patient while Seveces, with a foul and crooked mouth, smoked cigarette after cigarette, and cursed the winds. Juan Carlos had hoped to get this business out of the way early, and hurry back to the casino in time for the late show. But Seveces was as careful a driver as he was reckless in every other respect. Juan Carlos peered through the wet, wrap-around windshield. In the distance, he could barely make out the strings of light bulbs that adorned the gambling boats.

"This is the perfect night to talk to these people The water is too choppy and the boats are sure to remain anchored." Seveces said.

Yes, thought Juan Carlos, but it also would be a night when they were losing a lot of revenue, and everyone would be in a foul mood. These men were not known for their mild and gracious disposition even when the weather was fair.

When they finally arrived, Juan Carlos watched as the Cadillac headlights washed across the peeling boathouse walls as if they were two big yellow eyes. Seveces killed the engine with a swift turn of the key, and Juan Carlos prepared for the worst. Seveces looked at him with undertaker eyes, eager to get down to business. They both knew that business could get nasty: this was like walking into someone's house and telling them how to run their lives. Their only reassurances were the .45 caliber pistols each of them carried – gifts from Lansky.

The winds had grown even more furious. Giant waves exploded in quick succession onto the trembling pier. The air thick with sand and salt water slapped against it, forcing them to brace themselves. They walked as quickly as they could past the mouth of the long, narrow pier where six large boats, dark and empty, bucked like broncos against the turbulent tide.

"No one here's making any money tonight," Seveces growled, but his words disappeared into a gust of wind.

They continued past the dock and into the darkness, sand kicking up all around them, their suit coats flapping.

Bright floodlights shooting from the roof of the boathouse caught them by surprise, the harsh light momentarily blinding them, freezing them on the spot. They held firm against the winds as best they could. Juan Carlos fingered his gun. He didn't like carrying it, and so far he'd never needed to use it. He hoped this would not be the night. Seveces instinctively drew his weapon.

"Put it away," Juan Carlos shouted. The older man looked at the gun as if he had forgotten it was in his hand, and shoved it in his pocket.

They started for the boathouse, squinting against the powerful rays of the spotlight and the relentless spray of sand, their long, black shadows trailing behind them.

As they were about to step up to the front porch, the door flung open with a bang, and Felipe Arjuna, a silhouette in the doorway, his hair blowing wildly, greeted them with what, in the gloom, looked like a smile.

"I apologize for the lights," he shouted against the roaring wind, "they are completely out of my control,"

Juan Carlos and Seveces held their ground, assessing the situation. Arjuna motioned them towards him with a wave of the hand.

"You'd better come inside," he shouted, "or that wind will knock both of you on your asses."

Juan Carlos got to the door first. An awning protected him from most of the wind, and he was able to see Arjuna more clearly. Arjuna, he noted, was tall and muscular, with a sea-weathered complexion and shaggy brown hair. He was also much younger than Juan Carlos had expected.

The man extended a hand and Juan Carlos took it. They shook once, firmly, while Seveces kept his distance, one hand deep in his coat pocket. His gun pocket.

They followed the man who had become known as "The Buccaneer of Havana Harbor" into the boathouse.

"I'm Juan Carlos Talente," he said, eyeing the friendly stranger with suspicion.

"Oh, I know who you are," Arjuna interrupted, still smiling. "You are famous now."

"As are you," Juan Carlos replied, still not sure if he should return the smile.

"This is Señor Seveces."

"Ah, yes," Arjuna said. Seveces grunted the most minimal of

143

greetings.

Inside the boathouse the winds made everything creak.

Juan Carlos was surprised to see how empty the place was. He had expected bodyguards or at least a couple of lackeys hanging around, cleaning their rifles.

"Let's get to the point of your visit. Everyone knows," Arjuna said, "that you work for the Americans, and that you can close down our establishment just by whistling."

Juan Carlos pretended to ignore the remark, but he was delighted that his reputation preceded him to Jaimanitas.

"I'm just trying to keep things clean," he finally said, taking the chair that was offered. "For everyone's benefit."

Seveces took another chair and straddled it backwards. There were more chairs in the room, but Arjuna remained on his feet.

"I understand you think that's what you are doing, hermano," Arjuna said, with a smile, a smile that was starting to irritate Juan Carlos. He suspected the smile did not represent friendship but rather a patronizing superiority. "What I would like to know," he continued, "is, why us? And why are you, a Cuban, so interested in protecting foreign interests and so determined to slam us into the ground?"

Seveces jumped up, knocking his wooden chair over, and in a split second was thrusting his angry, red face towards Arjuna.

"I don't think you know what you are talking about," he growled at Arjuna, who took a small, measured step back and was no longer smiling.

"Hold on gentlemen," he said to Juan Carlos, purposely turning his back on Seveces. "I thought this was a friendly visit. I didn't realize I was going to need protection."

He spread his arms dramatically and pointed to every corner of the room.

"Look around," he said calmly. "I am alone and I am unarmed. And I can assure you, I have not made a fist since I was an infant."

Juan Carlos didn't know what to do next. If he called off Seveces, he would be disrespecting the older man and there could be repercussions when word got back to Lansky that he had backed down.

"Why don't you tell us what *you* think this is?" Juan Carlos asked, opting to act as the voice of reason.

144

Seveces turned to him, his face still red with anger. Juan Carlos motioned for him to be still. Seveces lit a cigarette and furiously turned his back to them.

"You want to take a look at my boats? Take a look," Arjuna started, taking the seat Seveces had vacated. "I am in business, just as you are. I don't know why I am your concern. I make a hundred to your thousand, a thousand to your million. I know there are rumors, but you have to ask yourself, who started those rumors? Who wants me down? I am a serious businessman, and I have every right to operate my business. You want to see what really goes on? Come back as my guest, when the weather is good, and I will be delighted to show you. Every boat is a little party. Very little."

He brought his index finger and thumb together to illustrate his point. "The games are clean, the girls are somewhat attractive, and everybody has a good time."

Seveces shot Juan Carlos a warning glance. Don't be swayed by this charmer, his cold eyes told him. Juan Carlos got the message.

Arjuna continued talking in a calm, world-weary voice, like a school teacher describing a particularly trying day.

"Sure, sometimes someone gets out of hand, but tell me that doesn't happen at the casinos. Tell me that every once in a while some pink-faced American doesn't get a little too resentful, a little rough when he loses more money than he intended. What you have that I don't are armed guards and undercover agents who can clean up the mess before anyone notices. Here we work with our hands, like we always have. We can either spend the rest of our lives cleaning fish or take our chances with an occasional drunken fool."

Juan Carlos continued staring at the young man's face, at the bushy mustache that contrasted with the round, almost childish eyes. Arjuna had been serious while he spoke but, as soon as he was through, that disturbing smile spread across his face again.

Seveces couldn't contain himself, his words cut deep and awkwardly through the air.

"You sing a pretty song, but I'm going to keep an eye on you," he said, making no effort to conceal his threat. "I'm going to keep an eye on you like a hurricane."

Arjuna nodded, still smiling.

Seveces, a man of few words, most of them ill-advised, started for the door. He signaled Juan Carlos to follow, but the younger man stood his ground.

"Before I go I want to make something clear," Juan Carlos said. "You are wrong. I do not favor the North Americans over the Cubans. That's the propaganda that's being spread on the streets. Naive propaganda, not fact. A smart businessman knows the difference. Every time I have closed someone down, there has been a legal reason for it. Go ahead, ask around."

His eyes burrowed into Arjuna's and he was happy to see the insolent smile disappear.

"Keep your nose clean," Juan Carlos continued, "and you will have two new friends who will lay it on the line for you."

He paused and walked to the door where Seveces waited impatiently. "On the other hand, if you are not as clean as you say, prepare yourself for the worst. We are in the gaming business, but this is not a game to us."

Everyone fell silent. The wind had lost its fury and now all they could hear was the creaking of the building, and the gentle crashing of the waves. Juan Carlos followed Seveces to the car. The storm had smoothed the sand and the moon had come out -- the area around the boathouse looked as if someone had spread an enormous white sheet around it.

Soon he was back in the luxurious embrace of the fine leather interior and was being transported back to Havana by the powerful and almost noiseless Cadillac engine. Seveces was still seething, but Juan Carlos was feeling very accomplished. It had been a business meeting. Nothing more, nothing less. He had followed Lansky's instructions -- he had squeezed tight but with soft gloves.

When Juan Carlos spotted the lights of the city through the windshield, he let out a sigh of relief.

He could almost hear the sound of the patrons taking their seats, the clinking of long-stemmed wine glasses, the dissonant sounds of the orchestra as it warmed up and tuned its instruments. His heart picked up the rhythms of the casino. With any luck, they would be safely back in time for the show, when all unpleasant business could be set aside, and he could bask in the glory of Estelita's luminous performance.

It's all worth it if it brings me closer to her, he said to himself, and smiled.

From the boathouse, Arjuna watched the red tail-lights of the Cadillac as it vanished into the tunnel. He went inside and double-locked the front door. He had been left somewhat shaken by the visit, but felt he had handled himself with dignity. In the morning he would have a talk with the boat captains. He couldn't afford to have those casino thugs sniffing around his business.

"You can come out now," he said wearily.

A door squeaked open and Delfino, a wild look in his eyes, stepped out. He was holding a gun so tightly in his long, aristocratic hand that Arjuna feared he might hurt himself.

"Did you hear everything?" Arjuna asked.

"Yes," was Delfino's surprisingly cool reply. "Lansky wants to control it all."

"This is how it starts," Arjuna said as he took the weapon from him, gently prying the fingers from the cold metal. "First, they drop by for a *friendly* visit."

The two men continued looking at each other, their hearts beating wildly. And without further words, they clung to each other for a breathless, desperate kiss.

15

The impossible had actually happened. Leonardo Delfino was in love and the man he loved, loved him too. For years it had seemed as if this would never come to pass, as if he was destined to live a life of affluent and tastefully decorated loneliness. After Spain and the success of his shop, Havana society had opened up for him. He was invited to all the right parties and met all the right people. Men who shared his proclivity and social standing had made advances. He had attended their secret dinner parties, pretended to enjoy the long nights of gossip and innuendo. He had pretended to enjoy their attention, made promises he knew he would not keep. But the time wasn't right, his heart still belonged to someone else far away.

At one point, he had started to think of leaving Cuba behind forever, of spending the rest of his life in self-imposed exile in Spain. But after what happened, Madrid wasn't home any more. A broken heart can make any place feel wrong and Madrid, once so warm and welcoming, came to feel hopelessly cold and stale.

Havana called out to him and soon he was boarding the airplane that would carry him home. He had been sad beyond reason but convinced that one look at the sea, at the silhouette of Morro Castle at dusk, at the green trees that never lost their leaves would restore him. He just didn't know that it would take so long, that Havana would also seem foreign.

He had no regrets but he was in a hopeless muddle. How could something so special have gone so wrong? Federico had been a difficult love, and as it turned out, an impossible love. Perhaps it had been a love of discovery, a dress rehearsal, the beginning of something. What that something was he would have to wait to find out.

MADRID

1950

He had arrived in Madrid in early October, sent by his parents ostensibly to study law but he had never once set foot near the Universidad de Madrid nor opened a single textbook. The European capital had immediately dazzled him with its ancient red rooftops, its clouded, cerulean sky, the endless ringing of church bells – chortles from heaven.

He was elated to be away from the hot, humid, salty air of Havana. His first days he'd spent outdoors, bundled in a gray overcoat and scarf. He'd walked the full length of La Gran Via, a majestic avenue lined with edificios so lavished with arches, medallions, and statues that they seemed to twist themselves into seductive positions as he passed.

In the weeks that followed he walked to all the great plazas – Neptuno, Cibelles, Cascorro – each one more beautiful than the last. He went to the Museo del Prado and Parque del Buen Retiro.

While winter deepened, the streets filled with people who spoke in loud voices, their lisping accent delighted him. He learned to pronounce Madrid as Madriz, the way the locals did. All around him they rushed from one corner to the next, the city, in winter, displayed a life he had not seen during his summer visit when everything had been empty and bone dry. Their exuberance was contagious, it inspired him to contact friends he had met on previous trips with his parents. Soon he was invited to join groups of people his own age at restaurants, excursions, and recitals. They wanted to know all about Cuba, about life on a tiny island in the Gulf of Mexico, an island that had been discovered and populated by the ancestors of the very people asking the questions. Some questions he found quite silly.

"Is it true that there is a Santera priestess on almost every block?" a woman named Nuria asked him.

"Is it true that a man's right to adultery is written into the marriage certificate?" a man asked with a hopeful tone of voice.

"It's all true," Delfino said each time. And they "oohed!" and they "aahed!" as if he was the most sophisticated savage on the face of the earth.

In Madrid, the social season started early and ended late. The round of parties, called festejos, seemed endless. It was at one of these gatherings that he first met Federico. Federico Bocanegra y Alcalá was the kind of man who filled a room the moment he walked into it. He kissed every woman on the cheek and greeted all the men with a bear hug. People were delighted to see him.

Although barely twenty-seven years old, he was elegant and imposing beyond his years, with dark brown eyes, a deep cigarette voice, his square masculine face softened by a luxurious mole to the right of a sensuous mouth.

"Yes, I've heard much about you," he said to Delfino when they were introduced. "You are the mysterious Cuban student all of Madrid is talking about."

Mysterious? Reserved, perhaps. Definitely shy. But mysterious? Delfino didn't know what to say to that. Federico noticed and leaned in and spoke in a voice as intimate as the rustling of bed sheets.

"Before you leave, there is something I must tell you," he said then he wandered off to join a group of people who were calling for him.

Delfino spent the rest of the night watching him from a distance. Wherever Federico stood was the center of the party. It was where women shrieked in shocked delight, and where the most raucous laughter of men erupted.

How does he do it? Delfino wondered. All that confidence. How do I become like that, are some men just born with the ability to enchant or is it acquired?

A new acquaintance, Lilia Lugo, moved closer to him and in a discreet whisper informed him that Federico was actually *Baron* Federico Bocanegra y Alcalá.

"But the title was purchased," she said, and taking him by the elbow led him to the other end of the salon. "The family history is fascinating, money and madness, more than most royals. I should know."

Delfino didn't offer a reply. He was too busy wondering how she knew that he found Federico interesting. Had he been that obvious?

"In this crowd," she continued, a scathing sweep of her judicious eyes taking in the entire room, "you must possess beauty or a title. I always had both."

Yes, but that hat! Delfino thought glancing on the creation that rested on her head. All the ladies wore them. Hats covered with so many silk flowers, curled ribbons, and sparkling trinkets that they looked almost too heavy for their heads. As if reading his thoughts, her gloved hand floated up and tickled an errant ribbon back into place.

Federico's laughter from across the room startled them, as if they'd been slapped by the same hand.

"But fun," she said. "Yes, he is a lot of fun."

The way she spoke implied, maybe deliberately, maybe as a warning, that Lilia Lugo was well acquainted with the Baron's bedroom. She looked up to the chandelier and her eyes reflected their shimmer.

By midnight, most of the guests Delfino knew had already said goodbye and drifted into the night. He felt he should leave, but couldn't. He desperately wanted to know what Baron Federico had to tell him, but couldn't think of a subtle way to approach him. Perhaps he'd forgotten, perhaps it had only been a joke. Reluctantly, he found his hostess and thanked her, kissed her goodbye on one well-rouged cheek as was the custom in Cuba and in Spain, and went to the entrance hallway to retrieve his coat.

"You thought you could get away from me?"

Delfino stopped and turned around slowly.

Federico was standing at the end of an archway that led away from the house.

"I thought you'd forgotten," Delfino said.

"I could never forget you," Federico said and moved towards

151

him.

Delfino looked around to see if anyone was watching. Is this what I think it is? Maybe this is the way it happens, maybe this is the way two men who know each other's secret meet. He wondered what Spanish society thought about this sort of behavior. Certainly in Cuba or anywhere else in the world, two men could have a conversation, alone, in a dimly lit antechamber, after a civilized party without arousing suspicion.

Dark clouds crowded his mind. What if Federico was not like him? What if this titled and sophisticated man was just like those back home? Maybe Federico was vicious and evil and looking to humiliate him. He felt as provincial as the day he had arrived in Spain.

Delfino took a step back. The thought occurred to him that Federico Bocanegra y Alcalá could easily grab him by the collar of his overcoat and drag him back into the salon where there were still enough people to make an embarrassing scene. He could expose him, accuse him of sinful suggestions, cast him out of Madrid like Adam from the garden. News would travel quickly from Madrid to Havana. His parents would be mortified. He could never return to Havana and he certainly couldn't stay in Madrid.

Where would he go?

Delfino took another nervous step back. Federico took two steps forward, still smiling. Was this a game? The man was now standing so close that Delfino could smell his cologne.

"Do you want to hear what I have to tell you?" Federico whispered, his breath brushing Delfino's eyelashes.

Delfino couldn't answer but he couldn't walk away, either.

"Promise me you will not be offended," Federico said, arching a menacing eyebrow.

"Go on," Delfino said, hating the sound of his own voice, so thin.

Federico lowered his face, and raised his eyes to meet Delfino's.

"Tonight," Baron Federico Bocanegra y Alcalá said without a trace of mockery, "I want you to spend it in my bed."

And suddenly all of Delfino's fears and doubts vanished and he couldn't say yes fast enough.

Yes, finally, at last. Yes.

They walked in silence to Federico's house but it felt as if they'd flown there, over the red rooftops he so loved.

They entered an old, three-story townhouse near Puerta Del Sol. Delfino later learned it had been granted to Federico by his family on his twentieth birthday. The living room wasn't so much decorated as crammed with lovely, old leather furniture. Thick velvet drapes, rioja red, covered every window. Above the mahogany wainscoting, the walls were a dark, green, and hung with enormous oil paintings of frowning ancestors.

That night had been magical, just two men under the full moon of Spain. Their time together had been like time stolen from heaven. Delfino had never been touched by a man before, in fact, he'd never been touched by anyone so intimately and tenderly. He fell under the baron's spell from the first caress.

Few words passed between them. They trembled at each other's touch. Their moans and sighs echoed in the large bedroom. Delfino was surprised that he knew what to do, that it all came so naturally to him. But he kept these thoughts to himself. And if Federico noticed that he was in the arms of a novice, he never said. For Delfino, it had been like falling into a deep, dark well of sweet, gentle water; water in which he would gladly have drowned. They dozed in each other's arms, face to face, their moist, hair-covered chests pressed against one another. The heat emanating from their groins a soothing comfort in the cool of the dawn.

Later, as if tapped by an invisible hand, without entering complete consciousness, they started again. At times, Delfino felt like a big rag doll as Federico lifted, bent, and twisted him. But he didn't care. Federico knew exactly what to do to him, and Delfino's surrender had been complete.

*

The months that followed were like living in a dream. Delfino had kept his room at the pensión, but at Federico's insistence now spent almost all his time at the house on Puerta Del Sol. In time, the house which on the first night had seemed a warm refuge from the outside world, began to feel like a prison. Although Federico was handsome, intelligent and charming, there was another side to him. Inside his house, he was warm and open.

But the moment they stepped outside, he was distant and short-tempered. Delfino understood that a relationship like theirs could not be shouted from the rooftops, but that was just exactly what he wanted to do. He was in Europe, after all, away from the stifling confines of Havana. But he quickly learned, although Spain lacked the inquisitive atmosphere of his native country, it could be just as ruinous to two men in love.

After every social event, Delfino came home feeling bruised, disappointed, and insulted by his lover's behavior. Federico explained the situation to him time and time again.

"We have to be careful what face we show the world," Federico said, his voice dark with impatience.

"But they're our friends, they like us. They know we are together."

"Yes, and they will look the other way as long as we play by the rules."

"And what exactly are the rules?" Delfino asked, his red-rimmed eyes wanting desperately to understand.

"They are not written down, exactly. But a man in my position could lose everything if he flaunts. I have seen it happen to men more powerful and respected than me. I have watched them crawl to Marueco and Tailandia, to wallow in degeneracy. Here, there is only so much people will tolerate."

"I'm not talking about flaunting, I just don't want you to be so cruel to me."

"I am sorry if you think that my behavior is cruel. This is not my intention."

Federico took him in his arms with a deep sigh of frustration.

"Try to understand, my young friend," he said. "Just to arrive at a party with you could be considered an indiscretion. They have chosen to look the other way, for the moment, but it could change just as easily."

"But you attempt to seduce everyone."

"Yes, but if you had paid close attention you would have seen that I do it with everyone equally, to the men and the women. The young as well as the old. It is a way of letting everyone know that I am still deciding. The moment they believe that I have come to a conclusion, that I am in love with a man, that I have decided that I will live my life as a-"

He stopped momentarily, incapable of speaking the forbidden word.

"You understand, mi corazón? Everything will change. Doors will close forever. This is the Spain of Franco, it is not like the little colony you come from where everyday it is a revolution or a carnival and people do what they please."

He stopped to make sure the insult had struck its target.

"And then," he continued, "there is the question of my family. Let us say that I do not care what those people think, that I am willing to give up the trips, and the parties. If my family should discover what I am, everything will vanish, my money and my title. This house was not meant for you and for me, it was meant for my wife and my children."

"So everything's accepted as long as you behave disgracefully at every party?"

"Do you find it humiliating, mi corazón?" he asked gently. "What about this," he said drawing him closer, "do you find this humiliating as well?"

Delfino felt the hardness against him and his heart turned liquid. He allowed himself to be taken, there, in the downstairs parlor, protected by velvet curtains, watched only by the unseeing eyes of Federico's ancestors. And when Delfino ejaculated, he did so with choking sobs, and nothing Federico said, neither apologies nor promises, could stop his tears.

That conversation had marked the beginning of a slow and inevitable end. He remained a guest in Federico's house, but a strange loneliness engulfed him. Delfino was used to loneliness, but now it seemed more pronounced, more specific because in his heart he felt he had found the answer.

Delfino found comfort in the cobblestone streets of Madrid. He walked endlessly. But bored with the great avenues and plazas, he took to the winding side streets, where he could get lost. On a summer afternoon so hot that the entire city was asleep and breathing the air was like breathing dust, a small shop window captured his attention.

On display in the window was a stunningly beautiful lady's hat. It was the lightest shade of lavender with a satin ribbon just a whisper darker woven through it. The hat was simple enough to seem naked and vulnerable, such was its delicacy. Years later he would be unable to say why he had stopped and lingered in front of that window. Why the single, solitary hat had moved him so. In Havana, only men, and the more eccentric women, wore hats. In Madrid, all the society women wore ornate hats, and he had accepted this as part of their ethos, like their accent and late hours. But none of the countless hats he'd seen had been quite so beautiful. This hat looked like a sculpture. A simple, exquisite sculpture.

"Simplicity is either a dying art, or one just about to be born," a man's voice said.

Delfino looked up. Although only in his sixties, Manolo Rejas Beato looked ancient to the young man. He was unusually tall and slender for a Spaniard; Spaniards generally got shorter and wider with age. His long, bony fingers pinched a hand-rolled cigarette.

"You make these?" Delfino asked, his eyes back to the shop window.

"Yes, these and many others," Manolo answered and motioned him inside. A long stream of cigarette smoke made a white, evanescent arch in the air.

The small shop was filled with hats so light they seemed to be floating on the mannequin heads. And as Delfino moved from hat to hat, Manolo whispered their colors, like an incantation.

"Ashes of Roses, Blue Waltz, Cuban Sand..."

Delfino immediately loved the smell of the shop, glue and fabric, cigarettes and dust. He loved that in the little room, a man could bend and shape material, finesse and adorn it, creating something that when it was finally set upon a woman's head, gave her unforeseen dignity and importance. Manolo moved closer to Delfino.

"Go ahead, touch," he said. "I can see you're fascinated, just as I was many, many years ago."

Delfino couldn't deny it, he *was* fascinated and excited, as if a wide door had opened. Suddenly his future made complete sense and he saw no point in fighting it. And just like a deeply troubled man who finally discovers just the right narcotic, the hats became his passion.

At Manolo's side, he learned the milliner's trade. Delfino was there early every morning and reluctantly left late at night. His days were spent measuring and blocking, inserting wire into brims and lining into crowns. He learned about trimming with pearls and ribbons, and how to create minute artificial flowers out of silk, felt, and crepe. As Delfino's hands became more agile, Manolo was happy to sit in a red leather armchair, smoke, and watch his protégé.

One morning, Delfino noticed Manolo staring intently at him. "You wonder why you're here, why it feels so natural. Do not question it. There is a reason why this has happened, in time you will find out."

"I think it's outrageous that you're spending all of your time in a dusty hat shop with that disgusting old man. What if somebody should see you?" said Federico who had never worked a day in his life.

"Who's going to see me? I work in the back room."

But as time passed, Federico started to get annoyed. No one he knew worked. Since he couldn't prevent Delfino from going to work, he chose to humiliate him.

"Delfino has a job," he announced to a group of dinner companions. Delfino remained quiet even though all eyes had turned to him.

"A real job?" Lilia Lugo asked incredulously. "What sort of job?"

When Delfino didn't respond, Federico answered for him. "Oh, it is a big mystery." Lilia Lugo continued looking at him, eyebrows arched with bored curiosity, her wine glass floating somewhere between the tabletop and her lips.

"It's something I'm learning," Delfino said. "I don't want to talk about it until I find out if I'll be good at it or not."

The topic was dropped. They didn't really care. He wasn't one of them, not really. He was an oddity, a young man from a little island somewhere in the Caribbean. Exotic, but not nearly exotic enough to matter for long. Boys like him were constantly dropping into their circle, from Morocco, Mexico or, on occasion, a good family from Manila. The new boys were a novelty at first but eventually became commonplace. And vanished.

Delfino was glad to be drifting away from the crowd. The only thing tying him to them was Federico, and that was quickly losing its allure. There was no denying it. Sex, once essential, was now rare and routine. The large house on Plaza del Sol felt overcrowded whenever the two of them were in it. He felt like he needed to get away, to think. He had no guidelines, no previous experience, and no one to talk to about it. If passion was the currency of their relationship and that currency was losing its value, what was left? Bankruptcy? He wished he could ask his father. His father would know. But approaching him with such problems would be equal to pressing a gun to his temple and squeezing the trigger.

The ideal opportunity to put some distance between himself and this annoying situation presented itself the following spring.

Encouraged by Manolo, he boarded a train to Paris.

"Go! See what real hats are like," the old man had said. "Think of it as an adventure. The most important adventure of your life."

Delfino looked into the old man's eyes and saw something there that he would not understand until he returned. At the moment he was too nervous and excited.

The trip completed the transformation that had begun in Madrid. Delfino suspected that Manolo had known it would. Paris was undoubtedly different from Madrid. In fact, Parisian ladies made the women of Madrid, who had seemed so sophisticated compared to the women of Havana, look absolutely dowdy. He hardly thought about Federico during his trip, concentrating solely on discovery. He visited all the famous fashion houses, entering those venerable couture establishments was a voluptuous experience, like floating in a cloud of Nina Ricci's L'air du Temps. Impossibly thin shop girls watched him from behind glass counters, but said nothing. Having no one else to talk to, he wrote long letters to Manolo every day detailing his adventures, telling him of the shops he visited: Chanel, Dior, Balmain, Givenchy, Balenciaga and even the shop of a young designer who was just starting to make a name for himself, Yves Saint Laurent.

Manolo never wrote back.

Several weeks later, armed with more information than he had ever imagined, an arsenal of elegance, he returned to Madrid, only to find that while he was away, Manolo had died in his sleep. He had been discovered peacefully resting in his red leather armchair, the artificial heads that wore his hats keeping silent vigil over him. Delfino found the shop boarded up. He peeked through the cracks and saw that all the hats and mannequins had been removed.

"Cousins from Malaga," the woman next door said. "They sold everything and what they couldn't sell they stole. They were quick like cockroaches in the night."

He looked at her as if she was speaking a foreign language.

"Here," she said, handing him a pack of unopened letters, "I think these are from you. Poor man, he never got to read them."

Delfino didn't take the letters. He turned and ran to Federico, pausing outside the house on Plaza del Sol just long enough to dry his tears and catch his breath. He hungered for the comfort of his lover's arms, but the reception he received couldn't have been further from what he expected.

Federico was sympathetic, in his own way.

"The death of a child, or of a young person is something to be grieved," he said with a sigh, "the death of an old man is just part of life." With that, he lifted his eyes to the sky as if to say "the rest is in the hands of God."

But Delfino wanted more. How could he make Federico understand what Manolo had meant to him? What the older man had given him? The patience, generosity, and guidance he had offered from the moment they met. How could he express to someone to whom nothing truly mattered, that in Manolo's shop Delfino had, for the first time in his life, felt useful, gifted, and truly loved?

"It's just that I'm going to miss him," he managed to say, choked by shameful sobs. He hoped for the comfort of his lover's arms, but when he looked up, he saw that Federico has moved to the opposite side of the room.

"What's the matter?" Delfino asked. "Why are you looking at me with such cold eyes? Why tonight when I need you the most?"

"It may seem cruel, but I am trying to help you," Federico said. He was standing next to the fireplace, the flames dancing in his eyes. The world must look so much better through such beautiful eyes, Delfino thought, but didn't have the strength to say.

"You are still very young," Federico continued. "What are you now, twenty?"

"Yes."

"Yes, well I am nearing thirty. It is time we changed."

"Changed what?" Delfino asked, not knowing where this was going, but sure he was not going to like it.

"Love between men, it is a game. A game played while we are young. Then it becomes a dream and eventually, like all dreams, it is forgotten."

"What are you saying?"

"I am saying it is time for me to grow up. In Spain all young men have these types of love affairs, like ours."

"All young men?"

"Well, the ones with our proclivity. But eventually we mature and marry. It will someday happen to you."

Delfino was shaking his head "no" before Federico was through.

"No, not me," he managed to say, willing himself to believe it.

Federico arched a cynical eyebrow; his lips, those lips that had once been Delfino's to kiss, to drink from, to get lost in, offered him an ugly smile.

"Then you will be very sad, very lonely, for a very long time and eventually die like your friend, in a rickety armchair, in some hat shop, alone. Without a wife and children, you are destined to die in your own embrace."

Delfino started to back out of the room, slowly at first, then faster as he saw Federico moving towards him.

"I never meant to hurt you," he was saying, "we can still be friends. You can come visit with your wife. Our children will play together..."

But Delfino couldn't really hear what Federico was saying. All he could hear was a horrible droning in his ears, like the motor of an airplane, but much louder. His back eventually hit against the front door.

"You already know and like the woman who will be my wife." Delfino's hand found its way to the doorknob, twisted and opened it.

"Lilia Lugo, she is a delight and much more sophisticated than..."

A hard blast of cold air met him on the other side. He was on the

sidewalk. Federico had not followed him. Part of him wanted to be
followed, to be begged, and another part hated the very thought of one
more word from Federico's lips. Part of him wanted to die and another
was afraid of that very thought.

He looked around at the ornate buildings topped by the red
rooftops that had once charmed him, the wide avenues, the bare trees.
He had been in Madrid for two years, most of them wonderful.

A week later, he was on a flight to Havana, convinced that he
would never, ever love again. But comforted by the thought that when
his time came to leave this world, it would happen in a comfortable
armchair, and he would not be alone, he would be surrounded by his
beautiful hats.

HAVANA 1952

He returned to his country on April 15, 1952 and when the
wheels of the airplane touched the ground, Delfino felt it in the pit of
his stomach – a sickening lurch. But from the moment he set foot on
Cuban soil, he knew he was finally home. Nothing in Europe had
moved him like the chorus line of palm trees that edged the highway.
He noticed that the driver of the auto de alquiler, mistaking him for a
European tourist, was driving a route that would add many miles and
several pesos to the trip.

"You're going the wrong way," Delfino said.

"The center of town is closed today," the driver said, and turned
the radio up louder. Suddenly Havana didn't seem so welcoming
anymore, but Delfino was too tired to argue. He settled back, closed his
eyes, and prepared to face his parents.

"A milliner?" asked his mother, a delicate teacup tittering in her
hand. A nervous smile danced on her thick and pillowy lips. She
covered her lips with the same pale makeup she applied to the rest of
her face, and then carefully painted them back on thinner with a ruby-
red pencil in a daily effort to make them appear less Cuban, more
European. How wrong she was, he thought. European women are
nothing like this.

"Ladies' hats?" his father said using the same tone he would for "dog shit."

The cigar in his hand burned in a perfect, orange circle, as a very good, very expensive cigar should. He occasionally brought it to his dark, purplish lips, which were framed by a narrow mustache kept perfectly trimmed with a straight razor. His father's mustache, Delfino noticed, was now speckled with white whiskers.

They had received him in the wide veranda of the Miramar house. The veranda overlooked a long green lawn that stretched perfectly to the sea, but somehow Delfino felt as confined as if they were crammed in one of the servant's rooms behind the kitchen.

"I have already thrown away enough money on you," his father said with the palpable traces of the anger and contempt that had always marked communications with his only son. This, in spite of his mother's efforts to keep the visit civilized.

His father went on to recount every cent spent in Spain, as if money were ever the issue. Money was never the issue, and the three people involved in the conversation knew what the resolution would be. It was simply important for his father to let his feelings be known so that, later on, he could say, "I told you it was a bad idea."

Delfino knew it was just a matter of waiting for his father to excuse himself on some pretext. Which he did.

"No le hagas caso," his mother said, following her husband's back with flat eyes. "Don't pay any attention to him. He's been upset about politics. Apparently, Batista is back in power and things, again, are insane."

She noticed that Delfino knew nothing of this.

"A military coup, of all things. There have been protests at the university and guns fired and all that nonesense this country seems to thrive on."

She sighed deeply while she searched for a checkbook in an embroidered handbag.

"Una trajédia," she went on. "It's all better now, but there will be more blood, I just know it. The Americans are backing the takeover. Your father is sick about it, he hasn't slept since it happened."

"Is that why the center of town was closed off?"

"I imagine so," she said, "nothing but tanks and guards and too much noise, too much fear."

With a quick hand she wrote him a check for twice the amount he had requested and signed it with a joyful flourish.

Shortly after Delfino opened his shop, his mother's friends started to arrive as if blown there by the afternoon breeze. They placed lavish orders. The first time they came as a social obligation, a favor to the family, but they returned because of his talent, and the lovely way he made them feel. They were his clients. He was the hat maker. He knew his place.

The shop bore his name, an elegant swirl of gold letters on a beveled glass door: *Delfino*.

Professionally, he felt happy and fulfilled. Even his father had stopped in one morning and expressed the closest he could to approval.

"Your mother says you're working too hard," he said, "I think that's good. At any rate, you seem to be getting results."

It was true. He was working hard because he couldn't yet afford an assistant. He spent almost every waking hour in his shop, designing, measuring, blocking, and trimming his simple-yet-elegant confections just as he had learned from Manolo.

He hadn't slept for two nights, the constant demands of the shop kept him awake and filled with manic energy when he received an unexpected visit from Maria Quintana.

He hadn't seen her in years and had given her little thought. It felt good to see her. She had always been a lovely girl, and now, with her long hair and simple dress, she was unforgettable. But there was something strange behind her eyes, in her manner. A shop like his should have been a place of comfort for a girl in Maria's position and she'd been stiff and uncomfortable. And then it all came pouring out – she was going to enter a convent. He had celebrated her decision, but after she left, as suddenly and unexpectedly as she had appeared, he worried and pledged to himself to stay close to her.

Delfino kept himself busy all day long, still, there were the nights, the long lonely, nights when his mind drifted back to Madrid, to Federico. Federico's last words to him had been right. The time they spent together did seem like a dream now, but not one Delfino felt he would soon forget.

16

Esteban de la Cruz dropped to his knees, hard. He had been standing in line in the dining room of the asylum, waiting to step up and collect his almuerzo when it happened.

It wasn't the first time he had been felled by a vision. Lately, the visions were coming with such force that they turned his legs to jelly. But at least he had not lost consciousness as he had several times before. This time he remained immobile, his unbelieving eyes staring at Estelita's lovely face. It hovered, like a resplendent moon over the thick cloud of steam that rose from the pots of boiling water on the dingy stove. She had been coming to him more and more frequently in visions and dreams. The dreams were always sad and he would wake up from his restless sleep sobbing; tears making pools around his eyes and rolling down into his ears.

The visions were different from the dreams, they were like a fast blow to his guts. There were others who appeared. Sometimes he would turn a corner and see his grandmother, Alejandra, long dead, standing still, her hands entwined, her thumbs making those familiar nervous circles she used to make when she was alive. It was her; there was no doubt. Or his Tio Juan Gomez, wearing the oversized suit he'd always worn to mass; the one he'd been buried in. The dead visited him all the time. They told him stories, sent him signs and warnings, they spoke to him with more clarity than they had when they'd been alive. Sometimes they appeared as a group and their voices would chorus and echo so strongly in his tormented head that Esteban had to shut his eyes tight and place his hands over his ears until everybody went away. This is exactly what he feared, what he'd avoided for so long and now his sober mind gave him no protection. He was at the mercy of the unseen world.

*

When he'd first arrived at the Casa de Socorros six months ago, he hadn't given Estelita or anyone else very much thought. But now he missed her with a grief so strong that it left him completely defenseless. Where was Estelita? What had become of his sweet girl? Was she dead? The visions of her were different, like memories but much more tenacious. Unlike the others, whom he saw as clearly as if they had just walked in from the terrace, he only saw her face, her pretty face looking concerned. He couldn't remember the last time he'd seen her, just some vague idea that she'd been singing on a tattered stage in some small town that resembled Camaguey. But her image got mixed up with other events: jails, motel rooms, a long procession of fun-loving painted ladies. His thoughts were blurred and scrambled. He would be mesmerized by Estelita's face and it would turn suddenly into the face of her mother, Belquis. Even in his confused condition, he knew that Belquis was dead; had been dead for many years. But it was difficult for him to understand that completely. Had Belquis really died, or was she still back in Pensamientos, waiting for his return? It couldn't be possible, could it? That the young and beautiful girl he had loved with all his heart could have died giving birth to his daughter? And that now his daughter was gone too? Had his life really come to this horrible conclusion?

He understood he was in an insane asylum. There was no doubt about that. He was reminded every night when he lay in his narrow cot and listened to the endless screams coming from other parts of the ward, piercing, heartbreaking screams of terror.

"They're here, they're here! Tell them to go away! Someone please help me!"

The shrieks and shouts were always the same, and no matter how many times it happened, they always alarmed him, because he believed the delusions of his horrified ward mates. They sounded so real. Every time he was awakened by the shouts, he expected to see someone, he was never quite sure who, but someone of authority, maybe an armed guard or an archangel, or a priest, to be standing at the entrance to the ward ready to take someone away. But where? To some torture chamber somewhere in the vast, sweltering basement of the madhouse? Or were the screams also fabrications of his own mind? No. They were real, and so were the hurried footsteps of the haggard-eyed doctors and starched, white-clad nurses who came in to harness and drag the troubled sufferer away. Not to the basement, he prayed, but to a private room. To a clean, sunny room where they would be sedated and gently rocked to sleep by somenone kind and caring.

After they were gone, he would look around the now silent ward. In the moonlight, he could see the other patients sitting up, wide eyed, and too frightened to speak. A few minutes later, everyone would return to sleep. Everyone except Esteban who remained awake, listening to the snoring and the farting. The horrible, constant snoring had become as familiar to him as his heartbeat. Night after night it was there: not just one man, but more than a dozen; whistling, snorting, gasping, grunting, struggling for breath. From a soft wheeze to a deafening roar, the nocturnal reverberations filled the room. Coughing, hacking, spitting was also part of the cacophony. Sometimes, the farts made sounds that challenged the snores. At other times, they were silent and wafted like evil spirits across his bed. The smell would hang from the headboard of his bed until pushed forward by yet another, even more awful odor. The farts came and departed as regularly as night trains. That was how he spent his nights, listening to the wet, struggling tongues, tonsils and uvulas of his ward mates, and inhaling the foul aroma of their bowels.

No one in the asylum ever slept well, so most of them had no energy in the daytime. They shuffled in a daze from room to room, unable to concentrate or make much sense of anything.

He only vaguely remembered arriving there and had no idea

how long ago it had been before he even knew where he was. At the time, all he could think of was liquor. He had wanted a drink so badly that, when a nurse had swabbed his arm with alcohol to administer a shot, they'd had to hold him down to keep him from licking the plump droplet that had escaped from the alcohol-soaked cotton ball. The fumes had pierced his nostrils like a cold, silver spear. The injection would take effect almost immediately, and he would stop shaking and drift into a black, soundless sleep. He didn't know how long he slept; just that when he had awakened, he no longer wanted to drink. He just wanted to die.

He vaguely remembered that Aspirrina had come to see him. Or maybe he had imagined it. He couldn't recall much of what she said to him, something about La Habana. Or maybe she hadn't come at all. Dreams, visions, reality; none of it made any sense to him. Not in this place where even the doctors and nurses seemed like mad, ghostly figures, and the rows of narrow white cots resembled tombs in a tattered cemetery. There was no treatment for madness. This was the land of the hopeless. The doctors reluctantly kept the patients alive, ministering to ailments like bedsores and convulsions, and rescuing suicides.

The nurses seldom spoke, for they had learned that a few words could get them embroiled in circular conversations from which there was no escape. They concentrated on keeping the place from exploding into total mayhem; tying up the aggressive patients with well-worn, dirty, straightjackets. Guiding the passive from bedroom to dining room to restroom; supervising the janitor whose job it was to clean up shit and vomit off the floors and walls.

"There is a way out," the visions whispered to Esteban time and time again, but he would not listen.

"You know what to do," the visions insisted. But he could not trust them. Only a crazy person would listen to apparitions. And then one day, it happened. He found the courage to look in their eyes, to see the kindness and concern in their faces. With time the fear vanished, and when they said, "You've always known what to do." He finally understood. He did, he knew exactly what to do. He had to accept responsibility.

He had to surrender.

That night, Esteban chose a corner of the dormitory, near his cot, and slowly, meticulously, started to build his first altar. He rounded up plaster statues of saints that lay scattered and forsaken all over the institution. They had been given to patients by their loved ones, parting gifts, consolation prizes.

"Pray to this," parents and guardians said after signing the official commitment forms with trembling but determined hands. He found statues under beds, in dusty corners, or half-buried in the backyard. All of them were damaged; chipped, broken, useless. San José lacked a head. Santa Barbara was missing an arm. La Virgen de la Caridad had had her eyes scratched out, (although she still fiercely cradled baby Jesus in her arms). He also collected discarded pictures of Christ holding a red bleeding heart in his nail-punctured hands, and of the Holy Trinity: The Father, The Son and The Holy Ghost, robed and bearded men floating above pink clouds.

He gathered yellowing pictures of dead relatives left behind by other patients and moldy greeting cards inscribed with long forgotten cheerful wishes or heartfelt condolences. He brought in smooth, round river rocks he'd found lining the garden paths, and desiccated pressed flowers that he'd carefully retrieved from inside the pages of old and ragged Bibles. With quiet, steady determination he wove big crosses out of the dry, fallen fronds of a Queen Palm tree that grew just outside the walls of the asylum. All this he pasted to the wall with shoemaker's glue so fresh it still smelled of horses. The altar reached from the floor to the ceiling. Candles were not allowed inside the asylum, so he stole sharp pieces of glass and mirror that the suicidal patients kept hidden. He positioned them carefully in such a way that they would reflect the sunlight coming through the windows. The result was dazzling.

When the altar was completed, the visions returned.

"Estelita is alive," they said, smiling with pride.

The news left Esteban with a strange new feeling, as if his soul had been washed clean. It was the feeling he used to get when he first discovered liquor; before he started to drink too much and everything got ugly. He felt as if he could go to the river and walk across the tranquil waters, as Jesus had done. It was a feeling so beautiful he would do anything to keep it. All his fears evaporated and were replaced with a powerful rush of hope and courage.

Now, when he turned corners or opened doors and saw his long dead relatives, he greeted them with smiling eyes and a gentle nod. He often found them gathered around his altar, sometimes praying, sometimes sitting quietly, or playing cards. After all those years of loneliness, it was as if he had a family again.

Most of the doctors and nurses ignored the gigantic shrine, while others, being people of faith, saw it as a good sign. But it was the reaction of the other patients that moved him. At first, they walked cautiously past his altar, looking at it fearfully out of the corner of their eyes, the way they would at a dead dog left on the side of the road.

They were curious but cautious. Little by little, one by one, they started to come around and kneel in front of the altar. Some of them brought their own personal religious items and offered them in the name of a favored saint, or in memory of a loved one: a small Psalter covered in mother of pearl, a rosary made entirely out of children's milk teeth, a golden locket containing nail clippings. Others, more commonplace objects began to appear: a glove, a coin, a flower. All this they placed on his altar. Esteban sat quietly on his cot and watched with peaceful satisfaction as the altar continued to grow like something living.

The patients started to refer to him as Don Esteban, a title reserved for Santeros. He acknowledged the honor simply by bowing his head humbly. Then something miraculous started to occur. At first he didn't notice, but the snoring stopped bothering him. The men had not stopped snoring, he simply didn't hear it. He started to sleep unperturbed and to awaken refreshed.

The clutter in his mind began to clear further. His memory began to improve even more, as if a veil had been lifted. He could remember far into the past, into his adult life, the time he spent singing and traveling with Estelita. The many stages he graced, the many times he drank himself into a stupor, the many strange women he took to bed. He could see it and acknowledge it all without even a wince, without guilt or regret, for everything now was as it should be. He could sit in complete stillness and recall the time before that, when he'd been a vibrant young man in a dank little town called Palmagria. He recalled his lovely bride, and his wedding, and was able to experience that rush of passion he once felt with Belquis. He remembered the horrible night when his daughter was born, and way back to his own birth, and before that, to his parents courtship and the starry night of his conception. The past became crystal clear, and in the midst of it all was his daughter, Estelita, the shining star that had guided all his days, even before she had been born to him.

The patients returned again and again to worship, pray and weep at his altar. They shuffled in and sat at his feet and looked adoringly into his face. The deep furrows between his brows were vanishing, as if an angel had passed a pale hand over them, erasing all his worries. It was a face that was becoming more beautiful with each passing day. But it was not a frivolous beauty, like in the old days when he had used his handsome looks to seduce audiences, to beguile women. It was the beauty of wisdom and inner peace.

The patients who used to irritate him daily with their screams and tantrums, he now regarded with compassion. They sat next to him on his cot, and he could see the source of their madness. He could see the broken hearts, the disappointments, the cruelties that had driven them to despair. He let them talk to him, he listened to their incomprehensible babbling.

"They don't love me, they don't want me, they want to hurt me, they want to hurt me," they'd mutter, spittle and drool flowing out of their shriveled, toothless mouths.

And now, he could see who "they" were. And beyond. He could see what had driven others to behave with such cruelty towards this individual or that, and back even further and further, to generations of brutality. Esteban let them talk until they had nothing more to say; until, depleted, they fell asleep next to him, their heads resting on his lap. Their hair always left a round grease stain on his trousers. The ugly blotch confirmed their existence. 'I am here,' it seemed to say, 'in all my human imperfection, in all my greasy, sweaty, drooling imperfection. I have been brought to a place where there is no hope, but I count, I deserve to be loved and I can pray at an altar, and this oozing of my scalp simply proves that I am human and that I'm still alive.'

Esteban no longer agreed with the wisdom of the day, the popular phrase: 'Nacen locos, mueren locos,' Born crazy; die crazy. That saying had prompted too many parents and family members to commit their loved ones to this and countless other institutions all over the island.

While they slept on his lap, he always repeated the same prayer, "as long as you are alive, there is hope."

Free of alcohol and with a renewed faith, he regained the dignity and charisma that had made him a popular performer on the stage. A vision told him he must always dress in white and so he did. But it was not the dingy white worn by the doctors and nurses. No, Esteban was resplendent in the purest shirts and trousers for miles around. Orquidea kept them that way.

Orquidea was the first patient to come forward. She had been brought to Casa de Socorros by her bewildered parents while she was still a young girl. Orquidea, they complained, couldn't stop washing her hands. Neither of them knew that the unfortunate girl was frantic with shame over the constant sexual manipulations of her uncle. The man was a loved and trusted family member. She knew no one would believe her accusations; all she could do was wash her hands raw. Her fingernails had fallen off and new ones refused to grow. Her fingers resembled red, bloody sausages. Now forty-seven years old, she had managed to channel her obsession with cleanliness into the service of God. In his name, she scrubbed and bleached Esteban's garments daily, so that he stood out like a beacon in the dirty, dreary asylum.

Orquidea took his clothes to the crusty old laundry tub early every morning. She prayed as she scrubbed Esteban's shirt and pants to her meticulous satisfaction. After that, she didn't touch soap and water again for the rest of the day. The next morning, she would return joyously to the laundry tub. As a result of this new and daily ritual, her hands started to heal. One day, when she handed Esteban his neatly folded clothes, he noticed something different about her hands. He saw small, almost childlike nails, delicate as rose petals, adorning each one of her fingertips.

"It's a miracle, Don Esteban" she whispered, her eyes glassy with tears.

"No, you're the miracle, my love," he said, taking her in his arms and holding her close to his chest. She wept for hours, her tears soaking his immaculately clean white shirt. He didn't move away, allowing her to let all the fear, anger, shame, and disgrace she had been holding in for so long to gently pour out of her. By the time she was done weeping, the sun had started to set. He walked the fragile woman to her cot and lowered her onto the grimy mattress. Orquidea nestled like a contented child underneath the dirty sheets, an ancient exhaustion completely overpowering her. And, for the first time for as long as he could remember, he took a woman to bed and allowed her to sleep. He felt the stirring of arousal but he disobeyed the command. He watched over her as she slept the slumber of the innocent. For the first time in all the years she'd been at Casa de Socorros, she did not wake up in the middle of the night screaming that her vagina was on fire. Screams that had led some of the more heartless nurses to refer to her as Senorita Chocha Ardiente - Miss Blazing Cunt, as they handed her a damp washcloth to press between her legs. The cool, soothing washcloth was the only thing that could calm poor Orquidea.

The same nurses had special names for all their charges. Senor Come Tu Caca, was the man who ate his own shit, Senorita Chupamela, was the lady who provided oral sex to any male who would stand still long enough. And so on. Many of the nurses had grown numb to the suffering and the insanity of Casa de Socorros, it was only through perverse humor that they could make it through the day. It was the nurses who first began to notice the change in Esteban, and they alerted the doctors. The doctors scratched their heads collectively, for they couldn't be sure if this so-called 'spiritual awakening' was a sign of regained mental health or just a further descent into madness.

"A tree that grows crooked remains crooked forever," one of the doctors insisted. But the nurses didn't see it that way. They had lived among the insane long enough to know the difference. It was clear to them that Esteban de la Cruz was changing for the better.

One of the nurses, a woman named Nelpidia Marron, was married to a man given to sudden fits of rage. His outbursts were so severe that they had devastated her family. All of her children had left home as soon as they could, and now were scattered all over the country. Some had gone as far away as Mexico and Guatemala putting miles of ocean between them. For years, Nelpidia, due to nerves, had been unable to maintain her weight above seventy-five pounds. One night she added her treasured graduation pin from nursing school to

Esteban's altar. She prayed that God would take pity upon her ravaged family. That he would quiet her husband's wild temperament, and bring her beloved children back to her. And from then on, from the moment when she placed her treasured pin among the other trinkets and offerings, she became Esteban's champion against the skeptical doctors. So sure was she of Esteban's benevolent powers. Her faith was not blind; she had seen the miracles, she had living proof. She had witnessed the soothing effect he had on his ward, where tranquility prevailed, and on everyone who came to his narrow cot for a prayer and a nap.

Esteban stood back and watched his good works change lives. His mind was clearer, he was helping the less fortunate. And he decided that it was time to take a little for himself. That night, when everyone had gone to sleep, he did something that was absolutely forbidden. He found a candle stub in the trash outside a doctor's office. It was white and all but wasted. But there was still enough wick left. He worked the wick with his thumbnail, clearing the charred wax around it until a tiny tip of wick stood upright. Then, he knelt before his altar and cleared his mind of everything except his daughter. When he was sure he had her attention, he lit the candle. A puny flame flickered shyly at first, then flared to a full, lovely glow, like a teardrop made of fire. For just a few seconds, it illuminated the darkened altar. And while its faint glare danced upon the suffering faces of the plaster saints, Esteban said the most important prayer of his life. His dead relatives gathered close behind him, joyously. Now that they had found their conduit to the living, they finally could return to their graves. Alejandra placed a reassuring hand on his shoulder and her cold touch made him tremble with ecstasy.

"Estelita," he whispered, "I don't know where you are, and I cannot be at your side to protect you, but with all my heart, I send this humble gift of light. May it brighten your path when it's dark, and guide you to safety whenever you're lost."

17

Estelita de la Cruz leaned into the warm glow of the dozen lightbulbs that framed the makeup mirror. Esteban would be proud, the show had gone well, she had been flawless, she knew it, she had learned to assess her own performances. Some nights were better than others, but this night had gone exceptionally well. The girls watched her every move, but she ignored their prying eyes, kept the eyebrow pencil steady in her hand, the ruby-red lipstick smooth and even. Calm, very calm. She brushed her hair as if she had all the time in the world, then walked to the wardrobe rack and debated between a pair of new blouses. She chose the more expensive of the two.

Once dressed, she took a last look in the full-length mirror and with the aplomb of a princess walked out of the dressing room. She moved leisurely down the now familiar hallway to the service elevator, to the pink hallway and to the private lift. It was bronze, not gold, she now knew. She smiled when she thought of how naïve she had been the first time she had been summoned upstairs. How silly. How needlessly worried! The last time a thug had come to fetch her.

This time, there had been a handwritten note from Lansky *requesting* her presence.

He greeted her with such ebullience that she almost didn't notice that they were not alone.

Juan Carlos Talente was there, too.

His presence paralyzed her. Why did he have such an effect on her? She became tongue-tied and stupid, awkward and unsteady. She cursed herself for allowing him, simply by being in the room, to challenge her confidence. All she could do was stand tall and try not to trip over the furniture. He was even more attractive than she remembered.

"How are you?" Senor Talente said with a quick smile.

She forced an impersonal airiness into her voice.

"I'm fine, thank you." And that was it, her mind went blank. Oh, what is wrong with me? It had been an almost physical effort to find her voice. And then what? He must think I'm the dullest girl on earth. She couldn't take her eyes off his face, his changes of expression, that smile. He was looking at her too, directly into her eyes. She felt herself blushing. He reached into his coat pocket and pulled out a packet of chewing gum. He extended it to her, smiling shyly as if embarrassed. She was about to reach for it but her hand was trembling. Something was definitely wrong with her. Why was she so flustered? She managed to shake her head no and he put the chewing gum back in his pocket.

She didn't know if she should be offended. Chewing gum is what an adult offers to a child. Did he think she was *that* young? She was almost eighteen. Still, she felt lightheaded, a funny weakness, beginning under her stomach, seemed to separate her head from her body. She feared she might faint. Slowly, she took some deep breaths.

She was so confused. Everything about him contradicted his reputation. If Senor Talente worked for Lansky, he was what the girls backstage referred to as "bad news," someone to be avoided even if they didn't always follow their own advice, even if they only talked about it after the fact. Maybe not all the men who worked for Lansky were thugs. Would a thug offer her chewing gum? If he had offered cigarettes, or a drink...

She wondered if he was armed, wondered if he'd kill for Lansky. She knew the types that were drawn to casinos, men who would do anything for money. Her thoughts were tinged with a memory: that first night, the unpleasant encounter with Aspirrina. He had seemed a bit rough but at the same time he had treated Aspirrina with care even as she hissed evil words at him. All she had were suspicions, guilt by association. Maybe Juan Carlos Talente was the one honest man in the casino. Why not? She was the one virgin in the chorus. There were exceptions to every rule, another side to every suspicion. He was just a man and there were plenty of those around. But she liked thinking about him most of all.

For weeks she had hoped to run into him alone so she could thank him. But she had never seen him again until now, and now didn't seem like the right time. She was relieved when he entered the elevator and after a brief, almost imperceptible wave of his hand, left her alone with Lansky.

Lansky had greeted her warmly, even called her "darling," and motioned her to the couch. She sat, making sure her knees were pressed together. Here she was, sitting with the most powerful man in Havana. What was on his mind? She'd heard of casino bosses who treated showgirls as their sexual property and she braced herself for his advances. Suddenly it was so clear to her, why she'd been summoned at this late hour, why Señor Talente had left them alone. Oh how she wished he'd stayed. No matter, she'd fight Lansky, she decided, she'd fight him all the way, she'd jump out of the window, to her death if she had to.

She eyed the window, calculating the time it would take her to reach it and how long the fall would be, when the elevator doors opened and Rosario and Barbarita rushed into the room.

They were a colorful burst of energy, giggling as if they had just stepped out of the liveliest party instead of out of an elevator. Their floral-print satin dresses were tightly fitted to their bodies, their long legs sheathed in shimmering silk stockings, their feet encased in elegant, patent leather shoes with high, thin heels.

Lansky greeted them with the same effusion that he had shown Estelita. The girls returned delighted greetings, and kissed him on both cheeks, European style, then sat down next to her before he even offered them a seat.

"I'm sure you know each other."

"Estelita? Of course," Rosario said with a wink.

"What a surprise to see you up here," Barbarita added. But they

176

both knew it was no surprise at all.

"You're probably wondering why you're here," Lansky said with a serious attempt at a smile.

"Yes," Rosario said, breathlessly.

"Yes," Barbarita echoed.

"Well, it's good news, so you can all relax," Lansky said.

Rosario and Barbarita giggled, and Estelita wondered why. Lansky had not said anything even remotely amusing.

"The casino is starting flights from Havana to Miami," he continued.

"Oh, that's wonderful," Barbarita said, as if he'd been consulting her for approval.

"Yes," he went on, "special flights to bring tourists to the casino. They will be flown in on an airplane especially designed to encourage and entertain very important patrons."

"Oh, the V.I.Ps!" chimed Rosario.

"Exactly, my dear," Lansky said, quickly, he was obviously not a man accustomed to interruptions. "There will be entertainment on the airplane, it has been modified to shove a piano in there, the center aisle will be your stage."

"Sounds marvelous," exclaimed Barbarita.

Estelita nodded, but she didn't feel she needed to say anything. What could she say without sounding like one of the chirping birds on either side of her?

"We have to make this flight exciting, as different as possible from the common carriers, like the festive atmosphere provided by the gambling boats, but more elegant and grander. You follow?"

"Oh, yes!" Rosario and Barbarita said at once, "what a wonderful idea."

They giggled at each other. Estelita only nodded to let him know she was listening and understood.

"Estelita," he said, making her heart jump a little, "I've heard great things about you, and I've caught your act a few times myself."

She was stunned. It never occurred to her that Lansky would be somewhere in the darkened audience watching her, but now she realized that it was only natural. He needed to see everything that was happening in his domain.

"You will sing and dance your little heart out for my customers. Think you can handle that?"

Rosario and Barbarita turned to look at her, tight-lipped smiles on their faces.

Before Estelita could answer, Lansky continued.

"I have no doubt that you can."

"I will do my very best," she replied.

Lansky continued looking at her, like a proud father, she thought. She couldn't help but smile at him, although what he was telling her was making her heart want to leap out of her chest.

"She's a lovely dancer," Rosario said enthusiastically. "A natural."

"And she sings like an angel," Barbarita added. "Without any training."

"Yes, she's a very special girl." Lansky said. "Now you two..."

Rosario and Barbarita leaned in, their eyes wide with anticipation.

"...will serve drinks."

Their gasps of disappointment almost sucked the air out of the room. Estelita noticed that Rosario's eyes had narrowed to slits and were directly staring at her.

"Which is just about the most important job on the plane, except for the pilot of course," Lansky quickly added with a laugh that was more like a snort.

All three girls laughed at his little joke, Barbarita laughing a little louder and a bit longer than Lansky's stab at humor merited.

"This is a very, very important job," Lansky said, meeting Barbarita's wide eyes. "You will be my ambassadors in the clouds."

He turned his face to Rosario.

"I'm counting on your exceptional grace and beauty, and on your warm, vivacious personalities. It will be a difficult job sometimes. The flight from Miami to Havana tends to be bumpy so keep everyone drunk full of mirth and your job will be a cinch. But the return flight, well, the house sometimes wins. So you may have some sour pusses."

He shifted his glance from Rosario to Barbarita, "Do you know what I mean?"

The two girls nodded somberly.

178

"And here's the best part," he said. "Ready? You will have your own suite here at the hotel. Free of charge, I hope you don't mind sharing. It will be a large room, a suite. We still expect you to do your two shows every night. It just wouldn't be the same without you. And we can't have you running home every night and then to the airport. It just wouldn't be fun. And girls, we want this to be fun. That's what we're all about here. Havana is all about fun."

He stood up, smiling.

"How does that sound?"

It sounded wonderful to Estelita. But the other girls remained silent.

"Well...?" Lansky asked, as if he had just unwrapped the most wonderful present.

Estelita nervously cleared her throat before she spoke.

"Will there be more money?"

Lansky shifted uncomfortably. He clearly didn't appreciate this question.

"Certainly. Not a lot at first, after all this is a risky experiment. I could lose my shirt. But more than you're making now, sure."

Estelita could hardly believe her good fortune, but the other two didn't immediately share her enthusiasm.

"What's the matter?"

"We've never been on an airplane before," Rosario said.

"Nothing to it, girls, these flights are safer than trains, you've been on a train before, haven't you?"

Rosario and Barbarita nodded.

"Fine," he said. "I promise you're going to love flying."

He then turned to Estelita with a questioning look.

"I'm ready to start right now, Señor Lansky," she said with the brightest smile she had ever offered anyone.

"That's my girl," Lansky said with American finality.

The ride down on the elevator had been silent. But when the doors opened, Rosario grabbed Estelita roughly by the wrist and pulled her to a dark corner.

"Hey, what are you doing? Let her go." Barbarita said in her defense.

Estelita was trembling with fear and surprise. She knew the girls would be jealous, but she didn't expect them to act like savages.

"It's okay," Rosario said, "I just want to make a little deal with our dancing songbird."

She locked eyes with Estelita.

"Not a word to the other girls, understand?"

Estelita nodded. Rosario put an arm around Barbarita, bringing her into the fold.

"As far as the others are concerned, we are all singing and dancing on that airplane. I don't want them thinking we're cocktail waitresses in the sky. Understand?"

"Perfectly," Estelita answered.

"Good thinking," Barbarita said.

Estelita narrowed her eyes and added, "I'll keep your secret under one condition, that room is mine."

"You can't be serious," Barbarita said.

"There's always two sides to a deal," Estelita countered.

Rosario and Barbarita stepped away to whisper with one another shooting hard looks in Estelita's direction, which Estelita pointedly ignored. They returned moments later, still furious but resigned.

Rosario said, "Who wants that stupid room anyway?"

Barbarita was about to protest again but Rosario squeezed her arm. They looked at each other with a portentous nod and walked away. Estelita stood alone in the hallway, her breath coming up short. At last, she had a home in Havana, a place of her own. It was temporary but it was a step in the right direction. Ahead, everything; behind her, nothing.

That same night she began to feel the chill coming from Barbarita and Rosario, even as they announced their new position to everyone in the dressing room, laughingly lying about what would actually take place on the flights. Barbarita went so far as to insinuate that it was Estelita who had a secondary position. It was a test to see if Estelita was truly going to honor their contract.

Estelita let it pass. Unlike Barbarita, she couldn't care less what the others thought. A part of her mourned that she had just lost two potential friends but she dismissed that thought. She had nothing in common with those girls, they were never destined to be friends. Estelita didn't come to Havana to make friends. Except maybe one, Juan Carlos Talente, if only she could figure out a way to be less nervous around him. She wished she could be more like those women who waited for her father after the shows and covered his face with kisses. Yes, that's exactly what she wanted to do to Juan Carlos Talente, cover his beautiful face with kisses. She smiled as she tucked that plan away in her palpitating heart. There was a definite possibility; if she could sing and dance on an airplane, anything was possible.

She loved Havana.

As soon as the second show was over Estelita quickly changed into her street clothes and ran to the convent to pack. A suite of her own in the hotel, it would be like living in a palace! No more sneaking into the convent and living in fear of being discovered. This was too good to be true. But it was, it was true! She was finally starting her life away from them all, and most importantly, away from Aspirrina.

"But you've never even been on an airplane, you'll get sick, you won't be able to sing, it will be horrible. And that hotel room, ha! I know what that's all about. Trust me girl, nothing is free in this world. You're going to pay for that hotel room with your ass."

Estelita wasn't listening. Nothing Aspirrina could say was going to stop her.

"What's going to become of me?" Aspirrina moaned. "I'm going to end up selling peanuts on a street corner. After all I've done for you. I watched over you when you were little and who was there for you when your father went crazy?"

"My father is not crazy."

"I know what I know," Aspirrina said. "I know that I was the one who brought you to Havana. Not Serpentina, not Lúcido the Magician, not the triplets. You had no one. I took care of you. I sheltered you from the nuns. Now all I have is nothing."

Estelita reached behind the dresser and pulled out the money she'd been secretly setting aside for her getaway.

"Here, this will help you get started," she said, handing the envelope to Aspirrina.

Aspirrina took the envelope and pulled out the bills. She looked at them and sniffed while she counted.

"Seventy-five pesos?" she asked, tears rolling down her fat cheeks. "How far is that going to get me? You selfish, ungrateful girl." And with that she threw the money in the air. The pesos flew around the room and landed at their feet. The two women stood facing each other. Aspirrina was breathing hard, fighting back more tears. Estelita still couldn't get used to Aspirrina without her excessive makeup. Nude, her face seemed even fatter, her eyes small and porcine, her nose barely there, the thick folds under her chin seemed thicker, vulnerable. Estelita's heart softened, in spite of everything, regardless of what Aspirrina thought, she was grateful for all that the woman had done for her.

"I'm going to make more money now," Estelita whispered, kneeling down to pick up the pesos she had worked so hard to save, "I'll send you more. I'll help you get out of here."

"Sure you will, just like you got your father out of that loony bin. You don't care about anybody but yourself. You're a selfish, ugly girl. Yes, ugly. You're ugly on the inside, and eventually it will show on the surface and you will be done, over. You remember my words."

Estelita was still on the floor gathering money when the door opened. She saw the shiny black shoes, the black hem. She looked up and met Sor Maria's stern gaze.

"What is happening in here? You want to wake up the whole house?" she said as Estelita stood up. Now she took it all in. Estelita was still wearing makeup and street clothes, her platinum hair was uncovered. In her high heels she towered over the nun. Aspirrina wiped her eyes and nose with the back of her sleeve.

"I'm leaving, Sister," Estelita said, and impulsively placed her arms around her. The embrace was not returned. The nun felt rigid to her touch. "Thank you for all your kindness."

"Where are you going, girl?" the nun asked, "Why are you dressed like that?"

Estelita didn't answer. She placed the money on top of the dresser, grabbed her suitcase and fled the room before anyone had a chance to stop her. She ran through the hallway and down the stairs. She didn't stop running until she was out on the deserted sidewalk. She took a deep breath, now that she was out on her own the city smelled different, fresher somehow. Her heels clicked on the pavement as she crossed the street and continued on into the night.

Aspirrina knew she had to think quick, act fast. She knew that with Estelita gone, her days at the convent were numbered. So she threw herself on the floor and uttered words she had never used before, not even when she was a child.

"Sister, help me," Aspirrina cried, crumpling to the floor.

Sor Maria fingered the money on the dresser with disapproval.

Aspirrina, still crying, rose to her knees, her arms encircling the nun's black skirt.

"She's a bad girl," she wailed, "we tried to show her the path to righteousness, but she's just a bad girl."

"Aspirrina, stand up, and stop with the dramatics."

Aspirrina swallowed hard and did as she was told.

"Where is that girl going?" the nun asked.

"I can't even bear to say it," Aspirrina whispered stalling for time.

The nun fixed her with a look, she wasn't going to let up until she got an answer.

"Oh Sister, she's gone to a brothel," Aspirrina finally admitted. "She has been recruited by some evil people to be a... a whore."

Sor Maria covered her mouth and her nose with both hands, as if the air had been polluted by Aspirrina's words.

"Our little dove, our precious little dove has flown away." Aspirrina continued, milking the moment. "Please, don't abandon me now."

"Stop talking, please" she said sharply. She needed to think. She cursed her vow of charity. What could she do now? She couldn't forsake this poor woman in her darkest hour. Why didn't she see it coming? Why hadn't she known that in her own house a young woman was falling into the clutches of depravity? But having failed at that, why would she want to keep this woman under her roof? This disagreeable, unpleasant woman who had allowed such a thing to happen to a girl under her care.

No, Aspirrina had to go. But she couldn't just throw her out into the street in the middle of the night. She would wait until morning, she would find a place for her somewhere, surely there were places in the city that would take her in. She could offer her services as a washerwoman. Even though she'd been out of touch with them, she still knew the wealthiest people in Havana. She could unload Aspirrina on one of them. In a house that employed so many servants, Aspirrina wouldn't seem like such a burden. She would just be one of many.

"We can figure something out," Sor Maria said, swiftly pocketing the money on the dresser, "in the morning."

But it was as if Aspirrina was reading her mind.

"You can figure whatever you want, *lady*," she said, biting hard on every word. "But I'm not going until I'm ready to go."

The two women continued to stare at each other. Sor Maria wasn't about to back down. More than ever, she was certain that Aspirrina had to go.

"You are here out of the charity of our Lord Jesus Christ," Sor Maria said.

"Bullshit!" Aspirrina said. "The only reason I've been tolerated was for the girl. And now the girl is gone. You hypocrite, you religious types are all the same. Under that boring dress you're just like everyone else, maybe worse."

"That's it, you devil of a woman!" Sor Maria cried out, never in her life had she felt the need to raise her voice and it scratched her throat. "How dare you speak to me that way? Here, take your filthy money and get out. I want you out of here immediately."

Aspirrina did not move.

"What are you waiting for? Pack your things, I don't care where you go or what happens to you."

Aspirrina smiled, wiping the fake tears on her face.

"I'll go if you insist," she said calmly, "straight to the police. Perhaps to them you can explain the crates of rifles down in the basement."

Sor Maria raised a hand to her aching throat, slipped her fingers under her the collar and tugged, then tugged again.

It felt very hot in the room, unbearably so.

18

Aspirrina was so happy she felt she could effortlessly soar into dance. Her heart was pounding, her arms wanted to rise above her head and sway, her hips wanted to swivel. She hadn't felt like dancing for joy in a very long time. But as she stepped out of the convent in her black dress, she knew some semblance of dignity was in order. She was free in Havana, free to do as she pleased. She walked down the uneven sidewalk and onto the main avenue where she easily fell in with other women in black. She looked around and noted that there must be hundreds. Some carried banners and placards with the words LIBERTAD and JUSTICIA furiously brushed on with dark red paint, long drips trailing from the lower part of each letter like tears of blood.

We probably look like a swarm of giant crows, she thought. No matter. She had on her full face of makeup again, it was her first act of defiance against the tyranny of the penguins.

She had been living in a coffin long enough. For months she'd cowered inside the convent while Havana bubbled over with excitement. She had become aware of the events taking place, events that she had always hoped for. She heard about them at the grocery stores and the fish markets, the only places Sor Maria let her frequent. But she had felt unable to do more than nod her head with a mixture of horror and excitement and hurry back to the confines of the convent. Now things were different. With Estelita out of the way and Sor Maria under her thumb, she could do as she pleased.

The protest had been organized by a woman named Hilda Llorente, whose two teenage sons had been accused of insubordination and thrown into El Principe Prison without trial, without evidence, without a second thought.

Hilda Llorente had rallied other mothers whose sons or husbands had suffered a similar fate, and now hundreds marched towards the Presidential Palace to let Batista know how they felt. Along came aunts, cousins, grandmothers, and friends. Others, inspired by the show of power, joined the march as they walked by, sometimes grabbing a black blouse and running out of the house while still unbuttoned.

Aspirrina had pushed and elbowed through the crowd until she was at the front. She found Hilda Llorente, whom she had never met, and linked her arm through hers. Hilda gave her a baffled, questioning look. Aspirrina looked back and smiled until she got a smile back. Before long, all the women had linked arms and were chanting together: "Libertad! Justicia! LIBERTAD!"

No, Aspirrina couldn't recall a day when she had been so happy. She was experiencing the rush of freedom again. She did whatever she wished in the convent, got out of bed when she wanted, helped out with some chores, but not with the same sense of indentured slavery as before, and no one dared to question her. No one dared to ask her where she went or what she did. Whenever one of the nuns frowned or was about to protest, Sor Maria intervened because she knew that one word to the authorities would not only land them all in a prison cell, but would also bring disgrace to the entire archdiocese, perhaps the entire Catholic church. *Nuns With Guns* was the sort of headline that easily traveled around the world.

Early that morning, Aspirrina painted on her eyebrows, rouged her cheeks, applied her favorite lipstick and was delighted to see her face return to normal. How she had missed those eyebrows. She not only had found her face again, she also had found a purpose. She was involved. Night after night she'd heard the explosions, the gunfire, the shouts, and had yearned to be a part of it. She talked to anyone who was willing to talk to her about what was really happening in Havana and indeed, all of her country. She heard about the freeze on civil liberties, the censorship of the press, rampant and wanton executions. Who did this Fulgencio Batista character think he was, anyway? Now, on this glorious day, people lined the sidewalks to watch her go by. She, little Aspirrina, once and often the subject of ridicule, linked arm in arm with Hilda Llorente, a woman many considered a hero, a saint.

Aspirrina eyed the crowd with pride and defiance. How she wished that Estelita would be there to see her. But the girl was nowhere in sight. She thought she might spot her among those who were too fearful to join the march, the ones who stood at the edge of the sidewalk, yelling at them to be careful.

"Cuidate!" they shouted, their voices full of dread. Be careful.

By one in the afternoon, they had walked a half a dozen miles, grown to number in the hundreds, and taken over the streets. Traffic was jammed in every direction as more and more women rushed in to join the march. When they turned a corner, beneath the baby-blue sky, Aspirrina could see the glass-tiled dome of the Presidential Palace rising above the rooftops, the blinding rays of the afternoon sun reflecting from it like a golden halo.

"You think Batista is in there right now?" Aspirrina asked Hilda Llorente. Hilda turned to Aspirrina and shrugged. She looked pale, Apirrina noticed, fear clouded her eyes. She's neither a hero nor a saint, Aspirrina realized, just someone's desperate mother – and she wondered how that felt.

*

Inside the Presidential Palace, Fulgencio Batista was laughing. It was a loud, short laugh; more like a bark, and not at all befitting a man in his position. The palace, which covered almost a city square, was under tight security.

A few weeks before, a small band of university students had stormed in and attempted to kill him. He had laughed then too, as his guards had annihilated the intruders, he'd laughed as he stepped over the bodies that lay scattered in spreading puddles of blood all down the winding marble staircase and across the white, sparkling, marble floors.

As he walked up the marble stairs, Juan Carlos had noticed that the bullet holes all over the marble balustrade and wall. It had been a serious attack yet the president was not only alive, he was sitting there laughing at him.

The President loved to laugh and he was laughing now, at the look of panic on Juan Carlos Talente's face. The young man had spoken out of turn. The words had flown out of his mouth and before he knew it, he had insulted Fulgencio Batista, a man who never in his wildest dreams he expected to meet.

Juan Carlos felt like a complete idiot.

Just a few hours earlier he had been standing outside the casino, looking over a racing form that held absolutely no promise. Lansky had come through the revolving glass doors in a mad rush.

"Come with me, Juan Carlos," he'd said without stopping, without explanation, without so much as looking at him. He followed his boss into a waiting car. Lansky sat where he always sat, in the front seat, next to the driver so he could give instructions without raising his voice. Juan Carlos sat in the back. Alone. He didn't know where they were going but knew better than to ask.

A short drive later he was following Lansky's squeaky shoes through the Presidential Palace and into the President's enormous office. Batista greeted Lansky like an old friend. The two men hugged and patted each other on the back. Juan Carlos was introduced and he shook the president's hand. Juan Carlos felt surprisingly at ease in the company of the two powerful men. Batista offered them his favorite cognac, Fundador Domec, which Lansky declined. Juan Carlos declined as well.

"How about a cafécito, then?" Batista asked as if they were visitors to a cozy cottage instead of this imposing room.

"That I will accept," Lansky replied. Batista picked up the solid gold telephone on his desk, famously given to him by AT&T, and placed his order. No sooner had he returned receiver to cradle than a uniformed maid came in without knocking. Silently, she passed around small cups of coffee and left as quietly as she had entered – Juan Carlos noticed that her eyes never made contact with anyone in the room.

Lansky took a small sip, set the cup down and got right to business. "Fulgencio," he said, "what is this I hear about you changing your mind about elections again?"

"The country's not ready," Batista answered. "Isn't it evident? A sudden change could place the wrong person in charge." He directed a sly glance at Lansky, "and no one can afford that."

"What can I do to keep you here?" Lansky asked as he swept the presidential office with his eyes.

It had been at that moment, just minutes after Juan Carlos met the most important man in Latin America, that the wrong words had come stumbling out of his mouth.

"But won't that be seen as another dictatorship?" Juan Carlos asked. "The people are not stupid."

There was silence, followed by that awful laughter.

Juan Carlos was momentarily relieved that the president was laughing. But he also felt a flush of embarrassment, as if a scalding hot towel had been dropped on his face.

Lansky didn't laugh. The situation couldn't be more serious for him. He had brought Juan Carlos along in case there were reporters, and he needed a Cuban at his side. But there had been no reporters, only militia. Now he regretted his decision.

"Yes, I've heard that once or twice before," Batista said, placing his empty coffee cup on the desk, "but I think the only dictatorship here is that which my wife and sons exert upon me. Do you have children, Señor Talente?"

His eyes were on Juan Carlos, a slight hint of a smile still in his dark lips. Juan Carlos had dealt with all kinds of men since he'd come to work for Lansky but this one was unique. In spite of the laughter, the jokes, the warm hospitality, there was something bone-chilling about the man. Juan Carlos and Batista continued looking at one another. The moment seemed like it was going to last forever. Juan Carlos began to get the feeling that he might not be walking out of that room with his life.

"Why don't you go sit over there, kid," Lansky told him, pointing to a chair in the back of the room. Juan Carlos knew what this meant - sit down, shut up, and let me handle this.

Juan Carlos Talente did as he was told.

Fulgencio Batista, the president of the Republic of Cuba, took a seat behind a big mahogany desk and placed his arms comfortably behind his head. This was his domain and he wanted there to be no doubt about it. The office was spacious, with long, French-style windows bordered with red and gold draperies. Lansky took a chair across from him, erect, his back barely grazing the back of his chair.

"I would like to know," Batista said, speaking directly to Lansky but loud enough for Juan Carlos to hear, and to hear very clearly and specifically, "how I could be called a dictator. What is a dictator? Is it someone who loves his country, who wants to do good things for his people? Look at the new highways, I have done more for transportation in the past five years than any other leader of this country ever has. Is that a dictator? No. A dictator by popular definition, is an evil tyrant. I am not that. Everywhere I go, my people embrace me, and so I know my people are happy with me. You are right, Señor Talente, the people are not stupid."

A satisfied smile brightened his face.

"Well, I have to tell you, I'm a little worried." Lansky said. "Frankly, I'm a lot worried."

Batista's expression did not change.

"I can understand your concern," Batista said. "But I am confident that my political enemies – and name me one world leader who doesn't have more than his share – cannot succeed in overthrowing this Government by revolt. I announced the restoration of full constitutional guarantees a week ago."

"But there's still trouble," Lansky added. "As our friend here implied, negative word is spreading. You have to excuse him, he is young. But he speaks what he hears on the street."

The president leaned forward, placing his elbows on the desk. His eyes coursed past Lansky, to Juan Carlos.

"Frankly, I don't know how anyone could arrive at that conclusion," Batista said calmly. "How could anyone call me a dictator? There are no restrictions on freedom of speech, freedom of press, freedom of religion. There are no concentration camps in my country. Congress can override any legislation I might veto, or refuse to

190

pass what I want passed. There is no libel law in Cuba. Everybody says what they want. Including this man, who insults me in my own office. A true dictator would have him arrested without hesitation."

Juan Carlos hardly dared to breathe, he was having trouble swallowing.

"What about this Castro fellow?" Lansky said. "It seems he's gaining more and more support every day."

Batista sighed as if he'd heard that question one thousand times too many.

"Fidel Castro is a criminal and a communist and I should have let him rot in prison," he said. "I do not understand why he is compared to Robin Hood, as he has been in the newspapers, mostly in the North American press – by the way. *The New York Times* seems to be running a political campaign in his favor. If you are worried, don't look to me for answers. Look in your own backyard. My side of the street is clean. You need to clean up yours."

"There's nothing I can do about *The New York Times*," Lansky said.

"What about Prio?" Batista asked, referring to Carlos Prio Socarras, the former Cuban president now residing in Miami Beach.

"My people tell me he has spent more than one million dollars to buy and ship firearms and explosives into Cuba, weapons intended to decimate my administration. I know because we have intercepted most of them, and that's just in the last couple of years. I believe the American Coast Guard likes to look the other way when arms are being delivered to the rebels. Call me crazy, but that's what I see. I, on the other hand, can't get anything through. I'm talking about training airplanes that were bought and paid for. I'm talking about two-thousand rifles that at this very moment are sitting in a warehouse because of paperwork. There has never been red tape between us before. Why now?"

"I know, I know," Lansky said. "That's why I'm here, it's all going insane. What about you? Do you still feel safe here?"

"Not entirely," Batista said, reaching into a drawer and pulling out what looked like a small .25 caliber pistol. The weapon cracked fire as he pulled the trigger four times. Bang! Bang! Bang! Bang! Right into the wall. Cement chips and dust flew in every direction.

Juan Carlos jumped behind a column, certain the next shot was coming at him for having called the president a dictator to his face. Lansky didn't flinch. Two armed guards charged into the room. Shouts and footsteps could be heard outside the open door.

"Blanks. Just to keep in practice," Batista said to the guards as he laid the pistol upon his desk. As the guards withdrew, Batista turned back to Lansky, his eyes, shining like two mad marbles.

"Yes, I feel somewhat safe," Batista said. "But now, let's get serious, shall we? What about this Prio? Maybe we can't do anything about *The New York Times*. But what can we do about this sonofabitch Prio?"

Just then, a strange sound started to fill the room. A thunderous, clicking sound.

"What is that? What's going on out there?" Lansky asked, rising to his feet and walking to a window. "Fulgencio, you better take a look at this," he added with a frown.

Batista joined him, parting the heavy drapes to get a better view.

"The women of this country have bigger balls than a breeding bull," Batista said. One of the phones on his desk rang; Batista picked it up with a deep sigh. "Yes, I see them, and I hear them." He paused to listen. "Yes, that's about all we can do. Yes, you can proceed, we have no alternative." His tone was suddenly tired.

Another phone rang. Batista picked it up, this time there was anger in his manner, his voice.

"Yes, that's what I said," he shouted into the mouthpiece. "It's either that or every day we're going to have some crazy march or demonstration."

He slammed down the phone.

"Demonstration my ass," Batista said to Lansky. "They're paid to do this sort of thing, you know. This is not how my people really feel. Degenerates and thieves are hiding behind each and every one of those women."

Juan Carlos walked to the window closest to him and looked down. The plaza was filled with women, all of them dressed in black, and they were all clicking their heels on the cobblestone street. In front of them was a line of soldiers, rifles at the ready. Behind them, a line of tanks created a powerful barricade. On the other side of the plaza, the sidewalks were filled with onlookers, both local Cuban and tourists, so many of them that they spilled into the street. Some were taking photographs with cameras they had brought to record their tropical vacation.

"Asesino! Asesino!" the women shouted in unison, holding up their placards, their voices echoing off the marble walls.

"This is not good, not good at all, Fulgencio." Lansky said. "Just one photograph gets out and it will be seen around the world. This is going to kill tourism on this island forever."

Batista remained silent, but veins were starting to show on his temples.

"How could you let this happen?" Lansky said, angry now.

"It's a free country, I told you. Just like yours," Batista answered matching Lansky's angry tone. "I can't control the actions of every citizen. Prio is behind all this. The women have been paid to do this. The women you see there would fall to their knees and suck my pinga if I walked up to them with a ten dollar bill."

Juan Carlos continued watching as half a dozen fire trucks rounded the corner of the plaza. Firemen scurried around quickly. They unloaded water hoses and aimed the powerful spray at the demonstrators.

Women dressed in black went flying and tumbling.

The crowd of onlookers scattered, pushing, screaming and running in every direction.

19

Felipe Arjuna sat alone at a bare wooden table inside the boathouse at Jaimanitas. He was counting dollars, not pesos, and shaking his head with astonishment at the amount of money that kept pouring in.

"This," he thought, "is going to change everything."

Cuban exiles in New York City and Miami were holding more fundraisers than anyone could have predicted, and sending cash to Havana almost every month. Money was coming from other sources as well; surprising, anonymous sources from all over the island. Now that Castro and his men had made it to the mountains, it seemed to him as if the entire country was getting involved and was determined to do whatever was necessary to squeeze Batista out of office.

For a brief period it had seemed as if all Cubans were involved, now there was plenty of evidence to the contrary. This worried him. Just a week before, on his way back from visiting with Delfino, he had stumbled upon an unexpected demonstration. About one hundred Batista supporters were rallying around the Presidential palace waving placards and banners that read: FOR BATISTA IN THE PAST, NOW AND FOREVER. To protect them, lines of uniformed policemen marched alongside of them. Also looking out for them were rows of soldiers, armed with telescopic rifles, crouched in the bulwark of the rooftops that bordered the plaza.

Nothing was simple anymore. It was getting confusing for Arjuna. At first the intent had seemed clear: get rid of the current president, who was not willing to step down without a fight and restore the country to some sort of democracy. But then other factors had come into play. The Auténtico Party, responsible for tossing Batista out in 1944, wanted it their way. But they were being countered by the Ortodoxo Party, who also opposed Batista, but wanted nothing to do with the Auténticos. The White Rose Movement was against both Batista and Castro, but didn't seem to have a serious candidate. People considered them radical malcontents and blamed them for the random violence that plagued the city.

"Thank God," Arjuna thought, "that Fidel Castro is up in the mountains of Oriente, far away from all this madness."

Felipe Arjuna didn't know Fidel Castro, but he was devoted to him. Castro had to be the answer. He was their last hope. The man was only thirty-years old, closer in age to everyone Arjuna knew and trusted. Certainly, he would bring about the changes the country needed. Above all, Arjuna shared with Fidel Castro a mistrust of the United States that verged on hatred. Castro, like Arjuna, believed in a free and independent Cuba. And that would be best for all. But Havana was suffering. Everyone was determined to topple Batista. Bombing, killing and arson had become commonplace. The average citizen had gone from fear and outrage to a suspicious silence punctuated by sudden bursts of civil disobedience. Batista struck back by censoring all news organizations. It was forbidden for periodicals, cable offices, radio programs, or television stations to report on riots or demonstrations of any kind. Tired of clipping articles with scissors, their fingers swollen like sausages, the censors had started to use a column-wide ink roller to delete objectionable items. Newspapers were sold on the street with articles literally blacked-out. But even without newsboys barking out horrifying headlines every morning, there was no denying that the country was at war with itself. Buses were set on fire. Power, electric and telephone lines were cut, store windows smashed, cars bombed, bridges burned. Trains were derailed, railroad stations burned down, all to prevent Batista's troops from reaching Oriente and its mountains.

Soldiers had been assigned to guard all railroad stations and public buildings. Planes and warships patrolled the coasts. Hundreds of suspected saboteurs were jailed. No evidence was necessary, just a rumor could ruin someone's life; destroy a family.

Corpses continued to appear mysteriously, at first in out-of-the-way places, then, right in the center of town. Many of the victims had been shot through the head. Others hung from trees and light posts.

Yet more and more individuals were climbing to the mountains every day. Most were former university students. All universities had been closed down for more than six months because Batista considered them breeding grounds of insurrection. And he was right. But now he had a whole generation of young men with nothing to keep them occupied. Armed with a suicidal sort of patriotism, they left home in search of Castro and adventure.

It was too much to think about. Arjuna finished counting the money one last time and was entering the totals into a coded ledger, when Delfino walked in.

"You'll never believe it," he said, barely able to contain his excitement, "four, maybe five hundred women, dressed in black, are demonstrating outside the palace."

Arjuna smiled. He liked how passionate Delfino felt about the changes they were working so hard to bring about. He claimed every act of sabotage as a personal victory. His attitude had surprised him at first; that the son of one of the most pro-Batista families in the city would invest so much of himself to bring down the regime. Then realized that this was just Delfino's way of getting back at a father he couldn't communicate with and a mother he felt was completely unaware of anything outside of her own protected, privileged world. The reasons didn't much matter to Arjuna. He liked seeing this young, melancholy and inexperienced boy turn into an impassioned revolutionary; a man with a purpose.

From that first night they spent together, under the shadows of the Framboyan trees near Plaza de Armas, to now, almost two years later, they had been inseparable. That whole first summer they had spent in bed, talking only about the revolution, and making love. Now they were warriors together. The true test of his commitment came when the shipments of arms started to arrive, and Delfino had persuaded his best friend, a nun, to store them in a convent. It was a brilliant move, for who would think to look there. But they wouldn't stay safe for long. Every day everything had to change. Constant change was the only invariable in an underground movement.

"Yes, the women are angry today," Arjuna said as he walked to embrace his lover. "Their children are being killed every day, or imprisoned. I'm surprised it took them this long to do something about it."

"I don't know how much they can do," Delfino said, breaking away from Arjuna, too agitated to be held. "But they looked fabulous. They were all dressed in black and were holding up banners that looked like they had been written on with thick red lipstick." He stopped to catch his breath. "Who knew Cuban women could get so worked up over political matters? My mother certainly wouldn't."

Arjuna took him firmly by the shoulders, it was the only way he was going to get him to calm down and listen.

"I have bad news."

Delfino met his eyes.

"What happened?"

"It's Enrique Fernandez. They got him."

Delfino walked to the window but didn't open it. When they were in the boathouse together, they always kept the shutters closed.

"What happened?"

"Somebody must have said something. The facts are not clear, but the front door was knocked clean off, and the house was swarming with police. Enrique wasn't even home, but he heard what was happening and he ran home as fast as he could. The idiot was trying to protect his wife. As it turns out, they were both arrested. We have enough cash to bribe him out. Maybe his wife too. I hope we can. Just the same, it's a huge loss."

"And everything else is gone too, I imagine?"

"No, we got them out. Twenty-seven machine guns, twenty-three rifles, about fifteen hundred rounds of ammunition. But they found some other stuff."

"What other stuff?"

"Twenty policemen's uniforms."

"Mierda. So now they know."

Arjuna smiled and nodded, his eyes sparkling with intelligence. "I think they've always known," he said. "Now they have proof. But one thing is clear, it's not safe anywhere in Havana, not even in a convent. We have to move the weapons. And we have to do it right away."

"Yes, Maria could be in danger," Delfino said.

"Maria has been in danger all along," Arjuna replied, "And so have the other women in that convent. But what concerns me are the weapons. We can't afford to lose them."

Delfino agreed. Lives could be sacrificed, were expected to be sacrificed. Like the women in black marching around the palace, everyone seemed willing. Uprisings and demonstrations were happening everywhere. It wasn't happening only in Havana. People were speaking out and demanding their rights in the most unlikely places. Sabotage had caused blackouts in small towns like Sagua La Grande, Remedios and Santa Isabel. The whole country was enraged.

Now, in the quiet of the boathouse, only the sound of the waves against the rocks of Jaimanitas indicated the constant passage of time. And an unspoken question hung in the air like smoke. How were Arjuna and Delfino going to get the cache of arms and money out of the convent and to Santiago de Cuba, nearly five hundred miles to the east?

20

Aspirrina was wet, angry and tired when she entered the convent. The march had been a resounding success, thanks in large part to her efforts, she thought. She had remained at the front of the crowd, her arms linked with the women on either side of her, and theirs, in turn, linked with hundreds of other women.

They had entered the plaza slowly, the presidential palace loomed above them. She could see the long, shuttered windows, and noticed that some of the lower ones were covered with sandbags. She could see the military tanks and guards. The sight had thrilled her, she enjoyed a formidable foe. But when the rest of the women saw what they were up against, when they saw the armed guards, the rifles aimed at them, they slowed down, almost to a stand-still as if an invisible shield was keeping them from moving forward. Their voices quieted. Fear reigned in everyone's heart. Everyone's but hers.

Aspirrina continued walking forward, pulling the other women along. Some of them unlaced their arms and started moving backwards, their faces twisted into masks of fear and confusion.

But the women in the back couldn't see what was happening at the front, so they continued marching forward, thrusting the reluctant ones towards the front entrance of the palace. Aspirrina found herself up against the rifles. A few more steps and she would have had a barrel poking into her chest.

"Step back," the soldiers barked, baring their teeth like rabid dogs, "step back!"

The front row stopped, and some of the terrified women turned to those behind them.

"Stop pushing," they shouted at each other, "stop!"

Finally, the mass of bodies came to a nervous stand-still.

Hilda Llorente turned to Aspirrina, her eyes anxious.

"Now what?" she whispered.

"We should kneel down and pray," a woman suggested in a whisper.

"They would love that," shouted Aspirrina. "Let's give them something better."

And with that she started clicking her heels on the cobblestone street. Hilda joined, and then the women to her left, then to her right, and then the row behind and on and on until every woman was clicking away. It was a marvelous, feminine sound, a powerful one. The clicking gave way to shouting and waving of placards and flags. They were not moving forward, but they were a force to be reckoned with.

Aspirrina looked around. All sorts of people, men in plaid shorts, women in flowered dresses and sunglasses holding children by the hand came running into the plaza to participate in the excitement.

She'd looked up at the windows of the presidential palace, up to the third floor, and had seen three men looking down on her. They were too far away to identify clearly, but she was almost sure that one of them was Fulgencio Batista. A shorter man stood at another window and him she did not know at all. But the last one, the tallest of the three, that one she could clearly see. It was that greasy Cuban mobster who'd thrown her out of the hotel: Juan Carlos Talente. He was someone she wouldn't soon forget. That he was up there with the tyrant looking down on her didn't surpise her at all. He seemed the type to look down on his own, he seemed the type to bring about destruction. It would have cost him nothing to let her see the show, but he had chosen instead to humiliate her. There was a special place in hell for men like him.

It had been after their encounter that Estelita had changed, that everything had changed. Perhaps instead of scorn she owed him some gratitude. After all, it was that night that had brought about her emancipation. It was that night when she'd suffered Estelita's first betrayal, but had also started her on the road to freedom. If she had never met Talente she wouldn't be standing here with these admirable women.

The women in black found their voices again and she joined in, never once taking her eyes off Talente.

"Mujeres, unidas, no seran vencidas," they chorused. "Women united will never be defeated."

Their voices were strong, loud, and angry. She could feel the energy course through her body, something akin to power, the power of voices united. But then without warning, the fire trucks had flown in like a red and evil wind.

And blown it all to hell.

Most of the women ran shouting and shrieking. Others, like herself, remained firm against the streams of water. But when the police arrived and started arresting women, roughly grabbing their arms and legs and tossing them into waiting vans like sacks of potatoes, she knew it was time to get out.

Aspirrina scurried through the crowd, as slippery as a greased pig. Women reached out to her, but she couldn't help them. She continued on as fast as her little legs could carry her until she found a narrow alley through which she made her escape. She could hear the screams and sirens for blocks afterwards. She was grateful that she did not hear shots and she was even more grateful when she reached the back door of the convent.

Inside, Sor Maria was waiting.

"Look at you!" she gasped. "Where in the world have you been?"

"I don't want to talk about it," Aspirrina hissed. She no longer needed to answer to this woman and could talk to her anyway she wanted. Make believe time was over. She could call herself Mother Superior, she could call herself Queen Of The Universe for all Aspirrina cared. To her she was just another woman trying to get in her way, another person trying to tell her what to do and how to live and

Aspirrina had had enough of that for one lifetime.

Without another word, Aspirrina started for the stairs, eager to get to her room and shed her wet clothes. She was about to climb the first step when, out of the corner of her eye, she saw two men she had never seen before.

They were standing in the front parlor, half in shadow. Her first thought was: Men! Inside the convent!

And then fear took over.

Policemen!

They've come to get me!

Her legs started to quiver. Whatever anger and the courage that it gave her, abandoned her completely.

She measured the distance between where she stood and the door. Could she make it? Her thoughts flew to Estelita. All differences aside, they had been a good pair, looking out for each other in this house of silent women and dark walls. Where was she now? The world seemed so big right now, and she felt so small. Small and alone and defenseless. But she was not going to give anybody the pleasure of seeing her cry. She'd rather die and dying, at the moment, didn't seem such a bad idea.

She felt Sor Maria take her by her damp shoulders and suddenly she was as pliable as wet clay. Sor Maria gently turned her to face them.

"These are my friends, Señor Delfino and Señor Arjuna," she said with a smile. Aspirrina stood shivering before them. Reluctant to step up and shake their hands, she remained where she was and nodded once. Only once. A polite, safe, and distant greeting.

The men returned her nod. Aspirrina, no stranger to disdain, noticed that their eyes couldn't conceal their disapproval of her disheveled appearance.

21

Estelita buckled her seatbelt as the pilot had instructed, closed her eyes and prayed. The airplane was skipping somersaults among the clouds, and so was her stomach. As the airplane lurched and bucked she told herself not to vomit. She told herself that the airplane would land safely. She felt dizzy and nauseous and a crippling agitation. She saw now how easily her every dream had come true, how quickly, and wondered what force, whether benevolent or malevolent had brought them about.

As the events had come she had accepted them gladly, proudly, her egress to Havana, finding shelter at the convent, obtaining the job at the casino and her rapid ascendance there. All this she had accepted as long overdue recompense for a childhood of poverty, loneliness and uncertainty. If she believed in God she would attribute her recent good fortune to his kind wisdom, his sense of fairness, but her father had not thought much of God. God, he said, had taken away his wife, his baby's mother.

Estelita thought of the many times her father had taken a crucifix off a wall, the times he had tossed the object out the window, the times when drunk he had urinated on it. But if not God, who? Who could she pray to now? And if it was the work of God, why would he bring her all this way just to let her die in a storm three-thousand feet above the earth?

The airplane took another tumble and after screaming she prayed as Sor Maria had tried to teach her. She prayed that she would be forgiven for all of her sins. She wondered what those sins might be. What was she so guilty of that God would place her in this appalling plight? Had she been too ambitious? Too selfish and thoughtless? Had she been wrong to stay away from her father? Every time she planned to visit him, something prevented it, something she just couldn't pass up. Something she knew he'd want her to experience. Still, her conscience nagged her as the airplane continued to rise and fall, turning this way and that, struggling to stay aloft.

Had she been wrong to leave the convent to seek her own fortune? She thought about Aspirrina. Estelita regretted the angry way they had parted. It had been three months since that horrible night when she had packed her bags, Aspirrina had thrown money in her face and Sor Maria had walked in on them.

Estelita was sure Aspirrina hated her and felt the hatred was deserved. But in a tiny corner of her heart, she had always hoped that one day she would get the opportunity to make proper restitutions. Not just to her but also to Sor Maria. She thought about the beautiful nun who had shown her such kindness. And looking back, the time she had spent with Aspirrina had not been so bad, or even the months at the convent. Yes, she had to make amends – but when? Between the shows and the flights, every moment of every day was booked solid.

She glanced at Barbarita and Rosario across the aisle, holding on to each other like two sisters and Estelita envied them. Yes, Estelita had the suite at the hotel but these two had each other. She had no one, she was going to die alone and she feared that the last emotion she would ever feel before she died would be envy.

The airplane tilted sharply forward and the seatbelt dug into her waist but she endured it for she was sure it was the only thing keeping her from crashing into the overhead compartment. The airplane lurched again. All the women in the airplane let out a synchronized yelp as if eminent death had eternally united them. It now felt as if the airplane was completely upside down.

The passengers, all Americans from Miami, looked at her with pleading eyes, as if expecting her to save them, and she knew there was nothing she could do for anyone on board except remain calm – on the outside, anyway. Estelita kept her eyes closed even if all she found behind her eyelids were unbearable thoughts. She did not want to make eye contact with anyone around her.

The airplane swerved again, various passengers shouted out prayers in English.

"Jesus help us!"

"Sweet mother of God!"

Others shouted in Spanish.

"Santa Barbara bendita!"

"Ayúdame Changó."

"Perdoname Yemaya."

Estelita felt a man's hand take hold of hers and she almost drew it back. The shock of his warm skin on her cold, clammy hands frightened her. She knew the hand belonged to the Mexican man who had smiled at her when he boarded, and fearing that these could be her last few seconds alive, she held on tight. But somehow, even at this desperate moment, it felt wrong. It had all been going so perfectly, and now it might all end in senseless tragedy. She kept her eyes closed and gripped the man's hand even tighter.

The night of that horrible scene with Aspirrina came rushing back. She had walked away from the convent as quickly as she could to the corner and hailed a taxi. She had sat in the back seat of the big Ford, trembling with excitement. Her life was leading her in directions that she had not anticipated, and it was her duty, her obligation, to gather her strength and follow.

The taxi took her to the entrance of the casino. Not the artists entrance in the back of the building she always used. No. This was the big, sparkling main entrance. She made the driver go around the circular driveway slowly while she checked her face in the rearview mirror. She powdered the shiny spots and carefully refreshed her lipstick. When she was satisfied, she grabbed her suitcase and went directly to the front counter in the grand lobby. She had never checked into a hotel without her father before, and never one as elegant as this. For a split second she worried that it had all been a mistake, that she had misunderstood what Mr. Lansky had said. But all her doubts vanished when she told the night clerk her name. The clerk had treated her as if she was visiting royalty.

"Welcome, Señorita de la Cruz," he said with a polite smile as he rang a tiny, almost inaudible bell. A uniformed bellhop appeared out of nowhere. So this is what it feels like to be on the other side, she thought, and pretended she had done it a million times before. Her expression didn't betray her – she kept her chin up and her eyes friendly but cool.

She recalled what one of the older showgirls had said backstage, "A beautiful face is the only passport you'll ever need."

The bellhop took her bag and introduced himself as Jorge. She followed him to the elevator and they rode in silence until the doors opened. He led her down a long hallway, and to the front door of room number 4219. He expertly threw open the door and there it was, her new home.

It wasn't at all what she thought a hotel room would look like, this was more like the living room of a very expensive apartment. And it was all blue, her favorite color!

The walls were pale blue, the drapes a little darker. The long, curving couch and the armchairs were upholstered in a lustrous blue fabric.

Jorge stepped in first, leaving the door open, and stood in the center of the room.

Her eyes grew wider and wider as she looked around. He grinned at her reaction.

"This is one of the many beautiful suites in our hotel," he said with pride. She was speechless.

Jorge moved about quickly, explaining everything to her.

"These switches control all the lights," he said and continued on slowly as if he had all the time in the world. "This controls the air conditioner. You can make it as cold as you can stand it. Let me show you the bar, it has every imaginable beverage and this is your own tiny refrigerator. If you need a larger one, it can be delivered."

He pointed out the blue telephone. The hi-fi stereo. Then, he pulled a cord that drew back the thick drapes, revealing a glittering view of Havana Harbor. From where she stood Estelita could see all the way from Morro Castle to Jaimanitas and to the vast expanse of black sea beyond.

"It's beautiful," she said.

"Wait until you see it in the daytime, it's even more beautiful," Jorge offered with pride. She doubted that anything could surpass this view and could hardly wait until morning.

He walked to a set of double doors and threw them open. Inside, in the same lovely blue, was a large bedroom and two double beds.

Jorge opened an even bigger door and beyond was a bedroom so elegant, and a bed so big, that she imagined only kings or presidents, or movie stars would sleep in there.

"Well, this is for you."

"But this room, it's too big, too beautiful."

Jorge looked at her for a second, searching for an appropriate response.

"The room is compliments of the hotel, but it's not all generosity. It is less expensive for them to give three girls one of these rooms than to give each of you your own room. Understand?"

She nodded, a delighted smile spreading across her beautiful face.

"Perfectly."

"I suggest you accept it graciously and enjoy it thoroughly."

"I agree and I will, Jorge, thank you."

"And now I must go," he said as he walked to the door, "please call the concierge if you need anything else."

She nodded.

"Perhaps I will see you again when I bring up the other girls."

There will be no other girls, she thought as she fished in her purse for a tip and thanked him. As his footsteps retreated down the hallway, she wondered if she had tipped him enough, but once he had left and closed the door, she forgot all about him.

Estelita spent the rest of the evening on the luxurious couch, looking out the window. Downstairs was a bustling casino and just outside, the streets of Havana hummed with activity. But she couldn't get herself to step out of the room. Hotel rooms were the one thing in life she knew well. This was nothing like the shabby rooms she had shared with Esteban, this room was a dream. She began to feel that old familiar loneliness, as if Esteban was out for the night and all she had to do was wait until morning. But Esteban was very far away now. Tears sprang to her eyes and she allowed them. A part of her wished she hadn't excluded Barbarita and Rosario. Perhaps if they were here, she thought, their mindless chatter would chase away the memories of endless hotel rooms in countless little towns, of hurricanes and unimaginable fear, of a little girl without a mother, of Aspirrina's knock on the door, how that knock had changed her life, brought her here, to this very moment, to opulence and success she had never imagined. She curled up on the couch, exhausted and she fell asleep right where she was. The luxurious beds, all three of them, remained untouched.

The following morning, after taking in the view from her window, which had been as breathtaking as Jorge had suggested, she dressed impeccably and went to the designated spot in front of the casino. She felt uncomfortable, the dark thoughts of the night before still swirling in her head. I will get used to it, she told herself. It's only a temporary room in a hotel. Hotel rooms were not a home. Home is what she was bartering for, home was a house by the sea with her father at her side and this job was one more step toward it.

Barbarita and Rosario were already there; their dresses too tight and their makeup much too bright for daytime.

"Good morning," Estelita said. Barbarita and Rosario looked at each other and giggled at a private joke. Estelita allowed them their childish pleasure, she knew the next few days were going to be difficult but she also knew she would get through these difficulties as she always had, but keeping herself calm, letting it all blow past her like dry leaves off a tree. She was not at all surprised when, the instant the car arrived, Barbarita claimed the front seat, hopped in, and locked the door.

"I get the front seat on the way back," Rosario warned her.

Estelita didn't argue. She couldn't blame the girls for being vindictive, after all, she had robbed them. For a moment she considered taking it all back, inviting them to share the room, but she couldn't. She needed something of her own and that room, sad and lonely as it was, was it.

The first week of training took place in a classroom near the airport. The room had evidently been used formerly for storage and lost luggage. In one corner, there were some cardboard boxes with faded addresses printed on them longhand as well as some sad looking suitcases and a smelly mop and a bucket. It had all been pushed to the corners to make room for their desks. The windowless room was so close to the runway that every time an airplane landed, the bucket rattled on the worn tile floor.

The instructor was Dorita Durán. Señorita Durán, as she liked to be called, was a fifty-something former stewardess for Cubana de Aviacion, Cuba's only airline.

She greeted the girls with a dissatisfied look.

"Oh, you're all much too tall," she said. "Legitimate airlines have a five-foot-five limit for stewardesses. But I suppose that in Lansky's world, there are no such rules."

Most of the first day, Estelita, Barbarita, and Rosario sat in uncomfortable desks - the kind you find in an elementary school classroom - and listened with indifference to Durán's life story.

"My father," she told them, "was fascinated with airplanes but never flew in one. Our house was decorated with model airplanes that he spent all his free time assembling. I finished high school and right after, started flying with Cubana. By the time I was twenty-two, I had been everywhere in the world, had served drinks and peanuts to some of the most famous and influential men in the world. That's how I met my husband, on a flight from New York to Havana. Now I'm both divorced and retired from flying. I have agreed to teach you what I know, not because I need the money, but as a favor to Mr. Lansky."

She did not ask the girls anything about themselves, much to Estelita's relief.

Barbarita and Rosario hated her on sight. Durán left them alone for the afternoon meal, choosing to go to a restaurant in the city rather than eat at the airport caféteria. And no sooner had she turned her back than Rosario and Barbarita unleashed a torrent of venom.

"Who does that bruja think she is?" Rosario asked.

"Yeah," added Barbarita, "I may be too tall, but not so tall that I can't bofetear su cara de culo all the way back to her daddy's house."

"Who knows," Estelita ventured, "maybe you'll also meet your husbands on one of the flights."

Barbarita and Rosario looked her up and down with unmitigated hostility.

"We're not looking for husbands, cariño," Barbarita said.

"And end up like Dorita Durán? Olvidate. Forget it." Rosario added.

Estelita remained silent. Meeting the man of your dreams on an airplane didn't sound so bad to her.

"And what is this favor to Lansky?" she heard Barbarita ask as they walked away.

"Do you think she's one of those degenerate gamblers and owes el patrón a lot of dólares?"

"I would not be one bit surprised," Rosario said.

The rest of the week they spent learning how to walk while in flight, and the proper way to bend over to serve a drink without spilling it. They learned how to greet the passengers as they arrived, the layout of the airplane, and all the safety regulations. Señorita Durán brought in maps and graphs and showed them routes and geographical details, preparing them for questions that may be asked. It was almost too much to take in, but Durán seemed to have inexhaustible patience and always talked to them as if they were children learning about life for the first time. This, Barbarita and Rosario didn't appreciate. By the third day Barbarita and Rosario had started to thaw towards Estelita, having now found a new adversary. They even asked Estelita to join them at lunch. She was surprised and flattered. She had never had friends her own age and as they walked to the restaurant she felt breezy, happy. The moment they sat down her tablemates began to complain. Ah, so this is what I've been missing, Estelita said to herself.

"She talks to us like we're mentally retarded," Barbarita grumbled.

"Why do we have to learn all that geography? It's only a half-hour flight," demanded Rosario. "I just want to get on that airplane and have some fun."

They complained endlessly at every meal, but in class they were surprisingly attentive.

At the end of each session, Durán stood in front of them, her fingers interlaced, her eyes narrowed, and always said the same thing.

"Preguntas?" Questions?

No one ever had any.

Every evening Estelita rushed back to the hotel, to her own spacious suite. As the days passed, it had become her place. The anxiety of that first night did not return. She moved her things into the master bedroom and had become addicted to long, luxurious bubble baths. She spent hours soaking in the warm, perfumed water before she joined the others in the dressing room. After the second show, there was no more running back to the convent, she simply dressed and strolled across the casino floor to the elevator, pressed her number, and she was home. Night after night, she sat at the window sipping a glass of Coca-Cola and looking out at the twinkling lights below. And every night, the late flight from Miami would cross the sky, its red light flashing. "Soon I'll be up there, singing and dancing inside one of those silver birds," Estelita would say to herself. The prospect felt unreal, and she could hardly contain her excitement.

The second week of training, they got to board the airplane that would soon become their second home. And the lessons became more practical, if somewhat more humiliating.

"Rosario," Señorita Durán screeched, "we do not stick our buttocks in the face of the man behind us! We bend our knees, my dear, bend our knees."

A week before the first official flight, Estelita was introduced to her accompanist, a man simply known as Tonti. He was a friendly black man with a humble manner when it came to everything except his music. The first time he set foot on the plane and took one look at the reduced, sawed-off piano he was expected to play, he shuddered.

"Oh, the indignities of a musician's life," he sighed. But he sat at the instrument and gently caressed the ivory keys, as though it were a sickly child. Soon, the cabin was vibrating with beautiful music.

Señorita Durán stood with arms crossed as the girls went through the paces. While Tonti played, Estelita was to sing and dance up and down the aisles with as much grace and enthusiasm as possible and without crashing into Rosario and Barbarita, who would be sashaying back and forth, taking orders and delivering cocktails and appetizers to imaginary passengers.

"Rosario, keep your eyes up," Señorita Durán said, "always look to see what's coming. You don't need to look at the passengers' faces to serve them. Barbarita, be aware that during this song, Estelita has turns, give her space."

They moved up and down the short narrow aisle again and again.

"All right now, we're going to pretend the plane is moving. Remember, if it tilts to the left, you place your right foot behind you. If to the right, the opposite. Now, pretend we're tilting to the left. No, Rosario, not that foot! If this was an actual flight, the passenger would be soaked in daiquiri right now. Do you have any idea how difficult it is to get the smell of spilled daiquiri out of airplane carpeting? I'm sure you don't."

It went on like that, day after day, with Tonti banging on the keyboard, Estelita trying to perform, and Barbarita and Rosario, according to Señorita Durán, incapable of doing anything right. Then rushing back to the hotel to get ready for the evening's performance.

The days passed quickly and ready or not, it was time for a real test-flight. Everyone was nervous, even Durán seemed more tense than usual. The flight was scheduled for later in the day. During the afternoon meal, Barbarita and Rosario were more vicious than ever.

"If she tells me one more time to get my ass out of somebody's face, I'm going to smack her," Rosario said.

Estelita barely heard them anymore. She was thrilled that in just a few hours she'd be on her first flight. They were only going to circle Havana a few times to see how everybody would do, and she was certain it was going to be all right. She liked the airplane, the red and orange seats, she even liked the red and orange uniforms they had to wear. Hers was trimmed with sparkles because she was the entertainer.

Barbarita's and Rosario's were not.

That day, they hardly touched their lunch, and returned to the classroom early. Durán was there, talking to a man in a dark suit. His back was to the door, but Estelita immediately knew who it was.

"Girls, this is Señor Talente. He was sent here by the casino to accompany us on our first flight."

He turned and his eyes went directly to Estelita, as if he'd anticipated seeing her.

"Call me Juan Carlos," he said, introducing himself. Barbarita and Rosario were immediately awash in a sea of fluttering lashes, giggles and squeals. But all of that ended when he turned to Estelita.

"You, I've met before," he said with a smile. She tried smiling back, but her mouth wasn't working properly.

"Yes," she managed to say, "it's very nice to see you again." Barbarita and Rosario exchanged a look that could only be interpreted as gut-churning envy.

"Fine, so now that we're all good friends," Durán interrupted, clapping her hands loudly. "Let's get on that airplane and show Señor Talente what we can do. We don't want him going back to Señor Lansky telling him you're all hopelessly clumsy."

Soon the motors were humming and the propellers were spinning. Tonti sat at his piano. Barbarita and Rosario were in special seats near the back galley, cocktail shakers at the ready. Juan Carlos sat in the fourth row, next to Señorita Durán.

Estelita waited in the galley, behind a sparkly curtain. She would make her entrance once the plane had stabilized. All her courage had vanished. It would be different, singing and dancing for a plane full of strangers. But this was just insane, to sing and dance not only for the demanding Señorita Durán, but also Juan Carlos Talente. How was she going to get through this flight?

They zoomed up to the sky, she heard the wheels retracting, they were up in the clouds. When Tonti started playing her introduction, all her apprehensions melted away.

She stepped out into the aisle and did the show she had rehearsed over and over. Rosario and Barbarita walked back and forth as if the airplane were filled with passengers. They brought out drinks expertly, and managed to keep away from Estelita as if they had been born with avoidance radar, like fruit bats.

Estelita fought a wave of nausea while she danced up and down the aisle and sang song after song. Halfway through her act she introduced Tonti. The words just came to her, recalling the countless times she had heard her father introduce the band.

"The man with the magic hands," she said, tossing her blonde mane in his direction, "now has magic wings as well!"

She sang a few more songs and wished everyone a happy vacation. Just as Durán had taught her.

"See you on the flight home!" she sang out and went back behind the curtain.

There was no applause, just the droning of the motors. Then she heard it, Juan Carlos clapping just for her. She smiled to herself, lost in a fantasy that would have made the nuns say extra prayers for her soul. They were descending, the voice of the pilot told them to get ready for landing. The wheels hit the ground with a gentle thud and the airplane came to a full stop. The stairs were rolled quickly to the door and attached. Barbarita and Rosario were the first to rush out, chattering with excitement.

Estelita walked down alone, Juan Carlos and Señorita Durán right behind her.

"I'm very impressed," Juan Carlos was saying.

"Make sure you share your sentiments with my old friend Lansky," Señorita Durán said with a sheen of delight in her voice. The motors of a nearby airplane drowned out the rest of the conversation.

The sun was beginning to set and Estelita inhaled the beautiful golden light. Suddenly someone touched her elbow. She turned to look.

"You were just great up there," Juan Carlos shouted over the noise.

"Thank you, I sort of felt like a trained monkey and I almost threw up," she shouted back.

"Well," he said, "what I saw was impressive." But she signaled that she couldn't hear him. They rushed into the small airport as the airplane took to the air and the world was silent once again.

"May I take you in my car?" he asked.

"Thank you, but I have to rush back and get ready for the show." Her hands were starting to shake, so she took hold of her elbow. Her heart was beating hard but she ignored it. She took a step back, the nearness of him was taking away her breath, she started to walk away.

"I have to return to the casino, too."

She stopped as if to consider his offer. Señorita Durán walked past them. Rosario and Barbarita were already out of sight.

"Sure, you can take me in your fancy car," she said with a teasing smile as she had seen women do. The smile was frozen on her face and she felt her cheeks begin to tremble. Was she flirting? The nausea she had felt on the airplane returned, but she fought it, took a

214

deep breath.

"I didn't say it was fancy," he teased back. "If you want fancy you may want to wait for a better offer."

Her heart soared. The ice had been broken. He drove slowly, as if he wanted the drive to last forever. The car was air-conditioned and the cool air soothed her nerves.

They drove in silence and after a few blocks she began to relax. She had to say something, but what?

"Do you like working for Lansky?" she asked him.

"Yes. Compared to where I come from, it's the greatest job in the world. And you?"

"I don't really feel like I work for Lansky. Maybe I'm crazy but I feel like I work for the audience."

He nodded silently.

"That wasn't my question," he said after a while.

"Well, I've only met him once," she answered earnestly, surprised at how easily the words were coming to her lips. "He's been very kind and very generous."

"He's been like that with me, too."

The car moved into the center of town; the streets narrowed. Estelita turned to look out of her side window. People crowded the sidewalks. She felt a churning in her stomach. She suddenly felt unsafe and unsure. She shouldn't have accepted this ride, should have returned to the casino with Barbarita and Rosario, but at the time, it seemed irresistible. She had thought about Juan Carlos so often and now, just sitting here next to him it felt as if maybe there was a chance that he liked her, that he'd like to know her better. But she'd had so little experience talking intimately with a man. What did the other girls talk about?

She allowed herself a glance in his direction. He was so handsome, particularly now, with his face set in a serious expression. He seemed almost sad. It made her want to run her hands through his dark, lustrous hair, to kiss his cheeks, to make him happy, to make him love her. His beautiful eyes were looking forward, set somewhere in the distance. She tried to think of something else to say, but her mind seemed stuck in this desire to touch him. She noticed that all the people on the sidewalk were going in the same direction, and moving very fast. Some were even running.

"Where do you think everyone's going?" she asked.

"There must be some trouble up ahead," he said calmly, like a man who was used to trouble. "Don't worry, I know my way around."

Seemingly out of nowhere, a mob came running out of a side street. There seemed to be hundreds of them. She could hear sirens and screams. A man threw himself on the hood of the car, banging on their windshield. Another tried to open the car door. Estelita looked around. They were doing the same to all the cars on the street.

Fortunately, their doors were locked. Juan Carlos quickly drew a revolver and aimed it at the man who was banging on the windshield. The man saw the weapon, shrieked, and fell away.

Juan Carlos placed the gun on the seat between them, turned the steering wheel sharply to the right and managed to get the car off the main thoroughfare and onto a narrow side street. People jumped to get out of the way, some of the pedestrians banged on the roof of the car and screamed curses at them as they passed. Juan Carlos continued, at first slowly, as slowly as it was safe, and then as the street cleared, he went faster until they had left the crowds behind.

"Another senseless demonstration," he said, his voice full of contempt.

She remembered that night when she'd had to run all the way back to the convent in her bare feet.

"Yes, I was trapped in one of these a few months back," she said, her eyes on the gun between them. "It's horrible, not knowing when or where there's going to be trouble."

She couldn't take her eyes off the gun. She had never been so close to one before and it made her heart beat at a gallop.

"Can you put that away, please?"

Juan Carlos looked at the gun as if he'd forgotten it was there. He stopped the car and with a swift movement reached his hand across her; his hand brushed her knee sending an electric charge up her spine. He opened the glove compartment and tossed the gun into it casually as if it were a pack of cigarettes or a pair of glasses.

"I'm sorry I frightened you," he said.

She nodded, but all she could see were those eyes, those beautiful eyes, and those lips. When he reached forward to kiss her, she didn't back away as she feared she might.

Instead, she moved forward to meet him, softly at first, then deeper and with more desperation. She was aware of their breathing. She clung to him, pressing herself against his chest, as if she were deathly ill and he was her cure, her medicine, her last bit of hope.

They continued kissing. She wondered how long a kiss should last – he kissed her for what could have been fifteen seconds or fifteen hours. She had lost all sense of time.

He kissed her again when he dropped her off at the casino. He encircled her waist with his powerful arms and brought her closer against him. She felt his hardness press against her, and it was nothing she had ever imagined. In all the nights she had spent wondering what it would be like to feel a man's desire, she had never conjured such a feeling.

She managed to break away and ran into the hotel, her sharp heels clicking loudly on the terrazzo floors. It was a happy, urgent sound. She rushed into her room, locked the door and collapsed on the couch. Now she understood what the songs she had been singing since she was a little girl really meant. She understood the emotions her father chased night after night, woman after woman. Finally, it all made sense. What had just happened with that man? What was this feeling he had brought to her and why did she want more? She imagined that her fingers were his fingers, let them travel up her thigh as she murmured his name, "Juan Carlos, Juan Carlos, JUAN CARLOS!"

When she stood up, her legs still quivered. She covered her face with her hands. She felt happy and confused. The world, which up to this point only encompassed as far as her eyes could see, seemed very big and frightening. She was aware that she had entered a deep, dark wilderness, and she was hopelessly lost.

And that she had no one to tell.

*

The airplane plunged faster, farther, bringing her back to a terrifying reality. All had gone so well on the practice flights, and now on their first flight with actual passengers, it looked as if it might be their last. The Mexican man's hand tightened around hers. Estelita prayed even harder. She prayed for the safety of this stranger who was sitting next to her. She prayed that she would see Juan Carlos one more time. Just one more time, God. But the airplane continued to buck as if it were riding over rocks rather than flying in the air.

Tonti's piano had flown open and its keys were making horrible sounds, nothing like music.

And then, just as suddenly as it had begun, the turbulence stopped. The passengers burst into nervous applause and shouts of gratitude to God, consecrating their lives to good deeds.

The captain's voice, haggard and raspy, announced that the turbulence had passed, they were safe and would be landing shortly. She wondered what it must have been like for him, there in that cockpit, wrestling against the winds, knowing so many lives were in his hands. She offered a quick prayer for the captain. She was still holding the stranger's hand and he was looking at her. Slowly, her face burning bright red, she withdrew her hand. He smiled. He was older than she remembered, maybe forty, maybe fifty. Dark skin, black eyes, and a mustache much too big for his face.

"Are you all right, Señorita?" he asked.

"Yes, thank you."

"Thank God," he said, then laughed at himself. "Nothing like a little trouble in the heavens to make everybody turn religious."

It sounded like something her cynical father would have said.

"My name is Hugo Benavides," he said.

"Estelita de la Cruz." They shook hands. Her heart was still beating fast, but as she heard the wheels descend and felt the airplane tilt slightly forward, towards earth, she started to calm down. As soon as the doors opened, all the American passengers stood up abruptly as if they had springs coiled inside of them. There was a frantic gathering of bags from the overhead compartments. Estelita remained seated, her stomach still queasy, her hands still shaking. Through the windows she could see the passengers running as fast as their luggage would allow towards waiting towncars and taxis. They had apparently lost what little faith got them through the chaotic flight, for they ran as if the airplane was on fire and about to explode.

"Look at them go," Barbarita said.

"They won't be getting on an airplane any time soon," Rosario added.

218

Estelita hadn't even noticed that the two girls were standing behind her, looking though the same window. As they watched her, a long, black limousine slowly appeared on the tarmac, cutting through the melee as sure as a shark. The uniformed driver jumped out, ran around and opened the door for Señor Benavides.

"Did you see that?" Rosario asked as the car silently vanished in the distance.

"See what?" Estelita replied.

"Your friend just got into the biggest, shiniest, most luxurious car I've ever seen."

"Oh, did he?" Estelita said as she gathered her things and stood up to go.

But Estelita had definitely noticed the car, the chauffeur, and the casual arrogance with which Señor Benavides had accepted both.

He was undoubtedly a man quite accustomed to the finer things in life. As she watched the car drive down the tarmac and onto the road that led to the city, she thought about her father, his failed dreams, his shattered life.

Soon, Papá, she told herself, I will come for you and bring you to this crazy city called La Habana where everything is bigger, shinier, and luxurious. This amazing place of tall buildings, big cars, and music. This place where everything you ever dreamed is suddenly within reach.

22

Aspirrina lifted the back of her black veil and mopped the sweat from her thick neck. But her efforts were futile. No sooner had she mopped than more rivulets flowed down her back and between her breasts. She had tried to remove her veil but Maria had forbidden it.

They were in an old Ford panel van, headed east on Carretera Central, the Central Highway. The van was filled to capacity with clothes, medicine, cans of oil, salt and powdered-milk purportedly for the orphans of Santiago de Cuba. But underneath it all they were also carrying ten machine guns, eleven Johnson rifles, two Thompson submachine guns and three crates of ammunition. No bombs or dynamite. It had been judiciously agreed that the trip was dangerous enough without explosives.

"I would go nude if I could," Aspirrina said.

"No amount of disrobing is going to change the temperature," Sor Maria replied. She was right, nothing was going to change the horrible, blistering humidity.

Aspirrina didn't have the energy to quarrel. It was just too hot, hotter than any hell she could have imagined. It had been raining since they left Havana. In between rainstorms, the full, fiery sun continued to shine, boiling the water on the ground, sending up waves of steam.

"I don't know how you do it," Aspirrina said after a long moment of silence.

While Sor Maria continued driving, Aspirrina tugged at the neck of the black habit she wore.

"All that fidgeting is just going to make it worse," the nun said.

Aspirrina looked at her, she seemed perfectly cool and comfortable even in the heavy black habit. Years of practice, she figured, that's why they call it a habit. Years of living in perpetual sacrifice had left her immune to discomfort. Sor Maria drove. Aspirrina had never driven in her life and Maria, who had learned to drive as a teenager at her father's hacienda, hadn't driven in a very long time. But she seemed to be doing well enough.

Traffic was light on the two-lane highway. Cuba had been sliced in two, the break came at Las Villas, in the middle of the island. The rebels had made sure of it by blowing up bridges and even the train-tracks that connected east and west. Batista's men were on full alert. Suspects were being dragged out of their homes at all hours of the night and taken in for interrogation. Reports of horrors being inflicted traveled by word of mouth from one end of the island to the other.

The president was feeling the pressure of the revolt and had seemingly abandoned all sense of humanity, people said. Tales of barbaric torture, of men stripped naked and covered with metal plates; days and nights of questioning, during which the soldiers banged on the metal plates with hammers, pulverizing bones, crushing ribs to powder.

Even after a confession was obtained, even if the confession was invented just to stop the pummeling, there was no healing, there was only death. Death, one blow of the hammer at a time; the loud banging of metal against metal competing with the screams. Metal against metal, neighbor against neighbor, brother against brother, Cuban against Cuban. The captive and the captor had the same face, the same language, only a murky political ideology divided them.

Sor Maria knew she could hide no longer. She clutched the steering wheel, grateful that the screams of injustice were louder than her fears. The road was pocked with deep holes covered by rivers of water that flowed with such force that it continually lifted the wheels and made the vehicle swerve from side to side. She had to watch for the holes the way a river-man watches for boulders below the surface, she had to keep ever vigilant.

The trip was an enormous sacrifice in a life already dedicated to sacrifice. It must be God's will. How else could she explain five years of living in the relative security of her convent and having this suddenly thrust upon her? Of course she had been apprehensive, she was, after all, a reasonable person, logical to a fault. But from the moment Delfino had returned to her life, from the moment she had opened the back door of the convent and allowed him to store contraband in the basement, she knew there would be no turning back. After years of hiding in obscurity she was forced to rejoin the human race.

Now, as she gripped the steering wheel, Aspirrina in a nun's habit asleep at her side, and the weapons of war in the back, she felt more human than ever, as vulnerable as a newborn baby. She had to have faith, but she was frightened.

She filled her heart with prayer, the prayers connected her to God and after that, it was up to Him. It wasn't all selfishness and patriotism that had put her on this hot, wet road. She needed to protect her sisters. Havana was so dangerous at the moment that she would have done anything to get the weapons out of the basement. She had gambled not just with her own life, but with the lives of the innocent women who lived in the convent and had no idea what was going on below. If she had to pay with her life, then so be it.

As she drove, Sor Maria was glad that at least the sisters back at the convent were safe for the time being. Aspirrina continued sleeping and Sor Maria was grateful for the silence. With all her complaining and nagging, it actually had been Aspirrina's idea to put on the habit. She had been rabid that night when she returned from the demonstration, wet and defeated.

She met Arjuna and Delfino in the little gothic parlor in the convent, said a cursory hello, and ran up to her room. She had returned a few moments later in a clean, dry dress, her face fully made up as if she were going to a dance, and had taken a seat among them. When she heard that Arjuna and Delfino needed to transport the weapons to

222

Santiago, Aspirrina had immediately volunteered to go.

"That's insane," Sor Maria had said to her with an apologetic smile to the men.

"Listen," Aspirrina said, her words serious as if she were an expert strategist, "you two will be stopped, searched and shot before you reach the city limits. Maria can drive. I'll go with her and I'll wear a habit. Who's going to suspect a couple of nuns?"

Maria had held the arms of her chair until her knuckles hurt.

"I can't let you do this, Maria," Delfino said.

Maria silently assessed the situation.

"Look," Aspirrina continued, impassioned, "nothing's going to happen. We'll cover the weapons with blankets and food and if anyone asks, we'll say we're delivering it to an orphanage in Santiago."

"You make it sound simple," Delfino said, "but if you're stopped, they will shoot you on the spot, for treason."

"They would never do that," Aspirrina countered. "Do you know what it would do to Batista if word got out that his men are shooting nuns? Nuns in Cuba are like cows in India. Kill one and that would be it. That would be the final victory. So, you see, we have nothing to lose. And, I'll bring a gun. You have a gun, right? If some bastard tries to look through our stuff, I'll shoot him between the eyes."

Maria and Delfino both shuddered at the thought.

"She's right, you know," Arjuna said.

"Damn right," Aspirrina added, then looked at Maria. "You coming?"

Maria remained quiet.

"Look, sister," Aspirrina said, "you can continue to waste away your life in this mausoleum polishing candlesticks and embroidering useless crap – or you can do something truly meaningful, something that could very well change the world."

Her words had stung Maria as an unwelcome truth always did. At that moment she could have jumped up and strangled Aspirrina with her bare hands. To say these things to her, in front of men, in front of her friend. What did she know? How dare she make her life sound so meaningless?

Delfino and Arjuna were clearly embarrassed for her, but didn't come to her defense. The reality of her life had been laid out before her

223

like a map. Now it was up to Sor Maria to choose which way to turn. She believed that there was a reason for everything. This must be the right thing to do, must be what God wanted of her. Why else would he have allowed this horrible woman to intrude so deeply into her life?

While Delfino and Arjuna packed up the van, Maria had retreated to her room and fallen to her knees. She prayed until she and she wept until she was shaking. Never in her life had she felt such terror. Where was her faith now? Where was her certainty that God would guide and protect her? She searched in the infinity of her soul, but could not find God. Maybe if she prayed harder, maybe if she searched further. But all she could find was darkness and despair. Like a sleepwalker, she stood up, walked out of the room and joined the others.

Aspirrina was waiting by the back door, dressed in a black habit with only her moonish face exposed to the light.

"What do you think, do I pass for a nun?" she asked.

Maria couldn't help smiling.

"You look perfect, sister," she said.

To her surprise, Aspirrina threw her arms around her. She held her tight, and Maria could feel the woman trembling. For all her bluster, Aspirrina was afraid too. At that moment, Maria found the God who had eluded her earlier.

The rains let up around Camaguey only to be replaced by thunder. Veins of lightning seared the sky. She stopped for gasoline just outside of Camaguey. The doors and windows of most of the houses were closed, as if they were vacant.

"This is rebel territory," the boy at the pump said, "everybody is gone because of the bombs."

"What bombs?" Sor Maria asked.

"Above and below," said the boy, "above and below."

From that moment on, she was even more vigilant. The thunder had stopped and she missed it. It was too quiet. Even Aspirrina, who seemed to have retreated somewhere inside herself, was silent, her eyes darting from one side of the road to the other.

For miles all she could hear was the crunching of the tires on the gravel and the whooshing wind. Suddenly, she heard the sound of an airplane. She looked up and saw a small one in the distance, it was flying low over the highway towards them. She could see the machine-gun mounted in one of its windows, aimed at them. Blood pumped hard in her temples.

"Estamos jodidas, sister," Aspirrina whispered, raising her eyes sky. We're fucked.

Maria ignored the profanity and kept her pace. Her foot on the accelerator felt numb but she kept her eye on the speedometer. Do not slow down, do not speed up, just keep steady. Just keep steady.

Aspirrina expected at any time to feel the impact of bullets ripping through her body.

"We're going to die, right here, in the middle of nowhere," she said.

"Don't say that," Sor Maria said, her voice louder and sharper than intended. "Just pray, Aspirrina. If you've never prayed before in your life, this is the time."

Aspirrina looked at her with a roll of her eyes, doubting that even a million prayers would help them now.

"For you, I'll pray, but not for me," she said.

"Fine," Sor Maria said, her eyes on the road, "Then I will pray for you."

They continued in silence, the sound of the airplane circling above. An eternity passed, but they continued moving forward. And then, the sound was behind them. The airplane had passed.

"God heard our prayers," Sor Maria exclaimed.

"Sure." Aspirrina didn't tell Sor Maria that she didn't know any prayers. That instead, while waiting to die, she had sung a song to herself from not so long ago, when Estelita was still in her care and had taken the stage because her father was too drunk to perform.

Take my heart, it is only a heart
Hold it in your hand
All through the night
And at daybreak, open your
Hand and let the sun's rays warm it...

For the rest of the drive, Aspirrina waited for the airplane to shower bullets upon them. Or to land in front of them on the highway, forcing them to stop. But nothing so dramatic ever happened. As they approached their destination, traffic started to get a little thicker, other cars and trucks passed in both directions. Soon, they were turning off the Central Highway and onto the uneven cobblestone streets of Santiago. The city was built on a sequence of hills overlooking a large bay, with the Sierra Maestra mountains in the background. The city of Santiago was fully awake when they arrived. People dodged cars and carts with ease as they walked along the narrow streets. The roofs of the houses were built so low that Aspirrina could see each curving tile. In all her travels, she had never been to Santiago, it was too big a city for Sabrosuras, and she could hardly contain her excitement. She sat back as Sor Maria guided them to the top of a hill on Heredia Street. From there she could see the copper-topped domes of the cathedral. Across from the cathedral was Cespedes Park and in that park was their contact. Arjuna said to look for a man named Jose Aguilera. He would be selling churros out of a cart. They arrived at the park and circled it twice, dismayed that there seemed to be a dozen men selling churros out of carts.

"I'll just have to get out and ask each and every one of them," Aspirrina said with irritation.

She left Sor Maria in the vehicle, the motor idling and probably attracting too much attention. She was back almost immediately.

"I found him," she announced.

"So fast?"

"I only had to ask one person, the churro vendors all know each other. They sent me right to him."

"What do we do now?" Sor Maria asked.

"We go to the Cemetery of Santa Ifigenia," said Aspirrina. "It's Sunday so everyone here visits the dead. It won't seem unusual that we're there. We need to go behind the Jose Martí memorial and all the way to the end, as far against the fence as possible, and look for a woman named Celia Sanchez. She'll know what to do."

"Where is this cemetery?" Sor Maria asked, frowning. "Why can't Jose Aguilera take the stuff out of the vehicle and be done with it? I'm not comfortable circling the city loaded with contraband. There are police cars everywhere and I'm not familiar with the streets."

"Relax," Aspirrina said. "He gave me directions, it's simple."

Everything was simple to Aspirrina, Sor Maria thought as she guided the car away from the park and followed her directions to the outskirts of the city and to the Cementerio de Ifigenia. Throngs of women, most holding at least one child by the hand, carried flowers through the gates of the cemetery. Just inside the gates, two gigantic marble statues of angels, with wide wings made of burnished bronze, greeted visitors. She had to drive at a snail's pace due to the groups of people who couldn't care less that a car was behind them.

Once inside the cemetery, they veered onto a small road. A large sign guided them to Jose Martí's tomb. From there, they continued to the back of the cemetery. They passed families standing around the large, above-ground marble graves. Some families had their heads bowed in prayer, others chattered to each other or weeded and raked leaves, some brought buckets of water and were busy washing the grime off the headstones. No one paid much attention to them as they drove past, and the ones who did waved pleasantly.

Aspirrina waved back enthusiastically.

"Don't do that," Sor Maria said, "remember who you are."

"Sorry, I forgot I was a nun."

They turned the corner until they were driving along the back wall of the cemetery. There were fewer people working on graves so deep into the cemetery, as if the dead in the back had no one left on earth to tend their graves. In the distance, they saw the figure of a small, thin woman, dark skinned and dark eyed, deeply sucking on a cigarette. As they drew closer, the woman tossed down the cigarette and ran to the driver's side.

"My name is Celia Sanchez," she said, her tone direct, her gaze firm. "Are you the friends of Arjuna?"

"Yes, I am Sor Maria and--"

But the woman had heard enough.

"Follow me," she said and hurried ahead of them to a narrow, vine-covered gate.

The lock, Sor Maria noticed, had been cut. Celia Sanchez disappeared for a second and returned with three young men. Without a word, the men opened the back of the van and started to unload everything so fast that it was dizzying. Sweat poured from their foreheads as they ran back and forth through the gate. Celia stood aside, keeping watch in all directions. When everything had been unloaded she stopped once more at the window to thank them and then she was gone.

"Wait five minutes, if I'm not back, go," Aspirrina said to Sor Maria as she opened the door and jumped out of the van.

"Aspirrina, you can't be serious," Maria said, but her words were lost in the silence of the graveyard, Aspirrina had dashed through the gate.

Sor Maria waited five minutes and then five minutes more. With a heavy heart she turned the van around and slowly made her way out of the cemetery. She passed the mourners and the giant angels, she found her way back to the cathedral and Cespedes Park. She stopped to consider her next step, feeling lost without Aspirrina. Across from the cathedral was a beautiful hotel called Casa Grande. Delfino had slipped money into her pocket. She had started to protest, but he had stopped her.

"In case of emergency," he had said. She counted the money – there was more than enough for one night. She parked the van and walked towards the hotel. On the sidewalk she was approached by a couple of beggars, a man and a woman. The man was silver-haired and was dressed completely in white. The woman met her eyes and extended a hand as pink and plump as a little girl's.

"Can you help us with some coins, sister?" she asked. Maria reached into her pockets, retrieved one of the bills. She handed it to her without looking at its value.

"Twenty pesos!" the woman said, her eyes lighting up, "that's very generous. Thank you sister, may the saints bless you."

The man looked at her with a touch of arrogance, as if begging was beneath him. His eyes were warm and she felt that he was not just grateful, but moved. She watched as they walked quickly down the sidewalk. Still distressed by Aspirrina's sudden departure, Sor Maria wondered what it would be like to have a partner who accompanied you through the ups and downs of life. Inside the grand lobby of the elegant hotel, a well-fed concierge greeted her warmly.

228

"Good afternoon, sister," he said smiling.

"Good afternoon," she responded, but didn't have the energy to smile back.

"I would like a room for the night," she said.

"Right away, sister."

She was exhausted and hungry. She removed her veil and her dress and dusted them. Her white head-band had brown sweat stains. She washed it clean in the sink, and then rinsed her brassiere and underpants and hung them over a chair to dry. She treated herself to a long, cool shower. Afterwards she put her black habit over her naked body. It felt strange but liberating to have nothing underneath.

She placed her black veil over her head, a strip of hair showed where the headband usually covered it. She had not shown her hair in public for several years and it felt as daring as exposing a rouged knee. But she decided not to care. No one knew her in Santiago.

She walked down to the lobby. The hotel reminded her of her parents' house. Everything about it was spacious and elegant. Chandeliers twinkled overhead. Thick Persian carpets covered the polished marble floors. Mirrors in gilded frames and oil paintings of sensuous dark women hung from the walls. She sat alone in the ornate dining room and ate her meal. Everyone who walked by nodded politely. She nodded back. No one knew, no one could tell, that underneath her habit she was completely naked, or that in the last forty-eight hours she had committed an act of high treason.

After her meal, she returned to her room feeling satisfied and overwhelmingly lonely. This was the first time since she joined the order that she had been alone, completely alone. She lay on the big, comfortable bed and thought back to the day's events. She wondered where Aspirrina was – probably in the back of some truck bouncing along mountain roads, sitting on a cache of arms. She said prayers for Aspirrina and drifted into a deep, dreamless sleep.

She woke up refreshed and relieved, as if the trip to Santiago had been merely a nightmare.

She ate breakfast at the hotel, this time fully dressed, and luxuriated one last time in the splendor of the dining room. She had earned it, she deserved it. The concierge gave her directions back to the

Central Highway.

The highway was clear and although clouds still loomed, the pavement was dry. She was happy to be on her way home, but still felt that strange loneliness, as if Aspirrina had taken part of her with her. Two miles outside of Santiago, she saw the same beggar couple by the side of the road. She had been apprehensive about driving back to Havana on her own. Without giving it too much thought, lest she change her mind, she pulled over.

"Thank you, sister," the man said, "may the saints bless your every step."

"Yes, sister, you are like an angel that has been placed in our path. Your donation last night bought us supper and a room for the night."

"You are very welcome," she said, stepping on the accelerator. "Where are you going now?"

"We're going to Havana," the man said. "Are you going anywhere near there?"

"That is where I live," Sor Maria said with a smile. "What brings you to Havana? It's very dangerous there right now, you know."

"That is precisely why we're going, sister," the man said with a frown. "We're going to find my daughter."

"Maybe you know her," the woman said from the back seat.

The man turned his head slightly towards her.

"Don't be silly," he said. "Havana is a big city, you can't expect everyone to know each other."

"That's right," Sor Maria said laughing, it felt good to laugh. "And the sort of life I lead, I know fewer people than most."

The woman giggled at the thought. "I suppose you're right, sister, I suppose you're right."

The man remained silent. They watched the trees go by, tall, stately palms washed clean by the rains, their fronds glistening in the sunshine. Ahead, the highway stretched forever, towards Havana. Above them the sky was a powder blue and the clouds had lost their heaviness, they were pure white and fluffy, like gigantic stuffed animals floating in air.

"What is your daughter's name?" Maria asked.

Time passed. No one answered. More trees passed. Road signs

230

passed. A truck bulging with sugarcane passed. A field of gardenias passed, the flowers looking like lovely white smiles in the distance. A soft wind picked up their fragrance and brought it into the car.

"Oh, I adore that smell, can you smell that?" the woman asked. But the man seemed lost in his own thoughts. "The gardenia is one of my favorite flowers. I could smell gardenias all day long. Sometimes I pin one to my chest and let the perfume follow me around all day long, even after the flower has turned brown around the edges."

Maria's veil tickled against the back of her neck. She breathed in deeply and smiled. The woman was right, the flowers smelled heavenly. She hadn't felt this good, this free, in a very long time.

They continued on as if the fragrance of the flowers had them in a trance.

"My daughter's name is Estelita," the man said with a long, deep sigh, "Estelita de la Cruz."

23

Estelita struggled out of her costume, a challenge without the help of a dresser. She had rushed out of the dressing room as soon as the show was over and taken the now-familiar back hallways and service elevators up to her room. Off came the bangles and spangles, the satin and tulle, the feathers and rhinestones. She peeled off the mesh stockings and dropped them in a ball on the floor. Once nude she refreshed herself with a light dusting of talcum powder and stood in front of the air conditioner until she felt sufficiently cool and calm. She only had a few minutes to put on her new linen dress and it went on like a dream.

She stopped and took a breathless turn in front of the mirror. She liked what she saw, and knew Juan Carlos would like it too. The dress was sexy, clinging lightly to every curve without squeezing. It was sleeveless, and cut high to the throat in a graceful semicircle, but scooped much lower in back, leaving her shoulders and most of her back exposed. Its gentle champagne color complemented her platinum hair and tan skin to perfection. The desired effect was casual elegance and as she slipped into high-heeled sandals, she felt she had achieved it.

She had come a long way from the faded cotton dress she had come to Havana wearing. Learning how to dress properly for the city had come easily, all she had to do was observe the other girls, leaf through their fashion magazines, figure out how she wanted to look, who she wanted to be, but most importantly how she wished to be perceived. She continued to look in the mirror and gave herself a playful wink as she reached for her perfume. She chose her fragrances with absolute care. Unlike other women who could be smelled yards away, Estelita strongly believed that her scent should only be detected by someone close enough to kiss. And with that rule in mind, she dabbed the tiniest bit of L'air du Temps behind her ears and at the base of her throat. As she did so, she imagined Juan Carlos' lips softly caressing those sensitive parts and a delicious shiver ran up and down her spine.

Downstairs, Juan Carlos watched Estelita floating across the lobby towards him, and could hardly believe his luck. Finally, this gentle beauty was his. Well, not yet, not entirely, but he knew the odds were in his favor. Their first kiss, only a few nights ago, was as fresh in his memory as if it had never ended. He could still taste the sweet flavor of her lips.

"Hola," she said.

She had kept him waiting for half an hour but he didn't care and she didn't mention it. She was worth waiting for, he would have waited all night for her. As the doorman pulled the door open for them, Juan Carlos placed his hand on her naked back, and his fingers tingled at the touch. They stepped out onto the street; it was a balmy Havana night.

"Let's walk," he suggested. He wanted to be seen with her, wanted admiring eyes on them.

She nodded in silent agreement as if she had wished for the same. He took her hand and the press of her flesh sent a shock of pleasure through him. "Does she know?" he wondered as he led the way. She must know, the whole world must know that he was, for the first time in his life, so obviously, so stupidly in love.

The sidewalks were filled with people relishing the summer breeze. Juan Carlos knew Havana better than anyone, and it thrilled him to show it off for her. Everywhere they went he pointed out something of interest, something out of his own past. He wanted to let her in, let her know him.

"That hotel," he said as they passed a crumbling little building awash in neon, "was the first place I ever lived that was truly my own. I was much younger when I lived there, young and broke with a head full of dreams."

He caught her eyes, they were so bright in the night air as he imagined his to be, sharing his memories. They passed a group of shoeshine boys arguing over a customer and as they walked around them, he said, "Those boys are my people, my family."

They walked for blocks and he told her about his childhood in the orphanage.

She told him about traveling with her father and the variety show.

"So, spectacle is in your blood," he said. "I always wondered how girls like you wound up on a stage."

Estelita laughed.

"I suppose you're right. It's all I've ever known, without my father's influence I probably would have ended up a chambermaid at one of the hotels."

"Not for long, I guarantee," he said giving her hand a tiny squeeze.

Neither had known their own mothers and both wanted to have children someday in order to enjoy the family life that had eluded them.

"I must admit, I'm partial to girls, little girls in starched dresses and pigtails," he said.

"Life can be hard for girls," she said. "I want boys, a lot of boys, a whole army of them to look after me."

"I can look after you," he said. "It would be an honor."

She looked away as if embarrassed by his words and he cursed himself for jumping so far ahead. He stopped to face her and looked at her with tenderness. He held her gaze as they waited to cross the spectacularly busy Via Blanca and her smile calmed him. He had not offended her.

"We're almost there," he said. "There's a magnificent singer at this club that I think you're going to love. Her name is La Lupe, have you heard of her?"

"Yes, the girls in the show are crazy about her," she said.

She loved it when he took her by the elbow and guided her across Zapata Avenue. All her life she'd walked alone, now someone was guiding her. They turned onto a smaller, cobblestone street and walked towards a big sign that flashed Club La Red. She was excited to be there and couldn't wait to tell the others that she had seen La Lupe. But, from the looks of it, she doubted that they could get inside. Let alone get a decent table.

There was a huge crowd at the entrance. Everyone was talking loudly to the uniformed doorman, waving money at him. Several photographers with big cameras leaned against a wall, smoking cigarettes.

"They're on the lookout for celebrities," Juan Carlos said. "Everyone in the world comes to see La Lupe."

"Are we going to be able to squeeze in there?" she asked.

"Wait here," he said with a confident smile and left her on the edge of the jammed sidewalk. She watched him work his way through the crowd. He walked right up to the doorman. They exchanged a few words and Juan Carlos signaled for her to join him. The doorman parted the crowd and led them to the door.

Inside it was only slightly less frenetic. The room itself was nothing special. Mirrored walls and round wooden tables. Every table was topped with a red candle and a small, crystal vase full of miniature red and white roses, and it seemed that every table was taken. There were full bottles of liquor at most of the tables and smoldering cigars in all the ashtrays. Bartenders rushed back and forth bringing buckets of ice, colorful bottles of tropical mixers, and silver bowls full of olives, tiny onions, and lemon slices.

A sweating waiter met them at the door.

"Just two?" he asked, mopping his forehead with a napkin.

"Just two," Juan Carlos said, holding up two fingers and smiling.

The waiter surveyed the room. The place was buzzing with joyous, boisterous activity. Dozens of men in fancy suits hopped from table to table, cocktails in one hand, cigarettes or a cigar in the other. The men greeted each other loudly by name, as if the room was filled with long-lost relatives. They shook hands, hugged, patted each other's backs, exchanged business cards, barked drink orders to bartenders.

Matronly women in elegant dresses grouped together sharing outbursts of laughter. Some couples remained seated, quietly sharing intimacies, the men murmuring into feminine ears. Younger women, their patent leather purses tucked under their arms, trailed each other to the powder room, squeezing through the narrow spaces between the crowded tables. They were beautiful women, both young and old, the cream of Havana, the people Estelita never saw for they never went to the casinos, which were for tourists. This was the smart set of Havana – well bred, wealthy and wild.

"I'm sorry sir," the waiter said, "but there are no tables for two available."

Juan Carlos placed a twenty-dollar bill in the waiter's hand.

"Here, my friend, maybe this will help you find one."

The waiter looked at the money with disgust.

"I can get you to a table," he sniffed, "but you will have to share it."

Juan Carlos didn't like the sound of that.

"I will be right back," he whispered to Estelita, and went back outside. He returned a moment later, with the doorman in tow. The doorman called the waiter to him. They moved away from Juan Carlos and Estelita. From where she was standing, Estelita could not hear what was being said, but she watched the doorman poke an index finger into the waiter's shoulder and leave. The waiter returned to them.

"Señor Talente," he said nervously, "I'm sorry about the misunderstanding, please come with me."

He led them to a table that had a 'reserved' sign on it, which he quickly removed. He pulled a chair out for Estelita. The table was so close to the stage that she could have reached out and touched it with the tip of her shoe. A bottle of champagne in an ice bucket and a bottle of Bacardi rum appeared at their table. The waiter poured their drinks expertly, taking his time, as if there was no one else in the room.

Estelita liked the taste of champagne, but sipped the bare minimum, just enough to wet her lips. She had a tremendous fear of alcohol. She watched as Juan Carlos took a large gulp of rum and she shuddered, wondering how that would feel. Memories of her father and what drinking had done to him haunted her.

"This is quite a crowd," she said.

"Yes," Juan Carlos agreed, "High society has taken La Lupe under its wing. Later you will see why."

The room darkened as waiters dashed to fill last-minute orders. All activity stopped, the audience grew expectantly silent. Blue lights appeared on the small stage, which was bare except for a black piano. The back wall of the stage had been painted to resemble a spider web – thin black lines crossed against a pale background. A saxophonist and a trumpeter in dark suits strolled onto the stage and struck the first melancholy notes. They were followed by the pianist in formal tails. He sat on the banquette without a glance at the audience and added a light twinkling of high notes to the already swooning melody. A timbalero joined them; his staccato pounding energized the room until every heart was beating to his rhythm. The other musicians on the stage picked up his tempo, rising to a sultry rumba.

A bright, white spotlight blazed center stage and La Lupe walked on, or rather, erupted onto it.

The audience went wild.

She was a short, curvaceous mulata in a tight, canary-yellow dress. Her processed hair was pulled back severely from her face and teased into a cylindrical sculpture several inches high. Her face was Afro-Cuban perfection, her blazing eyes outlined in thick black pencil, blue eye shadow, a wide, flat nose and full lips painted an incandescent pink. Big, gold hoop earrings dangled from large, mannish earlobes.

La Lupe grinned at the shouting crowd, then turned to her musicians and nodded fiercely. "Uno, dos, tres," and started singing over the boisterous ovation which seemed to go on forever. It was a long, harsh note that emerged from the bottom of her powerful throat and reduced her audience to worshipful silence.

She sang three guarachas in a row; big, rousing street songs sung at such a fast pace that the musicians were huffing to keep up. Her energy was boundless as she prowled the small stage. Thick beads of sweat jumped from her face at every turn. After the third song she stopped and the crowd went wild again.

"La Lupe! La Lupe!" they shouted in unison, banging the tables, stomping their feet.

La Lupe let the hand holding the microphone hang at her side, the other she lifted high in the air.

"Shut up, coño!" she joked, using Havana's favorite obscenity. "We have special guests in the audience and you're all acting like savages."

The audience roared with laughter.

"No manners, these Cubans," she continued. "Listen, you animals, we have a very important person here tonight. I'm not going to point him out because unlike you, I know how to behave in front of classy foreigners."

More laughter.

"Señor Pablo Picasso is here," she whispered into the microphone, as if betraying a confidence. Her announcement was greeted by stunned silence.

"The Spanish artist, you morons, aplauso!" Applaud.

The audience broke out into laughter and applause. La Lupe smiled innocently at someone in the back of the room.

"Before I sing my next song, which I'm dedicating to you, Pablito, I have to tell you a little story."

She paused for effect.

"El Señor Picasso said he wanted to paint me, but he couldn't because he couldn't get me to stand still long enough. As if that mattered, I mean, have you seen his work?"

She laughed holding her stomach.

"And I said, 'paint my soul Pablito, paint my soul!'" She smiled and winked at a short man in the back of the room. "And he said, in that funny French sounding Spanish of his, 'Lupe, it is your soul that cannot sit still.'"

And she slapped herself on her ass and let out what had come to be known as her expression of ecstasy.

"Aishhhh!"

With her thick, ravished voice she sang the most beautiful bolero Estelita had ever heard, "Con Mil Desengaños." (One Thousand Betrayals).

As she sang the slow, tragic song, she scratched at her arms and neck until red welts appeared. Tears blackened by eyeliner ran down her face. By the time the song ended she was slapping the piano player, not playful little pats but hard, painful, blows that threatened to knock him off his stool as if the musician was responsible for the suffering and heartbreak in the song.

Every time she hit him, Estelita cringed. Juan Carlos placed a comforting arm around her. The more La Lupe sang, the wilder and more vicious she became until Estelita wished she were sitting farther back.

A charitable waiter offered La Lupe a glass. She took it and sniffed.

"What is this? Water?" she snarled, "How many times do I have to tell you people, I don't drink anything fish fuck in. Give me something good, something hard."

La Lupe locked eyes with Juan Carlos.

"What are you drinking, handsome?"

He stood up and offered her his glass.

"Rum," he said shyly.

"Aisshhh, that's more like it," she said and drained the glass.

She handed it back to him, her eyes taking full measure of Estelita.

"That's a pretty girl you've got there. But very young."

Estelita felt all eyes turn to her. La Lupe looked at her with a wry smile.

"When you're ready for a real woman, come see me. I'm here every night. Except Sunday, when I'm in church...on my back."

The men started shouting again.

"La Lupe! La Lupe! La Lupe!"

La Lupe took a step back, taking in the clamor.

"You're so vulgar," she shouted at them, "Shut the fuck up!" Then softly, demurely, "I'm trying to sing."

She cued the musicians and continued with her crazy, exhausting, brilliant act. The audience refused to let her finish. She took bow after bow. The house lights came up but the applause continued, as did the table banging, foot stomping, and shouting.

"More! La Lupe! More!"

"All right," she said, "just one more. This one is for those crazy boys up in the mountains trying to make our world a better place to live, God bless their foolish hearts."

And she sang "La Virgen Lloraba" (The Virgin Wept), which

was like a prayer but as interpreted by La Lupe it was not like any prayer heard before. At the end, La Lupe stood at the edge of the stage frowning and as soon as she got her customary standing ovation, shrugged and left the stage.

The crowd milled around disoriented, chattering to one another in reverential voices.

"Isn't she amazing?"

"Can you believe that voice?"

"She's insane!"

Now Estelita understood why this woman was the talk of Havana. She had never imagined anyone could sing and behave that way on a stage. Not even Aspirrina, during her most misguided efforts, could compare. Of course, Aspirrina lacked something that La Lupe had in abundance, raw, peerless talent.

"Let's get out of here," Juan Carlos suggested and she followed him out, eager for fresh air and to recapture the romantic mood that La Lupe had all but demolished with song after song of love gone horribly, excruciatingly awry.

Back on the streets, in spite of the very late hour, Havana was alive and swarming with people. Estelita walked slowly next to Juan Carlos, the back of their hands brushed coyly against one another until he took hers in his and they intertwined their fingers the way she had seen lovers do all over the city. His hand felt large and warm, it enveloped hers completely, and she liked it.

"Did you enjoy La Lupe?" Juan Carlos asked.

"Oh yes, but I feel a little sorry for her, putting herself through all that night after night."

"And you would know about that," he said.

"Well," she said, "my father was a singer. A good one. And all my memories, as far back as I can remember are of the efforts of performers, how much they give, what they hope for in return, what they never get, what they regret."

"You've had a fantastic life," he said, then added, "For me, the sort of entertainment we witnessed tonight seems to be the way of future, and if those crazy rebels in the mountains get their way, it's only going to get more like that. Havana is going to sink further into pain and corruption."

"You truly believe that? Did you find her corrupt?"

"She's inmensely talented, there's no doubt about it, but so cynical," he said, "And I did not appreciate her little tribute to the boys in the mountains. Fidel Castro and his men have given rise to people like La Lupe. If they triumph, you can say goodbye to any sort of decency and restraint. Already, La Lupe imitators are popping up in other clubs, women who expose themselves, have nervous breakdowns and call it entertainment."

"La Lupe reminds me of someone I know," Estelita said, "a woman who came to the city with me. Her name is Aspirrina."

"That's her name?" he asked with a chuckle.

"Yes, you met her," she laughed.

"You mean the one who..."

They both smiled at the memory of their first meeting.

"Unforgettable, isn't she? I never found out if it was her stage name or her real name. She was a dancer but not anymore, she's older now. Just as well, she was an atrocious dancer. But that never stopped her from getting up in front of an audience. And every time she danced, she was shouted off the stage, but time after time she went back out, as if she enjoyed the punishment."

They passed a movie theater that was just letting out. On the marquee the name María Felix, the famous Mexican actress, appeared large above the title.

"I would like to meet this so-called Aspirrina again," Juan Carlos said.

"I haven't seen her in a few months. We had a little difference of opinion."

"About what?"

"About how to run my life."

"Where is she now, do you know?"

"Probably still at the convent."

"The convent?" he interrupted. "A woman who reminds you of La Lupe lives in a convent?"

Estelita smiled.

"Yes, we had no money so we lived there for a while. She probably still does. I left when I started working on the airplane."

"My God, you *have* had a fantastic life."

She was silent for a moment, hoping he didn't think her too crazy.

"It's becoming more fantastic with every step I take with you," she said at last.

He stopped, took her by the shoulders, and kissed her.

Estelita didn't want the night to end. As they approached the casino she considered inviting him up to her rooms for a drink and to watch the twinkling lights from her window, but didn't have the courage. What would any other girl in her position do, she wondered? She was sure neither Rosario nor Barbarita would have a moment's hesitation. But as much as she liked him, the idea of being alone in her room with him made her extremely nervous.

"Let's have a drink in the casino," he said.

"I know that most of the girls go there after the show, but I never have," she said.

"This is the perfect night for it," he said. "You should never go there alone."

He led her inside, where everyone seemed to know him. As she walked through, some men turned to look, perhaps recognizing her from her performances, but no one said a word to her. They walked past the blackjack tables and the baccarat area. The casino was teeming with tourists and local high-rollers zigzagging among the bartenders and cigarette girls.

Juan Carlos snapped his fingers and a waiter rushed to his side.

"Champagne?" Juan Carlos asked her.

"Just a Coca-Cola, please," she said. He ordered rum for himself. No ice. While they waited for their drinks, he kept his eyes on her, looking into her eyes playfully.

"Want to play?"

"I'd rather watch you play."

"I rarely do," he said, moving towards the blackjack tables. "The house always wins, you know, but I feel lucky tonight."

She took a stool, and when the drinks arrived she sipped the sweet sticky liquid and watched, he had joined a group of men who accepted him into their fold with ease. Juan Carlos had to keep his back to her, but glanced back every few minutes, showed her his hand, kept her in the game. He seemed to be winning.

She watched his broad shoulders, which he kept slightly bent forward to protect his hand, his arms turned up at the elbow, straining the material of his coat jacket. His jaw, square, firm. How old was he? she wondered. Twenty-five, twenty-six? And already so sure of himself. So grown up. Most of the men at the table looked twice his age, but he fit in. In between hands they joked with him and he laughed and collected his chips. He was a winner. A touch on her shoulder caught her attention. Turning, she came face to face with the man from the airplane.

"Señor Benavides," Estelita said, "How are you?"

He took her hand and held it for a moment.

"Much better now that I have found you."

"Thank you," she said.

He released her hand and from a pocket pulled out a silver chip which he twisted through his fingers as they talked. She knew it was worth two hundred dollars – but to him it seemed merely a toy.

"I saw you in the show and I went backstage to congratulate you, but they said you left in a big rush."

"I'm sorry I missed you."

"Yes," he laughed, still weaving the silver chip through his fingers, "but here you are. I suppose once two people have faced death together, they are destined to meet again."

Estelita wanted to forget the turbulent flight and the unavoidable flights to come, so she quickly changed the subject.

"What brings you to Havana?" she asked. "Are you a gambler?"

"Not in the conventional sense," he said. "I produce movies, so that makes me not only a gambler, but a foolish one."

Ah, so this is where all the money came from, the chauffeur, the big shiny car, the confident manner.

"I adore Mexican movies," she said. "There's a new one with Maria Felix that I'm dying to see."

"Yes, Mexico's biggest star, Maria Felix," he said, "I produced it and if I may say so, it's quite good."

"Now I *must* see it," she said.

Estelita's eyes darted to Juan Carlos. He had turned to look at

243

her. She waved. He frowned.

"And now we're planning a new one, only we're having trouble finding a star."

Juan Carlos had left the table and now joined them. Estelita introduced them. Juan Carlos shook Hugo's hand firmly.

"Señor Benavides was just telling me about a movie he's about to make," Estelita said.

"Really?" Juan Carlos said coldly. "What is it about?"

"Well," Hugo Benavides started, "it's about a virginal young woman who falls under the spell of a charming vampire. Arturo de Córdova is interested in playing the male lead."

"Oh, another Mexican vampire movie," Juan Carlos said, sounding bored.

Hugo didn't seemed disturbed by the comment.

"I adore Arturo de Córdova," Estelita said, trying to smooth things over. Juan Carlos's attitude disturbed her, particularly when he put his arm around her, as if she were his property. She knew where Hugo was going with this conversation, or at least she hoped she knew, and she prayed that Juan Carlos's rude comments wouldn't ruin her chances. A part in a movie, even a Mexican vampire movie would be like a dream. It didn't matter if it was a small part. She'd be happy to play a servant, even an extra.

"Yes," Hugo said, "another vampire movie, but we're trying to make this one a little different, it has been written from the girl's point of view. The trouble is, as I was telling Señorita de la Cruz, we've been having a difficult time finding the right girl."

"What about Maria Felix?" Estelita offered.

"My dear," Hugo said, twirling the silver chip through his fingers very slowly, "I love Maria, but she's a little too old now. It has been an arduous search. We have interviewed countless actresses in Mexico. The search has led me to Cuba. I thought I would never find her, but when I saw you dancing this evening I knew there was a reason why we had met on that airplane, under those terrible circumstances. Do you believe in fate, Señorita de la Cruz?"

"Oh, yes," Estelita said, touching his forearm. She felt Juan Carlos tighten his grip on her shoulder.

"What?" Juan Carlos said shaking his head in disbelief, "you think Estelita can be in a movie? Of all the cheap lines."

"Juan Carlos, please," Estelita said softly. Then, turning to Hugo, "Please excuse my friend, he is only trying to protect me."

And she flashed Juan Carlos a big smile. But her eyes weren't smiling. Not at all.

"I understand," she heard Hugo say. He was no longer twirling the silver chip, but rather had it clenched in his fist. "Any gentleman would. But let me assure you, Mr. Talente, my interests are purely professional. I have a daughter who is approximately the same age as Señorita de la Cruz."

"Then why don't you put *her* in your movie?"

To her relief, Benavides laughed, a long, generous laugh.

"Juan Carlos," Estelita said with a cautioning look.

Juan Carlos let out a deep sigh. Estelita took Juan Carlos's hand and held it tight, but his hand felt limp, as if his spirit had left his body.

"So this movie, Señor Benavides" she continued, "what will it be called?"

"It will be called *Jacqueline,*" Hugo Benavides said, tossing the silver chip high into the air, Estelita followed it as it spun and sparkled above them. When gravity pulled it back to earth, Juan Carlos swiftly snatched it and with a triumphant smile, handed it back to Hugo Benavides.

"Oh, I adore that name," Estelita gasped. "And the part you think I can play, what is the girl called?"

"Well, Jacqueline, of course," Hugo Benavides said, handing her the silver chip

24

Maria Felix's tearful eyes loomed large on the silver screen. The Imperial was one of the largest and most beautiful movie palaces in all of Havana, with two sets of balconies reaching up three stories. The immense ceiling was domed and delicately painted with pink and gold angels. On this hot August night, all seats were filled, as they had been every night since the movie opened.

In the film, *Miercoles de Ceniza* (Ash Wednesday) Maria Felix played a woman traveling on a luxury liner. But, in spite of her great beauty and wealth, she suffered and suffered and suffered and suffered. She suffered heroically in glorious black and white. She suffered so effectively, that night after night, she brought women to tears and made young men face the harsh realities of life.

Maria Felix was enjoying unprecedented popularity in Cuba. The public couldn't get enough of her flawless face and luscious figure.

But, just like the women she played to perfection, not all was well in Maria's personal life. Her equally famous husband, the actor Jorge Negrete, had died suddenly and unexpectedly. Maria had shocked Mexican society by wearing trousers to his funeral. The resulting scandal made headlines and was turning *Miercoles de Ceniza* into the most successful Maria Felix movie ever.

On this hot August night, the Cuban audience, which tended to be restless and given to catcalls, whistles and rude comments, watched the screen as if spellbound.

Just as Maria Felix, tears flowing down her sculpted cheekbones, was about to forsake her illegitimate child for the love of the Catholic priest who had stolen her heart, fireworks erupted inside the Imperial Theater.

The audience first heard a long, sharp whistle, then watched in horror as giant balls of colorful fire exploded, momentarily bleaching the movie screen white, then whizzing through the air, just missing the chandeliers, and scorching the painted angels above.

The audience screamed in unison and sprang up all at once, jumping over seats, pushing each other out of the way, jamming the aisles and blindly aiming for the exits. The fireworks stopped after the first explosion, sending down a shower of silver sparks – that's when the deafening string of Chinese firecrackers went off. The frenzy escalated for it sounded as if a machine-gun sniper had gone mad.

The audience, as if they were one body fused together, tugged and pulled each other, latching on to whatever they could, clothes were torn, handfuls of hair pulled out, anything that might get them out of there. Screams and curses floated above the swarm of bodies. On the silver screen, Maria Felix slapped the handsome priest who had done her wrong, then fell weeping into his arms.

In all the commotion, no one noticed the two men who had quietly lit the fuses and slithered out of the crowded theater.

*

Delfino followed Arjuna up the dark narrow staircase, nerves gnawing at his gut. He had started to develop the instincts of a clandestine operator. His hearing was sharper, his eyes keen to potential danger – any sudden movements, any strange sounds, any fleeting looks he noted and classified. He stood back while Arjuna rapped the secret signal on the door: the usual knock and a quick, almost imperceptible one-two twist of the doorknob.

The door opened and they quickly stepped inside.

"Fireworks inside a movie theater!" a man with white hair and round blue eyes was saying, "what a feeble excuse for a revolutionary action. We have to get serious."

"Calm down, Fructoso," another man said, "you know explosives get sent to the Sierras, we have nothing to work with down here."

Delfino and Arjuna silently shook hands with the men. They knew almost everyone there: El Cucuyo, Fructoso Varela, and Eusebio Nobar, but not the skinny young man with a severely pocked-marked face who sat quietly next to El Cocuyo.

Delfino took a seat next to Arjuna. He looked around the small apartment. He had been there before and wondered how long before the place was labeled "hot" and the meeting had to be moved to another location. It was a dangerous game they played with the police. The apartment belonged to Euscbio. He lived there with his wife and three children. On the days of the meetings Eusebio always sent his family out to the home of a relative. The apartment was ideal because it had a front and back door, and large windows to the street. A man could jump out of the second floor window if necessary.

But no one ever felt completely safe. This was Ventura Novo's territory.

Eusebio kept going to the window and peering through the blinds. "I stand by that action," Eusebio said, from his post at the window, "from now on people will stay away from the movie theaters. If the people of Havana can't go to the movies, they'll be aching to pick a fight. It could be the beginning of a general strike."

"That's absurd," Fructoso argued. "People aren't going to rise up because they can't go to the movies!"

"I've heard enough of this nonsense," Arjuna cut in. "What's this meeting about, anyway?"

"Novo's hyenas picked up some individuals responsible for distributing the newsletters," El Cucuyo explained. "We have to move the press immediately, before they seize the house."

A long time passed before anyone spoke.

"If someone is willing to deliver the press to the boathouse," Arjuna said wearily, "I suppose we can keep it there, but only temporarily."

Delfino tried to catch his eye, but Arjuna was purposely not looking his way.

"I can arrange that," El Cucuyo said immediately. "My brother has a panel truck."

"Excellent," Arjuna said. "By the way, we dispatched the cargo to Santiago. With any luck it is on its way to the Sierra. We have been in contact with Santiago and no one's heard of any recent captures, so we can safely assume everything went as planned. But now, we are defenseless. We have no arms. We need to figure out a way to keep the momentum going. We need more explosives right away."

The skinny man with the pockmarks raised his hand to speak. He was ignored, but he managed to stutter a question anyway.

"Well, what exactly is the real aim of any of this subversive activity?"

The room fell silent. Eusebio walked away from the window and stood across from the young man.

"It seems to me it's very dangerous," the new man went on with a little more confidence, "but no one here can tell me what exactly it's all about."

Frowning faces scrutinized him; his skinny frame seemed to shrink under their glare.

"Who is this cabrón?" Fructoso asked. El Cocuyo immediately stepped in.

"Excuse my friend," El Cocuyo said. "His name is Papo Rodriguez. I brought him, he's very smart and can be helpful. He knows about explosives. He just needs facts. You can't blame him for wanting to know what he's getting into."

There was a reluctant murmur of agreement around the room, but also of mistrust.

Arjuna nodded at El Cocuyo and turned to Papo.

"The ultimate aim of the revolt, my friend," Arjuna said, "is to establish a better society."

"I'm just not sure how you plan to accomplish that," Papo replied. "I grant you, Batista's is an illegal government, obtained through violence, but does that justify more violence?"

"No one enjoys the violence," Arjuna interjected. "We have given Batista every opportunity to hold democratic elections and every time he promises and promises and then he changes his mind."

"How can I be sure what you have in mind is better?" Papo
249

asked. "Word on the street is that people like you promise the farmers their own plot of land, but once you have power, you will give them just enough land to bury themselves."

"Word on the street?" Fructoso said, his patience reaching its limit, "is that what you listen to? I'm not sure why you are here. Maybe we should send you back out to the street, with your throat cut so you can't rat on us."

"Fructoso, you're out of line," Arjuna said, then turned to the young man, and very carefully, so that there would be no doubt left once he had spoken, he added, "overthrowing Batista and establishing an honest government is our aim."

Delfino's heart ached with admiration. Arjuna was always like this when he spoke at meetings – clear, intelligent, patient. Delfino not only admired him but also envied his convictions. Most of the time Delfino felt like a dilettante among these heroes. Sure, he wanted what they wanted, but he didn't burn with the same passion shared by the others. He wondered if he could have been swayed just as easily towards Batista had Arjuna been so inclined. Only one thing was sure, he would follow Arjuna to the ends of the earth. After Federico and all those years in Madrid feeling nothing, now he felt too much. But his love was mingled with fear. Day in and day out, fear tugged at his soul. He looked at couples on the street and envied their carefree, innocent devotion. He longed for the day when all the madness would come to an end and they could be free to be together without that nagging, insistent fear.

"Yes," Fructoso said, "our aim is simple, but it will not be accomplished with fireworks inside a theater. We have to get serious. Did you hear what the Socialist Student Movement did last Monday? Five of them, students, kids really, raided the fucking National Bank of Cuba."

"Yes, we heard," El Cocuyo said wearily and the others nodded and groaned, but Fructoso obstinately continued as if he'd heard nothing.

"In plain daylight, they walked in, one of them held the guard at gunpoint," he said, his voice rising with excitement, "while the other four splashed the place with gasoline, set it on fire and walked out. Now that takes cojones. Meanwhile we're moving a useless printing press around and justifying our ideals to this punk."

Fructoso glared at Papo until the young man spoke.

"I know where to get some bombs," Papo said. "I know where to get metralla and petardos. If anyone is interested, I can take them there. Tonight. "

The men in the room turned to Fructoso.

"Why are you all looking at me?" he said. "I don't know this man, he could be a rat for all I know."

"How do I know I can trust you?" Arjuna asked.

"You don't," he said.

Delfino joined Arjuna and Papo downstairs. The night was hot, without a lick of breeze.

"My car is over there," Delfino said, pointing down several blocks. He always parked far from Eusebio's house and always in a different place, fearing that the car would become too familiar to the patrols.

"No car," Papo said, "we'll take the bus. The place where we're going, very few people own cars, and any vehicle is suspect. The Number Twelve runs late and it will get us close without transfer."

Delfino walked a few steps in the opposite direction and called out to Arjuna.

"I need to talk to you for a moment."

"Go ahead, talk," Papo told Arjuna, lighting a cigarette.

Delfino and Arjuna moved a few steps away.

"Are you sure we can trust him?" Delfino whispered.

Arjuna shrugged.

"I think so," he said. "But if you don't want to come, just go back to the apartment and I'll meet you there later."

"I don't think either one of us should go. I have a bad feeling."

"I've had that bad feeling for years. It will not go away, it's part of what we're doing. Did you notice Eusebio checking the window every two minutes? We're all scared. We know the consequences. But if we don't do it, who will? Fructoso is all talk and the others have families."

"You're my family," Delfino said.

Arjuna placed a hand on his shoulder.

251

"Go home, I won't be long and I don't mind doing this alone. Perhaps it's better that one of us stays behind."

"No," Delfino said quickly. "I'm going with you."

"I admire your courage," Arjuna said.

"It's not courage," Delfino responded, and for a fleeting moment wanted to take Arjuna in his arms and kiss him forever, but he didn't. Instead, they joined Papo, and followed him to the corner to wait for bus Number Twelve.

They jumped off the bus in a neighborhood that neither of them knew. There were no sidewalks, just a flat dirt trail running along an exposed sewer. The water was covered with a thick coat of moss that appeared silver in the moonlight. Their feet slipped and stuck on the muddy trail. Two shirtless young men ran by chasing a third and yelling obscenities, their skinny torsos glowing with sweat. A toothless old man, his leathery face folded into itself, sat in a rocking chair near a dim doorway and stared blankly out into the street.

There were no street lights. The houses stood close together, as if leaning on each other for support, ancient coats of paint peeling from decades of salt air. All doors were wide open against the heat. Delfino found it impossible not to look inside as they passed. Bare lightbulbs cast shadows upon the desperate poverty inside. The smell of old cooking grease mingled with the stench of garbage. The misery was audible: babies screaming women shouting men arguing a bottle smashing insane laughter a cacophony of music distorted by static emanating from several distant radios.

Neither Arjuna nor Papo seemed to notice the sounds as they walked deeper into this dark world. They turned a corner and squeezed through a narrow alley between two buildings.

Papo knocked on a door. It was opened by a man wearing only his underpants. He eyed them warily, scratching at his bare chest with a gun.

"It's me," Papo said.

"I know who you are, but who are they?" the man said, pointing the gun at Arjuna's face.

"Just let us in," Papo said with urgency.

The man put the gun down and stepped back, making just

enough room for the three of them to enter. Inside it was dark and the air was heavy. In the darkness, Delfino made out a table covered with wires, pliers and cylindrical objects that he knew were homemade bombs. On a cot next to the table lay a dozen or so more bombs of different sizes.

"This is Rodolfo," Papo said, "the best explosives man in Havana."

Rodolfo stood firm. Arjuna extended his hand. Rodolfo looked at it as if Arjuna was holding a dead rat, but finally shook it. He directed Rodolfo's attention to Delfino.

"And this is--"

"I don't need names, and you can't stay here long," he said gruffly, "I assume you need bombs. Everyone needs bombs nowadays."

"Yes, let's get down to business," Papo said with the determined tone of a seasoned procurer.

Rodolfo stood over the table and launched into his sales pitch.

"These big ones here," Rodolfo explained, "are called Elefantes. We use them to blow up electric towers and stuff like that. These dark ones are metrallas, they are filled with nails, use them to hurt people you hate, it's a horrible way to die. Those small ones are petardo, a lot of noise, not much damage. And those little yellow ones are percussive, which explode when you pull them, like your dick."

Rodolfo picked up one of the yellow bombs and started tossing it from one hand to the other. Delfino took a giant step back, his heart pounding, his eyes following the arc of the bomb as it bounced from one hand to the other. Rodolfo laughed and continued tossing the bomb as if it were a rubber ball.

"Nothing will happen unless you pull on this little thing here," he said.

Delfino took a deep breath and stepped forward.

"I'm only familiar with the yellow ones," Arjuna said. "I'll take two."

"Excellent choice, my friend," Rodolfo said.

"We are going to do a little job tonight," Arjuna added.

"I don't need to know what you are going to do," Rodolfo said, and with the skill of a neighborhood butcher wrapping a cut of beef, he wrapped the bombs with two sheets of newspaper.

"How much do we owe you?" Arjuna asked.

"I don't know, I don't really sell them, I just blow things up. What do you think they're worth? Seventy-five dollars?"

"I'll give you a hundred for the two."

Rodolfo considered the offer.

"Be serious, it costs you nearly nothing to put one of these together," Papo said.

Rodolfo shot him an ugly look.

"Do it for the movement, brother," Delfino urged, anxious to get out of there.

"What do I give two shits about the movement?" Rodolfo said, "I don't have a dog in this fight, or better yet, I have too many dogs."

"But you are an anarchist," Delfino said, "you said it yourself, you blow things up."

"Yes, I do now, but if someone else comes to power, I'll still blow things up. The situation in this country is never quite right. I will always blow things up."

As if a light had gone on in the room, Delfino became wholly aware who this man really was, what this man did, had done, would always do, and nodded an agreement he did not feel.

"I'll give you one hundred or no deal," Arjuna said.

"I'll take it," Rodolfo said, "but what you do with it is your business. Do you understand me? We do not know each other."

Arjuna gave him the money and Rodolfo took it, smiling, a silver tooth and his eyes gleaming with the same intensity. Then he peeled a couple of bills and handed them to Papo who, with a quick sleight of hand, made them vanish.

Delfino tugged at the collar of his shirt, it was so hot that the air seared his throat but it felt good to be back outside.

"That man's insane," Delfino said.

"We're walking around in the middle of the night with two bombs wrapped in newspaper and you say *he's* insane," Arjuna whispered with a smile.

Delfino returned the smile; he liked the easy warmth between them. The way Arjuna could always, with just a few words, with a wink, with a firm hand on his shoulder or his back, put everything into perspective. He was no longer alone. There was someone who knew him, who cared, who would always understand.

"Since this one," Papo said, inferring Delfino, "has never done this before, he can come with me."

It pained him to be separated, but Delfino agreed that Arjuna would go on his own, find his own target. The explosions had to be set off quickly. It was already 11 p.m. The longer they held on to the bombs the more likely they were to be stopped and questioned.

"Don't worry," Arjuna said, "I'll see you back at your apartment in less than an hour."

Delfino stood as if rooted to the spot and watched Arjuna walk away until Papo tugged at him.

Papo carried the bomb. Delfino fell in next to him, but wished he could move to the other side of the street. He didn't know very much about bombs. Anything could happen. What if Papo missed a step, tripped and fell, what if he accidentally dropped the package? What would it feel like to be blown to bits? What would it feel like to be instantly transformed to liquid, or would it be to dust?

"Do you know where you're going?" Delfino asked.

"Yes, we're almost there."

Delfino looked around. They were close to the center of town. The streets were still filled with people coming home from restaurants and bars, from birthday parties or wedding celebrations, movies, the ballet. Life went on in Havana in spite of the men walking around with explosives wrapped in newspapers. Life went on.

"Not around here," Delfino said, eyeing a young couple with a stroller, "too many people. There can't be people."

"Don't worry," Papo said defensively, "I know what I'm doing. You can go home if you're afraid."

"I'm not afraid, I need to see how these things are done. Soon I will be able to do this on my own."

"Well, then shut up, stay close and watch what I do."

Delfino was amazed at how simple it was. Papo found a solitary streetlight near a vacant lot.

"This one is attached to the main artery," he said and crouched down at the base of the light pole.

He looked around. They were alone.

"Now watch this," Papo said and pulled out a roll of black electrical tape from his pocket. He held the yellow bomb against the pole and circled it with tape until it was firmly attached. Without a word of warning he pulled a tab. Delfino heard it click and his already racing heart now beat twice as fast. Papo stood up and looked at him.

"Run!" he hissed.

Delfino wasn't sure which way to go, so he followed Papo. He ran as fast as he could, the change and keys in his pocket knocking against each other, making a jingling sound that he was sure the whole city could hear.

They were barely a block away when he heard the explosion. It boomed in his ears. And then all the streetlights went out. He stopped running, afraid of falling in the darkness. He heard doors opening all around him and saw the dark silhouettes of people stepping into the street, talking in loud voices, sounding more annoyed than frightened.

"Another bomb?"

"Tonight of all nights!"

"I can't stand one more day of this."

"It's crazy, who can live this way? Never knowing when you're going to be blown sky high."

"All we can do is pray and wait."

"We're lucky to be alive."

Delfino had no idea where Papo had gone. He just kept walking and didn't stop, not for a second, until he reached his front door.

It was past four in the morning and Arjuna had not come home. Delfino fished around for a cigarette, but there weren't any more. He had smoked them all. He crumpled the empty pack and went to the window again. The street lights were still out, and the gray light of an early dawn was starting to wash over the buildings.

Where is he?

His eyes burned, his head was pounding. He wanted to stay calm, as Arjuna would have wanted, but how could he when only the most horrible thoughts came to him.

He tried to think positively, but that just started a jumble of arguments inside his already tortured mind. Maybe he's at the boathouse. Maybe he couldn't get back to the apartment for some reason. But he would have phoned. Maybe he couldn't, for some reason. What reason? What on earth could keep him from making a simple phone call? He's sure to be dead. No, not that. He is too smart for that. He's reckless. He's careful.

The sun came up full and bright, as it always did, but the morning felt different, horribly different. Delfino walked through the empty sidewalks back to Eusebio's apartment. He passed newsstands but didn't bother buying the morning paper. Sabotage was never reported.

His car was still there, just where they had left it the night before. So he's not at the boathouse. It was a long walk to the boathouse. Maybe he took a bus, or a taxi. Maybe he's all right.

Maybe he *is* dead.

The car still smelled of Arjuna, a scent only he would know. Delfino's eyes started to blur, but he fought against it. No tears, not yet. He needed to be clear. He needed to think clearly. He did not have the luxury of falling apart. He drove towards the boathouse. The streets were beginning to fill with people. Traffic grew thicker as he drove along the Malecón. The sea was as tranquil and placid as a lake. The morning had become brighter, almost impossibly glorious. He drove into the tunnel towards Jaimanitas and found the underground darkness comforting.

He kept his foot light on the accelerator. He was in a hurry, but reluctant to get there too quickly. Something inside of him was telling him that the news would not be good. He cursed himself for having such negative thoughts. He came out of the tunnel and the sunlight pierced his eyes. He turned onto the side road and heard the familiar crunching sound of the tires on the sandy gravel. He saw the boathouse in the distance, and the three shiny black cars parked outside of it.

His hands gripping the steering wheel so hard that he thought his bones would break, and with his body rigid from the sharp pain twisting in his chest, he drove past the boathouse hoping he wouldn't be followed.

25

"To a brothel!" Aspirrina had shouted on that horrible night, "she's been recruited by some evil people to be a... a whore."

The words had bruised Sor Maria's soul and the bruise still hurt, now with even more intensity, for she had Estelita's father sitting at her side. She knew that she would have to be delicate when breaking the news. How do you tell a father that his daughter has fallen into a life of infamy? She recalled how Aspirrina had used the words as a weapon against her. Sor Maria knew she had to tell Esteban, that sharing the terrible truth was the only chance they had of saving the girl.

It was dark by the time they reached Havana. In the distance she could see the lights of the city, then suddenly, as if someone had pulled a giant switch, it had all gone dark. She blinked to clear her vision. Had Havana vanished before her eyes?

She drove slowly through the narrow streets, the path illuminated only by the weak headlights of the van. People jammed the streets, crossing her field of vision like specters.

"Why is it so dark?" Orquidea asked.

"Someone must have blown up the power lines again," she answered, trying to sound casual, trying not to alarm her.

Esteban remained silent, probably frightened, she thought, not just for himself, but for his daughter, out there in that big, dark city, a city where people blew up power lines. She had no choice but to bring them to the convent with her. She couldn't just leave them out there in the dark. The sisters had lit candles and their three shadows danced on the walls. As she led them to their rooms, Sor Maria was angry with herself for having spent so much money on the hotel in Santiago. She could have given them all the money, wished them good luck and sent them on their way. Now she had no other alternative but to offer them shelter. For how long she did not know. For as long as it took him to find Estelita, she figured, resigning herself to another imposition from people she barely knew. Hopefully it would be a short stay, but Havana was a big city, and from what she'd heard, there wasn't a scarcity of brothels. But how and when would she tell him? So far she had revealed nothing. After learning that her passenger was Estelita's father, she pretended she was just making light, polite conversation, and had drawn the truth about Aspirrina from him. She had to hold the steering wheel firmly to keep from driving off the road, to conceal her shock, her abysmal sense of betrayal. Now what? she wondered. Who are these people? Why has God placed Esteban de la Cruz in her path? And if Aspirrina was not Estelita's mother, who was Orquidea?

"She is a postulant," Esteban told her with a warm, soothing voice. "She's a flower I discovered growing among the rocks. She's my greatest spiritual achievement. Perhaps when people see us, always together, thinking as one, they mistake our relationship as one of the flesh. But nothing could be further from the truth, it is much more. She is like family, but also more than that. Do you understand, Sister?"

Sor Maria nodded. Santeros! she thought. They believe in the same saints that we Catholics worship, but under other names. What difference did it make? Any faith is good, she assured herself. Hopefully, it all leads back to God, one God. She had learned a long time ago that it was not her place to judge, but to do good whenever and wherever possible. And here was another opportunity to put this belief to the test. She felt exhausted. So many tests!

Orquidea had remained quiet while she was being discussed. Through the rearview mirror, Sor Maria could see her narrow face; she was looking out the window, watching the road go by as if in a trance, as if the words being said about her didn't reach her.

"And your daughter?" Sor Maria asked, wanting to map out the situation further so that she could better prepare herself to deliver a tremendous blow.

"My daughter is my greatest joy but also my greatest personal failure," he said, "I failed her because my trajectory in life has been filled with deep tunnels and long detours into darkness. But those tunnels and detours have led me to the clear, bright open space I live in now. I intend to correct every wrong."

He turned to face her.

"Sometimes, sister, if we're not careful, that which is most precious to us becomes familiar and we neglect it."

His voice trailed off and he looked away, towards the passing trees and his next words were like a whispered prayer.

"I would give my life to see her again, to beg her forgiveness. Just to look at her." Sor Maria felt her heart drop even further.

"You will find her, Esteban," Orquidea said, coming suddenly to life in the back seat. Esteban did not answer. Perhaps there was no answer.

There had been grumbling in the chapel when she announced that Esteban and Orquidea would be staying with them. The sisters were just getting used to Aspirrina's and Estelita's departure, and now this, a man in the convent. They were somewhat appeased when she explained that Esteban was Estelita's father and that he was in Havana to find her. His relationship to Orquidea, Sor Maria left purposely vague.

Safe in her cell, she washed herself, and put on a clean nightgown. She momentarily wondered where Estelita was at that very moment. She imagined a world of dim lights, liquor and filth. It was a thought that never would have occurred to her before that fateful night when Aspirrina and Estelita had knocked on the convent door.

Sor Maria had been aware of prostitutes, but they had always been nebulous, and their activities even more so – and she preferred it that way. When she had read about Maria Magdalena in the Bible, she never once imagined her professional routine, what her life had been like before befriended by Jesus. She was a fallen woman, that was clear from the scriptures, but Sor Maria chose to think about Maria Magdalena's humility, how she had humbly washed Jesus' feet. But the more she thought about it, she realized that washing a man's feet was nothing compared to the many disgusting and humiliating acts Maria Magdalena performed day after day, year after year. Now, the scene of Maria Magdalena washing Jesus' feet didn't seem so lowly an act.

Sor Maria chased the nagging thoughts away with prayer and tried to sleep, but all she could think of was Estelita trapped in some hellish place, entertaining man after man, allowing them to touch her, to use her. She hated these thoughts. She longed for the days before Estelita and Aspirrina came into her life. She missed sitting quietly with her embroidery, surrounded by her sisters, her heart pure, her soul clean. Now her mind was like that of any other woman. The corruption that was strangling the country had seeped into the convent! The mere thought of it kept her mind blazing.

She thought about Delfino. She wondered where those guns and bullets had gone, what damage they were causing, how many souls would be delivered. Violence in the name of peace as it had been through the ages. And here, not even guaranteed peace, just, maybe it would get better. Maybe what the rebels were doing was for the better, but who knew?

If there was to be a revolution, she selfishly wished that it all could take place without her. There had been other revolts – military coups, bombings, uprisings and assassinations and she had been all but oblivious to them all. Presidents had come and gone. Batista, Grau, Prio, then Batista again. And now this, the battle for the soul of a country where most people were either too poor, too ignorant or like her father, too besotted with their own self-importance to know what truly needed to be done.

She wondered why a man like Delfino would get involved in the struggle. Delfino. Poor tortured boy. He had always seen himself as rebellious, so different, as if he were the first homosexual on earth. There had always been homosexuals. In her parents' circle there had been several, with varying degrees of what her mother called "discretion."

261

Sor Maria was glad that she finally had met Delfino's friend, or as Delfino had called him: "The true love of my life."

The contrast between the two men had been jarring at first. Arjuna, strutting, masculine, fires burning in his eyes. She hoped he was kind to her friend. She could see that Delfino, so gentle and vulnerable, was trying to measure up, to find his own virility through his attachment to this rugged man. And that Arjuna was trying to find his own virility through this so-called revolution. The logic of men remained a mystery to her. Again she tried to keep her mind from exploring deeper into their situation. Delfino and Arjuna were friends, just that. She didn't need to know any more, but scenes of their intimate life intruded into her imagination, and having no practical experience in the matter, they came to her in the form of sacred paintings, the sort one finds printed on the devotional cards she used to bookmark her bible.

La Piedad: Delfino's nude and tortured body draped over Arjuna's lap.

La Resurrección: Delfino emerging from his sepulcher at Golgotha, Arjuna falling to his knees before him.

La Crucificción: Delfino dragging crates of weapons through the streets of Havana, Arjuna the Roman soldier urging him on with a spear.

La Traición: She saw herself washing her hands as Pontius Pilate had done, and with the same bowl of water, Delfino washing Arjuna's feet.

The lurid images tortured her well into the chill of dawn. She wondered why her life had taken this sudden turn, how she had become so deeply involved in a world of prostitutes, homosexuals, santeros and revolutionaries. Would it all have been better if she'd kept the door closed that night, if she had never opened that door, if Aspirrina and Estelita had never walked into her life? Sor Maria allowed herself, just for a moment, to imagine the life her parents had traced for her, a life like her mother's, of privilege and distraction.

She saw herself in pretty dresses in all the colors of spring. Her hair long and well past her waist for she would have had others to look after it. She pictured herself in a house filled with light, an exquisite home where there was always a cool breeze, lovely music and a cold drink. Her family would consist of a handsome husband approved of by her parents, and healthy, intelligent children who her parents adored and spoiled. Who would she be? What would she think about? Who would be her friends? Would she have given revolutions, homosexuals, prostitutes or santeros a second thought on those cloudless afternoons when she met her girlfriends for Canasta? Would she think of the poor when she attended charity balls and galas? Or would she have been content to keep them as an abstraction, regularly dropping checks into velvet-lined collection baskets. Checks her husband had signed. Would it ease her conscience? Would she have a conscience? She had closed so many doors trying to find her place in the world, but now it was obvious. No matter how many doors one closes, all it took was a twist of a doorknob, the opening of a car door, for all of it to come gushing in like sewage.

She did not get a moment's sleep. She knew she was postponing the inevitable, wasting precious time. Each moment that she kept the truth from Esteban was one more moment Estelita would spend in a strange room with some strange man. She grabbed a robe and made her way to his room. She had placed him in the room that Aspirrina and Estelita had vacated. She had situated Orquidea on the other side of the convent. Esteban had pointedly told her their relationship was not of the flesh – but Sor Maria was not taking any chances, not with anyone, not anymore.

She knocked lightly on the door and hearing no response twisted the knob and entered. Esteban, fully dressed, stood by the dark window, his face reflected in the dark glass. He turned when she entered.

"I can feel her here," he said.

He walked to the bed and touched it. "This is where she slept?" he asked.

"Yes, that was her bed for the short while she spent with us."

"She's still here," he said touching the walls. "She has left so much of herself behind."

"Señor de la Cruz," she said, "there is something very important that I feel you should know."

The words had come to her slowly and she was glad. She had feared that nerves, the trip, and lack of sleep would conspire against her, make her clumsy and unnecessarily harsh. But she had spoken her words well, with delicacy and tact. His face collapsed, as if all bones had been removed. She watched his shoulders sag and his whole body melt to the floor.

"Señor, I wish I could help you more," she said, standing tall above him. She had been forced to speak the unspeakable to a man she barely knew; a man who at the moment lay sobbing at her feet.

"Where is Aspirrina?" he asked, his voice choked with pain.

"She promised me she'd take care of my girl, she promised…"

They sat in a thick, heavy silence. How could he not have regrets? How can he not feel the pain of a million bad memories? It was a different pain than what Estelita must have felt when she was small. At the time he'd thought there was no greater suffering than to lose his love, to remember Belquis still and lifeless on that bloody bed, to hear the newborn child crying out for her. But he had been wrong, even that pain was nothing compared to this. He had selfishly taken the baby away from a grandmother who loved her because he believed he could do better. But he hadn't. What could he have been thinking all those nights, before he blackmailed Aspirrina to sit with his daughter, when he'd left her alone in strange rooms. What does a little girl know? What does a little girl feel? He knew nothing about it, thought nothing of it. The most difficult part was her quick forgiveness when he returned, her constant adoration whenever he looked at her. What sort of woman had Estelita become? What does a little girl become when she'd been exposed to someone like him?

He dared not speak in fear that if he opened his mouth just a bit, he would weep forever and ever.

He had to find her, if only to save his own soul. He was better now, the past could not be undone, but the future could be everything she'd ever dreamed.

26

Aspirrina was uncomfortable, there were flying bugs in her hair and strange sounds all around and every bone in her body ached. No matter. She had achieved what she had set out to do. She had joined the revolution. And not just in the city, where all a woman could do was march and protest in vain. She was a part of it now, high up in the mountains of the Sierra Maestra, living among the men who were going to change the world.

She'd had to do some quick thinking and fancy footwork after she'd hopped the truck outside of the cemetery in Santiago – Celia Sanchez had not been easy to convince. But Aspirrina had seen the opportunity and grabbed it the way a farmer grabs a chicken by the neck and twists it until it becomes food. She jumped into the truck and squeezed herself in, deaf to Celia's shouts of protest, shoving the indignant woman, with a bump of her hips, to move up against the driver.

"Sister, what are you doing? Are you insane?" Celia said, her face so close that Aspirrina could count the beads of sweat above her upper lip.

"I'm no sister," Aspirrina replied, ripping the veil from her head and tossing it out the window. "My name is Aspirrina Cerrogordo, and

I want to come with you to help any way I can."

The truck had picked up speed on the highway and even the hot wind coming through the window felt good, although the black habit she still wore was strangling her.

"Universo," Celia had said to the driver, her voice frighteningly calm, "pull over and let this woman out."

Aspirrina watched the truck slow down as Universo released the gas pedal. Fortunately, they were rounding a curve and Universo couldn't come to a complete stop.

"Please don't leave me here," Aspirrina pleaded, "I promise you, I can help. I'm sure you could use another nurse."

Celia looked at her, taking her measure with cold, calculating eyes. "Keep going," she said to Universo.

He shifted gears, the transmission making a struggling, scraping sound.

"You're a nurse," Celia had said, more a statement than a question.

"For many years," Aspirrina said, looking her in the eyes. She knew only liars looked away and she had to convince this woman that what she was saying was true. "That's why they call me Aspirrina, I take away the pain. "

The lie came so easily to her, it might as well have been the truth. If she only knew why my mother actually gave me that name, she thought, she'd never stop laughing.

"I was going to be a nurse," Celia said, as if the thought was too disgusting to mull over for long. "My father is a doctor, in Manzanillo."

"Oh, so you're from Manzanillo," Aspirrina said with a note of admiration, hoping to steer the conversation away from her nursing qualifications.

"You've heard of Manzanillo?" Celia's voice was flat and even.

"Sure, everybody's heard of Manzanillo," Aspirrina answered, keeping up her tone of admiration, which was as false as anything could possibly be.

"Manzanillo is a small town full of big heroes," Universo said. "But now it's fallen on hard times because all the men have come up to the mountains and there is no one left to do the fishing."

"It is the women of Manzanillo," Celia said, "who are the real heroes."

"Like you, patrona," Universo said staring straight ahead. Then he turned to Aspirrina with a smile. "They call her the Native Flower of the Revolution."

"At the moment I feel more like the *wilting* flower of the revolution," she added with a chuckle. Aspirrina took this split second of levity to make a case for herself.

"And that's what I want to be, too," she said enthusiastically, "I want to be one of the flowers of the revolution. Please let me come with you, I promise you will not be sorry."

Celia didn't answer, but the truck kept moving with no further attempts to slow down and let her off. Aspirrina began to breathe a little easier.

Aspirrina was familiar with Celia's voice because she'd heard it on Radio Rebelde, the clandestine station that broadcast from the Sierra. Those who dared could hear her impassioned dispatches urging the people of Cuba to join the revolution, to revolt against the government. She couldn't believe her luck, to be sitting in a truck with a woman she admired above all others. This is my destiny, she told herself as they turned off the main highway and the truck started to climb. The road to the Sierra was narrow and rough, better fit for mules than a truck. Aspirrina's discomfort as they continued to climb and hug curbs that overlooked steep embankments was palpable.

"If you think this is frightening," Celia said, "prepare yourself because where we are going there is not one moment when you won't be afraid for your life."

"I'm not afraid," Aspirrina said.

"Just tell me if this is too much for you, because I can always send you back with Universo."

"You don't know me very well yet," Aspirrina said, "but you will discover that I am not the type of person who ever takes a step back."

Celia smiled at her for the first time.

"We sure could use a good nurse," Celia said.

"After what happened to Doctor Lapasmada," Universo added sadly.

"Universo, watch the road," Celia cautioned.

"What happened to Doctor Lapasmada?" Aspirrina asked.

"Nothing," Celia said with finality and the topic was closed to further discussion. Aspirrina didn't care what had happened to Doctor Lapasmada, he'd probably been shot dead. No matter. She was actually relieved that there would be no doctor there to greet her, a doctor who would immediately have exposed her as a fraud.

"The job is hard," Celia said. "Bullet wounds are the least of it, we all know how to retrieve a bullet, sew up a wound, set a bone. There is so much more, my friend, infections, insect bites, fevers, diarrhea, dehydration, it goes on and on. Sometimes you'll feel like you're drowning in a sea of shit."

They continued climbing, the gears of the truck grinding and screaming, she feared that at any moment the truck would completely give out and slide back into the darkness below. Aspirrina didn't know how high they had climbed, but she knew it was far, her ears had become blocked, as if sealed with wax. After what seemed an eternity, they reached a field where a group of peasants were harvesting malanga. Her stomach was growling.

"Do you think we can ask them for something to eat?"

Celia looked at her with disgust.

"Learn this lesson now," she said, "each peasant is a potential informer. Every person you see between here and our camp could be the enemy."

Celia then told Universo to pull over, and Aspirrina learned a lesson: Only Celia Sanchez says when to stop and when to go. When to eat and when to shit. Celia approached the peasants carefully, and that day they ate boiled malanga without salt or lard. The thick white paste caught at Aspirrina's throat, forcing her to gulp down hard, but at least it satisfied her stomach if not her tastebuds.

"The peasants are always suspicious at first," Celia said. "Who wouldn't be after what they've suffered at the hands of Batista's soldiers? The threats, the tortures, the burning of their homes, not to mention rape and murder. Of course they support us. Of course they give us their children to be combatants and guides, of course they let us use their houses, share their food. They're poor but they're not stupid."

Before leaving, Celia handed a few pesos to one of the farmers.

The man refused the money, so she stubbornly thrust it into his shirt pocket.

They climbed into the truck and were off again. Aspirrina had no idea how much farther they needed to travel, how high was the mountain they needed to climb.

"Fidel has rules we must follow at all times," Celia recited like something memorized, "never pass a farmer without shouting a greeting. No matter how much danger you are in, never take away their hunting weapons. Never eat or drink without paying. Never trifle with their women."

"Sounds reasonable," Aspirrina said, thinking that the one about giving them money was just plain stupid.

"The rules work in our favor," Celia said. "They separate the rebels from the soldiers. The soldiers believe they own the island, they do as they please, they take what they want, they have no respect for the farmers."

Shortly before nightfall, they arrived at Charco Redondo, a tiny village in the most remote part of the lower Sierra. If it wasn't for the altitude it was just like the many tiny towns where Sabrosuras had performed only once for lack of attendance, zero profit. Charco Redondo was even smaller than that, only those who lived there even knew of its existence. The villagers must have heard them coming because as the truck traveled through its narrow street, every family stood outside their house holding red candle lanterns to catch a worshipful glimpse of them, the saviors of Cuba.

"They know me here," Celia said with obvious pride as a woman ran into the road and handed her a paper bag containing several loaves of bread.

"Universo, stop the truck a moment," Celia said.

Universo did as he was told. Celia jumped out of the truck and ran after the woman. Aspirrina looked back and saw Celia thrust a few coins into the woman's hands.

Celia returned with a look of contentment and they started off again. Aspirrina eyed the dark, crusty loaves of bread like they were the last meal of the condemned. But Celia wrapped them tightly and placed them behind the seat.

"The men will be happy to get bread, won't they Universo?"

269

Universo smiled and nodded in agreement.

"They haven't seen fresh bread for a long time," he said.

The smell of the loaves filled the cabin of the truck, making Aspirrina's mouth water uncontrollably. She wanted to turn around and tear herself a piece and savor it slowly; Celia Sanchez be damned. But she managed to control herself. Another lesson learned: Everything is for the rebels.

It was pitch black when Universo pulled the truck into a grove.

"From here on," Celia said with a resigned sigh, "we walk."

"Walk?" Aspirrina said looking into what seemed to be a dark, impenetrable wall of jungle. Universo jumped out of the back of the truck and camouflaged it with branches until it could not be seen. They set off on foot, slogging their way through the muddy undergrowth in pitch black.

"There is often patrol around these parts," Celia whispered, handing Aspirrina a pistol as casually as if she were handing her a purse. "Keep your ears open to any sound, any at all, you understand?"

All Aspirrina could hear was the pestering squawks of wild parrots. There seemed to be hundreds of them.

"What about the truck? The cargo?" Aspirrina asked.

"Universo will stay here to guard it. The camp is not far, I will send men back to get it all."

The moon came up full, illuminating their steps. The ground played tricks on them, leveling out, but then dipping suddenly. She followed Celia down into a deep ravine. She clung to branches to keep from collapsing. She had only looked away for a moment, but when she looked back, Celia was not there. Then, she heard her voice on the other side of a tree.

"Come this way, quickly," Celia urged.

Aspirrina brushed aside a heavy curtain of fronds, and there, in a clearing lit only by the moon, was the rebel camp, her new home. She was as far away from Havana as a person could get without actually leaving the island. She was high above it all, exactly where she should be, where everything was happening, everything that mattered.

27

As soon as Estelita boarded the jet bound for Mexico City, she began to regret her decision. But it was too wonderful an opportunity to pass up. Lansky had made that perfectly clear. It had all happened so quickly! Only two days ago Hugo Benavides had walked with her into Lansky's office. The two men seemed to know each other well.

"So," Lansky had said, "our little star is going off to make a movie. Well, why not? All a woman needs in this world is to be young and breathtakingly beautiful and doors will open for her. Isn't that so?"

She dropped her eyes, she still couldn't get used to the effect her looks had on the most important people of Havana. *A pretty face is the only passport a woman will ever need.* Apparently she was beautiful, apparently it was true.

"Here are her visa and work permit," Hugo said, placing an envelope on Lansky's desk.

"And the contract?" Lansky asked.

"All there."

Lansky leafed through the papers.

"Thank you for letting me go," Estelita began, she had planned a little speech but she didn't get to finish it.

"Well, I don't *own* you," Lansky said without looking up,

"although to you girls it probably seems like I do. You know, in America we are strong believers in overnight success. It's what we live for."

And without a hint of hesitation, he put his signature on all the papers and passed the pen to her. She quickly signed. She had read them before. At first she thought she would make a lot of money, and when she returned she would have enough to send for her father, get her own place. But she had discovered, to her dismay, that most of her salary would go to Lansky. She would only make slightly more money than she was currently earning, and a lot of it she already had spent on traveling outfits. No matter what Lansky claimed, he did own his girls – or as Juan Carlos proudly said, *the house always wins.*

"Are you all right?" Hugo asked.

"Just a little nervous, that's all."

"There's nothing to be nervous about," Hugo said. "I've been doing this for a long time, I wouldn't gamble on you if I didn't believe you have what it takes."

"The man don't lie," Lansky cut in. "Now, let's see that gorgeous smile, girl, this should be one of the happiest moments of your life."

Lansky was right, it should have been one of the happiest moments of her life, certainly one that would have made her father proud. She remembered how much her father had loved movies, particularly the ones that allowed him to visit foreign lands. When she was a little girl they rarely went to a movie but he'd kept her entertained during their long car rides by recounting the plots to movies like *West of Zanzibar, South of Pago Pago, East of Borneo*, and his favorite, the one he talked abut the most, *North of the Rio Grande.* He had always said that the island he was born on was just too small for him. She wondered how he was and wished she'd had time to take the train to visit him, to tell him the news. But train travel was more dangerous than ever. Since the rebels had cut the country in half, few trains could make it safely to Santa Clara. And now it was she who was off to a foreign land.

Yes, it should have been one of the happiest days of her life and it would have been if only she'd gotten Lansky's cut of her salary. Still, it was a step in the right direction. After this she wouldn't just be a

272

showgirl or even a featured dancer, she would be an actress with a movie under her belt. The money was sure to come then – or so Lansky had assured her.

Estelita had left Lansky's office in a daze. She did the shows, not mentioning her plans. Lansky said he'd take care of it. The show, her last, had gone smoothly. But leaving the others without a word left her feeling empty. She sent a message for Juan Carlos, but hadn't heard from him.

For hours she had been unable to keep her eyes off the phone. Where was he? He'd been angry because she paid too much attention to Hugo Benavides, but she was sure he would come to his senses, understand what a fantastic opportunity this was. She saw the last airplane sail across the sky, the familiar red lights blinking. Midnight. Her bags had been packed for hours. She had carefully folded all her new clothes into her new suitcase; she had spent too much money, but she was satisfied. She had no idea what kind of people she was going to meet or what was awaiting her in Mexico City. She imagined the Mexicans would be sophisticated and fashionable, and she was determined to make a good impression. She didn't want to be perceived as the dusty, provincial girl she was deep inside. She had visited the best shops in Havana and was surprised at how helpful everyone had been. She tried on countless dresses, raw silk and linen for daytime, in soft pastel colors that complimented her skin tones. For the evenings she picked two elegant dresses made of satin and covered with organza. One was black with white trim, the other dusty rose.

"The very latest designs," the saleswoman assured her. Estelita had never purchased jewelry, and she didn't own any. But she did stop by the jewelry counters and admired all the glittering stones. She stood for such a long time that the saleslady stopped asking her if she needed assistance. She lingered over the diamonds, rubies, and emeralds, her eyes tickled by their sparkle. But with a sigh, she declined the saleslady's offer to try them on. Jewelry will come soon enough, she said to herself.

"You will need hats," the saleswoman said as she rang up the purchases, and handed her a business card. "This place is the best."

She was looking forward to seeing Delfino again and hurried to his shop. But it was closed. She peered inside, it was dark in there and felt as if it had been dark for some time.

It was well after midnight and still no word from Juan Carlos. She couldn't wait all night, she had an early flight – a flight she was looking forward to and dreading at the same time.

"To hell with him," she said, plopped down in front of her mirror and began to remove her makeup. She didn't like the look in her eyes, sad, hurt, confused, lonely. She had just wiped her lips clean when there was a knock at her door. She ran to it, looked through the peephole. It was Juan Carlos. She forgot she was angry and forgave him for staying away all night when she was about to leave for a long time.

When she threw open the door, she didn't notice that the knot of his tie was loose, or that his suit was wrinkled, or that his face was oily and haggard from the hours he had spent sitting alone in a smoke-filled bar, nursing a scotch and fingering the tiny velvet box in his pocket. All she saw were his eyes, and that was all she needed to see. A warmth washed over her, a peace, a calm. He no longer made her nervous, not in the same way he had before. But still he had a disorienting effect, whatever she felt was heightened in his presence. She did not stop to wonder why this man, almost a stranger, made her feel this way. She simply stepped back and he walked in. The room was dim, only a small lamp illuminated the space between them. Juan Carlos kept his back to her while he took it all in, the sparkling views, the flawless furniture, the thick, luxurious carpeting. He let out a low, slow whistle of admiration,

"Nice place."

"Yes, but tomorrow it turns back into a pumpkin," she said.

He turned to face her and they smiled at each other. His smile vanished when he saw her luggage neatly piled in a corner.

"Would you like a drink?" she asked, hoping to find something to do with her hands.

"Just water," he answered.

She walked slowly to the bar hoping not to stumble, afraid she would give herself away with an awkward step, a false move. She made it to the bar, and filled one of the cut crystal glasses that she had not had an opportunity to use yet. With her fingers she took a couple of ice cubes out of the silver bucket. The ice tinkled happily as the clear, fresh water filled the glass.

"I came here to convince you to stay," he said, taking the glass from her, "but on the way up I realized that it would be foolish, so instead I came to wish you a good trip, and to give you something to remember me by..."

"Juan Carlos," she said, stepping up closer, "there is no way I could possibly forget you."

"Is this true?" he asked, taking a drink and setting the glass down on the coffee table, never once taking his eyes off of hers.

She nodded. They stood staring at each other. She wanted to be kissed, she wanted to be kissed hard. She wanted to feel his lips on hers, on her neck, on the back of her neck. She wanted to feel his strong arms around her. It was as if her skin was reaching out to his. She was having trouble breathing. She wanted to be taken, and she was. Nothing else mattered. She hadn't felt this joyous, this free since she was a little girl, swimming naked in the blue waters of a deserted cove.

Look papá, I'm a dolphin, I'm a mermaid.

Except now, her father wasn't sitting on the shore making sure she was safe. She let the image of her father slip away and vanish until all that was left was the memory of the warm waters, the beautiful, gentle sunsets and the delicious sensation of Juan Carlos pressing himself against her. He placed a hand on the small of her back, bringing her closer than she ever thought possible, the other hand reached farther up, trapping her against his chest. She felt as if she could disappear inside him and hoped that she would.

His lips were on her cheek, then moved to her brow, then lower to her eyelids. No one had ever touched her there, no one had ever kissed her like this. She shuddered again and again, pressing herself tighter, her hips grinding involuntarily into him, finding his erection and rubbing herself against it as his hands moved lower down, bringing her tighter. His lips moved from her eyes to her ears, his tongue working its way in there, sending up flames of desire all through her.

"Don't go," he whispered, and she knew he meant it. She pushed him away gently and stared in his eyes.

"Please, don't torture me," she said, her eyes filling with tears, tears she did not want to reveal. And then her hands went to his face, pulling him in, and this time, it was she who kissed him, pushing into him, digging her sweet tongue deeper into his mouth, licking his lips and his rough chin, then lower to his muscular neck. She wanted him to know how difficult this separation was going to be for her, that it felt like a flower being torn from the branch before it had a chance to bloom. But in that room, at that moment, all words seemed false. Instead of speaking, she took his hand and led him to her bedroom. They stopped at the edge of the bed. He lifted her skirt and his hand worked its way up to the tender skin between her thighs and then higher, to the place which was covered, for the moment, with black lace. She felt his hand expertly push away her panties. Without thinking, she instinctively parted her legs slightly to give him access, and when his fingers found what they were searching for, she thought she would explode. Her breath picked up speed, almost embarrassingly so.

"Do you need to slow down?" he asked in a hoarse whisper.

Her eyes told him no while she unknotted his tie, letting it drop to the floor. He removed his coat while she unfastened the buttons of his shirt. She spread the white material to reveal his chest and bent down to kiss him there. Together they tumbled onto the bed, landing awkwardly, but to her it seemed like floating.

They were tangled now, half dressed, half undressed. His lips searched for hers once more and while they kissed the rest of their clothes continued to fly off, even more urgently now, until they were both naked and beautiful, her deliciously satin skin contrasting against his darker, masculine body. Estelita felt cold, the room felt cold, everything about the world felt cold, except for the man on top of her and she burrowed into him for warmth, letting him cover her completely. His face moved to her chest, his lips teasing her nipples, then farther down. She felt cold again, but when he buried his face between her legs, a lash of heat ripped through her and suddenly she was perspiring as if the room were on fire. His body was moving, his hands turning her upside down, she took him in her hand, feeling its hardness, unsure of what to do. He stopped what he was doing and looked up for a moment, a glimmer in his eyes, and pushed his hips closer to her. She was surprised when the delicate foreskin slid back. She closed her eyes and she did what she knew he wanted, she licked her lips wet and allowed him to ease into her. She heard him groan with pleasure and decided to make him groan again and again. Nothing mattered but his pleasure.

He returned to what he had been doing and she allowed herself to moan, to make noises she had never made before. The room was filled with the sounds of their passion as she sunk deeper into a dark abyss where only pleasure exists. She felt him ease out of her mouth and suddenly his lips were on hers. She felt him hard between her thighs and stiffened slightly, suddenly frightened, but his kisses relaxed her until she felt her whole body go limp, she couldn't have raised herself off the bed if she'd wanted to. Juan Carlos leaned himself on one elbow, as if levitating over her body, while his other hand took hers and guided it down. She grasped his penis and guided it into her. She felt it rub against her, parting her, and then gliding deep inside. The stab of pain shocked her and she let out a little yelp. His eyes opened to meet hers, and she felt him withdraw.

"Continue," she begged, "I want you to."

When he broke through, she moaned, making sounds only he had ever heard. He was above her, covering her completely, and as he moved inside of her she clung to him ferociously. And when he pulled out and wanted to turn her over so that her back was to him, she let him. He entered her again, this time with ease, for now this territory was his. She pressed her back against his chest, feeling the heat of his skin while his arms encircled her, his hands softly grasping her breasts, his hot breath on her neck. In that moment she felt happy and sad all at once, secure and in a panic, loved, desired and terrified, all the emotions she had always wanted to feel, and others that she was hoping to avoid. She knew that in the morning, when she boarded that airplane for Mexico, an important part of her would remain on the island of Cuba.

The first class cabin was nearly empty. Hugo Benavides slept soundly next to Estelita, his eyes covered with a black mask. His peaceful slumber was aided by the glass of champagne he had gulped down before the plane had even left the ground. But Hugo was used to long flights and he always traveled first class. The stewardesses had greeted him by name, and he was even on friendly terms with the pilots. Estelita fidgeted in the wide, comfortable leather seat. She wished she could sleep, but it seemed impossible. She hadn't touched her breakfast, and the thought of champagne nauseated her. She'd settled for a few sips of guava juice, hoping that the tropical nectar would calm her nervous stomach. The script to *Jacqueline* sat dog-eared on her lap. She'd read it from start to finish. It was all right for a vampire story. She was relieved that although her character appeared frequently, she didn't have much to say. Mostly she wandered in a hypnotic trance wearing diaphanous gowns. The way she felt at the moment, it wouldn't be too much of a challenge.

She kept replaying the events of the morning, the morning after. They had been awakened by a knock on the door, the wake-up call she had requested and completely forgotten. She had disentangled herself from her lover's arms. He didn't want to let her go and playfully clung to her. She could have stayed snuggled next to him for an eternity, and for a split second she entertained the idea of doing just that. She could easily telephone Hugo Benavides and tell him she wasn't going. But agreements had been made, contracts had been signed.

Juan Carlos remained in bed while she showered. She liked having him there but was unaccustomed to someone being in the room while she went through her morning routine. She had her hair to think about, a night of love, she discovered, wasn't gentle on hair. She brushed it back and tied it with a black chiffon scarf. She looked at her face before applying fresh makeup, and wondered if there was anything new in the mirror. Did she seem different? She peered closely into her eyes, and she saw it, yes, way in the back, in a place no one could see, was a woman who'd just made love for the first time.

Delicious, decadent love with a man who knew his way around a woman's body. How many have there been before? A man who looked like him, she told herself, many. Too many. The thought strengthened something inside her. What if she was just one of many, with many more waiting in line? Sure, the night before he had spoken the language of love, but was love really this easy? Could it be this simple? She tried to convince herself that a separation would do them good. When she returned from Mexico, she would know for sure if this was real or just a crazy fling, like the other showgirls regularly enjoyed.

He was dressed and sitting on the living room couch smoking a cigarette when she emerged from the bedroom. He was staring out the window. The morning sun was busily painting everything outside pink and gold. Juan Carlos whistled when he saw her, and she liked it, she liked his long, slow whistle of admiration. She knew she looked good in her new dress and expensive shoes. He stood up to kiss her. She held back a little, afraid that if she gave him too much encouragement she would never get on the airplane. He settled a soft but lingering kiss on her cheek.

"I know you won't believe it," he said with a smile, "but the real reason I came here last night was to give you this."

He held out his hand. In it sat a small black velvet box, like a baby bird he had just captured.

She took it and opened it. Inside were two tiny diamond earrings. She was speechless. This was no ordinary present. If it had been flowers or a heart-shaped box of chocolates...but this. This had taken thought and money. Her apprehensions vanished, and because she couldn't find the words, she kissed him, forgetting all about her lipstick and her hair. She held on to him and he to her, crushing her new dress but it didn't matter. Nothing mattered.

"Hurry back," he said and left. That was it. The door opened and closed and he was gone. She stood still, listening to the sound of his footsteps as they faded into the distance. When she came out of her delicious daze a bellhop was carrying her bags to the elevator and she was trailing behind.

The flight to Ciudad Mexico seemed to last forever. Hugo Benavides continued to sleep in the next seat, not a care in the world.

Hurry back. She couldn't get Juan Carlos's words out of her mind.

She searched the seat pocket for magazines, anything that would distract her.

There was only an airline newsletter and a package marked with the airline's logo. She opened it. Inside was a sleeping mask just like the one Hugo was wearing, toothpaste, a small toothbrush and a miniature sewing kit: little scissors, a needle, a roll of black thread. She placed the sewing kit in her purse and made her way to the bathroom. She locked the door and wiped the counter dry. Then calmly and methodically, she took the needle out of the sewing kit and drove it through her left earlobe. The pain shot through her body, but she liked it. It reminded her of him, of the pain of the previous night. Wishing the pain would go on forever, Estelita then pierced her other ear. Pearls of blood appeared on both wounds, and she dabbed them with a napkin soaked in perfume, glad to feel the burning. She took the velvet box from her purse and, gently removing one diamond earring at a time, she pushed the studs through.

A few minutes later, when she returned to her seat, she was proudly wearing her two little earrings. The diamonds were beautiful. Perfect.

But they did not sparkle nearly as brightly as her eyes.

28

Delfino parked in the wide, circular driveway. His eyes were burning with exhaustion. As he stepped out of the car, he felt pain shoot through every muscle in his back, his neck was so stiff he had trouble moving his head. He stood for a moment on the carefully manicured lawn where bird of paradise grew in thick round clumps, their stiff orange blossoms staring up at the rising sun. His mother hated them, always used to say they were the most unrefined of flowers. But despite how many times she had them cut down, they returned and she eventually learned to live with them. But she always stared at them with a frown as if her disapproval should be enough to make them wither.

He crossed quickly to the front door feeling dwarfed by the large pale-blue house. The twelve windows extending from one side of the facade to the other were dark, like mouths caught in a big black yawn.

He knocked hard. Something in his chest tightened while he waited.

"Who is it?"

Even through the thick varnished wood, he knew it was Clotilda. He had been a boy when she came to work for them, a skinny girl with tiny braids all over her head and a loose, faded cotton dress over her bony frame. He remembered how frightened she had been to find herself in such opulent surroundings. Her nervousness had caused all sorts of disturbances those first weeks, dishes had shattered, beverages were spilled. But his mother had inexhaustible patience with new girls, the way some people have with puppies. Eventually Clotilda had been trained, housebroken, and the family was much the better for it – she was faithful, over-protective, and she didn't steal. He remembered the thefts, how the house would be heavy with suspicion for days. There would be interrogations, accusations, tears and dismissals. Clotilda had survived them all.

"It's me," he said just loud enough that she could hear it.

The door remained closed.

"Who is it?" she repeated.

"It's Leonardo, Cloti, open the door."

The bolt slid fast, the door opened and her big eyes lit up when she saw him.

"Ay, Leonardito," she said, "where are your keys?"

She moved aside and he stepped into the foyer. She was close to him in age, but seemed much older. He wondered what troubles could possibly be aging her so rapidly. Certainly life with his parents was as good as any poor black woman could possibly hope for. Or was it?

"I don't carry the keys to this house with me," he said and walked quickly into the house, propelled by an energy he didn't trust. He had to keep moving or he would simply collapse. "I need to see my mother," he said, "where is she?"

"Ay, your mother is in Nueva York," she said. Her voice always sounded worried.

"Well, where's my father?"

"In his room, sleeping, of course. Is something wrong, Leo?"

He left her without an answer and walked through the dark living room to the wide curving stairs. He took the steps two at a time, found his parents' bedroom and entered without knocking.

His father was asleep, alone in the big bed. Delfino stood in the middle of the bedroom, taking in its aroma. The scent was as familiar as anything could possibly be. He had been a child in this house, in this room. He remembered coming here when he woke up too early, and crawling into bed with them, feeling safe next to their warm bodies. That was a million years ago, before the change, before he'd had to withdraw, before he'd been told big boys didn't do that. In this room he had learned that being part of a family didn't guarantee access. The big bedroom had turned into a place of mystery and longing. His parents had each other. He had only himself. It was a strange loneliness that had only subsided when he met Arjuna.

He loved waking up and keeping his eyes closed, knowing he was not alone then, opening them slowly, he would turn to find Arjuna's face in profile, peacefully sleeping next to him. He loved knowing his friend was there, sharing the same bed, breathing the same air. It was all he needed, all he'd ever wanted. He wondered if his parents had felt the same about each other, if he missed her when she was in New York.

"Papá," he called out. He meant for it to be a whisper, but it came out loud and harsh, like a demand. His father sat up, immediately wide-awake as if he hadn't been asleep at all.

"Leonardo?" he said as his eyes adjusted in the darkness, "What in the world are you doing here?"

Delfino froze. All along it had seemed as if this was his only recourse, but now he was filled with doubts. He would have to tell his father everything and it wasn't going to be easy.

"Leonardo?" his father said again and yawned.

Delfino walked around the bed and sat at one of the armchairs by the cold fireplace. He realized that he was acting like a madman. What was he thinking, crashing into his father's bedroom like a wild animal? How would he feel if his father had broken into his apartment, invited himself into his bedroom? Delfino detested his desperation, wished that he could start all over again, calmly. Everything his father thought about him, that he was immature and reckless would be confirmed in the next few minutes, and he hated that.

"I need your help, it's urgent," he said in a rush of words.

"Well, it must be, what the hell time is it?" his father said, with an irritated look to the clock. Delfino remained quiet while his father eyed him suspiciously.

"I was up late playing cards," his father said. "Why don't you go downstairs and I'll meet you in a while."

"I need you now."

"Very well," he said, swinging his feet over the side of the bed and fishing around with his toes for his slippers, "will you at least give me time to take care of business?"

Delfino nodded and watched his father shuffle to the bathroom. He heard the powerful stream hit the water. No one had more of a right to be here, he thought. The same spout that is emptying his bladder is where my life began. No two people could be more closely related. So why did he feel like such a complete stranger, an intruder? How was he going to find the words to tell him the truth? He placed his shaking hands lightly on his lap. He had to calm down, he knew how his father liked problems presented calmly. Nothing irritated his father more than hysteria. But Delfino had now been hysterical for hours. After driving past the boathouse in Jaimanitas, he had returned to Havana, to Eusebio's house. Eusebio's wife had opened the door and her eyes had been wide with fear. The fear turned to anger when she saw him.

"We heard," she said, before Delfino had a chance to speak. "Eusebio has gone into hiding and so have all the others. I'm packing up the kids and going to my sister."

"But why?" he asked.

"Why?" her voice was low, "because, you stupid, stupid man, Arjuna's going to talk. He's going to name each and every one of you."

"Arjuna would never do that."

Her face twisted into an exhausted sneer.

"Everyone who falls into the hands of Ventura Novo talks."

"How do you know that's where he is? He could be in a hospital, or–"

She cut him off fast.

"We know."

She started to close the door, but opened it again.

"All you can do now is pray he doesn't play the tough guy and that he talks, talks plenty and quickly. Pray they kill him fast. I'm not one to give advice, but if I were you, I would hide my ass for a good long time, or you'll end up just like him."

Her words hit their mark. His eyes crystallized with fear.

"Don't look for any of them, they can't help you. Just disappear. If you know what's good for you, Delfino, you will disappear."

And she had closed the door.

Delfino heard the toilet flush, the sound of water running in the sink. His father returned to the bedroom and took an armchair opposite him, then clicked on his mother's exquisite tulip-topped floor lamp. Even its soft light made Delfino's eyes hurt.

"What's wrong with you?" his father asked.

"This is going to upset you," Delfino warned.

"Stop it with the hysterics, son, what's on your mind?"

He wanted to meet his father's eyes, but he couldn't. He found a place over his shoulder, an oil painting of a pink ballerina caught at the highest point of a sublime grand jeté, and tried to stay focused there. His mother's touch again. Paintings were all over the house. In her bedroom, ballerinas. In the living room, giant landscapes. In the dining room were his favorites, water flowers: lilies and lotuses. It was part of her inexhaustible effort to bring civility to what she considered a savage island. It would be so much easier if his mother were here. Or would she be horrified? He found the courage in the ballerina, masterfully rendered on canvas, her arms and legs perfectly horizontal, back arched, chest upwards, chin forward, trapped in flight forever in his parents' bedroom, never landing, but always graceful.

"I have a friend," Delfino said, his words started out clear and firm, but a spasm caught on the word 'friend.' "He is in terrible trouble, Papá. I'm hoping that you can help me."

He knew that tears were dammed inside of him and the dam was just about to overflow, but he couldn't let that happen, not here, not in front of him. He had to be strong, the strong man his father had always wanted. He looked away from the ballerina and met his father's eyes. Any improper display of emotion would ruin everything.

"This *friend*," his father said, carefully measuring every word. "What sort of *friend* is he?"

Delfino felt all the tears inside of him dry up. He looked deeper into his father's eyes.

"What does it matter? He's a friend. The point is," he said trying to control his impatience, "is that I need your help. Will you help us?"

His father shifted in his chair.

"All right, this friend of yours, this evidently a very important friend, what has he done? What could be so dire that you grace me with

285

a visit?"

He hated to say it but each minute wasted was one more minute Arjuna would be at the mercy of Ventura Novo.

"He was caught with explosives."

"Por Dios, Leonardo."

"I know, he was stupid."

"Beyond, beyond," his father said shaking his head. "Do you know where he is?"

Delfino nodded.

"Ventura Novo has him, that's what I've been told."

"Ventura Novo?" his father said with an ugly smile. "Ventura Novo?"

Delfino continued nodding, his face bobbing up and down and then his whole body was shaking.

"Son," he said, standing up, "there's nothing anyone can do. Your *friend* is dead."

Delfino stood up to leave but something was missing. He felt as if everything beneath his neck was gone. He knew he had a face because he was looking at his father who was moving quickly about the room. And he knew he had legs because he was still standing. But where his heart should be, his guts, his lungs, all of that was missing.

"Don't go," his father ordered as he hurried into his clothes.

"But you won't help me."

"Oh, I'm going to help you all right. You're going to New York."

"What?"

"I know what you're not telling me, Leonardo, I've known you your whole life. I know you're involved, I know," he said, shaking his head. "Look son, your mother is there, she will help you find a place. You cannot stay in this country."

"I'm not going anywhere," Leonardo shouted, "I have to find him."

He started for the door.

His father blocked his exit.

"You know what you're going to find? Maybe a hand, a leg; if you're lucky, his head, but you will not recognize the face."

Delfino recoiled, his father was standing so close he could smell his stale breath, his unbrushed teeth.

"You will not want to look at your lover's face after Novo is done with him."

Delfino gripped the doorknob.

"Yes, I know who this man is to you, this rebel or whatever you call yourselves," his father whispered. "I know what this so-called revolution is all about."

Delfino pushed past him, opened the door and ran across the long hallway, down the curving stairs, across the vast floor of the living room. "I never thought I'd see you fall this low," his father shouted after him. "The Hyenas will tear him to pieces."

Delfino didn't stop until he was inside his car. As he gunned the engine he looked back to see if his father had followed him.

He hadn't.

They had stripped him naked and thrown him into a narrow, putrid cell. The floor was hot and smeared with dry blood, vomit and shit. The cell was without windows and filled with suffocating smells. Every breath he took was tainted. How many others had died there, he wondered as he sucked on the raw patch at the end of his little finger, where his nail had once been. They had held him down while he struggled with all his might. At first his sweaty body had been hard to grasp, and they had laughed and made jokes as if this was some sort of game to them. But soon they tired of it and got down to business, their powerful hands sinking deep into the muscles of his arms and legs, paralyzing him.

The two men held him still while a third ripped the nail off with pliers. The pain of the small pink shell ripping apart from his skin had sent arrows of fire to every part of his body. He was astonished that he could withstand the burning pain. He saw the butt of a black pistol swing towards him, the impact, an explosion of lights and then it was dark.

When he came into consciousness he immediately knew where he was. His wounded finger was in his mouth, the saliva kept it from burning. He kept his eyes closed, kept still. He knew that they would return as soon as he stirred, this was all part of their game, one nail at a time until they wore him down, until he told them what they wanted to

Eduardo Santiago

know. And he knew that after the fingers and toes came the testicles, then his penis, and then, if that didn't do it, if they still believed he was holding back more information, they would go for his eyes. He knew who was behind it all: Ventura Novo. The man who never got his hands dirty but was responsible for atrocious deeds. He'd seen his photograph on the front page of newspapers dressed in his customary white suit, looking like a bad actor in a gangster movie, a sardonic smile on his face. In the background there was always a group of detained youths whose lives he had spared for the sake of publicity, or a room of confiscated weapons.

His name inspired horror and repugnance. Ventura Novo, the killer from Havana's Fifth Precinct, as famous for his massacres as for his stylish suits. His guards were even more loathsome; people called them the Hyenas. All who saw them coming up the sidewalk, even those who were clean beyond any possible reproach, crossed to the other side of the street and prayed to every saint they could name. He could hear them now, outside his cell, talking and laughing. Life went on outside while he waited, for what? More pain? More questions? Death? Was he willing to die or would they break him? It wasn't so much the moments of excruciating pain that the Hyenas relished, it was the time in between tortures; they knew it was the anticipation of even harsher punishment that made prisoners talk. Like the interminable moments of silence while the firing squad reloads. Moments that made even the most courageous patriots beg for a blindfold.

He had to think fast. He didn't know how much longer he could stand the torture. He had to have a plan. When the Hyenas returned, and it could be any at any moment, they may forget all about the fingernails and go straight for his testicles. If he started to crumble, he would give them Delfino's name first. Delfino had rich and powerful parents who could bail him out of any situation. Delfino's father probably played dominoes with Batista. The others had no one. The others would end up like him, stuck in a cell without a prayer. Yes, even if it tore his heart to pieces, if the pain became unbearable, if it was more than he could stand, if they went for his balls or his eyes, he would give them the name of the only person he had ever truly loved: Leonardo Delfino.

Delfino pulled the car into the long, tree-lined drive.

Seated next to him, Sor Maria took in the magnificent house. The stone columns and lace ironwork that surrounded the entrance to her parents' estate were exactly as she had left them. But something was different. More than a dozen new, shiny, American cars were lined up along the drive. She fingered her rosary, repeating unspoken prayers. She invoked the Hail Mary, the Our Father, the Soul of Christ, finally settling on her favorite childhood prayer to her Guardian Angel, for it seemed, given the circumstances, the most appropriate:

> *Angel of God, my guardian dear*
> *To whom God's love commits me here,*
> *Ever this day, be at my side,*
> *To light and guard, rule and guide.*

"We're here," Delfino said.

"I know."

Delfino opened his door, but she stopped him.

"I should go in alone."

"Are you sure?"

"Yes."

She hadn't set foot in the house since the day she had left, hadn't seen her parents in nearly the same amount of time.

"I'll never stop being grateful for this," he said, settling back behind the steering wheel, "for all you've done. I always knew you were the one person in the world I could count on."

She took him in her arms in a long embrace. He was trembling. She had never before held anyone who trembled so.

He had been trembling when he arrived at the convent an hour ago, lost and desperate, interrupting Sunday services. The horrifying story had come gushing out. He'd told her what she needed to know and more than it was safe for her to know. She had felt pity and annoyance. Hadn't she already done enough? Was there no end to his demands on their friendship? She had hoped her vocation would shelter her from the world and the world had come crashing in. Had she willed it or was it God's will? She could never be sure. As her pulse quickened, she knew she had to help him. He had no one else and if she refused him it would only be out of arrogant pride. Was she too proud to try to save a man's life? Was she too proud to assist her one and only friend? She had made her decision fast, afraid that too much thought, too much reasoning, would keep her from doing what she had to do.

"I'll talk to them," she said.

"Are you sure?"

"Of course not," she replied, hurrying to his car. "It is not a matter of being sure, it's a matter of being willing."

The drive had seemed long, although her parents lived just outside of Havana. But it had been like traveling back through time, taking a route at once familiar and absolutely foreign. Sor Maria broke away from Delfino and made it to the tall front door. She was here, where everything began where everything ended. It was like opening an old favorite book and discovering someone had translated it to another language. She knew the story but couldn't read it. She could hear the distant music of a guitar coming through the wide open windows, as if the music itself was causing the soft fresh-scented breeze that flowed through the veranda and made her veil flutter. She saw herself reflected in the glass panes of the front door and wanted to back away. So much of the young girl who had once lived in this house was still there. But the black habit and veil, she knew, identified her as an alien, a woman from another place.

Her knocks went unanswered. She tried the door, it was unlocked. Suddenly she was inside, in the big living room with its intricate marble floors and mirrored hallways. Everything looked just the same, the walls seemed freshly painted but they were still a delicate peach, the furniture was still white, French and frail.

A black maid wearing a black dress and white apron hurried towards her.

"Welcome, Sister," she said smiling respectfully, "you're just a little late. Isn't the music beautiful?"

"Yes, it's lovely," Sor Maria replied.

"It's la señora's favorite."

"Yes, I know."

The maid's eyes quickly searched her face, then she turned.

"Come with me, please," she offered.

290

They walked across the wide living room and towards tall French doors that opened onto the wide stretch of lawn, green and tidy. Two dozen guests sat at small round tables arranged in a circle around a guitarist. Everyone was listening intently.

Sor Maria stopped.

"Could you tell El Señor that his daughter is here?"

The maid turned to face her, a smile of recognition in her eyes.

"Ah yes," she said, "I thought you looked familiar."

"The photographs," Sor Maria said.

"I dust them," the maid said. "There are dozens of them all over the house."

Sor Maria nodded.

Without another word, the maid descended the few steps to the lawn. Sor Maria watched her lean to whisper in her father's ear. He turned as if he'd been jolted with electricity, knocking over a champagne flute, which the maid quickly retrieved and set upright. Neither the guitarist nor the guests seemed to notice. Her father tapped the elegant woman sitting next to him and whispered in her ear. Both stood up at once. Others turned to look but only briefly, their attention held captive by the magical sounds of the guitar.

Her mother reached her first. They took each other's hands wordlessly and looked into the other's eyes.

"Maria," she said, a lilting question in her voice.

"Si, Mamá."

Her father took her in a powerful embrace.

"Papá," she heard herself whisper, her breath on his neck. She had no idea she missed him so much. No idea it would be as simple as walking in the door.

"What is it, Maria?" her mother asked, "what's wrong?"

"I am here to ask an enormous favor," she said, "I hope you will forgive the intrusion."

Her parents glanced at each other.

"Yes, my dear," her father said. "Anything."

Her mother and father nodded in agreement.

"Are you ill?" her father asked. "You're so skinny."

Maria dismissed the question with a shake of her head.

"Is it money?" her mother asked.

291

"No, no," she said quickly, noting the expression change on her mother's face. Money would be easy.

"Let's go where we can talk," her father said taking his wife's hand. Maria followed them into his study. The familiar smell of leather-bound books and polished wood greeted her. Her mother closed the door firmly.

"Sit down, Maria," her mother said, "sit wherever you want, this is still your home."

Sor Maria's heart filled with a strange joy at the sound of those words.

"Thank you," she said, feeling as if her manner was too formal, too stiff, hoping she could feel less like a nun, more like a daughter. She took a chair and sat very straight, her back hardly touching wood.

"I don't have very much time," she started.

"Naturally," her mother said.

"Be direct," her father said with a sharp glare at his wife. "We are your family."

Maria turned to her father. She spoke quickly but clearly.

"I have a friend in a terrible situation and I believe you can help."

"What sort of situation?" her mother asked.

"It is dreadful," she said. "He has been arrested."

"Arrested," her mother said. "What has this friend done? Is it one of the nuns?"

"Elena, please," her father said. Her mother placed a hand to her chest as if to stop something pounding there.

"No, mother, it's a man. He's been detained and worst of all, my friend is undeniably guilty."

She stopped and searched their eyes.

"He's being held by Ventura Novo. I believe the charge is treason," she said and watched her father's face cloud with worry. Her mother's eyes flickered towards the windows. "They will kill him," she continued, "unless we intervene. And it has to be immediately."

A silence followed. Her father was looking at her the way he did when weighing a complicated situation. This was so wrong, why had she come? How could God allow her to make such a grave mistake?

"I will understand if you refuse," she added, "all I can do is present the situation and let you decide. But I must know your decision right away."

"Maria, are you involved in this?" her mother asked.

Maria lowered her eyes.

Her mother's hand floated from her heart, where it had been clenched, to her lips. But a hand to the lips could not stop her from speaking.

"You disappear from our lives and now you return, with this?" her mother said.

She walked to the window. Maria saw her part the drapes and knew she was checking on her guests.

"I'm so sorry. This is an unforgivable imposition. You have no reason to involve yourself in these affairs. I see now I've made a terrible mistake."

She stood up to leave. Her mother turned away from the window and came to stand next to her father.

"Maria, sit down," her father said. And he said it with such force that she was compelled to do as he said. It was as if her body remembered, much more clearly than her mind, who he was to her.

"I've never asked you for much," Sor Maria said, "I thought just this once..."

"Never asked us for much?" her mother said. She couldn't disguise, not that she was trying, the anger in her voice.

"Elena, no," her father ordered.

"Why not?" her mother said, looking away from Maria. "She's asked us to forget we have a daughter. She has asked me to forget that I carried her in my womb, fed her from my breast, taught her how to talk and walk. She has asked us to forget that we wanted grandchildren, and the company of our only daughter."

"Elena, no," he repeated.

"Alberto, she has to know," her mother continued, now looking directly at her. "Do you have any idea the darkness you left behind? The sadness? The humiliation and pain I endured every time I went to that place and was told that you could not see me? And for what, Maria? So that you could serve Jesus Christ? Who is this Jesus Christ? We are your parents."

"Elena, there's no point," her father said.

"No point?" her mother continued, "After all these years she returns to tell us that now she's traded Jesus Christ for Fidel Castro! What are we to make of all this? What are we worth to her? Less than nothing, that's what."

And with that she crumpled into a chair, convulsing with sobs. Her father pulled out a handkerchief and offered it to her mother. She smacked his hand away, the sound of it crackling in the room.

"I can't tell you how sorry I am that I came here today, how I regret opening this wound for you, Mamá. But sometimes we need to think of the greater sacrifice. Yes, what has happened to our family is unfortunate and I know it was all my fault. I cannot ask you to forgive me. But please, open your hearts for just a tiny little moment, and think of a young man who, because of a stupid mistake, a lapse of judgment, is also suffering."

"Shut up," her mother said, "you sound just like I always feared you would, like a pathetic little nun. You bring light to the lives of others and only darkness to ours. I want nothing to do with this," she said with finality, patting her hair into place and smoothing down her dress. "I have guests. Some of them are friends and some of them are strangers, but none of them have ever treated me with as much disrespect as my own daughter."

She flung the door open and she was gone. Only the lilac smell of her perfume remained.

Sor Maria stayed seated. Her father towered above her. She couldn't look at him so she fixed her eyes on his feet, the expensive leather shoes shined like black mirrors.

"I always knew this day would come, and now it's over and done with," he said with a sigh. "Your mother has missed you so much, but you remember how she is, she gets upset, blows up, cries, rants and raves, and then she comes around. She's not always happy with me either. You've missed some good fights around here."

He was smiling down at her, but she continued staring at his shoes.

"Maria?"

She did nothing.

"Maria," he called out again, "if I help this young man who means so much to you, will you...promise to disengage from them, from people like them?"

She looked up, tears streaming down her face. She couldn't recall the last time she had wept so much, tears just kept coming and coming.

"Maria?"

She nodded slowly as if her head was too heavy for her neck to sustain.

"You still have the face of an angel," he said.

Tears welled in his own eyes. She looked up, he was dabbing his eyes with a handkerchief. He offered it to her and her tears mingled with his. He walked to the window and motioned for her to join him. She did.

Outside, the guitarist was still playing. Her mother had returned to her seat, her hands tightly grasping and releasing a linen napkin.

Maria felt the warm comfort of her father's arm around her shoulders and thought about Esteban. He'd been leaving the convent for hours every day searching for Estelita.

She shuddered to think of the horror and pain that must be churning inside of him, hoping to find his child while dreading where he would find her, and in what condition. It had only been a few months since Estelita left the convent, but who in heaven knew what could have happened to her during that time, what level of degradation she had reached. Esteban was not an easy guest. Maria had looked the other way when she found all the plaster saints in the chapel turned backwards, white candles burning, and a small bowl of honey placed as offering at their feet.

But the others were outraged.

"He's worshipping the devil in our chapel," Sor Beatriz cried.

"No he's not," Sor Maria had responded calmly, "just God, the same God, in a different way. Try to be tolerant, he won't be here for long."

Daily, Maria set the statues back to the way they should be, facing forward. She removed the rocks and the cigars, the honey and the rum. She let the candles burn, and didn't say a word to him. If this was what he felt he needed to do to strengthen his faith, she would not stand in his way.

"You know, you're not that different from my people," Maria's father was saying. "You were born into all this, I wasn't. I wasn't born into a house with marble floors; our house had no floors at all, just dirt. You chose to walk away from it, and that's all right. Your grandmother would have been proud. She detested the rich. Ultimately, we can never really please our parents, can we?"

He tightened the arm around her shoulder, bringing her even closer. The guitarist finished playing. Maria heard the applause, watched her mother stand up and walk to the guitarist and shake his hand.

"You see that man over there," her father said, pointing with his chin, "the one in the white suit?

"Yes."

"That's Ventura Novo."

From Delfino's description, she had expected the personification of the devil, but Ventura Novo was simply a man, dapper in a white linen suit. He held his glass of white wine elegantly and looked like any other of her parents' friends.

"How could you allow such a man in your house?"

"Better a friend at your table than an enemy at your door."

Maria made the sign of the cross slowly, taking her time letting her thumb travel from her forehead to her navel, to one shoulder and her other.

"Yes, Sister, pray that he listens to me. Pray that he grants me this favor."

He kissed her cheek and walked out of the room. He had called her sister. He accepted her as she was, as a nun.

Maria remained at the window and watched her father return to the party. Rather than pray to God that Ventura Novo release Arjuna, she gave Him thanks, and she thanked her guardian angels and prayed for her mother's soul. She saw her father approach Ventura Novo's table, watched her father reach into his coat pocket and take out a cigar and offer it to Ventura Novo. She watched the man in the white suit stand up, watched her father light the cigar for him.

Her father then placed an arm around the man and led him away from the party, towards the house. They were facing her now, she could see that her father was doing all the talking while Novo sucked happily on his cigar and nodded respectfully.

29

Esteban de la Cruz walked through the teeming streets of Havana, dressed in his clean white shirt and pants, a ghost ship in a turbulent sea of strangers. In 1958, one million people lived in Havana, and from what he could see most of them were orphans, cripples or derelicts. Not just one or two, as had been the case in the small towns of his past. In Havana, armies of beggars roamed the streets at all hours. Every day he passed the dark, blank-faced women who sat huddled in doorways holding infants in their malnourished arms like afterthoughts. He walked past dithering men who all seemed to be missing something essential, an eye, an ear, an arm. Some of them had open sores, their faces red and raw. All of them watched him pass with craving eyes.

He always walked alone, leaving Orquidea at the convent. At first she had tearfully pleaded to come with him, but now seemed happy to stay. She helped the nuns with the laundry, and had started attending mass. He set out every afternoon at the same time. This was the time the taxi driver had suggested. This was when the las mujeres de la vida, the women of the life, as the taxi driver called them, started to emerge from their hangovers and their exhaustion.

Every afternoon, at three, Esteban walked past the same beggar, the one missing both legs, the one who sat in a child's red wagon and was pulled down the sidewalk by a little girl in a bright yellow dress. They fascinated Esteban, the legless man wore a dirty khaki shirt that had been mended over and over again, while the little girl blazed like a sun in her perfectly clean and starched dress. Many coins were dropped into his hat because he gave the illusion, warranted or not, that in spite of being a beggar, he was a good father. It was the girl's dress. Anyone could see that every night he washed and ironed it, her hair was clean and neatly braided. Even her teeth gleamed with wholesome whiteness. The little girl seemed happy to be with her father.

"She doesn't mind pulling that wagon as long as he's in it," Esteban thought.

The two always took him back to the times when his Estelita had tried to look after him. He had both his legs, yet she had a much heavier load to pull. A father who disappeared for days on end, a father who left her alone in strange hotel rooms. If he could just find her, he'd make it all up to her. He would never stop making it up to her. He walked past the lottery peddlers, their hoarse voices a beacon of hope.

!ONE PESO COULD WIN TEN THOUSAND BY NIGHTFALL!

He no longer trusted games of chance. Not that money had ever been significant to him as long as he had enough to pay for a hotel room, and a few drinks at a bar. Now he had no money at all, not even for a lotto ticket with the promise of ten thousand.

The day after his conversation with Sor Maria, he had set out to find her, driven by demons named Shame and Regret. He took to the unfamiliar streets without a plan. He knew taxi drivers were a good place to begin. He found a large group of them outside the Hotel Inglaterra, their shiny cars parked like a multicolored wagon train, in the shade of the Framboyan trees, away from the scorching sun. They were an intimidating group, clean-shaven and smelling strongly of cologne. Successful businessmen who could take you to any corner of the big city. It showed in the confident, joyful way they talked to one another, their hands cutting the air wildly. Their voices were deep, lacking any doubt. They could tease one another, they could argue with each other without ending in fistfights. They were in control. This had once been his tribe, back then, back when he could stand at a bar and talk sports and politics and sexual conquest, just drunk enough to be amusing, before he crossed over to annoying, and finally boorish and violent. But he found them intimidating now. He watched them from a distance. How to approach them? In the old days he would have offered to buy them a drink, or point out a poster with his picture on it. Esteban de la Cruz, the famous singer! The man their wives wouldn't stop chattering about to each other. That was back then, back when he held the winning hand. Now he held nothing. How could he tell them he was looking for a daughter who had become a whore in Havana? He dreaded finding her through them, discovering that they knew her, had maybe even been with her, for a few pesos or a late night cab ride back to town. He stood watching them for a long time, hoping he could figure a way to get in with them without showing his hand. So many people in Havana! He walked among the taxi drivers without eliciting even the slightest glance. He saw well-dressed people emerge from the hotels that lined the boulevard.

"How much to Marianao?"

"How much to Varadero Beach?"

"How much to Regla?"

All the taxi drivers would shout out prices and conditions, trying to outbid each other.

"Regla? You need a boat for Regla, my friend."

"Tres pesos!" they shouted.

"Cinco pesos."

"Seis pesos return trip, and I wait for you."

"Diez pesos to Rancho Boyeros Airport, luggage included."

The rich ones who didn't haggle took all the fun out of the game. They just opened the door and jumped in while the driver ran around the car and settled behind the wheel. They were the big fish, Americanos who didn't care what anything cost, only how long it would take to get there and back. They always returned, and they always tipped. Not all the Americans were rich, many were there for a cheap vacation.The Cubans didn't tip, they only used the taxis for emergencies, so nobody jumped at the chance to drive them. Everyone wanted Americanos, that's where the real money was. A round trip to Varadero Beach or Santa Maria del Mar provided enough money to keep a family fed for a week. As the afternoon wore on and the heat began to subside, all the tourists came out at once, as if synchronized. One by one the taxis were taken. They pulled away from the curb and vanished to all parts of the city. Esteban waited until only one taxi remained. The driver leaned against the hood, peacefully reading the racing form and smoking. He smoked luxuriously, inhaling deeply and deliberately, then slowly releasing long funnels of smoke into the crystal clear air. He was a little older than the others, and he seemed completely unconcerned that he wasn't making money, content to be left alone for a few minutes. Esteban saw his opportunity. It was now or never.

"Mi hermano," he said, approaching the taxi driver with an outstretched hand and flashing a smile he did not feel. The man almost reluctantly opened the back door to the car.

"Adelante, señor," he said with enthusiasm. "Right this way."

Esteban stayed where he was.

"I need to ask you a question," he said.

The taxi driver eyed him suspiciously.

"Mira, I have this problem," Esteban said. "I don't have any money to hire you, but I have to ask you a very serious question."

The man nodded.

"I'm not from Havana, and I need to find the prostibulos, you know, where the women are."

The man closed the car door.

"You don't have any money but you are looking for a whore? Nothing in Havana is free, amigo, and particularly pussy. Suerte, my friend, good luck."

And he went back to leaning against the car and to his racing form. Esteban got closer to him and leaned against the car.

"It's not what you think," he said, his voice quivering, "it's my daughter, man, I think..."

The man lowered the racing form. Esteban could tell that the man knew the story, had heard the story many times before. The taxi driver raised a hairy eyebrow.

"You think she's..."

"Yes, that's what someone told me, that she's taken some wrong turn."

"That's tough, viejo" the taxi driver said, "but what are you

300

going to do? The girls today they do what they want."

"I have to find her."

"Sure, I understand, but even if you find her, there's a good chance that she'll tell you to go fuck yourself, that's what they're like today, you know."

The idea that Estelita could feel that way had not crossed his mind. But he accepted the possibility. He realized that he had no way of knowing how much she had changed in the two years since he'd seen her. For all he knew she'd grown tough and hard in order to survive.

"I'm willing to take that risk," Esteban said, "I just have to find her, find out for myself that this is what she really wants to do, that someone isn't forcing her."

"And maybe she'll share some of the money with you?"

Esteban didn't answer, but his hands formed into fists. Back then, back when, the man's teeth would soon be scattered all over the pavement. But he chose to let it go. Let him think what he wants.

"I have to find her, but I don't know where to start. Can you help me at all?"

"Look, friend," the man said, "there are as many whores in Havana as fish in the sea. Just walk around the big hotels, you'll find them. You can always tell who they are because they all walk the same."

Esteban wanted to slap him, again and again. *I know what a whore looks like. I know what a whore looks like.*

"But my daughter," he said calmly, "she's a really beautiful girl, they said she was in a prostibulo, a real exclusive place."

"Sure she is," the taxi driver began, but something in Esteban's eyes cautioned him against it.

"There is a street that's full of them," he said, "it's called Calle Virtudes. If she was my daughter, I would look there and when I found her, I would cut off her tits."

Calle Virtudes was not so much a street as a narrow, curving alley with three story buildings on both sides, bars, stores and cafés on the ground floor and apartments on the two floors above. It was early evening by the time Esteban found his way there. He was reluctant to ask for directions because there was only one reason why a man would want to find Calle Virtudes. He had circled the center of the city, making narrower circles until he'd stumbled into it. The taxi driver had been correct. The street, even at that early hour, teemed with women of all ages in tight revealing attire. There were tall mulatas in bright satin dresses crimson red, celestial blue, coral pink, making their skin look as dusky and delicious as a Marroo grape. Their hair was hot-iron straight and piled high up. They paraded back and forth, restless as birds. The other girls, varied in skin tones from cinnamon brown to creole pink, stood on the shady side of the street, leaning against the cool cement walls, their hard, often homely faces painted like masks. Thick maquillaje covered blemishes and discolorations. Rouge redefined puffy cheeks, long black lines enhanced beady eyes. Blue powder shadowed droopy eyelids. Homemade beauty marks were strategically drawn to distract from noses too big or too wide. Any shadow of mustaches shaved clean, any errant chin hairs plucked. This was not the cream of the crop, these were common streetwalkers, most of them past their prime, if they ever had a prime. Thick tummies protruded through the flimsy fabric, breasts hung heavy with age, varicose veins ran like blue tracks up and down tired legs.

Men pulled wooden carts loaded with vegetables, or chickens or garbage pails down the middle of Calle Virtudes without so much as a glance at the girls they could never afford. Half-naked children played games on the sidewalk, still too young to be aware of their mothers' vocation. On the sunny side of the street, foreign men strolled, casually eyeing the prostitutes. Some wore their Sunday best and reeked of cologne. Many wore the naval uniforms of their native countries. The women on the opposite sidewalk tossed sassy, well-rehearsed invitations at them.

"Don't be shy," they would say, "Come talk to me."

"I don't bite, unless you want me to."

Occasionally a man crossed the street and, like a fly willingly surrendering to the sticky fragrance of the Venus flower, vanished into a dark hallway. The woman always led the way, she knew that as long as she could keep his eyes riveted to her round, undulating ass, he wasn't going to change his mind.

!ONE PESO WINS YOU TEN THOUSAND BY NIGHTFALL!

Esteban didn't know whether to be disappointed or relieved that none of the girls was Estelita. He took a seat at Café Las Virtudes, directly across from the girls, and waited. He would wait all night, he would wait the rest of his life if he had to. A scrawny waiter in a dirty black apron, with greasy hair and shaking hands came to take his order. Esteban asked for a glass of water and the waiter brought it to him without complaining. Esteban sipped his water slowly, keeping an eye on the activity in front of him. He didn't want to listen to the voice of fear in his head. Instead, he concentrated on the sounds of the wooden wheels of the carts on the bumpy cobblestone street, the constant hawking of the vegetable vendor and lottery peddlers, the barking dogs. As it got darker, more men, now fortified by an afternoon of drinking, ventured across the street. Balconies that had been closed to the afternoon heat now opened and music poured into the air. More women appeared on the sidewalk. The children vanished as if an invisible hand had whisked them away. Esteban had sat there for hours and there had been no other customers at the café.

"Want some company?" the waiter asked not waiting for an answer but taking a seat and lighting a cigarette. He offered one to Esteban, who declined.

"Business is slow," Esteban said.

"The only ones who make money on this street is them," he said, pointing to the women across the street with his cigarette. "We get the spillover, after they've done their business, some of the men stop in for something to eat. Usually they go to the bars to drink. Sometimes the girls get hungry and send one of the kids down for a sandwich. We do all right. Some days are better than others. Today is not a good day."

Esteban nodded.

"And you," the waiter said with a wicked smile, "can't decide which girl to take?"

Esteban considered his answer.

"I'm here for another reason."

"The healing powers of my tap water?"

Esteban noticed little scabs in the crook of the waiter's elbows and between his fingers, as if insects with long sharp needles had been feeding there.

"Maybe you can help me," Esteban said, "I'm looking for someone who is very important to me. Her name is Estelita de la Cruz."

"I know girls named Estelita," the waiter said, "but I don't know their last names. The girls, they don't use last names and most of them, even their real names are a mystery. What do you need with her, she owe you money?"

"No, nothing like that, I just need to find her."

The waiter shrugged.

"You are welcome to sit here as long as you want," he said crushing the cigarette butt into the tin can that served as an ashtray. "My name is Eleguá."

He took off his apron and underneath he was dressed all in white. White shirt, white pants, white shoes.

Esteban shook the man's hand, it felt as if it was made of glass.

"Me llamo Esteban."

Eleguá made no further comment, and no further comment was needed. Only santeros wore all white, only santeros had that instant recognition, whether divinely inspired or just common sense, the link had been made, the relationship had been established. It needed to be simple, and it was. They sat in silence looking at the colorful parade across the street, listening to the music and the catcalls, the laughter, united by their anomalous faith in all thing seen and unseen. Esteban was glad for Eleguá's company, and particularly for his silence.

*

Listen to me Changó
Hear me Ochún
Attend to me Yemala
Watch out for me, Obatala
Don't desert me, Ogún
Grant my favors, Orula
Intercede on my behalf, Elegúa

For weeks, Esteban sat at the same little table daily, inwardly reciting a prayer and drinking a glass of water that lasted forever.

"You are penniless, but you ask for nothing," Eleguá said. "You look at the girls but not like other men."

It took days before Esteban trusted Eleguá with the truth. Together, they watched the women across the street, watched their demeanor change from the lazy afternoons when they reclined peacefully against the wall, to the carnivorous frenzy of the nights when they tried to snag as many customers as possible, trotting up and down the dusty stairs to the shabby rooms as fast as their high heels let them. They had watched fights break out, eye-scratching, hair-pulling fights – altercations that did little more than send the customer in dispute running.

"I enjoy your company, but you're not going to find your daughter here," Eleguá had told him. "If she's as young as you say, and as pretty as you say, she has never been to Calle Virtudes."

"Where else can I look?" Esteban had asked.

"You wait for Angustia," he said. And together they waited in silence.

She was known simply as Angustia. And Calle Virtudes always received her as if she were visiting royalty, for she brought with her the possibility of a better life for the lucky girls who met with her approval. No one ever knew when she would show up, but everyone lived in anticipation of her arrival. She was announced by the little boys. The moment they spotted her long, red-and-white Ford Fairlane turning into the block, its headlights bulging like those of a gigantic, curious insect, they would run to greet her. They ran noisily just steps ahead of her car, clearing the streets of pedestrians and slow moving carts, kicking sleeping dogs out of the way. The boys considered this their job, and Angustia always rewarded them with a new penny, which she bestowed with the slow, calculating hand of a monarch.

"She's here," Eleguá said with a tired voice. Esteban nodded. He watched as Angustia took in the sidewalks with a long, exhausted glance. She looked to be about fifty years old, but carried herself arrow straight, her shoulders locked in military style, her hair black and thick, her pale skin tight. She took small, firm steps on the dirty sidewalk, easily sidestepping those who crowded her, the way others walk around dog shit. Some of the younger girls were practically jumping up and down for her attention.

"Hola, Señora Angustia," they yelled out flirtatiously, waving arms that rattled with plastic bracelets. Angustia greeted them with a sneer. The older whores sniffed and turned their haggard, clownfish faces away, as if a bad smell was wafting through. They had been passed over many times before, and knew they didn't stand a chance of being asked into the back seat of the two-tone Fairlane, of being whisked away to that place where the job would be the same, but much more profitable. Where life was luxurious and the customers more refined. If they had to fuck for money, why not fuck a diplomat or a sultan? Why not fuck in a house with running water instead of a rusty pail, and mattresses that weren't crawling with chinchas that left ugly welts on their skin. Angustia, in her ice-gray tailored dress and her flawless black suede shoes with sensible heels and silver buckles, represented all that. She was the lottery, the windfall, the cash cow. She was the one-way ticket out of Calle Virtudes.

"What are you going to do?" Eleguá asked Esteban.

Esteban watched Angustia stop and talk to a round-faced girl with eyes the color of heaven. He could tell from the girl's smooth complexion and skinny legs that she couldn't be more than thirteen-years old. He watched the other whores turn to monitor the exchange, the few words that passed between Angustia and the girl, the brief negotiation. It was as if the entire street was holding its breath. He watched Angustia place an arm around the girl and walk her to the car, whispering an intimacy that made the girl giggle. He watched as she opened the passenger door, watched the girl bounce in, as happy as if she'd won the national lottery.

¡ONE PESO GETS YOU TEN THOUSAND BY NIGHTFALL!

When the car door slammed shut, some of the whores broke out into wild applause, while others wiped away black tears. All of them shouted good wishes to the thirteen-year-old girl, who waved and smiled back as the car pulled away from the curb and vanished into the sultry night of Havana. And then, it was over. Everyone went back to business, no more excitement until Angustia returned the next time with the promise of a better life for the chosen one.

"Why didn't you do anything?" Eleguá asked. "You sit here for weeks and you do nothing."

"If my Estelita got into that car," Esteban whispered, "there is nothing I can do."

30

MEXICO

1958

Estelita leaned back inside Hugo Benavides' car and tried to mask her disappointment. Hugo was driving her right through Mexico City at a very fast pace. He only slowed down once they approached what looked like a gigantic prison. Miles of tall brick walls surrounded an even taller array of concrete buildings. As he drove through the huge iron gates, Estelita found herself staring at a world that was at once foreign and yet surprisingly familiar. Instead of her father, Aspirrina, Lúcido the Magician and the triplets, she saw a werewolf, a group of mummies, and several robots casually strolling through the narrow alleys between buildings. To her right, three midgets dressed like dolls laughed and chased each other with curved sabers. To her left, beautiful girls in Mayan and Aztec costumes giggled in groups, their faces thick with theatrical makeup.

"Churubusco Film Studios," Hugo said as he maneuvered the car though the throngs, "is one of the most exciting places in the world right now. In soundstage one they're making *Face of the Screaming Monster*, which should do well. In stage two, *Curse of the Hand Of Stone*, which has been made and remade so many times, I don't know why they are bothering to make it again. All the versions I've seen have been dreadful. But people like the idea of a huge hand that comes to life and strangles peasants," he said with an eye roll. Then there's *The Severed Head Returns*, which is just like the movie about the hand, except the head appears and hypnotizes the villagers into killing people. *Attack of the Black Butterflies*, I don't know anything about.

"How much harm can a butterfly do?" Estelita added with a smile.

"Exactly," Hugo laughed as he pulled over and parked the car.

"And finally," he said, "Our movie, *Tinieblas: Bride of the Vampire*."

Estelita turned to him.

"*Tinieblas*? I thought our movie is to be called *Jacqueline*."

"I forgot to tell you," he said, "the studio wanted to change the name to something more commercial."

"But that's a horrible title," she offered.

"Maybe. We'll let the public decide. Anyway, the name of your character is still Jacqueline, if that makes any difference to you."

"Shouldn't it be Tinieblas?"

Hugo shrugged.

"What difference does it make? You're here in Mexico City, you're going to be in a movie with Arturo de Córdova, one of the biggest stars in the world. You should try to enjoy yourself and let me do the worrying. Chances are by the time the movie opens it will be under yet another name. And if that name doesn't draw an audience, they'll change it again. This is the movie business, my dear, it's not about us, it's all about the audience. We give them what they want."

"Or what you think they want," Estelita said, stepping out of the car.

"It's always a gamble," he said and ushered her into the sound stage, dark as a grave.

Estelita had no idea that acting in a movie could make her feel so lonely. She was always early on the set, her nervous stomach waking her up with the sun. The set consisted of several rooms in a medieval castle made mostly of cardboard walls covered with dust and spider webs. Only the construction crew would be there and, although she greeted them with a friendly smile, they largely ignored her. Her work was dreary. The first few days the director had her standing in what was supposed to be her bedroom and looking around frightened at specific places on the walls, pretending she could see a giant bat flying around.

"The actual bat," the director explained with great enthusiasm, "we put in later with special effects, but you have to make your terror real."

Time spent inside the makeup room was not much better. The hair and makeup women talked mostly to each other and were clearly very old friends. So different from what she was used to, a dressing room full of bickering showgirls and dressers who told jokes and dirty stories as they worked. The Mexicans she found to be much more subdued. They were kind and polite but distant. After a couple of days she stopped trying to engage them. She showed up, sat down in her makeup chair and let them do whatever they wanted until she was called to the set. Once there she would do as she was told.

"Pretend you're scared!"

"Turn to the window!"

"Run out of the room!"

"Come into the room and act scared! More scared! Open your eyes wide!"

"Scream!"

After each take she would return to her chair in the shadows until they called her again. She spent a lot of time in her chair, sipping water through a straw (to keep from smudging her lipstick), and dreaming up passionate letters for Juan Carlos. A week into shooting the rest of the cast arrived, and the set took a different tone. Suddenly, it was full of life, just as she had imagined. She met Mecha Ruiz, who would play the malevolent housekeeper, and Susana Santiago, who would play her ill-fated best friend, and a young man named Pablo Paredes, who would play her fiancé. But where was Arturo de Córdova? She had been anxiously waiting to meet her famous co-star. She knew that Arturo, with his aristocratic dark looks, would make a wonderful vampire. She had been working on the film exactly ten days when an older, short, plump man introduced himself as, "Your vampire, at your service."

His name was Guillermo Villa and apparently he'd been acting most of his life – in regional theater. Estelita shook his hand with as much warmth as she could muster then ran directly to Hugo's office. He was shouting into a telephone, but winked at her. She paced the room until he hung up. "Hugo, what happened to Arturo de Córdova?" she asked him without bothering to mask her displeasure.

"Oh, yes, I was going to talk to you about that," he said, offering her a chair. She remained standing, her arms crossed.

"Arturo had to back out of the project at the very last minute," Hugo said. "That's why for the past week we've been shooting all your scenes where you are alone. Didn't you wonder about that?"

She had, but figured that was the way movies were made.

"Why? What happened?" she asked.

"He's making another movie," Hugo sighed. "We thought he would be done by now but they've had problems and we can't hold up production any longer, we tried to wait for him but it's clear it's just not going to happen."

"And that man, Guillermo Villa, is the best you could find to replace him? I think..."

Hugo Benavides silenced her with a serious look.

"You're in this business one week and you pretend to know more than me?"

"It's just that," she started.

"It's just what? You don't like Guillermo? He's an experienced actor. A professional. You don't see him here interrupting my business and complaining that I've paired him up with a girl who until a week ago had never even seen a movie camera, do you? I'm sure he was perfectly charming to you, wasn't he?"

She had to admit, he was right on every point.

"Yes, he was," Hugo continued, without waiting for her answer, "and that's what I expect of you, too. Now go back to work, my dear, time is money."

She had no choice but to return to the set and try to get along with everyone. But someone had heard her complaining, someone had talked, someone had told the others about her outburst and they shut her out even further. She went out of her way to be sweet, but it was one cold shoulder after the other. And she had to endure it. She continued to show up on the set and do what the director told her without question. Every night she returned to her room aching from loneliness and frustration and tried to pour her heart out in letters to Juan Carlos. But, in spite of Lúcido's best efforts, her vocabulary was limited, and although she had all the words and feelings inside of her, she found it increasingly difficult to express herself in writing. She found it impossible to explain her professional struggles, so she only talked of love, she wrote about how much she missed him and how much she was looking forward to coming home and seeing him again. She knew her letters were simple and repetitive, but they comforted her. As long as she had Juan Carlos waiting for her in Havana she could endure anything. But her first scene with Guillermo Villa made her question her resolve.

In the scene, she was lost in a foggy cemetery. After a few steps and turns which she performed to perfection, she entered an abandoned crypt. Inside the crypt was a coffin. She stared frightened and mesmerized as the coffin lid began to open. Suddenly, Guillermo Villa sat up and looked at her. She was supposed to be overcome with desire and run to him, offer him her white, virginal neck. Instead she burst into nervous giggles. No matter what she did, she couldn't stop. His little round face, even with the pale makeup and prosthetic fangs looked irresistibly funny.

They performed the scene over and over again. The director screamed at her. Hugo Benavides was brought in, and he screamed at her, too. Guillermo Villa, humiliated, threatened to walk out. It was all a horrible mess that reduced her to tears. She ruined her makeup. It had to be reapplied, but the makeup woman was nowhere to be found. Finally they found her on the set of *Curse of the Doll People*, where she'd been transforming midgets into murderous toys. The makeup woman was in a foul mood, practically smacking her with the powder puff. Estelita returned to the set sick with embarrassment and somehow managed to get through the scene. That night she phoned Mr. Lansky. The following morning, Hugo Benavides called her to his office.

"Estelita," he said, his voice kind and paternal as it had been in Havana when they first met. "Every movie I have ever worked on has had its challenges. That's the nature of filmmaking. We're always in a hurry, there's never enough money, tempers run hot. I brought you here with the best intentions. And I have no regrets. In spite of what happened yesterday, your work on the film so far is magnificent. Do you believe me?"

She managed to nod and shrug at the same time.

"Well, it's true. And I hold myself responsible for some of the mishaps you've suffered. I know you've been disappointed. A lot of first time actresses are; making a movie is never as simple as watching one. And this experience has been compounded by the fact you have no one here, and I have many responsibilities to attend. I cannot be always at your side."

"I understand," she said.

"We must always remember that we started out this venture as friends," he said with a smile. She returned the smile, remembering the turbulent flight that had brought them together.

"So I want to make it up to you. I have arranged for you to meet the most famous man in all of Mexico, a true star."

She met the most famous man in Mexico that same evening, after completing a scene where she stood at a balcony and stared at a painted moon while an electric fan blew her hair and gown all around her and wolves howled in the distance. The most famous man in Mexico arrived with Hugo and the entire cast and crew clamored to shake his hand. He was tall, over six feet, and dressed in an elegant grey suit. He cut quite a figure, except for his head, which was completely covered by a silver leather mask. There were holes for his eyes that resembled exclamation marks, two little holes to breathe through and a larger hole for his mouth and a zipper running along the back, from the crown of his head to the back of his neck. The effect was quite ferocious.

"Estelita de la Cruz," Hugo Benavides said, "I want you to meet Santo."

She smiled, a little confused, but willing to be a good sport. Surely this is some kind of joke, she thought, but from the reaction of all the others, she doubted that it was. This truly must be the most famous man in Mexico. So she offered her hand, which he took in his large, thick paw. Estelita hardly had a chance to say a word to the man before he was engulfed by people who wanted to meet him. All those on the set who, up to now, had acted superior to actors and celebrities were thrusting scraps of paper at Santo, vying for his autograph. Estelita backed out of the crowd and signaled for Hugo's attention.

"Who is this?" she asked, more amused than annoyed.

"Santo?" he exclaimed, "He's the man in the silver mask!"

"I can see that," she responded, "but who is he?"

"Only the most famous wrestler in the world, the most..."

"The most famous man in all of Mexico," she cut in.

"Yes," Hugo said without a trace of irony, "and I have arranged dinner for the two of you, tonight, at the most glamorous restaurant in Mexico City."

She wanted to say, "You can't be serious," but it was evident that he was absolutely serious.

"But why?"

"Trust me dear girl, Santo can do for you what no one else in Mexico can. I can put you in a movie, but I can't make you a star. Your timing couldn't be better. I only know him because we're just about to close a two-picture deal. He's going to your country next month to make two movies. When I told him you were the rising star of Cuba, which, by the way, in spite of your trantrums, I still believe you are, he jumped at the opportunity."

"The most famous woman in Cuba?" she mocked.

"Soon, if you play your cards right."

This was no time to be difficult, she told herself. What could it possibly hurt her to have dinner with Santo, the most famous man in Mexico?

Hugo Benavides had insisted that she look spectacular for her date with Santo ("there will be photographers"). Estelita chose a glamorous, black sequined dress she had purchased in Havana. But game as she wanted to be, something about the venture didn't feel quite right. As she fastened her diamond earrings, she realized she felt as if she were betraying Juan Carlos. It's only for publicity, she told the frowning face in the mirror.

When she heard the knock on the door to her room, her heart felt heavy and she moved as if in a trance, like the girl she played in the movie. Santo was not alone. The two bodyguards with him were just as

313

imposing in stature as he, if a little thicker around their waists. Santo was dressed in another expensive suit and tie. And he was still wearing that silver mask.

"You look very beautiful tonight," Santo said, and although his words were delivered in a sincere, almost sweet voice, the mask rendered them null.

"Thank you," she said, concentrating on his eyes, which, although framed by the silver mask, looked kind. She left him standing at the door while she reached for her purse, afraid that if she invited the three towering men into her room, it would be so crowded that the walls would have to expand to accommodate them. They didn't seem to mind, and she didn't keep them waiting long. Santo walked alongside of her while the bodyguards trailed a few steps behind. Suddenly she felt unsure, going off into the foreign night with three enormous men.

"Will you introduce me to your friends?" Estelita suggested before she entered the car.

"They're not my friends, they are yours," Santo said, a smile in his voice. "Hugo Benavides hired them to protect you."

Her first thought was, does Hugo think this man is dangerous? Santo must have seen the thought cross her face, because he added, with a laugh, "Certainly not from me, I'm a harmless hero."

She looked back at the two men and they both bowed silently. She started to relax a little. She smiled at Santo as he ran to the other side of the car to open the door for her. Santo drove. No one said much until they neared their destination.

"There it is," Santo said.

They were approaching a building that looked like a gigantic concrete butterfly or seashell, or an undulating parasol. It was completely encircled by a narrow moat filled with colorful, little boats loaded with flowers and candles.

"Welcome to Los Manantiales," Santo said, "isn't it something? It's named after the natural springs under it."

In the back seat the bodyguards whistled with admiration.

"It's beautiful," she said.

"Hugo Benavides has very good taste," Santo said with a flirtatious tone that she decided to ignore.

Hugo does have good taste, excellent taste, Estelita thought as she walked over the curving bridge that led to the front of the restaurant. Santo walked next to her, and as they approached the entrance two men in tuxedos ran to greet him. Seemingly out of nowhere, photographers jumped up to take their pictures. Santo placed an arm around her shoulders as flashbulbs exploded in their faces. The two bodyguards stayed outside. Santo and Estelita followed one of the tuxedoed men through tall, metallic doors.

Inside, the restaurant was even more astonishing. It was round, as if a movie spaceship had been converted into a swanky dining room. Santo seemed to know everyone. He even hugged some and called them hermanos. They in turn glowed with the honor of his presence. He failed to introduce her and she kept a frozen smile on her face until he was done with his greetings. When they sat down, complimentary bottles of champagne and bottles of Scotch began arriving at their table. Santo waved his massive arm in the direction of the people who had sent them.

"Mexican people are very kind, no?"

"Yes," she said, glancing at the menu. She was hungry but too nervous to make a choice.

"Why don't you order for us?" she said with what she hoped looked like a smile.

"The usual," Santo said to a waiter. He waited until another waiter poured the champagne and made a toast.

"To Cuba," he said, lifting a glass that seemed diminutive in his hand.

"To Cuba," she answered, her eyes fixed on his silver face.

Estelita stormed into Hugo Benavides's office the next morning, her face flushed with anger, a bundle of newspapers in her arm.

"This is crazy," she shouted, tossing the newspapers on his desk.

There she was, on the front page, smiling like an idiot, with Santo's arm around her. The photo would have been fine, but it was the headlines she found most offensive.

SANTO: ¡AT LAST I FOUND THE WOMAN OF MY DREAMS!
¡HE'S EVERYTHING I EVER WANTED SAYS CUBAN BEAUTY!
SANTO AND MYSTERY GIRL EXPECTING MASKED BABY?

That last one really got to her.

Hugo Benavides laughed at her.

"Calm down, Estelita," he said, "this is exactly what we wanted. You can't buy better publicity."

"Better publicity?" she said. "This is a disaster."

"Listen to me, girl," he said, suddenly serious, "there are seven films in production in this studio and each film has a leading lady. But you're the one grabbing headlines. Don't you see?"

"But this is scandalous and untrue," she insisted. "This lie about a baby could make a lot of trouble for me."

"Hardly," he said, "nobody pays attention to *La Verdad*, every one knows it's just a scandal sheet. Tomorrow there'll be another two-headed goat born and you'll have to fight to be noticed."

"I don't know what to do."

"You do nothing," he said using the fatherly tone she no longer trusted. "Word is already spreading. A reporter from *El Machete* has asked for an exclusive interview. Isn't that fantastic? You can clear up any misunderstandings and make good publicity for the film."

"I don't know..."

"Estelita, the only really bad thing that you can ever find in a newspaper is your own obituary," he added. "As long as you're alive, you can face anything."

"*El Machete*? I've never heard of it."

"It's one of Mexico's best newspapers," he assured her, "very reputable, not a rag like *La Verdad*. Just make sure you talk mostly about the movie."

"I'll tell them the truth."

"That would be a mistake," he said. "You can tell them you're not pregnant, but keep the romance vague. Tell them you're just good friends, that always translates as lovers and it will keep the attention on you a little longer, until Santo is seen with someone else and they start calling you the poor victim."

Estelita returned to the set. Somehow, she managed to get through her scenes, which consisted of endless dialogue with the evil housekeeper. It was the most talking she'd done in the movie so far. In between takes, Guillermo Villa had grabbed her and tried to wrestle playfully with her. She couldn't find the humor in his antics and pushed him away.

"What's the matter?" he'd said with a leer. "Didn't Santo teach you any of his signature moves last night? Maybe The Camel Clutch ha ha ha or The Diving Head butt ha ha ha?"

The crew laughed, and he took an exaggerated bow while she seethed with embarrassment. She couldn't wait until someone put a stake through Guillermo Villa's heart so she could return to Havana once and for all. She'd had about as much of Mexico City as she could stand. As soon as the director was satisfied, she rushed to get out of her costume. She was removing the last of the pale theatrical makeup she detested when Hugo Benavides walked in.

"I thought you'd like a few tips on how to conduct yourself in an interview."

"Sure," she said, determined to cooperate until she could be done with it all.

"Well, first you offer to give him a tour of the set, tell him a little about the plot, not too much, mind you. Although with vampire movies everyone knows how it's going to end. But you can hint that this one's going to surprise him."

"I understand."

"He will probably want to know more about you, but always bring it back to the movie. You can tell him about how I discovered you on an airplane, make it sound like a fairy tale."

"Well," she said, "at least that part is true."

"Exactly," he smiled, "so make that the better part of it all. And when he brings up Santo, which he undoubtedly will."

"I know," she cut in, "we're just good friends."

"Sounds like you're ready," he said, and with a quick pat on her shoulder, he left her alone.

The reporter wasn't at all what she had expected. She was a woman. She had dark, short cropped hair, a hollow face and wore a tailored tweed suit. She introduced herself with a firm handshake.

"Ana Verdugo," she said, " with *El Machete*."

"Very nice to meet you," Estelita said.

"Well, let's get started," she said, pad and pen at the ready.

"Do you want to start with a tour of the set?" Estelita offered. "I can tell you about the movie and--"

"I'm not here to talk about the movie," Ana Verdugo interrupted. "Who cares about one more Mexican vampire movie? I'm here to talk about your country."

"Cuba?" Estelita asked surprised. "What about it?"

"Well, let's see," Ana Verdugo said with mock innocence, "how about we start with your reaction to what happened last night, and then we'll take it from there."

"Oh, that," Estelita said with an eye roll. "Sure, let's get that out of the way. Nothing happened, Santo and I are just good friends, not even that, we only met yesterday. But what does that have to do with Cuba?"

The reporter was staring at her.

"Santo? I couldn't care less about that masked moron," Ana Verdugo said and her face then brightened as if she'd just heard something terribly amusing. She leaned in to Estelita, fixed her sights on her.

"So, you're not aware that as of yesterday, November 3, 1958, your country, Cuba, has a new president-elect?

"No," Estelita said with a tentative smile, "I am not aware of that."

"You're not aware of that." Ana Verdugo's eyes were still on her, they were hard eyes, and her voice had taken a judgmental tone. "Well...no."

Estelita felt ambushed. She was not prepared to discuss politics with this woman, hadn't even looked at a newspaper until her face appeared on it. Cuba has a new president? Now she understood the look on Ana Verdugo's face, she thought her an imbecile, a showgirl in a vampire movie. She wished Hugo had not left her alone. She'd gladly talk about Santo now, even own up to the baby, just to avoid this line of questioning. Ana cleared her throat as if to get Estelita's attention. And then she was on her – ratatatat – like a machine gun.

"So you don't know that the new president of your country is named Andres Rivero-Aguero, that he was backed by Batista, that he was prime minister under Batista and is probably one of his closest friends? That there are rumors, *strike that*, that there is evidence that

318

ballots were tampered with, and that Fidel Castro, you've heard of him, of course, called for the assassination of all candidates and threatened to gun down anyone who showed up at the polls to vote?"

Estelita's head was spinning. Surely this woman didn't expect her to know all of this.

"No," she said again, "I am not aware of any of this. I've been locked in a soundstage making a movie."

"And we can assume that this is not your natural hair color."

"Well, no. It's usually blonde but for the movie they made it more silver. They told me it would photograph better."

"I see," the reporter said but did not write anything down. Estelita flashed her her best smile, which the woman did not return.

"Are you, Estelita de la Cruz, aware that a great percentage of the people fighting alongside of Fidel Castro to free your country from foreign oppression and the dictatorship that condones it are in your age group and even younger?"

"No, I was not aware of that, until now."

She watched as Ana Verdugo closed her pad and put it away.

"Wait," Estelita said, "don't you want a tour of the set?"

"No, dear," Ana Verdugo said with a smile that would have been unbecoming on a shark, "that is all I need for now."

Eduardo Santiago

31

Aspirrina had heard the signature motto of Rebel Radio countless times and it still thrilled her.

Aquí Radio Rebelde, transmitiendo desde la Sierra Maestra, territorio libre de Cuba.

The words ran over and over in her head as she looked around the makeshift station, just a shack with a Collins transmitter and a gasoline-powered generator. And yet, from this little corner of the world, high in the Sierras, her words would reach all of Cuba. Her heart was pounding with excitement. She wiggled her big ass into the chair. Fidel Castro and Che Guevara had sat in the same chair she now occupied. As of late, Celia Sanchez had been the voice of Radio Rebelde. But all three of them were far from camp. Celia went wherever Castro went, she followed him around like a faithful dog.

After months of trying to win her over, Aspirrina had given up. She found Celia disgusting. It was obvious to her that Celia was not only driven by revolutionary zeal, she was as deeply in love with Castro as Castro was in love with war. But Fidel Castro had no time for conventional romance. The more Aspirrina got to know her leader, the

320

more she respected and admired him. Not the way Celia did, like a lovelorn schoolgirl, but in the true sense, something she felt in her gut every time she thought about the man. She was in awe of Fidel's courage, his determination, and his generosity. He had given himself completely to this effort to liberate his country.

She respected him because he wasn't just one of the many starving, disenfranchised, and resentful men who daily joined their cause. He was a rich man's son, and a lawyer! He was a man in his prime who could be fishing from a swanky yacht, drinking cold cocktails and enjoying every comfort, or gambling at a luxurious casino with other young men of his class. She admired him because he was a man of principle and determination who was making enormous sacrifices, living in mud, deprived of every comfort, like everyone else.

Because of him, Radio Rebelde had become a phenomenon, an unbeatable weapon, a convincing blow against the false reports disseminated daily by the dictatorship of Fulgencio Batista. Batista controlled all the media, but hard as he tried, he could not control Radio Rebelde. Every day the broadcasts contradicted the fabricated headlines:

FIDEL CASTRO SHOT DEAD
CHE GUEVARA SHOT DEAD
INSURGENT MILITIA SURRENDERS

In rural zones, tuning in to the *barbudos*, the bearded ones, became a nightly ritual. Neighbors, largely isolated from each other, would congregate in a bohio with a transistor radio, illuminated by the light of a kerosene lantern and the hope each broadcast created. In the cities, deep in the recesses of private homes, families gathered to listen to Radio Rebelde with the same eager anticipation usually reserved for popular shows like *El Hit Parade Cubano*.

Aspirrina knew how important this moment was. She took a deep breath as she waited for the signal from Chano, the short-wave operator. He had been fiddling with knobs for an eternity. When he gave her the signal, she was ready. She wasn't sure what she would say, but the broadcast had to go on, as it had every day of the struggle. As she leaned into the microphone, she feared her voice would crack from excitement and nerves.

She'd much rather express herself through dance and movement. But to her amazement her voice came out strong and clear.

"This is Radio Rebelde, coming to you from the Sierra Maestra, the free territory of Cuba," she announced, just as she had watched Celia do so many times, perhaps even a little better. She had to do it better – Fidel might be listening. This was her opportunity to show him and the world that she wasn't just some kind-hearted woman who was willing to bandage the wounded, happy to sit on the sidelines while day after day men and women became heroes. She was a true rebel now, an authentic warrior, a passionate liberator of her country.

"I have good news," she went on, "very good news. We've taken Oriente province, and Holguin province, too. We're moving fast towards Las Villa and Santa Clara, so they better run. They had better run." She paused knowing the effect her words would have on the listeners. She could practically hear their sharp intake of breath, see their eyes wide with awe. She didn't know if any of the information she was dispensing with such conviction was true, but she wasn't going to let that stand in the way of her fervent message. The Batistianos lied all the time. To hell with them! She had always relished a good lie, it felt good on her tongue. If Batista could make shit up, so could she.

"Listen to me, my people," she continued, growing excited by the sound of her own voice, "we're coming and we can't be stopped. Freedom can't be stopped. Fairness and equality can't be stopped. We are like a volcano here, high in the Sierras, and we have erupted."

Again she paused, letting the words take effect.

"Like lava, we are flowing down, destroying everything that is evil, everything that is oppressing you, everything that is keeping our beautiful island in the grips of foreigners and corrupt leaders. I have been living here among the rebels for months now, and I can tell you…"

Emotion choked her, she wasn't lying, this was the truth as she had lived it. She raised her voice in order to continue. "I can tell you that I have never in my life seen more courageous men, the men here go days without a piece of bread, but are willing to take up arms against injustice. The men here go days without a glass of milk, but are willing to walk miles to give you back what is yours. The men here haven't

322

seen their wives, their mothers, anyone who could give them comfort, encouragement."

She was on the verge of tears. She put a hand over the microphone and looked up at Chano who was standing at her side. 'How am I doing?' she whispered. She didn't need a reply, the glint in his eyes said it all.

"You have no reason to believe me," she continued, her words taking on an intimate tone. "You don't know me, but you've met me. Every time you've seen a baby crawling on a dirt floor, crying from hunger, you've met me. Every time your children go without shoes, without education, without a future, you've met me. Every time you see a man who wields a machete in a sugarcane field but doesn't know how to write his own name, a man who worked from sunrise to nightfall but can't support his family, whose spirit is slowly broken by poverty day after day, you've met me."

Aspirrina stopped, the emotion was overwhelming her. She felt as if something was squeezing her heart. All those memories of her slow, pregnant mother, the dirt floor covered with sick children, her father's acceptance of his dreary poverty, the inescapable misery. She stepped back from the microphone, fearing that she was going to lose consciousness. Chano placed a hand on her back and gently pushed her back to the microphone.

"Sigue, " he said. Keep going.

"Every time a mother has smeared rouge on a daughter's face," she went on, her voice choked with anger, "and sent her out to the streets to grab the tourist dollars because she knows that only by sacrificing one child can she save the others, you've met me. Every time you've looked in the mirror and seen the face of despair and frustration, you've seen my face. Not all of us can climb up to this mountain and take up a rifle. I understand that. But there is much you can do down there in the plains, in the cities, in the sugarcane fields. You can do your part, too."

Aspirrina could feel her strength returning, and with it, an inexplicable feeling of joy and euphoria. Her thoughts were taking her back to Batey Oriente, her mother, her father, her brothers and sisters. The Haitians and her thoughts were coming out of her mind and through her lungs as if she had planned it that way.

323

"You can make the sacrifice." She was so enraptured she felt like she was dancing. The people listening were the same people who had once laughed at her, thrown rocks at her. Maybe even Diego Cervantes Murillo, who had once used her, slapped her and thrown money at her, was listening. She could forgive him now, at this very moment in the middle of a clandestine broadcast, she let him go. She could feel years of bitterness leave her body.

"The enemy loves money and only money, yes they do; that's what this is all about. They love money more than they love you. They love money more than they love our beautiful country. So, this goes to those of you who have more than the others, we urge you, don't give it to them. Don't buy anything that is not essential. Stop shopping. Stay away from the cinema and the cabaret. Stay out of the jewelry shop and the department stores, the restaurants. It is through this action that you can show them that you have the power and the discipline, that you have the control."

She stopped and wiped away the beads of perspiration clouding her eyes. Her words were coming fast, maybe too fast. She slowed down as she would when dancing on stage, when she wanted every gesture to matter.

"We will continue to fight for you. We will continue to bleed for you. We will continue to die for you. You can count on that. You can be sure that our effort will continue until one day, and it won't be long in coming, the day will come when the whole country, not just the mountains, are territorio libre, when any one of us can go into any radio station, or stand on any street corner in any city or any town and safely say without fear, without misgivings: This is Radio Rebelde, coming to you from the free, fair, independent country of Cuba."

Aspirrina took a deep breath. She didn't know where all those words had come from. They had flowed from her as if from a wellspring. Everything she had ever felt, every idea she had ever had, had become suddenly lucid, clear, powerful. Everything she had ever wanted to express through her dances finally had become a coherent message. Not until Chano put his arms around her did she realize that she was sobbing.

"Aspirrina, you have to introduce the singers," he whispered.

"Oh, you're right," she said, wiping away the tears and leaning into the microphone.

"All right, my people, the sermon is over. You know what you have to do. Now, let's have some fun, because this isn't just a revolution, it's a revolution with rhythm, a revolution with guarachas, rumbas, and pachangas. So it's my pleasure to introduce the joyful voice of the Sierra Maestra, the talented troupers you've taken into your hearts, the radical sounds of The Rebel Trio."

Aspirrina stepped back and three bearded men, guitars hanging from their necks like rifles, stepped up to the microphone and quickly launched into their first song. The trio's lively music and harmonious sounds did little to disguise the message of their lyrics. Their most popular song was a humorous ditty called "El Mono," (the monkey). It directly and unabashedly ridiculed Fulgencio Batista, a dark and scrawny man who many said resembled a simian.

We've cut off the monkey's balls.
The monkey walks with a limp now.
The monkey can't climb no trees now.
The monkey can't make you laugh.

They also sang songs about the horrific things that were going to happen to *chivatos,* informants and traitors. But mostly, The Rebel Trio sang songs that glorified Fidel Castro, whom they called "El Caballo," the horse. In the Fidel songs, he was always idealized as a powerful beast with enormous genitals. Aspirrina loved the songs. She stood back and sang along. Other men from the camp joined in on the choruses, turning the broadcast into a boisterous party that spread throughout the camp.

When the broadcast was over the technician buried the radio equipment behind the house, lest it be stolen or damaged in a skirmish. Once the final shovel of cold, wet dirt had been dropped and a thick camouflage of leaves had been spread, the group walked back to the camp together. Even in the damp November night, their spirits stayed high as they trudged through the dense foliage, leaves and branches scratching at their faces, feet sinking into mud. No one was happier than Aspirrina. All the rebels congratulated her, commenting on her broadcast, praising her dedication and devotion.

"Gorda, you told them!"

"You showed them your cojones and your corazón."

They did not say what she longed to hear: You did better than that stuck-up-old-cunt Celia Sanchez. No matter. Aspirrina was in heaven. These were her people. This was her tribe. She had brought almost each and every one of these men back to life. She was no doctor but it didn't matter, there was no medicine to speak of. But she was strong. She could deal with the shouts, the screams, the blood. She had nursed them through fevers and terrors. The ones who survived were eternally grateful, the ones who died, they buried. Celia Sanchez, because she was literate, had the relatively easy task of writing the letters home. They were short and dispassionate.

On such and such a date your son so and so died a hero.

"Who should I write to in case something happens to you?" one of them asked her.

"No one," Aspirrina said.

"There is no one?"

Aspirrina thought about a time when there had been. Esteban, Estelita. Who knew where they were now. She saw no point in notifying the convent. What did they care?

"There is no one and it doesn't really matter," she said, "only the survivors matter."

Only survivors mattered, and on this night, they were in high spirits. They would have carried Aspirrina on their shoulders if she wasn't so fat. Instead they sang, risking discovery, forgetting for the moment that mountains carry voices far and wide, that their shouts of joy could jump ravines, echo through canyons. Before Aspirrina knew what was happening, there were masculine hands at her waist and she was leading a conga line through the jungles of the Sierra Maestra.

"El Mono se va/ the monkey is leaving," the rebels sang, their rifles clanging against their canteens.

It wasn't just a song, they believed their words. They believed that victory was at hand, that little by little, step by step, one town, one province, one mountain at a time, they were going to drive the tyrant out once and for all.

The smell of roasting goat greeted them at the camp. They were tired and dirty, but happy, alive, and pulsating with the spirit of the

326

revolution. She had nursed each and every one of them back to health, as she'd done her brothers and sisters so many years ago – quickly and efficiently. Who knew back then in Batey Oriente that all the work she had resented would prepare her for this, that so many of her early experiences, miserable as they were, would bring her such joy.

She watched them seated around the fire pit, chomping on succulent chunks of goat and passing around a bottle of agua ardiente, a local rum. Soon they were singing again, the members of The Rebel Trio passing their guitars to anyone who was willing to strum. Drums were fashioned out of boxes and crates. A set of timbales appeared out of nowhere. A cowbell added to the percussion. A group of men, their spirits warmed by the alcohol and the goat meat, took off their shirts, braving the cold, and formed a circle. Aspirrina didn't touch a drop of the agua ardiente, but she was drunk with excitement and impetuously moved to perform one of her dances. She just couldn't help it. She had to express herself, she needed to move. She stood up in front of the fire, the red flames tinting her face into something wild – and once she was sure she had everyone's undivided attention, she started to shake and jump and twirl.

Delighted, the rebels strummed the guitars harder, pounded the drums louder. But her dance wasn't coming out the way it always had. Instead of the Isadora Duncan-inspired movements that had become her trademark, she found herself shaking her shoulders, swaying her breasts and undulating her hips and her ass. For the first time in her life Aspirrina was dancing like a Cuban woman, like the queen of the carnaval, like a goddamned rumba goddess. The rebels loved it. They encircled her, chanting and clapping their hands; big, open smiles on their bearded faces. They took turns, pushing each other out of the way for a chance to twirl her around, to rub up against her.

Aspirrina was soaring. She had never been so happy in her life. She was at a zenith, at her most gloriously, deliciously ecstatic peak when the sounds of whistles pierced the air.

The whistles were a warning.

All activity stopped. The men picked up their weapons and ran. Click, click, click. As they broke and loaded their rifles. Thomp, thomp, thomp. Their heavy boots on the cold, hard ground. One by one they vanished into the dark thicket, took their places. Held their breaths.

Aspirrina continued to dance. She was used to dancing alone.

"I don't care what happens now," she sang softly to herself. "If Batistiano troops come in and kill us all, I will die a happy woman."

32

Delfino sat on the floor of the boat and leaned back against a coil of thick, wet rope. He stretched out his legs in front of him and turned his face up to the sun. The sky domed above him, the air so clear and pure that it would make even the most hardened atheist believe in heaven, if only for a moment. Delfino did believe and he momentarily closed his eyes in gratitude.

When he opened his eyes again, he cast them on the horizon. The Atlantic Ocean was serene and seemed to go on forever. All around the boat, colorful fish, their translucent tails swaying with the tide, could be seen circling deep below the surface, oblivious to the violence that roared on land. Through sleepy eyes, he watched Arjuna expertly navigating eastward, towards Oriente province. It was a long trip, easily 500 miles from Havana. But this was the only way to reach the eastern end. All ground transportation had ceased; military roadblocks and checkpoints had been set up every few miles. Bridges had been blown to pieces, train tracks dismantled. The island was at a standstill. Only a fool, or a very desperate man, would dare to brave the Central Highway. It was a chance neither Arjuna nor Delfino was prepared to take. But they couldn't stay in Havana.

Arjuna's release had been swift. After a frantic, bloody stop at an emergency room in Miramar, Maria had driven them to Jaimanitas where Arjuna kept his boats. To his relief, the cars he had seen the day before were gone.

"You both should stay in the convent," Maria said. "At least until your hand has healed. Considering the circumstances, an infection is still probable."

"You've already done enough," Delfino said. "We can't put you in any more danger."

"I agree," Arjuna added. "Besides, I think this all was meant to happen. I'm excited by the adventure, I can't wait to join the rebels in the mountains."

"That's fine for you," Maria said, "But why does Delfino have to go? He is not a warrior."

"I'm going with him," Delfino said. Maria argued against it but nothing could keep Delfino away from Arjuna. How do you explain to a nun the kind of love he felt? He couldn't and he didn't. He knew that Arjuna's decision was crazy, hasty, but they were in too deep to stop now. The revolution had to triumph, and they both had to do what they could to make it happen. Otherwise, they would have to leave the country. Arjuna was a marked man. It would only take one more slip, one small indiscretion, even a rumor. Maria's father saved him once, but he couldn't ever again. Arjuna had used up all of his blessings. And he was not the kind of man to just sit at home and wait it out. This was as much his revolution as anyone elses. Delfino knew that. So he had returned to his shop, emptied the safe and met him at the boat. His peaceful life of creating hats for the aristocracy was over for now. For a while. Until things changed again. He was sure they would change, they always did.

Delfino watched the muscles on Arjuna's back ripple under his sun-browned skin. To think that if it weren't for Maria's intervention, this skin would now be cold, rotting in a shallow grave in some field somewhere.

"Do you want me to take over for a while?" Delfino asked.

"Sure," Arjuna said, turning the wheel over to him. Delfino

grabbed it and held on tight.

"Keep on course, now," Arjuna teased, helping himself to water from the canteen. Delfino stared into the horizon, a soft warm breeze in his face. If only they could stay like this forever. With little effort they could reach Jamaica or one of the Bahamian islands. But he knew better. Almost two years into the war, every man counted. Every effort was needed.

They reached the Bay of Antilla after nightfall. They would have to cut across the widest part of Cuba to reach the Sierra, but there was no other way. He was hoping to find transportation to Holguin and from there to Bayamo. They had the name of a man in Bayamo who could point them in the right direction. But at the moment, Bayamo seemed as unreachable as the North Pole. Arjuna knew that by staying north, always north, of Guantanamo, Santiago, and Manzanillo, where active fighting had been reported, they would be relatively safe. They docked in Antilla as planned. The basin was calm with only a few small fishing boats tethered to the docks. After securing their boat, they walked into the town hoping to find something to eat. Although the sun had just set, all the shops were closed; all lights were out, not a soul in the streets. They returned to the boat and waited until morning. The soft rocking put them to sleep in an instant, and they didn't wake up until they heard the hungry gulls, their relentless squawking sounding to Delfino like a warning. In daylight, the town was only slightly more animated.

"The people are strange," Delfino said.

"They're cautious, or frightened," Arjuna said. "Something must have happened here."

On the way to the bus stop they saw something they had not noticed in the night.

Every light post and tree trunk had a poster nailed to it, it was government-issued and yellowing in the sun:

SE OFRECE

$100,000 PESOS

POR LA CABEZA DE

FIDEL CASTRO

"Like something from a cowboy movie!" Delfino said, tearing off one of the posters.

"Yes," Arjuna answered looking around. "No wonder the place is so quiet. Either they're still here or they just left. Either way, we're not safe."

Delfino folded the brittle sheet of paper and stuffed it in his pocket. They hurried on, their footsteps echoing off the cement walls. They were dressed humbly, better to fit in wherever they went, but still they felt as conspicuous as tourists. They passed an old woman sweeping the sidewalk and asked her when the next bus was due.

"There is no bus, there is no bus anymore," she said and made a hasty retreat into her house. They could hear her bolt the door. They continued on the main road, their spirits starting to flag. Chances were they would have to get back on the boat and round the tip of the island, past Baracoa. But that would place them past Guantanamo Bay and increase their chances of being questioned by a patrullero.

"Look," Delfino said, pointing to a rusting old car.

They walked up to the front door of the house and knocked. A disheveled man in his undershirt opened the door. They had obviously awakened him.

"Are you the owner of this car?" Arjuna asked, extending his hand with what he hoped was a friendly smile.

The man eyed him suspiciously.

"What if I am?" he said with an unnecessarily long yawn.

"We'll give you twenty pesos to drive us to Bayamo," Arjuna said.

"Bayamo!" the man said as if they had just mentioned the farthest point on any map. "That's a two-hour drive, and the road is full of holes."

"That's why we're offering twenty pesos," Delfino said.

"That town is very dangerous right now," the man countered.

"Forty pesos, cash," Delfino said. "Twenty now, and twenty when we get there."

The man grumbled an acceptance and walked back into the house. They heard some shouts coming from inside and a woman's voice, nagging.

"You're crazy to do it, Soledad," the woman said. "Crazy."

He returned a moment later, at a clip, buttoning up his shirt as he walked.

"Let's go," he said without stopping, the woman was at his heels. She said nothing, but she looked at Delfino and Arjuna as if she were cursing them to death.

The drive to Bayamo was silent, interrupted only by Soledad's curses every time they hit a pothole.

"They promise to fix the roads, and nothing happens," he grumbled. "Every year it gets worse. And now there's no buses, no trains, nothing. This whole country is turning to shit."

"Things are changing," Delfino said.

"Oh, yeah," Soledad sneered, his eyes fixed on the road. "Where are you from?"

"La Habana," Delfino answered.

"Sure," Soledad said, "things are always changing in La Habana, but not out here. Nobody cares what happens to us out here. Even the fish stay away."

Miles before they reached Bayamo, they started to see Batista soldiers along the side of the road. They didn't stand like soldiers, but rather like the boys who loiter outside of movie theaters smoking and waiting for something to happen.

"They're all here," Soledad said, nodding at the soldiers. "The command post is in Bayamo."

"Why Bayamo?" Delfino asked.

"It's always been Bayamo," Soledad answered, "to protect Santiago."

Delfino realized how little he knew about this remote part of the island. Bayamo was a small town, but a bustling metropolis compared to Antilla. There were people in the streets. Large, leafy trees shaded the narrow sidewalks. And among them, Batista soldiers, in groups of two and three at every corner, their uniforms worn and soiled, as if they had been away from soap and water for a very long time. Soledad didn't bother to kill the motor; he took his money and got out of Bayamo as fast as his old car would take him. Without a good-bye or good luck.

Arjuna and Delfino made their way to the address where their contact, Armando Peña, lived. The door to Maceo 53 was clearly marked. A sign hanging from a window advertised a notary public. "El Señor Peña no esta en casa." Mr. Peña is not at home, a woman, who they presumed was his wife, told them, her eyes flickering between suspicion and fear.

"When can we expect to see him?" Arjuna asked. "This is an urgent matter."

Delfino took in her flowered house dress, wide and flowing, with large pockets at the hips. Camouflage for a figure that had seen better days.

"Come back later," she said. When later? Delfino wanted to ask. An hour? Two hours? Tomorrow? They walked back to the center of town. Horses clopped by, children played in a park, and their joyous screams filled the air. Milling around them were Batista's omnipresent soldiers. Some sat on benches and stared into the distance as if anticipating some arrival. Others chatted and played games, tossing bottle caps at a circle drawn on the sidewalk with a piece of chalk.

"So this is Bayamo," Delfino said, looking around.

There were wanted posters nailed to trees and the light posts, just as in Antilla.

"Why is it that no one dares to tear these posters down?" Arjuna asked. "What's happening in Bayamo, this place was once so brave? This is the kind of place where the people would have challenged the soldiers by now, torn down the posters, ripped them up in their very faces."

"I suppose Batista knows all about Bayamo," Delfino offered. "Maybe that's why the town is so thick with soldiers."

"The history lesson every Cuban boy learns in school," Arjuna said with a sigh. "Bayamo, the town that set itself on fire rather than continue whoring itself to Spain. And the town where La Bayamesa, Cuba's national anthem was composed."

Delfino vaguely nodded, not really interested in Arjuna's history lesson. His stomach was grumbling with nerves and hunger and his feet hurt. They found a place to eat, to wait. But the pork sandwich stuck in his throat. Sugarcane juice, guarapo, pushed it down, but it only fermented in his stomach. Everything was souring.

"Just think," Arjuna said, "less than one hundred years ago we kicked out the Spanish and now we're going through it all over again with the Americans."

"It's never been right, has it?" Delfino said, pressing a hand to his sour belly.

There was nothing more to say. They were both exhausted. Bayamo was hot, dry and dusty. As the day grew hotter, everyone vanished from the streets and into the relative coolness of their homes. Only the soldiers remained. The afternoon wore on like an eternity. Arjuna paid the bar bill and they started back to the house at Maceo 53.

Delfino was worried and tired. Nothing was going as planned. Maybe it had been a mistake. What did they plan to do? Join the rebels? Grow beards? Shoot people? He suspected that actual warfare would be much different than setting off bombs. It required courage to look a man in the eye and pull a trigger. He doubted that he could do this, but he also knew that he did not want to be separated from Arjuna again. Wherever he went, they would go together. With any luck Armando Peña wouldn't be home. With any luck they would return to the boat and go off somewhere for a while. Why did they have to get so deeply involved? Why not just lie low for a while? The revolt couldn't last forever, could it?

Armando Peña *was* home. He came to the door himself, dressed in a white guayabera, his gray speckled hair neatly combed through with Brilliantine.

"I'm Felipe Arjuna and this is –."

Armando Peña grabbed Arjuna's arm and pulled him into the house. Delfino followed.

"Quickly," he urged.

Once inside, he bolted the door. They sat in the living room, the drawn shades made it dark and cool.

"Luz," he cried out to his wife, more a command than a request, "make us a *cafécito*."

Delfino was relieved just to be indoors and away from the

prying eyes of the soldiers. He longed for a nice bed, clean sheets. His feet hurt, his guts were in knots. The life of a rebel was not for him, but he wasn't about to say so.

"I've heard good things about you," Peña said to Arjuna. "I'm sure they could use a strong boy like you."

Arjuna lowered his head. Peña tapped his fingers on the table, one of his eyes twitched uncontrollably.

"I'm always willing to do what I have to," Arjuna said, and with a glance to Delfino, he added, "we both are."

"Glad to hear it," Peña said, "now we have to get you to El Hombrecillo, that's where the camp is. But it won't be there for long. I can arrange transportation to Rio Cristal, but after that, you're hiking." He turned to Delfino so abruptly that Delfino almost jumped. "You're going to be hiking a lot and uphill."

"What are the dangers?" Delfino asked, his feet throbbing at the mere thought.

"It's all danger, my friend," Peña said. He seemed to have taken a dislike to Delfino and wasn't bothering to disguise it. "If you don't think you are up to it, don't go. The last thing they need is a burden."

Delfino stared at him hard. No one said a word. Peña continued tapping and twitching. Fortunately, Luz entered with the steaming coffee. They sipped in silence.

"I'm going to draw you a little map, I know the area well, I grew up near Hombrecillo," Peña said taking a pen out of his pocket. He searched through a pile of documents on the coffee table.

"Luz," he cried out, "grab me some paper!"

Delfino dug in his pocket and retrieved the wanted poster he had torn from the lamppost in Antilla.

"Here," he said, turning the page over so that it offered a blank surface, "you can use this."

Peña grabbed it from him and carefully outlined a rough map. They watched as Peña moved the pen slowly, methodically tracing lines, jotting down names of rivers; he even drew trees and rock formations.

"It looks like a treasure map," Delfino said.

Peña looked up at him with a scowl as Luz lumbered in, waving a clean sheet of paper. "Never mind now," Peña said to her. He returned to his drawing, adding a little dry cough to his repertoire of nervous tics. Luz picked up the empty coffee cups and retreated awkwardly to the back of the house.

*

They all heard the warning whistles.

Aspirrina took cover behind a large rock. She knew that if there was gunfire, the rock would offer scant protection, but it was the best she could think of at the moment. The night was dark, without even the hint of a smile from the moon. Only the remaining embers of the fire-pit illuminated the small clearing. From where she crouched, she could see the backs of her men; their knees bent forward, their arms at the ready.

In the silence that surrounded them, she heard their breathing, even the clicking sound of their fingers as they nervously played with the triggers of the old rifles. Fingers that itched to pull, to fire, to defend their camp. The whistles grew louder, closer. The rebels turned in the direction of the piercing sounds. Aspirrina heard the breaking of dry branches as they approached. There was a group of them. The rebels kept their shoulders tense, their heads leaning forward as if their eyes were pulling them forward, wanting to see into the darkness ahead. A branch moved. The soldiers turned in the direction of the movement, automatically, functioning only on instinct. The branches parted. Aspirrina shivered behind the rock. She heard the metallic sound of rifles cocking. She watched as two blindfolded men, their arms up, their hands on their heads, were pushed forward, into the clearing. Three rebels walked closely behind, the barrels of their rifles poking the two men in the back. One of the rebels laughed when he saw the looks of fear on the faces of the squad.

"Put down your weapons," he said, "it's only us."

With ridiculously exaggerated sighs of relief, they did as they were told.

"You should see yourselves," another one said, "it's obvious you've been away from combat far too long. Is that shit I smell? Did someone shit his pants?"

Aspirrina stood up on the rock to get a better view.

"Maybe it's your mother who shit her pants," one of them said

337

as he put away his weapon.

Aspirrina appraised the two blindfolded prisoners.

"Look what we found wandering around El Hombrecillo," the rebel said.

"We're not the enemy," one of the prisoners argued. "We're with you. Armando Peña sent us."

"I don't know any Armando Peña," the soldier said. "And how do you explain this?"

He waved the map around.

"I found this in his pocket, a ransom poster and a map that leads them right to this very spot."

"I told you a million times," the second prisoner said, "we needed paper, it was something I stuck in my pocket, it means nothing."

"Maybe it means nothing to you, idiota," the soldier said, "but this isn't just treason, it's an insult. One hundred thousand pesos for Fidel Castro's head. Not even dollars. Pesos!"

"What do we do with them?" another solder asked. "Do we shoot them?"

Silence swept the camp.

"We don't shoot unarmed men," Aspirrina said.

"But they're already blindfolded," the soldier said, "ready to go. Two bullets and they're not a problem anymore."

Aspirrina noticed a dark stain spreading down the leg of one of the captured men.

"If we don't shoot them we have to feed them," another said.

Arjuna had felt his bladder giving way, the warmth running down his leg, and he cursed himself. Maybe it would be better if they just shot him. He could not stand the humiliation. The time he spent in the hands of The Hyenas had left him vulnerable, had given him a deeper understanding of imminent death. But here? In the hands of the very people he had come to assist? The car had taken them over bumpy dirt roads to the edge of the foothills. There, the driver had pointed a finger up and left them, like two unwanted dogs. Peña's map had been useless, nothing was where it was supposed to be. They had stumbled about for two days, like a couple of idiots. The further they climbed, the colder it got, until the warmth of the plains was a distant memory. Arjuna had spotted the rebels at a distance, but instead of hiding, he shouted at them, waved his arms at them and waited. The idea that they would be mistaken for the enemy, or worse, bounty hunters, never crossed his mind. Who knew it would turn out this way; so ugly, so unnecessarily vicious. But in a war, the slightest misunderstanding could turn fatal.

Everything would have been fine if it were not for that map, the ransom poster, tossed into a pocket as casually as a souvenir, a memento. The moment it was discovered, everything had changed. No amount of reasoning or pleading had changed their minds. The rebels branded them mercenaries, out for Fidel's head. For money. Arjuna couldn't imagine a greater insult. Not even the time he had spent naked, vomiting and begging for mercy in Ventura Novo's shit-filled cell had been as torturous and humiliating. He'd lost three fingers by the time Maria and her father showed up, but he didn't give up one single name. If he had to die, at least he could die with that certainty. He wondered how Delfino was holding up. Arjuna felt completely responsible for the fate of his friend. He wished he had left him alone with his money and his hats. He should have forced him to stay in the convent with Maria. Now strangers were deciding his fate.

"Do we shoot them or not?"

"I say shoot them and throw them in the river, let their bodies float downstream as a warning to anyone who might get the same idea."

Arjuna heard laughter, the laughter of his own men. His life was a joke to them. And he heard a woman's voice. She seemed the voice of reason.

"Remove their blindfolds," she ordered. "We don't shoot unarmed men here, you all know that. Think about it, would bounty hunters come up here unarmed?"

Arjuna felt fingers at the back of his head and he bucked away from them furiously. But they persisted until his blindfold came loose and dropped around his neck. His vision was blurry. He could see a round clearing. In the center there was a large hole full of burning embers, the half eaten carcass of a goat and bones scattered about. There were about a dozen men, bearded, haggard, and most of them bandaged. They had rough-hewn bandages around their heads or their arms, or on their legs. One even had a patch taped over an eye. Two of them stood on crutches fashioned out of tree branches. This must be some sort of rebel hospital.

He was disappointed. He always dreamed that his death would come in a place of honor, in a raging battlefield or at least in front of a military firing squad. Not at the hands of this scraggly bunch.

He looked to his left as a man removed Delfino's blindfold. Delfino's eyes, red-rimmed and swollen, met his and sent him a silent message: I love you.

Arjuna nodded, taking it in. His heart was beating hard, gulping blood. The pounding was so loud that it affected his hearing, was as if there were waterfalls in his ears. But a voice cut through the droning.

The woman's voice again.

"I know these men," Aspirrina said.

33

Lansky was looking at his bowl of white rice and black beans with disgust.

"You don't like it?" Juan Carlos asked from across the small, rickety table.

"It's all right," Lansky said. "Ten thousand Jews in Havana and not one decent deli."

They were at Bodeguita del Medio, and it was filled with tourists trying to get a gander at Ernest Hemingway.

"Look at all these people, hanging around, chewing on pig, just to get a gander at some fat writer," Lansky said. "When I first came to Cuba I ate whatever they placed in front of me, pork, bacon, lard, just to close a deal. If Cubans could, they'd eat every part of the pig, from snout to tail."

Juan Carlos laughed.

"You're right, boss, we love our puerquitos."

The moment was light, but Lansky was making him uncomfortable. Why had he brought him here? Did he know about his night with Estelita? Is that what this is about? How could he know? Well, he knew everything else. He prayed Lansky didn't but without one moment's regret.

"You know I didn't bring you here just to feed you," Lansky said.

Juan Carlos stopped chewing. He knows!

"You're not afraid of me, are you?" Lansky asked.

Juan Carlos smiled at him, he could tell Lansky was half-joking.

"No, boss, I'm not."

"And you trust me some," Lansky stated.

"Is there any reason why I shouldn't?"

Lansky pushed his untouched dish with disgust.

"Let's get out of here," he said.

They left the restaurant and walked toward Lansky's car, Juan Carlos watched Lansky take in the landscape, the well-dressed people moving fast, up and down the sidewalk.

"Such a beautiful country, such a marvelous city with the kind of energy that can't be replicated," Lansky said. "Only New York City exudes this kind of energy. Havana! So beautiful and so fucked up."

They got into the car. Before they circled the plaza in front of the embassy building and the Ayuntamiento and then turned onto O'Reilly Street.

Juan Carlos tried to see the city through Lansky's eyes: The size of the waves in the mouth of the harbor and the heavy rise and fall of the channel buoy. In the mouth of the harbor the sea was very wild and confused and clear green water was breaking over the rock at the base of the Morro, the tops of the sea blowing white in the sun.

"All this is mine for the moment," Lansky said. "I just have to make the moment last."

Lansky was silent for a moment.

"So you trust me, you say?"

"You've never given me any reason not to," Juan Carlos said. "And I think there is something on your mind. What do you want me to do?"

"Goddamn it all, if you're not the greatest find in all the Caribbean. I knew from the moment we met that there was something special about you. You can't really trust the Jewish boys anymore. Ever since the Holocaust, tough Jewish boys are hard to find, and even harder to train. They're all college boys now, brainwashed by the cult of the survivors. *Never forget,* they said. But they forgot. They're not hungry anymore. You are, though. Hungry like I was, maybe hungrier."

"Not as hungry as I was before you hired me," Juan Carlos said. "I'm talking about a different kind of hunger, ambition. Ready to do anything to get out of where you came from, to get what you want."

"That I am, boss."

"Horny, too. I've noticed the way you look at the showgirls, and one in particular. The girl is worth it."

So he knew, had known. Juan Carlos braced himself.

"I knew the girl was special from day one," Lansky said, "but I also knew that just a few days in the gambling world would destroy anything that was special about her in short order. So I put out the word – she was not to be used like the others. Sure, everyone immediately thought I wanted her for myself. To hell with them, let them think what they want as long as they kept their greasy paws off her. Estelita is and will remain under my protection. In spite of my warnings, I could see the sharks circling her."

"Boss, I would never..."

Lansky squared with him.

"Yes you would, and you did. That's all in the past now."

Juan Carlos was starting to sweat, he knew his face was wet and that Lansky could see it. He was both ashamed and terrified.

"You never told me not to," he stammered, "if you had, I never would have touched her."

Lansky smiled. A closed-lip smile.

"I didn't think you stood a chance," he said. "You had millionaires up against you. Expert seducers. Sons of bitches!"

"She's not like that," Juan Carlos ventured.

"Calm down." Lansky said, " it's all in the past now. Look in my eyes, Juan Carlos, see I'm not angry. I took care of it. I sent her away. I knew she would be safe in Mexico. When she returns she'll no longer be a showgirl up for grabs, but a movie star. A star I created myself. I'm through spending hundreds of thousands for name talent. That Rogers dame cost me a fortune. From now on, I intend to create my own stars. Hugo's movie is going to be crap, but I'll make it a hit, it's going to take a bit of capital, but it can be done. Anything is possible on this little island as long as I stay close to the man in charge. But nevermind the girl, if the reports on the radio are to be believed, we're in for some serious changes."

"You listen to Radio Rebelde?" Juan Carlos asked, surprised.

"You bet I do," Lansky answered. "I get it right here in the car. I roll up the windows, turn up the air and listen. And if what they're saying is true, we have to move fast."

"From what I hear, a lot of those reports are made up, just to frighten the army."

"What if they're not? I can't risk it. I have too much money, too much of my life invested here," Lansky countered.

"But you've got Batista on your side. He's not going to let anything happen to you."

"Feh. Batista only believes in Batista, I hear he's already packing bags of dough, that's what I hear."

"What does Batista say to this?"

"Say? He doesn't say anything. I can't get him to talk to me. They call it a security measure. I call it bullshit, Fulgencio knows the jig is up and doesn't want to face me."

Juan Carlos nodded seriously. He could see in Lansky's eyes that he was burning with fury. If he ever got within ten feet of Batista, there would be serious trouble.

"How can I help, boss?" Juan Carlos asked. He started to feel safe again. He stopped sweating, Lansky wasn't going to banish him from the casino. His future was safe.

Lansky remained silent for a moment, he pulled the car over so he could look Juan Carlos directly in the eyes. "We have to get to Castro," he said. "And you're the only one who's smart enough and trustworthy enough to manage it."

"That's quite a job."

"You can do it, I have no doubt."

"But it's almost impossible to leave the city now," Juan Carlos said. "There are roadblocks, the trains have stopped. I'd be lucky enough to make it as far as El Escambray."

"You can do it," Lansky flashed him a confident smile.

"Campechuela." Juan Carlos said easily.

"Yes, Campechuela, maybe Pensamientos. Stay out of Bayamo.

It's too risky there right now. I hear they're shooting people just because they look suspicious. So you have to be careful where you go and who you talk to. But you have to talk to Castro, face to face."

"I can try."

"You can't just try," Lansky said. And there followed a long silence.

"You have to get to him," Lansky continued. "Let him know that I'm willing to deal, that this Batista situation is no longer feasible for me. That there's a lot of money for him and his people to make. Millions. Tell him five million. Enough money to fund all the revolutions he's ever dreamed of and more. And as for you, my Cuban friend, if you can pull this off, for the rest of your life you never have to worry about money again."

One thing Juan Carlos had learned on the streets – if it sounds too good to be true, it probably is. But if he understood correctly, Lansky's entire fortune was dependent on him. This was the moment he had been waiting for. The chance to show Lansky what he was made of.

"Do you have a plan for me?" Juan Carlos asked.

Lansky turned to him and smiled, the kids wants a piece of the pig and he wants it bad. "I always have a plan," he said.

"I'm listening."

"You must travel unarmed," Lansky had said.

"No gun?"

"No gun. If they stop you, a gun's not going to help you. One lousy gun against twenty. But it will blow your cover and that will be the end of that. You are a grief-stricken son on his way to his mother's funeral, your sainted mother whose heart could take no more."

Juan Carlos had listened carefully as the plan was laid out for him. He had never known his mother – and here he was, burying her.

"The car must be humble, take an old one from the heap, buy one off some poor bastard on the streets, it should be just functioning enough to get you there and back, even if it breaks down from time to time. It must look borrowed, don't take that one in the fleet you seem to be so fond of."

Juan Carlos reddened. He didn't realize he was so transparent, that his ambition was so obvious. Nothing escaped Lansky.

345

Eduardo Santiago

"Listen carefully now, what I'm about to say will change your
life more than money. You do what I ask, you do it effectively, and the
girl is yours."

Juan Carlos secured a beat-up old car without too much trouble,
a rusting old Ford with no windows. Something no one would suspect.
The night winds flowed through it freely, like the caress of ghosts on
the back of his neck. It was quiet. Only the rattling of the hood escorted
him; the rustling of the trees, the constant crunch of tred. The light of
the one headlamp that still worked dimly lit his way down the Central
Highway. Lansky had it all figured out. Juan Carlos would be like
anyone traveling on the highway. A husband, a father, a victim of
circumstances, anyone desperate enough to take to the road when the
country was about to explode.

"They will let you through because your mamá has died,"
Lansky had said as he handed him a photo of an old woman. "If anyone
stops you, show them this, they will understand. They would do the
same. They would race to her graveside, nothing could hold them back.
I know you people, you Cubans. In many respects, you're just like the
Jews."

Juan Carlos took the picture, looked at it closely.

"It's my mother," Lansky said. "Nice lady, a face like a fist."

"I don't have one," Juan Carlos started.

"Yes, I know," Lansky said, "that's why you're taking mine.
She will bring you luck."

How did he know? Juan Carlos never talked about it. Lansky
knew everything. He had to trust the plan would work. As he drove on,
his confidence soared. He would return to Havana a rich man. He
would return deserving of Estelita's love. He would give her everything
her heart desired. He would put the past behind him forever, the
orphan, the shoeshine boy, the black fingers, the poverty, the shame.
He kept her letters in his breast pocket, close to his heart. Her sweet
letters, written in pencil, lightly, almost illegibly, like a whisper. The
paper, touched with perfumed hands and covered with lipstick kisses.

Sometimes the letter would be simply a page filled with the
words "te amo," I love you, over and over and over again. Those were
the letters that made him smile the most. Or she would write:

346

"I miss you with all my heart, with all my soul, with every breath I take."

They were lyrics he recognized from popular songs. He understood that those were the the words she knew, the poetry of guajiros, field hand serenades. Songs that tasted of guarapo, sugarcane juice, on a hot summer night. But no matter what she wrote or how she wrote it, whether she made it up or stole it, he loved her. He loved imagining her beautiful face scrunched up over a blank sheet of paper, her perfectly arched eyebrows knitted into a frown as she tried to put down on paper the emotions that floated through her sweet soul. Te amo, te amo, te amo, he shouted back to her out the car window, the words flying like doves into the December winds. Can you hear me in Mexico? How far away are you? Are you looking at the same moon?

Juan Carlos's mind stayed on Estelita as he drove. He'd read her letters a hundred times. She missed him, she wanted to be with him, she was his. She wrote to him about her father, locked away in some institution. That the only reason she had gone to make the movie was money. Money to bring her father to Havana. She was such an amazing young woman. Deep down inside, Juan Carlos had been feeling unworthy and unsure. For whatever reason, Estelita de la Cruz was in Mexico City becoming a movie star.

But what did he have to offer her? Who was he? Nobody, that's who. But now, suddenly, everything was different. He would get to Castro if he had to crawl on his belly to do it. He would make this happen. He would make Estelita proud to be his girl, and with Lansky's blessings, his wife. They would send for her father, if that would make her happy. At the moment, the only thing that sustained him was his desire for her and his desire to make her happy. He daydreamed of the curves and fragrances of her body. Her kiss like an abyss, a bottomless well of sweet, dark water, had awakened the poetry in a soul hardened by circumstances, by his past. He was discovering what love really was, where it could take you, what it could do. He looked at everything differently now. He always knew that eventually a woman would come into his life; after all, they were all around him. But he never imagined that she would have such an effect. That love would turn him into a man he hardly recognized.

It was well past midnight, there were no other cars on the

highway in either direction. No lights burned in the fields. He was driving through a silent, gray landscape, a place where all the rocks and trees had turned to velvet. Juan Carlos kept his eyes on the road. He wanted to make the car fly. But it refused to go any faster. He had to press the accelerator to the floor, gasoline vapors wafting all around him. Even the slightest hill proved a challenge. Now, as the road headed straight up the hillside, the car chugged along, sounding like it was choking.

When he reached the top, he heard it. The sounds of combat. The rat-tat-tat of machine guns, punctuated by the sudden booms that could only be tank cannons. Bright flashes of light tore into the night sky. But his car could be heard above all else. He shifted into neutral, he was coasting, picking up speed as the car rolled down the curving mountain road as if pulled by an invisible force. He was going much too fast, much faster than he had intended. He pumped the brakes, but they were useless. He caught a glimpse of an old road sign that read Pueblo de Moffo. And then he was careening towards a deep gully that had been dug in the road.

This was a trap. He tried to turn away from it, but he was traveling too fast. The car was suddenly airborne, a heap of metal flying in the night, life had suddenly taken a giant step forward, too big and too quick for his mind to identify. The moment of impact was blessedly fast, a blunt, crashing thud. His head bucked forward and hit something. Hard. And that ended all motion. Men crawled out from the thicket, they swarmed the smashed car. He couldn't make out their faces in the moonlight but he could see their eyes, which were wide and furious.

He felt himself being dragged out of the car by clamp-like hands. His legs had turned to water, and when they let go, he dropped to the ground. He lay by the side of the road; a painful knot formed in the pit of his stomach making it impossible to speak. Juan Carlos never had felt paralyzing fear before. Not as a youth when he walked the cavernous night alleys of Havana among cutthroats and thieves. Not even as an adult when he'd raided sleazy gambling dens, squaring off with some of the most violent individuals on the island. But now he could feel his every muscle contract, like a dead body reaching towards rigor mortis. Lansky's plan deserted him, he couldn't remember, couldn't think. His mind was locked into a singular image. Estelita on the casino stage, performing her fire dance. Her lithe and graceful figure dancing in a circle of light, moving sensuously, magically, a white flame. A porcelain figurine in a jeweled box. An enchantress. He felt the hands of the men pick him up again and drag him, face up, away from the highway, into the thicket. He made an effort to struggle, but it was useless. His body would not respond. Thorns clawed at his legs, tearing his pants and into his flesh, one of his shoes came loose and came off. The men were moving fast, dragging him deeper into the jungle. They kept low, stray bullets zinged all around them. And then they dropped him again. He could hear them cocking their rifles. The sharp sounds of gunfire pierced his eardrums.

A boot turned him upside down, another on his neck pushed his face deep into the ground, into the sacred dirt of Cuba. And there he found some comfort. He felt a knee on his back and realized that one of the men was using him as a rifle brace. Were these men Batistianos or rebels? It didn't matter. He never had figured out which side he was on. He breathed in the sweet smell of the damp soil, letting it soothe his mind. He didn't know how much longer he would be alive and he wanted to make every last moment count. He could feel the slight bulk of her letters pressing against his chest, his heart beating against the envelopes of perfumed paper.

As he lost consciousness, he offered a small prayer.

"Forgive me, Estelita de la Cruz, I have failed you."

34

On Christmas Eve, Sor Maria led the way through the dark alleyways and twisting, narrow roads of Old Havana, towards its majestic cathedral, San Cristobal. From a distance, framed by the dark sky, she could see its mismatched towers, to her a reminder of man's imperfection.

The rest of the sisters followed her in their usual silence. They kept close together, their earnest faces intermittently illuminated by the ornate lamps that hung from the humid cement walls. This was a special night for the sisters of Convento de la Santa Caterina, the only night when, as a group, they stepped out of their solitary, shadowy existence and merged with the other residents of the city. A strong December wind blew in from the Malecón, bringing with it the dark-blue scent of the sea. The nuns walked on bravely, their black habits pressing hard against thin bodies, their veils lifting and falling with the will of the wind.

Sor Maria looked around her and frowned, merriment prevailed and she couldn't help feeling a twinge of envy. Everyone seemed so excited as they rushed on ahead to find seats before the clanging bells announced the beginning of the mass.

The birth of Jesus brought out those who seldom stepped foot in a church. They tore themselves away from after-dinner conversations, after gorging on the traditional Christmas Eve fare, roast pig. Some came in romantic pairs, strolling as if in a dream, holding hands, the light of love shining in their young eyes. Married couples walked with other married couples. The women in red, low-cut Christmas dresses that out of respect for the church they covered with somber, knitted shawls. Groups of darkly-dressed matrons, their Spanish lace mantillas already draped over their stiffly coifed hair followed closely behind. Portly men, their round faces still flushed from one after-dinner cognac, walked in groups of three and four, slowly savoring the last of their fat cigars. Among them also walked ascetic ladies who wore no makeup at all, not even a trace of lipstick. They were dressed in frequently washed frocks, fading flowers and lackluster plaids. They kept their hair cut short and practical. Their shoes sensible and scuffed. Sour-faced widows dressed in the dark colors of eternal mourning arrived alone. Young mothers carried bundled babies, whispering little prayers to keep them from crying.

Many greeted the nuns with a cheerful, "Feliz Noche Buena" as they passed by. The nuns, so used to being invisible, responded with a nod. The last groups to arrive at the wide, ornate cathedral doors came in long, shiny cars. Black-suited chauffeurs offered white-gloved hands to the older women, whose thick, freckled wrists were heavy with bracelets and rings, their nails filed and lacquered to perfection. Elegantly dressed and expensively perfumed, they entered the church, some followed by much-younger husbands in three-piece suits with London cuts. They walked down the red-carpeted aisle, all the way to the front of the cavernous cathedral, their eyes fixed on the altar of Carrara marble, gold, silver and fine, polished wood. They took their honored, reserved seats at the very front, as close to God as money could buy.

The plaza outside the cathedral was filled with those who never went to church, for whom this night was simply a holiday, an excuse to celebrate. They sat in the cafés that bordered the plaza, chatting and laughing while street musicians strolled by singing Christmas carols. Beggars asked for alms, as they always did. And on this night they actually got some, for this was the eve of the most important birthday in the Catholic world.

As Sor Maria walked up the steps towards the church, she noticed a young man in a dark blue suit, defiantly wearing a red-and-black 26th of July armband, darting through the crowd. She motioned the others to go inside and stood watching. She watched the young man as he approached various people in the plaza and whispered to them. She saw people turn away, or shrug him off. She walked down the steps and moved closer to hear what his message might be.

"The rebels have taken Santa Clara," she heard him say.

No one seemed to care.

"The rebels have taken Santa Clara," he shouted as the cathedral bells began to clang. His eyes were wide with the crystalline look of a fanatic.

"Listen to me," he shouted even louder as the crowd that had been loitering in the plaza started moving towards the door of the cathedral. Enraged by their indifference, he climbed on top of one of the café tables and shouted again, this time much louder.

"The rebels are in Las Villas! They've taken Santa Clara. Don't you understand what this means? Wake up people, wake up!"

If this was true, what did this crazy man expect anyone to do? Did he expect them to rise up and take to the streets, on Christmas Eve? What would this mean for Delfino? No matter, Santa Clara was more than two hundred miles away. A lot can happen in two-hundred miles.

Sor Maria wondered. Was he safe now, past Las Villas? She would say another prayer for him. As the massive bells above them began to ring signaling the beginning of the mass, she felt the young man run past her with a greater force than even the raging winds. She followed him in, watched him rush up the center aisle to the holy epicenter of the cathedral.

"They've taken Santa Clara!" he shouted from the altar. The gasp must have made him realize where he was, because he lowered his voice and in an urgent whisper, as if divulging a secret, he said it again.

"They've taken Santa Clara."

A few of the men in the front pew stood up grumbling and stepped towards him.

But the young man slid past them and ran back towards the front door. When he was gone, there was only silence. When the bishop appeared at the altar, all eyes centered on him as if the disturbance had never happened, as if the young man did not exist. And although Sor Maria loved the pageantry of the midnight mass, the thick clouds of incense that wafted from the illuminated altar, she was having trouble concentrating. While all the others marveled at the altar boys who, on this special night, wore large, white angel wings made of goose feathers, and admired the bishop, resplendent in his red and gold vestments and rejoiced to the choir's soft, heavenly serenade, her mind was locked away elsewhere. She looked at the altar, gleaming because she and her sisters dusted and polished it every night, but she could take no pride in her work; her thoughts were still with the exuberant young man and the trouble in Las Villas. She forced herself to set aside all disturbing thoughts, tried to wash her mind clean of anything unrelated to the birth of her savior. While the bishop said a silent prayer, his arms extended towards the giant crucifix that hung over the altar, Sor Maria begin her own silent prayer. Her first prayer was for Orquidea, who had resolutely refused to attend mass.

"I just can't, Sister," she'd said, lying in a heap on her unmade cot.

"It will do you good," Sor Maria had urged.

"I know, but I just can't, please forgive me."

Poor Orquidea, she missed Esteban. It was so obvious and sad. Sor Maria wondered what it would be like, to have your heart and soul so consumed for love of a man that even the birth of Christ didn't matter. She was about to start her second prayer, the one for Delfino – when a searing sound from outside severed the silence. And then two more. They were gunshots, as clear and jarring as if the bishop had fired them from the altar. First one, then a brief silence, and two more in quick succession. Everyone looked at each other, eyes wide, ears sharp. A murmuring crescendo swept from the first pew to the last. Even the bishop, his arms still raised to the sky, seemed to have skipped a word, a syllable; had somehow stumbled, missed a tiny, almost imperceptible beat as he spoke the ancient words of Isaiah.

> For unto us a Child is born,
> Unto us a Son is given; and

The government will be upon
His shoulders...

Then, as if the church had suddenly burst into flames, everyone who could stand up did, and whether it was fear or curiosity or some sort of demented self-protection that leads people to do what they do, they ran towards the door.

"Please remain seated," the bishop ordered, but Sor Maria was the only one listening, for there was an upsurge of sound, a violent jostling of bodies and the stomping of feet. Sor Maria didn't join the stampede, for she knew exactly what she would find out there – the young man with the armband, the one she inexplicably loved, face down in a dark pool of his own blood. While insanity raged around her, Sor Maria remained seated, and she added another prayer to her list, for the young man who lay dead in the Plaza de San Cristobal.

35

Café Las Virtudes was bustling with tourists on Christmas Eve. The narrow street was jammed with people, the bars were packed with men of all shapes and sizes, their colorful shirts, hot pink, turquoise, sunflower yellow open to the navel, the dark and hairless chests slick with sweat. Everyone laughed uproariously at anything anybody said, many pissed on the walls, others threw arms around each other, singing in drunken celebration.

It looked like happiness, but Esteban knew better. He was busy helping Elegúa keep up with the demanding crowd; his fingers stiff from slicing roast pork to perfect thinness. They hardly could keep up with the demanding hoards. Their hands became slick with the delicious grease. To give their pork sandwiches a special flavor, they dipped each slice of bread in a mixture of raw garlic, olive oil and dry cooking wine. The work was unrelenting but their pockets were thick with cash. It was exciting, there in their little corner of La Habana that had become his home, the slice of the city where no one went to midnight mass or cared whether it was the night before the birth of Christ or not. To them, it was Noche Buena. The Good Night. A good night to forget, a good night to chase the devil, grab it by the horns and ride the December winds.

The profligates came from all parts of the country and all corners of the world. Sailors took to the streets in garrulous groups, overjoyed that this year their holiday leave was on the island of illicit pleasures. Farmers who came to the city to sell their pigs at mercado stayed late that night to grab a few drinks and maybe some paid-for loving before returning to the monotony of their bohios.

On Christmas Eve, the men of Havana walked out of their homes without explanation; deaf to the threats and shouts of their wives, to do what men do. Their festivities began on Noche Buena and most of the men wouldn't come to their senses until well into the New Year, when they returned home, sick, exhausted and broke, but without apology. Some would be welcomed back with hugs, kisses, and others with a disdainful roll of the eyes and a cold shoulder.

Christmas Eve on Calle Virtudes was not just festive, it was as if everyone in the world had lost all sense of shame. Streams of lights were haphazardly strewn from one balcony to the other, radios placed on the windowsills blared bone-rattling music. The rousing, drum-driven songs filled the narrow street. Melodious and contagious, the kind of music that keeps away dark thoughts and worries.

The whores across the street were the busiest of all, and they liked it that way. They moved fast to the midnight rumbas that gushed from the radios. They wore their shiniest blouses, tightest skirts, biggest earrings. Bright flowers bloomed behind their ears and between their breasts. They squeezed their calloused feet into towering heels. In those spiked and curved shoes, they trotted up and down the stairwells to their rooms with one man after the other. It was a contest among the whores to see who was the most desirable, the most expert, the one who could service the most clients, make the most money.

As the night wore on, they got careless and returned to the sidewalk with their blouses half undone. Their lace undergarments, torn by impatient, fumbling hands, lay discarded on the pink tile floor. All night the whores of Calle Virtudes pushed themselves to the limit. Their eye makeup smeared. Their lipstick smudged by frenetic kisses and the savage tongues of strangers. A night like this was like heaven to these whores, their gift from baby Jesus. In these few hours and all the way to New Year's Day, they were sure to make more money than they would make any other night.

It was in this crowd of inexhaustible revelers that Esteban saw her, or thought he saw her. His beloved Belquis. Her black, lustrous, shoulder-length hair. Her smooth and creamy shoulder, tan and perfect. He heard her laugh, deep and dark as a night river, exploding above the din. But it couldn't be her – Belquis had been dead for almost two decades. Could it be Estelita? Could it be his little girl grown up in the image of her mother? Could she be here, on Calle Virtudes, as he had long suspected? Could this be the moment? Could this be she?

"What do you see, Esteban, un fantasma?" Elegua asked seriously, for it was not uncommon for men like them to see ghosts. But Esteban didn't answer. He put his knife down, and deaf to the complaints of his customers, took to the streets. He rammed his way through the thick crowd, shoving drunks and hookers out of his way. When they complained he shoved harder.

"Mira viejo," they said with annoyance, "get your greasy hands off me."

But Esteban pushed on, through and through, until he was standing behind her. The dancing crowd around him ebbed and flowed, a stormy sea, making it difficult for him to maintain his balance. She was just ahead. Just beyond his reach.

"Estelita," he shouted above the noise and the music, "Estelita!"

The woman didn't respond. He squeezed closer, knocking over a marimba player with great clatter. He extended his arm as far as he could, over the bouncing shoulders of others, past their faces. He meant to tap her lightly on the shoulder, but suddenly the crowd changed direction and he was knocked into her, pressing the palm of his hand into her naked back. The woman turned around, a frown of intense displeasure obscuring her face. No, she was not Estelita. Everything about her was wrong. She was a beautiful woman, but there was no subtlety to her beauty. Her eyes were too large, her lips too thick. He closed his eyes for a moment and when he opened them, he was staring into Orquidea's face. He saw her sweet gentle smile, her soulful eyes. He wanted to hold that moment for all eternity. But just as quickly and clearly as her face appeared before him, it was gone and he was once again staring into the angry face of this strange woman who for a moment had so resembled his daughter.

"¿Que le pasa a este tipo?" she asked, both frightened and defiant. What's the matter with this guy? A man was pushing Esteban away from her, back into the crowd. His fists clenched, his hard, hairy knuckles aimed at Esteban's jaw.

The crowd pushed back. The man pushed Esteban again, this time with greater force.

Esteban walked away while others around him shouted with derision. "¡Cobarde!" they said laughing. Coward. A group of men picked up the word and chanted it. Coward, coward, they sang. Years before Esteban would have fought them to the death but now he kept walking. And he didn't hold their attention long. They returned to their beer and their dancing as if nothing had happened.

Esteban walked through the crushing crowd on Calle Virtudes, this time staying close to the walls, away from the churning mob. The illusion of Belquis and Estelita had left a deep and powerful yearning to be held, to be with someone, to look into eyes that were familiar. He walked deliberately until he was well beyond Calle Virtudes, until he had left the party far behind. He entered other more respectable neighborhoods, passed houses where all the furniture had been pushed aside and families were dancing as if they wanted to tear up the floors. He walked past the peddlers offering lotto tickets.

"One peso wins you ten-thousand by New Year's," they shouted at him. And on towards the convent. As he neared he heard the sound of bells clanging loudly. He must be near the cathedral. He let the bells guide him, and then, suddenly, the unequivocal crackle of gunshots. First one, then silence, then two more. He crouched in a darkened doorway, his heart pounding. Nothing happened, no more gunshots. Must have been some crazy drunk trying to shoot down the stars. He walked beyond the boulevards and past the glittering, high-rising casinos where elegant couples streamed in and out of revolving glass doors.

He turned into the narrow street that led to the convent, avoiding the beggars who extended grimy hands. He passed a street corner where a group of men much younger than he were playing conga drums, maracas and the flute, and passing around a bottle of rum. They were beating on the drums fast, as if in competition. The flute sent long, measured notes into the night air. The flute transported him to his

358

hometown of Pensamiento, and he stopped to listen, to drink it in. Then, as if playing just for him, the musicians slowed down to a soft, burning, beat. One of the men took a big gulp from the bottle and started to sing a ballad, an old one. He remembered singing that song many times and in a much better voice.

"Me conoces," the man sang, "you know it."

Esteban nodded. While he sang, the man smiled and offered Esteban his bottle. Esteban looked at the swirling, amber liquid. It would be so easy, he thought, to just take it and drink it down. All of it. And then another. And another. He would be just like them, happy until dawn. It would be just like the good old days. He could stand on that street corner and sing all the songs he used to sing. He would swagger just like he used to. A crowd of available beauties would gather around him. He would end up on a rough-and-tumble mattress in some hotel and it would be like heaven. He would never have to walk away from a fight again, he never had to feel shame or regret, he would never long for anyone, hurt for anyone. The bottle felt good in his hand, so familiar, so comforting, just the shape of it, the weight of it. He brought it to his nose and inhaled the cool vapor and felt dark corners of his mind light up and twinkle like the happiest of stars. He smiled at the singer and shook his head no. The man shrugged, took back the bottle and continued to sing.

"Me conoces," he sang. It was that song he had taught Estelita so long ago. The one she had sung so beautifully, even better than he ever had. He broke away from them quickly, continuing back towards another destiny. But the melody of that song stayed with him as he walked. Without realizing it, he picked up the pace, his heart took on the beat of the drums, and his veins flowed to the sweet whisper of the flute.

When at last he saw the crumbling walls of the convent, his soul rejoiced. He had been so afraid of this, of love, thinking love was only something that was offered and then taken away. But now, as he reached the door, he was no longer afraid. He was twenty-two years old again, ready to defy the devil, ready to give away his heart even if it got torn to pieces. He knocked on the thick wooden door. Nothing. He knocked again, harder, louder and placed his ear against the door, his heart racing. He heard footsteps approaching and he knew they were hers. It seemed an eternity, waiting there, listening to the footsteps, remembering the frail woman with the raw and ravaged hands. All this time he'd believed it had been a miracle, something the saints had done. But now, listening to her footsteps, waiting for her to reach the door, he realized how wrong he had been. So obstinate, chasing after ghosts when all this time she had been there, waiting patiently.

"Who is it?" Orquidea's timid voice asked through the slab of wood that divided them.

"Orquidea," Esteban whispered, "Orquidea, mi amor." Never before, in the long history of el Convento de Santa Catalina, had those doors been flung open so fast, so wide and with such joyful abandon, for a man.

36

Estelita looked out of the small, round window of the airplane that was returning her to Havana. It had been a long flight, but finally her island was in sight, an emerald alligator asleep in a sapphire sea. All through the flight she was impatient, wanted to make the airplane go faster, arrive sooner. She had been gone such a long time. Her senses, dulled by the flight and the monotonous whirring of the propellers, now sparked at the sound of the landing gears, the creaking and cranking of the wheels being lowered. She saw the golden silhouette of Morro Castle, majestic in the harsh afternoon light. And then a dazzling blur of blue, white and green and she was soaring dangerously close to the water and the sand and the palm tree-tops and everything that was good in the world.

She was home.

They hit the runway hard, the airplane bounced slightly as it came to its noisy stop. She jumped up as soon as she heard the pilot's voice say she could, gathered her things, and ran for the door and down the rickety, metallic stairs. She rejoiced to the feel of the hard ground of Cuba beneath her feet. In Mexico, she had always felt as if she'd been walking on quicksand, as if at any moment she could vanish and no one would hear from her ever again.

Her stay in Mexico had lasted much longer than she had anticipated, two-and-a-half months. She had missed Christmas in Havana. Hugo Benavides wanted her to stay, but she had been determined to be home for New Year's Eve, to welcome 1959 in the arms of Juan Carlos. Hugo made her sign papers promising she would return if they needed her for looping or publicity. She had agreed, just to get out, and he let her go, albeit with much reluctance.

On the drive to the hotel, as the taxi neared Havana, she thought only of Juan Carlos. Tonight she would be in his arms. They would dance all night, and into the clear, blue dawn; they would escape to a small beach somewhere, far from everyone. She had so much to tell him, so much more to show him. It amused her that love could be so strange, that the deepest feelings she had ever felt were for a man she hardly knew. Now that she was back she would never leave him again. They would be inseparable. She couldn't wait to introduce him to her father. They would go see him together. She imagined sitting back and feeling safe while the two men smoked cigars and shared stories of their past. Esteban would tell him about their life together, of his days as the most popular rumbero in the eastern provinces.

Juan Carlos could tell him of his days at the most popular casino in Havana, the powerful men he'd met, the movie stars. Her heart pumped with excitement at the very thought.

From this day forward, it was going to be perfect.

Her musings soothed her, she felt like another person, a woman who knew what she wanted, who wasn't content to let life toss her around like a scrap in the wind. From now on, she would go where she wanted, do what she wanted, get exactly what she wanted. From now on she would make plans.

As she entered the hotel, the turquoise walls welcomed her. She stopped briefly, taking it all in, letting it make her giddy. This was her world, and she was thrilled to return. This lobby was her lobby and everything in it was perfect. Crowds of tourists streamed through the revolving doors, followed by bellhops loaded with suitcases. Many of the faces now crowding the front desk she recognized from her flight. Their voices filled the vast room. Different accents: Mexican,

Venezuelan, Portuguese. Foreign languages: English, French, Italian, Japanese. She strolled through the casino and its scent of danger and desire, she followed the buzzing of the sexy cigarette girls and barmaids. She eyed the bejeweled women who loved their dogs more than their children, the men who loved money more than their wives, the sounds of quick deals and broken promises, the hushed voices of steely-eyed men who believe luck is a lady, men who lived with the certainty that adamant ambition was enough to rule the dice, and that the next roll would send them home a winner. At the baccarat tables, ladies without strategy, in flowered hats and white gloves, daintily sipped colorful daiquiris, their tired eyes listlessly following the hands of the dealer as cards were expertly laid out in front of them.

Everyone was here.

A freshly painted banner hung across the ceiling, gleefully announcing Feliz Año Nuevo! Happy New Year. An even bigger sign tempted tourists with the New Year's Jackpot. The amount of the jackpot reflected the coming year: $1,959,000.00!

For a moment she thought about what Ana Verdugo had said to her in Mexico and shrugged her off as a malcontent. After her bizarre interview with the reporter, she had started to read the newspaper every morning, at once curious and dreading what Señorita Verdugo might have written about her. She tortured herself with imagined headlines: Cuban Actress Hopelessly Out of Touch, or Showgirl Turned Actress Is All Show, or worse, Santo's Cuban Concubine Is A Moron. No such story appeared – apparently, the journalist had not found her interesting enough for the pages of El Machete. She did find almost daily articles about the so-called Revolution which she read voraciously. And she had worried. But as far as she could tell, nothing unusual was going on in Havana.

Everything was as she'd left it. In a corner of the lobby, reporters and photographers surrounded someone important. Several flashbulbs exploded at once sending a thick waft of smoke up to the ceiling fans. Someday that will be me, she thought as she walked past them. She slowed for a moment, hoping to catch a glimpse of the celebrity creating the commotion. It could have been any of a dozen stars that regularly came to Havana: Frank Sinatra, Nat King Cole, Tony Bennett, John Wayne.

Then she saw the silver mask.

Santo, the most famous man in Mexico! She vaguely recalled him mentioning he was coming to Havana to make movies. She hadn't thought much of it, but apparently he had been telling the truth. She backed away carefully, hoping he wouldn't see her. She was not in the mood for a chat with Santo, and she certainly didn't want her name linked to his in the Havana papers. That would be catastrophic.

She hurried back to the front desk hoping the crowd had diminished, but it was still bustling. There were the usual arguments and complaints about bungled reservations. Indignant guests, cranky from their flights and anxious to get going, were shoving each other out of the way and shouting their frustrations at the overworked clerks. Estelita stood back for a moment until she got the attention of one of the hotel managers.

"Welcome home, señorita," he said. A snap of his fingers brought a bellhop to her side. She followed the uniformed bellhop to the elevator and up to her old suite. Like an inveterate gambler who perceives fortune in the minutest details, she construed as a good omen that her room was still waiting.

"You don't remember me, do you?" the bellhop asked.

"Sorry?"

"Jorge," he said, smiling and extending a white-gloved hand, "from your first day here. I brought you to your room."

"My first day? Yes, I do remember you now, Jorge," she said, taking his hand. But she didn't remember him at all.

"I hear you've been away," he said, effortlessly hoisting her heavy luggage onto the stand.

"I have, yes."

"Mexico! I've always wanted to visit there."

"Where did you hear that?"

"Everybody in the hotel knows it, Señorita de la Cruz," he said as he opened the door and deposited her bags, "everyone knows you went to Mexico to become a movie star."

A movie star! If they only knew, she thought to herself. But to the fawning bellhop she offered her brightest smile. A movie star's smile. And a big tip. And then he was gone and she was left alone with just her pounding heart. She took a moment to take in the familiar surroundings. She looked out the window at the panoramic view. Everything looked just like she had left it. Nothing had changed. The sea still extended blue and sensuous to the horizon. Her sea. Her sky. Her clouds. She recalled how she used to watch the airplanes from that same spot, dreaming of the day when one would take her far away. Now she dreaded the very thought.

She was glad to be home. This hotel was the only place that had ever welcomed her. Where she had been appreciated and celebrated. Sabrosuras had been uncertain, and life on the road with her father even more so. The convent had never seemed like a real home to her. Kind as they had been, the nuns had never allowed her the freedom she'd known here. Not with Sor Maria and Aspirrina constantly looking over her shoulders.

The time spent in Mexico had been a mixture of elation and torture. She did not regret having gone. How could she? She'd had been incredibly lucky that she was the one chosen. She was grateful for the experience of acting in a real movie. But looking back, it puzzled her, almost scared her. She had left her father and Juan Carlos behind. While in Mexico she'd thought of her father daily. She'd wished he could've been there with her, to see the sights she'd had no time to see: its pyramids, cathedrals, museums. She comforted herself with the knowledge that she had done it for him. Now that she was back, her desire to see her father was overpowering.

Now she was ready to properly care for him. She was a woman with a career and a man, the sweetest of men. Her father would be so proud. She looked around her, at the elegant suite. He was going to love this life! She turned away from the window and took an envelope out of her suitcase. She spread its contents neatly on the bed, then carefully counted the bills one more time. She had saved enough money to send for him. Better yet, she'd get Juan Carlos to drive her there. She would be safe with him, she thought, remembering the gun in the glove compartment. She recalled how the gun had frightened her, but now she would be much more frightened without it. The trip would bring them closer. They would begin the year together. A fresh start!

They could spend the rest of their lives here, at the top of the world. She would get her father a job at the hotel. He would sing again.

Eventually they would find an apartment of their own in Havana. Now that she was older, she could take much better care of him, keep him from drinking too much, from thinking too much. She knew memories plagued him, but perhaps in Havana, she could help him forget. From now on she would always know where he was, what he was doing. Juan Carlos would help keep him sober and sane and productive.

Their apartment would not be as lavish as her suite, but comfortable enough for the three of them. She had no doubt that their fortunes had changed. Her movie was not going to be a classic, but she had done it, she had made a film. This would guarantee a preferential standing among the other girls in the show. Lansky had all but assured her of this. She began to regret not having wired Juan Carlos. Prepared him for her arrival.

Now she wished he'd been waiting for her at the airport with roses. It had been childish wanting to surprise him. She still had so much more to learn about how one went about things with men. It was not only her father, perhaps all men were unpredictable, liable to go missing when most wanted, to be where least expected. But no, Juan Carlos was different. He had written to her, only once, but the letter was everything she had hoped for. He was a busy man, not sitting around a movie set as she had been with nothing else to do but daydream and write letters. She couldn't wait to see his look of surprise when he saw her. She had changed, not just on the surface, but deep down inside. She was a woman now. In just a few short days she would be twenty years old and everything she ever dreamed of would be at her feet.

Filled with a new optimism, she took a look in the mirror, the face staring back convinced her that she needed a bath and some rest. She had to look spectacular tonight when she saw Juan Carlos and set her new plan in motion. It was New Year's Eve, after all, the perfect time for a new start.

Estelita tried to nap, but couldn't keep her eyes closed for more than a minute. A long bubble bath had done the trick, though. She felt refreshed and ready as she strolled into the bustling lobby.

"Estelita de la Cruz!" Juancho, the doorman said as she passed him, "you look like a million American dollars."

She smiled. Juancho had never commented on her looks before. He had always treated her with the same studied politeness he offered all the hotel guests.

"Juancho, have you seen Señor Talente?" she asked casually, careful not to set off a wave of gossip. The man stopped to think, as if remembering was the hardest work he'd done all day.

"Come to think of it, I haven't seen him for more than a week," he finally said.

"A week?" This was not the answer she was anticipating. This answer didn't fit in with her plans.

"Where did he go?"

"I don't know, cariño," the doorman said with a playful grin. "But if you're lonely, you know where to find me."

She forced a little smile, but was not in the mood for flirting with a doorman. She returned to the elevators and pressed the button that would take her directly to Lansky. Lansky would know. Lansky knew everything. And she had promised to check in with him as soon as she arrived. She would play it cool, pretend she was just in for a quick visit. Wish him a Happy New Year. He'd want to chat about Mexico, the movie, her future. She would be patient, answer his questions carefully, and somehow work Juan Carlos into the conversation. She knew exactly what to do.

She entered the small, private elevator, once so daunting. She allowed herself a final check on the polished brass doors. She smoothed down her dress, inspected her lipstick, and calmed herself. She was no longer intimidated by Lansky, by his big office, or his frightful reputation. He was her friend now, her protector, her benefactor. Without his intervention, her time in Mexico would have been a series of indignities. But when she phoned him, he had taken care of the problems without question. He'd protected her, treated her like a daughter. There was nothing to fear.

When the doors slid open, she stepped into the hallway. She stepped up to the big, solid door and knocked gently. It was eerily quiet in the hallway. The air-conditioner was blowing from a vent above the door. She felt a chill run up her spine, and wondered if it was the air conditioning, or just the feeling of loneliness that was starting to course through her veins.

She wrapped her arms around herself against the cold and waited, her impatience increasing with every passing second. She thought back to all the times when just on the other side of that door, in the spacious, book-lined office, her life had suddenly changed. It was in that office that she had first met Juan Carlos. She remembered his first words to her, "This woman claims she is your mother."

And the look of horror on Aspirrina's face when Estelita answered.

Poor Aspirrina, their friendship never had recovered from that moment. A tiny instant in time when Estelita hadn't been as kind as she should have been. But at that moment, she felt she had no other choice. She knew that one day she would make it up to Aspirrina. She would go to her, make amends.

In this office she had been promoted from showgirl to star. She smiled at the memory of Barbarita's and Rosario's expressions when Lansky had turned to her and said those magic words:

"You will dance and sing."

And in this office, barely three months ago, she had become an actress with a movie contract. She recalled how swiftly Lansky had signed the contract, like waving a magic wand. The other side of the door was her lucky corner of Havana. So why wouldn't it open?

She knocked again, a little louder this time. The sound that came back to her was hollow. She tried again, rapping hard, until her knuckles hurt.

There was no one behind that door.

She ran back to the elevator and took it all the way down to the ground floor. She walked quickly, almost running through the maze of hallways that led to the dressing rooms. The girls would just be arriving and starting their transformation – from ordinary girls to gorgeous chorus girls. Certainly one of them had seen Juan Carlos.

She could hear their cackling voices as she approached the dressing room.

And then she heard her name.

"Estelita..."

She inched closer and stopped just outside the door.

"Oh, she's back all right." It was Barbarita's brittle voice. "She checked in this afternoon."

Estelita could tell the others were hanging on Barbarita's every word.

"La princesa is back in her old suite. I've said it before and I'll say it again, she's giving the mean old Jew something more than a good performance."

She heard laughter. They were laughing at her, telling lies and laughing. Then, she heard an unfamiliar voice.

"Is it true she was discovered in the casino and sent to Mexico City to star in a movie?"

More laughter, dark and horrible. Estelita clenched her fists so hard that her nails dug into her flesh.

"Eso es lo que dicen," she heard Rosario say. "What really happened, and I was there to see it—"

Rosario paused, allowing the curiosity to mount before she spoke again.

"What really happened was that she pounced on the producer during one of our flights from Miami," Barbarita cut in. "Wait until you meet her, you've never seen such a manipulator."

There was another brief moment of silence. She could imagine all the girls stopping whatever they were doing to pay rapt attention. Lipsticks and powder puffs suspended in mid-air.

"She puts on airs of innocence and propriety," Rosario continued, her baby voice rising, "but you should see the way she always got everything her country-girl heart desired."

"She was the new girl, just like you," Barbarita said. "And next thing you know she's got a solo dance number and a suite in the hotel and she's flying around from here to Miami singing and dancing and shaking her maracas at anybody in a three-piece suit."

"It's true!" cut in Rosario. "She threw herself at that producer like a snake falls from a tree. He gave her a ride in his chauffeured car all the way back to the hotel. I don't know what she did in that car, but by the time they arrived in the hotel, she had a movie contract."

Estelita backed away from the door. "Chismes y envidia," her father used to say. Gossip and envy. Oh yes, Rosario and Barbarita were eating themselves up with envy, rotting away in that stuffy dressing room night after night while she was off making a movie. She determined then and there that she wasn't going to let them upset her,

369

she was above their cheap gossip. She was above them in every possible way, and she was going to make sure it stayed that way. She raced back to the front desk. Perhaps one of the managers could tell her where Juan Carlos lived. Maybe he was ill. She had to calm down. She was starting to feel frantic. Maybe things were not the same after all. Maybe her luck had not changed. Maybe. Maybe.

"Estelita?"

The deep, familiar voice made her cringe. She turned and came face to face with Santo's silver mask.

She forced a smile and before she knew what was happening, she was being embraced. She placed one arm around his massive back and gave it a light, friendly pat.

"Santo," she said, disentangling herself from him. "How nice to see you again."

"When did you return?" he asked.

She reached for the elevator button and pushed it several times.

"Just a few hours ago."

"It's wonderful to see you here. So you made it out of Mexico in one piece?" he said. "And just in time for Año Nuevo."

"Yes, just in time."

She checked her wristwatch, stole a look at the elevator needle. Why was it taking so long?

"What's the matter, pretty girl? You seem sad."

"No, just a little tired from the flight."

"You're too young to be tired on New Year's Eve!"

She didn't know how to answer. She didn't want to tell him she was on her way up to her room and planned to stay there. That she didn't have one single friend in this city. That she had just heard the women she was closest to in all Havana saying terrible things about her, and that the man she loved was nowhere to be found. The elevator was taking forever.

She pushed the button again, scraping a fingernail. It hurt. Everything was starting to hurt.

"Listen," Santo said, "you probably already have plans, but I would love it if you came to a party with me tonight."

"Thank you, Santo, that's very kind, but I--"

"It's at Batista's house in the country. Have you heard of it? It's

370

called Coo—"

He stumbled over the word. The elevator finally arrived and she entered. He followed her.

"Kuquine?" she said, impressed. "You travel in very important circles."

"I'm the most famous man in Mexico, didn't you know?" he said, laughing. His booming laughter always disturbed her, as his mask never changed expression. It remained frozen in a fierce grimace. But he seemed to be in great spirits. Santo was a man who enjoyed his celebrity, his success, and at the moment he seemed particularly jolly, as anyone should, on New Year's Eve in Havana.

What was wrong with her? She hadn't felt so out of sorts since those nights long ago waiting for her father to return to the hotel. In Mexico she got used to being alone, but tonight she was feeling not just lonely but hopelessly lost.

"It's going to be a big fancy party," he continued, "a lot of fancy people. The men who are producing my new movies here in Cuba will be there. I would love to introduce you. We're still looking for my leading lady," he said with a teasing lilt. "And Batista is a big fan of horror movies," he continued. "Did you know that? I'm sure he'll want to hear all about *Daughter of Dracula*."

"It's called *Tinieblas*," she said.

"I heard they'd changed it," he said.

She felt a current of excitement and dread course through her. President Batista would chat with her about her movie! But she pushed the thought away. The mocking words of Barbarita and Rosario were still haunting her —La Princesa, the opportunist, the girl who would do anything to get ahead. Her churning insides were telling her she should go to the party with Santo. She should make the effort to meet these producers and the president. Keep the momentum going. She wished she had someone to consult, someone who could advise her. She wondered what her father would say to this invitation. Santo remained silent, watching the numbers as they lit up, floor after floor.

The elevator door opened to her floor and she still had trouble finding the right words.

Finally, she turned.

"I don't know if I'm up to a big party tonight," she said,

371

stepping out onto her floor. He was holding the elevator door open with his massive hand.

"What? A beautiful young girl like you!" he said, then noticed a shadow of sadness cross her face. She seemed about ready to burst into tears.

"Think it over," he said with a note of kindness, "If you should change your mind, I'm in room 811."

"I will. Thank you. And happy New Year, Santo, I'm sure we'll see each other again soon."

That was it. She had told him "no" without having to speak the word. It was all she could do. The last thing she needed was a scandalous headlines linking her to the most famous man in Mexico. She barely made it back to her suite. As her hands reached out to push the doors open, it felt like they were weighed down. And although her body felt heavy and lumbering, her thoughts were racing, stumbling over themselves. Her stomach was tightening with doubt, squeezing itself upwards inch by inch. She looked at the clock, it was almost nine and she had absolutely nothing to do for the rest of the long, long night. Outside her window it was dark and moonless. She considered dressing and going downstairs, watching the show to see the new girl, her replacement. But she couldn't muster the energy. She wanted nothing to do with those hypocrites, those two-faced phonies in the chorus. She also didn't want to be wandering around the casino alone. Too many romantic couples toasting with champagne, dancing slowly, looking into each other's eyes, and too many drunk, ass-pinching men looking to score for the night. It would be like spending her New Year's Eve in hell.

She stared out the window. One of the dozens of yachts that bobbed in the bay was already shooting fireworks, red and orange and gold glittered into the dark sky. Instead of beautiful, she found them annoying, for they prevented her from believing that this was a night like any other.

She walked to the phone and checked with the front desk again. There were still no messages for her, not from Lansky or from Juan Carlos Talente. She hung up; looked at the four walls and at the jumble of dresses still strewn across her bed. She was considering hanging them when a clear and specific thought cut through the welter of unhappy thoughts. She suddenly recalled seeing pictures in newspapers and magazines of Lansky and Batista together! They were the best of friends.

Surely, Lansky would be at the party tonight. And he would be able to tell her where Juan Carlos was. Wherever he was, she would go to him.

The nine o'clock cannon pounded the sky like a fist. All over Havana people scrambled to make decisions. Well, she was a woman of Havana now. She ran to the telephone and dialed the front desk.

She asked for room 811.

"Santo?" she said, her heart buzzing with excitement and anticipation, "It's Estelita de la Cruz…yes, much better thank you…listen Santo, about that party tonight…"

From the moment she'd joined him in the lobby, he'd been a perfect gentleman, as he had been that night in Mexico City. He greeted her with compliments, opened the car door for her. In spite of his formidable appearance, there seemed to be a gentle soul behind the silver mask. Surely, a famous and sought-after man like Santo didn't need to force himself on young girls. He had beautiful women throwing themselves at him all the time.

Soon, they were alone in his luxurious car and it was slow moving. Boisterous throngs filled the sidewalks and spilled onto the streets. Cheerful conga lines interrupted the traffic, laughing, shouting, dancing. The garish parade of tropical happiness only reminded her of how heavy her own heart felt. She wanted some of that happiness for herself. She couldn't wait to get out of the city, to arrive at Kuquine and talk to Lansky. Santo drummed the steering wheel to the music on the radio and pointed at people he found particularly amusing: the woman with fruits and bells on her hat, the group of men dressed in rumbero costumes, the pretty girls in short, yellow and orange dresses looking like tropical fruit come to life.

"Look at that one!" he shouted as another drunken conga line stumbled and weaved in front of them. "There's a happy group. They'll be sorry tomorrow!"

Estelita smiled and nodded. The men in rumbero costumes stumbling drunk in the middle of the night frightened her. Papá, she thought, soon we'll be together. She missed him to the point of heartache. She almost said as much to Santo, told him the whole sad story but she didn't want to encourage him with intimacies. She also didn't want to be rude but silence was all she had to offer tonight. She was relieved when he turned into a side street and on to the open highway. It was dark and quiet now. Santo fumbled with the radio dial and different music filled the car. They were driving along the coast with all windows rolled down and she let the fresh air of Cuba caress her face, as lush and romantic as the music. She allowed herself to relax, glad that she had accepted his offer. A part of her felt it was an act of revenge against Barbarita, Rosario and all the others. They would be shaking their asses on stage all night long while she welcomed the new year with the most interesting people in Havana. With Mr. Lansky and the president and other powerful men. Let them eat their hearts out. They were wrong about her. Could she help it if opportunities came her way? That she had the courage to take advantage of each one?

There wasn't one single thing she had done since arriving in Havana that hadn't terrified her. They had no idea how horrible it had been for her on that movie set. But she had learned, and she had managed. In a few months, the movie would be in theaters, and then everything would change again. When it did, she would be ready. And most important, she would have Juan Carlos at her side, holding her hand, protecting her. Loving her.

"About that business in the newspapers," Santo said, interrupting her reverie.

"Oh, that," she said with an amused smile. They had turned off the main highway and onto a long, narrow, dirt road. She hoped Santo knew where Kuquine was. The last thing she needed was to get lost with him.

"Yes, that." he said. "I assure you I had nothing to do with it. They print whatever they want."

"I figured it out," she said. "Hugo Benavides did it. It's all part of his publicity scheme."

"Just so you know," Santo said.

"I do," she replied, turning to look at him, letting him see that her answer was sincere. She liked this big, strange man, even if she had never seen his face. She wondered how long it had been since anyone had.

When she turned again to stare down the dark, narrow road, she noticed headlights in the distance. Soon, big, fancy cars filled with elegantly dressed people started driving past them. They seemed to speed up as they approached Santo's car and swerve by with a whoosh.

"Hugo is a businessman through and through," Santo said, squinting against the oncoming headlights.

The cars kept coming, about a dozen of them, Pontiacs, Buicks, Cadillacs, followed by military jeeps. Santo had to pull to the side of the road to let them pass. She wondered where they were all going.

"The party couldn't be over, could it?" she said.

"Not a chance," Santo assured her. "It's not even midnight."

They were driving deeper into the countryside. The dirt road was getting narrower. On either side thick palm trees grew tall, high into the dark sky.

"Santo, are you sure we're going to the right house?" she said. "Everyone seems to be leaving."

"I've been here many times before," he said, "it is up ahead just at the end of the road. You can't miss it."

"I hear it's like a castle," she said.

As they rounded a sharp curve, more cars came at them.

"Look," Santo said.

In the distance, she could see the house. Kuquine. And as they drove in closer, she could see that it wasn't like a castle at all. There were not just one, but two spectacular houses, colonial in design, luxurious, large, and expensive. A tall, ornate, wrought iron fence surrounded the houses. The large gates in the center were wide open. They were rounded, like big, hunched angel wings, but from the top edge, sharp metal spikes, painted red and gold, protruded skyward.

Santo had to pull the car over to the side before entering the gate, for there were several cars waiting to get out. Estelita could see anxious faces inside them. She detected the women's jewels and furs, tall, lacquered hair, the men in suits and ties. Santo managed to squeeze through onto a vast, unpaved drive. There, other cars were making desperate circles, trying to be next in line for the exit. The tires of the cars kicking up dust, which filtered through the glare of the headlights, giving the place a gloomy look, as if they were deep in a foggy swamp.

Santo swung wide around the other cars and pulled his car close to the house. As soon as he shifted into park, both their doors swung open and uniformed guards roughly pulled them out of the car and into the dusty darkness.

"What do you want here?" one of them barked as they were led up to the expansive front porch where there was more light.

Santo stood up to them, puffed himself up like a big cat.

"We were invited here," he said, searching in his coat pocket and thrusting an invitation at them.

"Why are you wearing that mask?" one of them asked. Before Santo had a chance to explain, another cut in.

"Take off your mask and show me identification."

"This is outrageous," Santo's deep voice was rising.

One of the guards still held Estelita's arm. She tried to shrug him off but he held on.

"Take off your mask," the man ordered again, pointing his rifle at Santo's head, the two black holes of the barrel staring him in the eyes.

"I never take off my mask," Santo said, "I am Santo, the Mexican wrestler."

"He's the most famous man in Mexico," Estelita added, almost an apology.

"We're here for the party."

"There is no party," the guard said.

"There is always a party on New Year's Eve, I've been to several," Santo insisted.

The guard placed a hand on his revolver.

"Either you take off your mask," he said, "or we're taking you in."

"What is happening here?" Estelita asked the man who held her. He didn't answer. They were all waiting for Santo to remove his mask. Instead, Santo reached into his coat pocket and showed them his passport.

"This doesn't tell me anything unless we can see your face."

"And then you'll let us go?" Santo asked.

"And then we'll see," the man said without a trace of humor.

Santo took a deep breath.

"Estelita," he said softly, "please don't look."

As his massive hands started to reach up to his head, Estelita turned away. She heard the sound of the silver zipper being pulled open. She realized that in Havana, the most famous man in Mexico was just another man.

From where she stood, she could see through the wide open door and into the house, to the glowing, wooden floors of the entry hall. There were wide-open windows to the right and she could see past an archway, into the main room. Enormous vases held crisp white roses. A grand piano sat silent. Dozens of golden candles still burned, the shadows of their flickering flames the only movement in the room. Her attention was drawn still further into the house, towards the back of the living room where two black maids in gray and white uniforms wept into each others arms. What horrible tragedy has taken place in this house? Eselita wondered.

"Are you satisfied now?" she heard Santo say. She wanted to look, but she didn't dare, he might just leave her here at the mercy of the guards.

"You must leave immediately," the guard said. "And I strongly suggest you go straight to your home or your hotel, this is no time to be on the streets."

Santo was no longer listening to the guard.

"Come on, let's go," Santo said to her. She turned. His mask was back on. All other cars were gone. Only the guards remained. Santo took giant steps towards his car, she followed him and quickly got in. He reached over and locked her door then his own.

When he turned on the engine, the car radio came on.

As the car crossed the gate, the guards offered them a military salute that Santo did not acknowledge. His eyes were fixed on the road ahead, his hands hard on the steering wheel.

"I don't understand," he said. "I was invited to a party here. Something's wrong. Something serious."

The song on the radio ended softly, and a male announcer's voice said, "*Feliz Año Nuevo. Happy New Year to all of our listeners. May 1959 be the best year of your life.*"

They continued listening to the music, waiting for a news report,

377

anything that might explain what had happened to the president.

But the announcer never returned. Music continued to play, one bolero after another, romantic music for people in love, for those who were still dancing out there somewhere, still clinging to one another, their hearts full of hope. Songs for those who believed that 1959 was going to be the best year of their lives. Songs her father had sung, and new ones that she had never heard before. Beautiful songs of love, love lost, love found, unattainable love, vengeful love. It felt to her as if at that very moment, the whole island was swelling obscenely with love. And it felt wrong to be in a dark car on New Year's Eve with someone other than Juan Carlos, someone whose face she had never seen.

They drove back to Havana in silence, the music filling the widening space between them. Neither had anything to say. Something had happened to Santo when he was forced to reveal his face. She realized at that moment that she was not his trusted friend, that she was just a girl he'd picked up in a hotel.

Once back in the city, the streets were wilder and more densely packed. Men carried bottles of rum, swinging them above their heads to the beat of the drums. Everyone was singing, confetti rained from balconies. As Santo's car inched through the narrow streets, costumed revelers banged on the windshield, drummed on the roof and then danced away.

Santo pounded on the car horn, shouted at people to get out of the way, but they thought he was playing with them, that he was a Cuban in a costume, and ambled up to his window to offer him a drink from their bottles.

He wouldn't lower the glass.

"Idiots," he said.

The people of Havana danced in spite of the explosions that had plagued them all year long, in defiance of the shootings and the hangings, they danced under the surveillance of the armed guards who milled amongst them, their eyes sharp, their fingers on the triggers. They danced and drank to ward off the devil, the dark angels, the vengeful saints and evil spirits. They celebrated the moment as if suddenly aware that it was a moment that would never return. They danced as if they would never be so young again, the music as seductive, the colors as bright, the world as full of promise.

Estelita wanted the night to end. Nothing had worked out the way she had planned. There had been no Lansky. No Juan Carlos. Nothing. But neither did she want to go back to her hotel room and sit anxiously waiting for the telephone to ring. As they slowly rounded a corner she recognized, a corner as familiar to her as her own face, she opened the door.

Santo slammed on the brakes.

"What are you doing?" he shouted over the cacophony.

"Santo," she said, "I need to be alone for a little while."

It was all she could think to say. He didn't even look at her.

"Go," he growled, and dismissed her with a wave of the hand. She knew what he really meant was "go to hell," and even in her haste, she appreciated the courtesy of his omission. But his voice had been so brusque, so dry and rude, that it didn't sound like him at all. For the first time since she'd met him, it sounded like the voice that should come from behind a ferocious silver mask.

She squeezed onto the sidewalk. Men tried to grab her. One took her hand and spun her around, then held her close, sang in her ear. She pushed him and he fell away laughing.

"¿Que pasa, nena?"

She walked faster, turning corners and crossing streets until she was far from everyone, until she was on a narrow familiar street; she ran through the night and didn't stop until she was at the convent's door.

She knocked loudly, aware that it was a very late hour and the nuns were sure to be asleep.

But she didn't have long to wait. The door opened just a few inches, held in place by a safety chain. She saw the annoyed face of Sor Maria.

"Sister, forgive me," Estelita said, "I had nowhere else to go."

"Estelita?" the nun asked, blinking as if her eyes needed a moment to adjust to the sight before her. The door closed. Estelita could hear the safety chain being unhinged. Sor Maria opened the door wider now. She looked the young girl up and down, taking in the elegant gown, the expensive shoes, the blue eye shadow, the diamonds sparkling in her ears, but most of all the lost look in her brown eyes. The same look she'd seen on her the very first time they met.

"Estelita de la Cruz?"

37

Estelita gasped, a fluttering hand flying up to cover her mouth. "Sister, that's not true. I've done many things since I left here, but never that."

Sor Maria looked the girl over with a narrowing gaze, she seemed sincere. Had Aspirrina lied to her to save her own skin? Of course! She knew the crazy little woman wasn't above such calumny. The devil incarnate, that one.

"Forgive me, my dear. I should have realized I'd been lied to..."

With some misgivings, she motioned Estelita inside and led her to a chair in the front parlor. She took in the exquisite outfit the girl wore; how every part of it had been carefully tailored. Everything about her was so different. She watched Estelita sit down and elegantly cross one leg over the other, one expensive, high-heeled shoe pointing sharply towards the ceiling, the other perfectly arched on the polished wooden floor.

In spite of her agitation she was poised and assured. Every gesture the height of femininity. An air of sophistication that she had not detected in her before now punctuated Estelita's presence. When she spoke, she did so softly, but directly, her thoughts coming easily to her. There was no trace in her of the country girl Maria had met almost two years ago.

Sor Maria listened patiently as Estelita, with a growing sense of pride, described the events of the past year. Working as a showgirl in a casino didn't seem such a far cry from prostitution to the nun, but clearly the woman Estelita had become was enormously proud of her career –a career she'd made entirely for herself. From her lips, such a life sounded like the pinnacle of success.

"I entertained, that's all," she explained, her manicured hands resting lightly on her lap. "I grew up with performers. My father was a singer, it's all I know. I have done nothing shameful, nothing."

"Your father will be greatly relieved to hear this," Sor Maria said. Estelita's face softened.

"My poor father," she sighed, " He's in Holguin, at a sanatorium and I'm determined to get him out of that horrible place as soon as possible."

Sor Maria couldn't control a slight smile. She leaned forward and touched the girl's shoulder.

"Your father is in Havana."

Estelita's eyes flickered, as if trying to ascertain that she'd heard correctly.

"Yes, in Havana, looking for you," Sor Maria added softly. She could see a jumble of questions gathering in the girl's mind, so many so fast she couldn't decide which to ask first.

"God works in mysterious ways," the nun said.

Estelita jumped out of her chair.

"But where is he, sister?" she pleaded. "How did you come to know him?"

"He was placed in my path," she said, "just as you were, my dear. We sheltered him a while, and then, just as quickly as he came, he vanished into the night. All I can tell you is that he's here, in Havana. Or rather, out there," she said motioning towards the city that hissed and sizzled like the devil's cauldron. "He's somewhere out there, searching for you."

"And you told him?" she asked.

"I told him what I knew, or what I thought I knew," the nun said. "I thought it would help."

"What he must think of me!" Estelita said, moving towards the door. "I have to find him right away. Who knows where this search has taken him.

Sor Maria nodded. Estelita seemed to be spinning in circles. "How did he seem to you, sister –did he seem...well?"

"He's a strong man, with a kind heart, and there is no doubt that he loves you very much."

The words released the torrent of tears she had been holding back all night.

"Where do I start?" Estelita whispered. Then, as quickly as the tears had come, they stopped. She wiped a hand across her eyes.

"Where is Aspirrina?" she asked, a new resolve in her voice. "Did she go with him?"

"No, my dear, Aspirrina left here long ago. I'm afraid I don't have the slightest notion where she is. I wish I could tell you that all your loved ones are upstairs sleeping. I wish I could tell you that all you need to do is run upstairs to find them. But just like you, they all left, without warning, without so much as a word of gratitude."

"I'm sorry if we... if I seemed ungrateful to you," she said. "Please forgive me for all the lies, for betraying your trust in me. I truly beg your forgiveness."

"For a very long time now I've known that my job in this world is to show love, not to keep score," Sor Maria said, walking to the entryway. "I hope that you will remember that. In the short time since you left, I have done things I never dreamed of and I did it all out of love, just as you have. I took great risks, placed my life and the lives of others in danger, but it led to something I never imagined, a reconciliation with my father. We see each other frequently now after a long estrangement. I'm convinced that my father would not be in my life if I hadn't opened the door to you that night. I am in your debt. Now my only prayer is that you find yours."

She opened the door and the night swept in and stood between them, the nun and the showgirl. Sor Maria looked at Estelita with tenderness, studying her as in the early days of their acquaintance. How quickly time passes, how indelibly people change. Estelita was no more the shy country girl who had once knocked at her door seeking refuge than she herself was the rebellious girl who had traded a life of luxury for the most humble of convents seeking the very same. Sor Maria was satisfied with her choice and hoped that Estelita would one day come to terms with hers.

"You can stay the night, you know," she said. "It's wild out there."

Estelita paused for a moment, taking in Sor Maria's sweet face, the genuine kindness of her eyes and secretly hoped that one day she could achieve even a modicum of that serenity, that gentle, unwavering munificence. But if she stayed she wouldn't get a moment's rest, she would toss and turn and grow even more agitated. She knew herself well enough, she had to stay in motion.

"Thank you for all your kindness," she said, throwing her arms around Sor Maria and holding her much too tight, the way she imagined she would hold the mother she never knew. And, almost fearfully, she whispered, "I hope we can still be friends."

The nun allowed herself to be held, feeling the girl's hands on her back, feeling the heat coming from her anxious face, the heaving of her sorrowful breast.

"Yes," Sor Maria nodded, "We will always be friends. Now, go find your father. Go with God."

38

By dawn the next day Estelita had rushed from one end of Havana to the other. The elegant gown she had put on the night before with such illusion was now grimy with soot and ash from the fires. She realized she must appear as she had when she was a little girl except she was no longer running through the muddy streets of some small, nameless town looking for her father. Now she was stumbling through an enormous city that had burst into flames, a city where all music had stopped.

"*In an effort to maintain some sort of order, truckloads of soldiers rolled into Havana,*" a radio blared. She need not be told. She could clearly see them, she felt their rumbling coursing through her, reverberating and pulsating as if they were driving into her soul.

They came in conjunction with Fidel's "26th of July" Militia, armed with machine-guns and rifles; the number *26* painted on their helmets with white shoe polish.

But chaos and mayhem still held sway. Everywhere she turned, stores were being gutted; houses set on fire. People waved torches and red-and-black flags. Young men, in groups of five and seven, ranged through the crowds like feral dogs. She quickened her pace, took turns into unfamiliar alleyways trying to stay one step ahead of the fear grabbing at her heels, shadowing her relentlessly, threatening to take over and weaken her resolve.

But the events of the day had taken over the entire city. Even in the most remote neighborhoods, from all the houses she passed, radios thick with static blared the latest news: *Batista has fled, taking with him the national treasury. The army had surrendered to the rebels.*

Estelita remembered not long ago when only music emanated from Havana's homes, now strange voices pitched with excitement or hoarse with hysteria reported the position of the rebel forces, and neighbors reiterated the news from door to door, window to balcony, shouting the latest as if to convince themselves that what was being reported had any relation to the truth. She overheard at a gallop that all the radio and television stations had been penetrated by revolutionaries at gunpoint, that the president was gone, the country was bankrupt, and the city had exploded in a tidal wave of maniacal celebration.

She made her way back into the city center where she was one of thousands on the sidewalks, found herself in front of the luxury hotels where the lobbies were mobbed with frightened guests demanding to be checked out as quickly as possible. She saw tourists throwing money on the counter and jockeying for a taxi to the airport. They had once been her adoring audience, now they were a sweaty, hysterical crush of red-faced men barking demands, shouting for this and that: their cars! and their rights! their ambassadors! as if anyone was listening while next to them pale, swooning women gripped their patent-leather purses, their pearls, their nerves.

Estelita felt an urge to offer some words of comfort, to magically transport them back to those nights of sipping sugary drinks and watching the colorful parade of showgirls from ample, cushioned chairs. And always the music, the rumba beats heard around the world, the dark rhythm that brought them in, kept them coming, welcomed them to the island of unimagined joy, to the tropical vacation *you won't soon forget.*

She turned from them, determined to feel no pain, to simply forget or at least forget that they had once had any meaning, she turned

385

from them as if they had never existed.

All around her streets were jammed with honking, overheated cars filled with nervous, overheated passengers, the lucky ones who'd managed to snag a car, bribe a driver, figure a way out. For a moment she considered abandoning her search, jumping into one of those cars, talking her way into their good graces and away from the tumult but she couldn't move in that direction. Somewhere in the burning city was her father, who knew in what condition, physical or emotional. She imagined him frail, huddled in a doorway, helpless as a child. She chased that thought away and imagined him drunk and pretending the party was just for him, stumbling through the minefield, blissfully unaware, miraculously safe. She wished that just for one moment God would grant her the voice that could cut through the clamor, "Papá, I'm a dolphin! I'm a mermaid!" and his eyes would light up with the sun and she would be at his side.

Night shrouded the city with a stupefying calm. But this brought her no comfort. She returned to her hotel room, exhausted, drained. She watched the sky endlessly, unable to sleep, eat, or sit still. She was filthy but the thought of undressing for a shower made her feel as if she weighed a thousand pounds. Any simple action, running a brush through her hair or applying lipstick was an indomitable task. Her legs ached with the desire to run, search, find.

Day after day she had left her room at sunrise, and with diminishing hope, made her way out into the rubble that was once Havana. Each day she chose a different direction. She covered every crevice of the ravaged city, fearing the worst. She battled the constant, nagging dread that her father was trapped in one of the impenetrable hospitals, or now lay in one of the blood-lined gutters somewhere. But regardless of the horrible thoughts that pushed in on her, impervious to the sad and incomprehensible brutality all around her, she kept looking. She moved fast through the smoke and the flames, raging violence and the stench of death, past screaming sirens, deafening gunshots, shattering glass.

She saw hundreds of faces that week. The bearded faces of the olive-green clad soldiers that were starting to swarm into the city. It was a strange sight to most people of Havana, where even the humblest men prided themselves on their neat haircuts and meticulously trimmed mustaches.

She saw the clean-cut faces of American sailors rushed in from Guantanamo to protect the American tourists who'd come to celebrate the holidays and now found themselves trapped like rats on a sinking ship. She'd seen the retreating faces of Batista's supporters scurrying in shiny automobile armor through the desolate landscape, still haughty in their suits and ties and furs and pearls. She kept moving, catching glimpses of every form of anguish.

She saw too many people as those days aggregated into a week. So much sadness and confusion, so much derangement.

As the days of January wore on, a strange calm washed over Havana. The smoke cleared. The screaming sirens subsided. And eventually everything stopped. Fear emptied the streets almost completely. Havana was silent and stayed that way for two days. After the initial frenzy, it was as if everyone had retreated indoors, as deep inside the dark shelter of their homes as possible.

The radio continued to announce the advance of the people they were calling the Heroes of the Revolution. They had made it to Santa Clara, the radio said, which meant they were roughly 200 miles away.

What Estelita did not see during her relentless search was one single face she recognized.

It was January 5th and still no word from Juan Carlos, no sight of her father. From her window she could see military airplanes flying low, cutting through banks of white clouds that floated in stark relief against the black sky. Were they clouds or was it smoke? She couldn't tell the difference anymore.

For a week she had searched every corner of Havana, even through hospitals full to capacity with wounded men and weeping women, all victims of the violence flaring and growing around her. Overworked hospital attendants turned people away with vicious, unmeasured words. A cold, heartlessness was the new currency. Fights broke out as desperate men turned savage, demanded medical attention, or tried through brute force to make their way to the front of the line. Blood smeared the floor and the furniture of the waiting rooms.

Furniture rained from balconies and was doused with whatever fuel was handy. Bonfires blocked the streets. She saw pink damask sofas, gold-gilded mirrors, carved armchairs, oil paintings of great beauty and taste, treasured family heirlooms, crash to the ground to be instantly engulfed in the ravenous, spiraling towers of flames.

Restaurant, café, and grocery storeowners boarded their doors and windows as the looting and rioting spread. Mobs broke windows and swarmed in anyway. The overwhelmed police force, no longer sure who was in charge, or if they still retained jurisdiction, fired their guns listlessly and without aim, further arousing the already inflamed and impassioned crowd. The mangled bodies of the wounded writhed and panted on grimy, ash-covered sidewalks.

Estelita continued to push her way through crowds of people, fighting a fear and a sadness she'd never known. As she neared the center of the city, she saw more and more men dragged – kicking and pleading – out of their homes and into idling cars to be taken to places where there would be no mercy.

She heard that anyone associated with Batista was being taken to a field outside of town where a massive grave had been dug with a bulldozer. That those who resisted arrest would be labeled traitors and shot on the spot, their bodies falling backwards into the pit.

On empty sidewalks, blood mingled with the confetti and colorful streamers from nights before. In other parts of town, hordes took to the streets screaming for justice, lifted the injured and carried them away to the relative safety of their homes or out-of-the-way alleys and junkyards.

The word TRAITOR appeared scribbled large on walls and sidewalks. Posters and billboards of Batista were defaced; crossed out, declaring a new day, the number 26 painted across his face with a furious, swift motion. Bodies of men hung from trees. Groups of women gathered around them, wailing and shrieking with escalating abandon, as if their very souls had been set afire.

As Estelita crossed to the other side of the narrow street, she saw two teenage boys climb a rickety stepladder, knives clenched in their mouths like pearl divers, to cut a man down from a makeshift gallows. They worked fast, eyes wide with mounting panic, aware that at any moment someone could take them out with a single bullet. At a glance, she knew it was their father. She moved on as the lifeless body dropped to the pavement with a sickening thud, thinking only of her own father, adrift in a godless world. A group ran by shouting that fires were breaking out near the docks. She kept moving. Mobs had destroyed the new casino at the Plaza Hotel, she passed a gutted café where a radio still blared. All radio stations had been seized, the broadcasts were calling on everyone to rise up and join the Revolution one minute and to remain calm the next.

No one was listening.

She reached the Banco de la Construccion in the Central Plaza where those trying to withdraw their savings were savaged. Her money was in that bank, careful deposits from her earnings, now she had nothing to show for her work, nothing to offer her father. No matter, she had been poor before, she knew what that was like and so did Esteban. She hadn't been any happier with money in the bank, had not felt any more secure. Together they would forge ahead somehow. She knew things that could never be taken from her, she had a wealth of experience now. She knew how to get that little house by the sea, how to earn a living, how to use her talents. All she had to do was find him and everything would be fine. Surely they could find another road show, she would sing for their supper, dance for their rent, whatever lay ahead, she was ready.

Farther ahead, the Latin-American embassies were crammed with officials begging for political asylum.

The words of Ana Verdugo, the Mexican journalist, drummed in her ears, "Are you, Estelita de la Cruz, aware..."

Yes, she was. She was all too aware now.

The hotel was mostly empty now. All performances had been canceled; the dressing room, once so bustling, was completely still. Gambling had stopped. Every last green felt table was deserted. The roulette wheels sat frozen in time. The lights of the slot machines continued to flicker and beckon to no one. The hallways echoed with melancholy and regret. At times she felt as desolate as a princess in a cold, bleak fairy tale, living in an abandoned castle with no sentinels to protect her. She lay on her bed, fully dressed, not bothering to pull back the bedspread. But in spite of the exhaustion and the relative safety of the elegant room, a room untouched by the events of the outside world, she could hardly summon one hour of sleep. Something was pressing down on her, she felt it pushing her further into the thick and downy mattress until all consciousness abandoned her. Sleep would come fitfully and she would awaken over and over again throughout the night.

Eight days into the disastrous new year she rose with less stamina but even greater determination. She had slept longer than she had in days but a vague sense of nausea and disorientation prevailed. She took the elevator down and walked quickly through the deserted lobby, towards the revolving doors.

A scruffy guard in crumpled olive-green garb and a red-and-black armband sat on a folding chair exactly where Juancho once sat, guarding nothing and no one. He saw her approach and spread his knees, defiantly, an unlit cigarette dangling from his leering mouth. He had a small transistor radio with him, pressed close to his ear. The radio was bright yellow, made of plastic, resembling a child's toy. But the voice emerging from it was not playful. The announcer talked fast, his words bursting like gunfire, as if the excitement of the moment was too much to convey.

"They're here," the guard said as she tried to walk past him without making eye contact.

She heard the announcer as she pushed through the revolving door

"The Heroes of the Revolution are less than twenty miles from La Habana."

What did this mean to her? Hopefully that all this revolution nonsense would stop, that the world would calm down. She didn't care who was in power, she just wanted everything to go back to how it had once been. She wanted the gloom to vanish, she wanted her fairy tale back, she wanted the hotel to reopen, the casino to start up again, the din of happy gamblers to rumble through her ears and her bones as it once had. If the casino would return to normal, everything else would fall into place.

She would find her father.

Juan Carlos would return.

She would be happy again.

It didn't seem like too much to ask.

She stepped into Havana, a city waking as if from a coma, heard the honking horns, saw cars, jeeps, trucks moving slowly down the crowded street, flags draped across hoods, trunks, and windows, convertible cars full of boisterous young people. Bicycles and motor scooters snaked through the sidewalks – a pulsating procession of people and machines. Crowds of men and women grinned from ear to ear and waved gigantic red-and-black banners, and shouted "Viva Cuba Libre" to the four winds.

She moved on to the wider avenue where she encountered hundreds more bursting out of the city's buildings and spilling into the streets, a flood of humanity flowing torrentially in the same direction, a cacophony that spoke only of elation.

Red-and-black 26 of July flags hung from balconies so packed with people that they seemed in danger of collapsing. Red-and-black confetti rained down on the boys who waved newspapers on street corners.

"*Fidel Castro enters La Habana!*" they shouted echoing the headlines they held in their grimy hands.

Women in red blouses and tight black skirts – living, breathing flags, shapely monuments to the revolution, hurried in joyful groups. They walked fast and Estelita fell in with them, melding into the surge; curiosity and momentum pulling her towards the center of the city.

Fidel Castro's name was on everyone's lips. They simply called him Fidel, the way one would a relative or friend. Fidel was marching into the city and everyone wanted to see him, to watch him up close, to test the sincerity in his eyes.

The farther she moved with them, the thicker the crowd became, the hotter the sun. Every possible smell wafted over her, from nauseating perfumes to grilling meats to garbage. And sweat. Sweat everywhere, sweat and cigars. This was a day for cigars, it was a day of celebration. Men discarded all formality and came dressed in colorfully plaid shirts, as if for an afternoon party or a picnic. They wore jaunty straw hats, and the dark glasses that American and Italian tourists had made popular. Some entrepreneurial citizens sold ice-cold watermelon juice and sugary lemonade, which people paid for gladly, tossing coins into tin cans, quickly gulping the refreshing beverages as they walked. Many linked arms and sang the hymn of the republic, or a popular conga song, or made up lyrics, composing them as they went along.

Estelita couldn't believe that a city that had been so beleaguered and frightened could change into uproarious merriment in just a matter of hours. There were gleeful shouts and screams. People – black, white, brown– pushed each other along the way, a massive quilt of bobbing heads, hats, flags. Others stood firm, parting the sea of bodies with sharp elbows only to allow a child or an elderly person to break through the crush, and she was among them, an ant in a sea of ants, one of them.

She searched every face until she felt a throbbing in the back of her eyes. The January sun was too bright, the cheering too loud, the people pressing in too close to her. Her hair felt dirty and heavy, and she lifted it to allow the warm air to dry the back of her neck. Earlier, a quick glance in the mirror had revealed the dark roots emerging. She needed a hairdresser and as soon as this was over, she would find one. A surge pushed her towards the edge, towards the narrow opening in the middle of the avenue where muddy military jeeps, tanks and trucks were moving along, keeping steady pace as if bound by invisible chains that pulled them inexorably towards the plaza. Estelita felt herself being pushed farther and farther towards the edge of the sidewalk. She held steady with one foot on the lip of the curb and the other in the gutter. The rumbling mob pressed hard against her and she had to fight hard to keep them from toppling onto the street, to be thrown under the enormous wheels of a passing truck.

She returned to the hotel again that night, eager to remove the shoes from her painful, swollen feet, to remove every item of clothing and soak in a nice hot tub, pretend for just a little while that outside everything was as it was. But a new guard barred her entrance.

"I live here," she insited.

"No one lives here," he said, "I strongly suggest you go elsewhere."

She was not going to back down.

"You don't understand," she said with her softest voice, a

seductive smile on her lips, "my things are in my room, it is number sixty-seven. You can check."

From her purse she dug out the key with the number sixty-seven clearly etched on it. The guard didn't bother to look at it, he simply backed into the entrance and locked the door. The door was glass and she could see him as clearly as he could see her, but he wouldn't look at her. She dangled the key in front of his face, but his eyes were blind to it. She could have stripped naked and that man would have remained resolute. As she walked away her arms felt light, and she felt completely unencumbered. Furious, yes, but surprisingly light. Her only burden was this thought: the game has changed, the rules have changed. You have to learn to play the new game.

39

Delfino and Arjuna marched by so close Estelita could have reached out her hand and touched them. But dark beards and mustaches, overgrown and dusty, masked their handsome faces and matching olive green caps and made them look almost identical to all the other young men marching along.

They marched proudly in their olive green uniforms and *"26 of July"* armbands. Their hearts were together, full of possibilities and jubilation. They had walked hundreds of miles towards a future for which they'd fought so hard, a future where the value of a man would be measured by his sacrifice and commitment, and not by how much money he had, who his father was, or what he owned.

In front of them, and for close to a mile behind them, marched other young men and women just like them who had risked everything for this glorious moment in their nation's history.

As they continued on, Delfino gazed at Arjuna out of the corner of his eye, as he had been doing throughout the long, joyful march – just to catch a glimpse, to briefly share with him all that was happening around them.

His life was so different now. He thought back to that time –

was it only five years ago, when he had returned to Havana, opened his shop, and tried to forget Madrid. He was invited to parties by all his clients, all of them eager to claim him as their "discovery," but after attending a few, he stopped going because they left him feeling even more lonely and isolated than he already felt. There were other men like him in Havana. Hundreds of them, it seemed. He saw them at the parties, among white tuxedos and crisp, pastel evening gowns made of silk organza, taffeta or lace; laughing to draw attention, hands aflutter. Delfino felt their eyes scrutinize him from head to toe before they brazenly introduced themselves. He could tell who they were, one diamond too many on their tie clips discretely set them apart from all other men. They praised his designs and offered him their friendship, recognizing him as one of their own.

He accepted politely, and promised to call, but never did. He had learned his lesson in Spain. Society ladies will tolerate effeminacy in a man, and in Cuba it seemed to be encouraged. But he knew a serious liaison with someone of his own class could only lead to scandal, and scandal to ruin. It was better to keep them guessing.

The daytime streets were just as treacherous. Men who walked alone, men who carried themselves in a particular way, were mocked and taunted with whistles and catcalls. He saw it happen time and time again, so he adjusted his walk to seem more masculine, almost threatening. No one whistled at him, no one dared to mock him, ever.

The nights were somewhat safer. He went for walks, always lying to himself about the reason, but deep down inside he knew what he was after. He wore dark clothing to better merge with the Cuban night. He found what he was looking for behind the arched columns in the Plaza de la Catedral, the center of Old Havana. There was no denying who they were and why they were there.

They, he soon discovered, would do anything to a man for a few pesos. He hired a few of them, quite a few times, for quick, furtive trysts inside one of the cathedral's confessionals. But the more he did it, the more these young men appeared to him dirty and indiscreet. They began to call out to him the moment he stepped into the plaza. He had made up a name for himself, Guillermo, and that's the name they called out.

"Guillermo," the voices were hard and thick; and so familiar as to be frightening. Later, they started demanding more money than was agreed upon. Always an unpleasant experience that, if handled incorrectly, could lead to violence. They were used to American tourists, the ones who grew tired of blackjack and roulette and sought another diversion, or those whose trip to Havana had been for the sole purpose of buying a cheap pound of flesh. Just as Federico had said, Cuba was the little colony where every day was revolution or carnaval and people did what they pleased.

Delfino liked to walk farther, through Parque Central, which was always filled with pretty girls in the same line of business as the men at Plaza de la Catedral, and were slightly more discreet than their masculine counterparts. They wore the latest fashions, colorful, ruffled blouses that bared creamy brown shoulders and tight skirts. They didn't call out but fixed their eyes on men as if they could paralyze them with a look.

And when they did speak, they called him, "Señor."

The older, less attractive women could be found at the other end of the park. They were more aggressive. They grabbed at men's crotches and yelled out to them making their intentions unmistakable. They were noisy, desperate, and competitive with one another. They pulled each other back, ran each other down to get the business. They said terrible things about each other.

"You don't want her, she's crazy."

"She's contagious."

"She's pregnant."

"She'll rob you."

He would walk past them quickly, swatting them away like gnats, crossed the street to the Paseo del Prado, past lovers entwined in shadows on to Plaza de Armas, and beyond, past the docks, behind the tunnel entrance to Jaimanitas. Men gathered there late at night. These men were not after money, just pleasure. As much pleasure as they could pack into a few heart-pounding moments.

The place was so isolated and so thick with ceiba and framboyan trees, that couples could enjoy themselves without fear. And not just couples, groups often formed, men of all shapes, sizes and ages, quietly vying for position, elbowing their way in, eager to get their turn at the best looking morsel in the crowd. The group would grow, looking to

Delfino like something savage, as if a fly had accidentally wandered into a beehive.

It happened there, with the full moon shining through the branches of the framboyan trees and casting shadows that made him feel as if he was walking on an enormous lace mantilla.

One man's face stood out, as if the moonlight favored him above all the others, and Delfino felt his hand being taken, firmly. He let himself be led away from the pack, deeper into the thicket. Once alone, they tore into each other, a dazzling mass of fingers and tongues.

"My name is Felipe," the beautiful man said into his ear.

Delfino's heart was pounding so loudly he didn't have time to think of his other name.

The name of the night.

"Delfino," he whispered as teeth bit into his neck and every little hair on his body screamed. They were not alone. There were crickets and frogs, footsteps on dry twigs, wind through branches, waves lapping against a pier, and the horn of a distant liner, but he only heard the man's breath, or was it his own.

He turned and gave himself to the stranger and cast his eyes up through a clearing of branches, to the moon, the same moon that shined on Madrid and now shined in Havana. Behind him, he heard the man spit on his fingers, then felt the cool, wet sensation of his touch and when the man opened and filled him, he was suddenly convinced that all was good and pure, that the world was not the cesspool he had come to believe it was, but rather an enchanted playground of infinite possibilities.

As the gentle rhythm gave way to a frenzied, passionate dance, and the man (did he say his name was Felipe?) whispered magical words of love into his ears, Delfino knew without a doubt that his life was about to change again. And he could not wait.

So much of his life had taken place in the dark, behind closed doors, in forced silence.

After midnight.

The sun was beating on him, the crowds were cheering. He had never been happier in his life. He had Arjuna to thank for all this. Had they never met, at this very moment Delfino knew he would be at his father's house, packing the family's finery into trunks and suitcases, preparing for a one-way trip abroad, rushing to forsake his country. If he had allowed himself to be guided by his father, he never would have known this joyous satisfaction. For the first time in his life, Delfino felt like a real man, a grownup. Walking through the cheering crowds, arm in arm with the man he loved, Delfino felt ten-feet tall.

Arjuna was not looking at Delfino. His sights were set farther ahead, beyond all the cheering faces, the waving hands, the flags. Just steps ahead, high atop an army tank, Fidel Castro himself was cheering and waving back. Arjuna knew that this march across the island, from Oriente to Havana, would be hailed as one of the great marches in history. It sickened him to know that Fidel Castro, the reason everyone had taken to the streets, the man everyone was so excited to emulate and rally behind, whose footsteps they planned to follow into the future, had traveled by helicopter, had flown from point to point in comfort while everyone else walked, or bounced around in a jeep under the scorching sun. He knew that Fidel had only joined them earlier that day in Matanzas, just outside Havana.

Arjuna wished he didn't know so much, wished he was as happily ignorant as the millions along the parade route, but he wasn't. Fidel Castro's mode of transportation brought to mind Benito Mussolini's triumphal march into Rome. Il Duce had not marched at all, but had traveled by train, first-class, in opulent and unrepentant luxury.

The more he thought about it, the more the knot in Arjuna's gut drew tighter. Would the struggle never end? Was all the pain and bloodshed in vain? For the moment, he waved and smiled back, feeling the comfort of Delfino's hand on his shoulder. But the comfort was insubstantial. Arjuna hoped with all his heart that his misgivings about Fidel were unfounded, that his doubts were just typical of a man who was used to struggles, a man who had never accepted an easy victory, a man used to wondering what waits beyond what he's been shown, around the next corner, behind the closed doors. A man who had given up three fingers of his right hand for the revolution couldn't afford to take anything at face value. He resolved to play along for the moment, but silently vowed to keep a close eye on Fidel Castro. He continued on, waving, smiling, shouting the slogans, enduring the painful blisters and punishing calluses raised by the stabbing leather of his boots, the ceaseless and continuous cutting into his flesh.

40

Aspirrina's short, squat figure was precariously balanced on the sturdy hood of a jeep. She was thinner now, and had decorated herself with now-wilting sunflowers she had picked along the way. She was flanked by young, bearded, long-haired men, most of whom were bandaged and scarred, and much thinner than the ones on foot, but just as spirited and delighted to be alive and triumphantly parading through Havana.

This was a parade! What a joke it had been, Esteban's car and that struggling truck that had comprised Sabrosuras. All that honking of the two wheezing horns, the contortionists and the magician on top of the truck. Pathetic. It was hard for her to believe she had once been a part of such a disgrace, that she had once believed that if she had been ousted from Sabrosuras that her life would have come to an end. She had been so sure that each performance would be her last that she had agreed to watch over Estelita, just to make sure she had a place to dance, a place to display her art. What a laugh, what horrors that arrogant Esteban de la Cruz had put them through. Disappearing for days, no one knowing if he was dead or alive. The little girl in hysterics. The little girl missing in the morning, combing the streets and alleyways of strange towns looking for him.

But it had been that moment, when he'd winked at her, letting her know she had no other option, that had led to this, had brought her here, to this moment. Her life had been a series of moments, of sudden decisions – leaving her family, finding employment, getting involved with that worthless cretin, Diego Cervantes Murillo. The memory of him no longer hurt, it just made her nauseous. No matter, here she was, on top of the world.

As the jeep inched forward, she shook her wide hips and waved her flabby arms to rambunctious music only she could hear. Her smile so big it threatened to split her face wide open. Those who stood near clapped to her rhythm and she shook her fleshy breasts and shoulders at them, as if voluptuous currents were shooting through her. She was the firebrand she had always wanted to be. She was an audacious agitator dressed in someone's sweaty, olive-green military shirt. On her head, a black beret flirtatiously tilted above one eye, her face a circus of eye shadow, rouge and lipstick.

The soldiers in her jeep were singing, and she sang with them, leading them from song to song. This was the true moment she had worked for all her life, and particularly all those months up in the mountains. This was her moment of glory, and she was drinking it up, owning it, savoring every drop of adulation. She had traversed the island in full glory, through the same towns where she had played with Sabrosuras, where she had been jeered and mocked. She had looked at the smiling faces and wondered how many remembered her days in chiffon, her days when only anger and resentment against everything had fueled her dance. As they made their way through Campechuela, she had scanned the crowd for one man and one man only, there had been hundreds gathered at the dusty highway, but she did not see the one she hoped for. So many years had passed, would she even know him if she saw him? How much had he changed? What would he look like now? Probably a married man, with the big mustache and the bald, greasy pate typical of the provinces. She wondered if he ever thought of her. How could he not? She had been significant. As she had danced and waved and shouted, she imagined the look he would give her if he saw her, his eyes shaded by regret, an inconsequential woman at his side, just a small-town girl who was once pretty, and now, not even that, holding the hand of a snot-nosed kid or two. And here she was now, Apirrina Cerrogordo, the one that he had called a pig, at the pinnacle of the greatest event the island had ever seen.

She was shocking. She was glorious. And Diego Cervantes Murillo no longer mattered. Only Fidel Castro mattered now. He had made this happen for her. Fidel was her saint, her imaginary lover, her reason for living, he hadn't failed her. He had brought her back to the capital in style, on top of a jeep, surrounded by the fawning, grateful rebels she had helped bring back to life. All to the intoxicating rhythm of the cheering hordes. She was back in Havana now, where other ghosts tried to haunt her, but she chased away all thoughts of Esteban and Estelita de la Cruz, she was well rid of them.

Aspirrina was where she always intended to be, at the center of everything, dancing like the wind, alone and without music.

41

Night came slowly, a lingering rosy glow rested above the city until shadows at last descended, swooping down, a swift and noiseless shroud. A million people crowded into the sprawling plaza, eager to hear the heroes of the Revolution determine the future for them. The plaza was packed, but the rest of Havana was empty, a desolate city, a glorious ghost town.

The walls, still warm from the afternoon sun, stretched long and silent, winding and turning, sometimes disappearing entirely into complete and total darkness. The sidewalks were interrupted only by occasional lengths of muddy, unpaved patches of dirt covered with bottle caps and dry, yellowing weeds. Squares and rectangles of light streamed from vacant windows, embroidering the streets with luminous geometric patterns that followed one another, stretching on and on into infinite darkness. Soft shadows borne of the dim streetlamps extended along the cracked pavement, folding and dipping, molding themselves onto the terrain, wrapping around trees, creeping through gutters and dipping into watery, quivering potholes, elongating into the distance, pointing the way, offering vain direction like enormous, cautioning fingers.

For the moment, Esteban de la Cruz was content to sit with his woman at one of the outdoor tables, enjoying January's evening breeze and the emptiness. For the first time since he'd stumbled onto Calle Virtudes, at once hoping and dreading finding his daughter, there were no women on the sidewalk, nobody making lewd suggestions, or flashing a breast, or engaged in a hair-pulling, name-calling fight. Even in this far recess of the city, the thunderous applause coming from the plaza could clearly be heard. A million citizens clapping madly, two million fervent hands meeting in euphoric celebration.

He could hear Fidel Castro's virile voice, assured and unwavering, shooting through loudspeakers, followed by its own distorted, metallic echo. It bounced off rooftops, flowed into the winds and carried over all the oceans in all the world. Eleguá, too, had put on his whitest white suit and bounded out, his face shining with something that resembled hope.

"He's one of us," he'd shouted to Esteban, but it was more like a song. "I will turn into a dove and perch upon his shoulder."

Esteban had never been one to rush to anyone's celebration, he stayed behind, with Orquidea at his side. Every day he counted what he had, forced himself to appreciate what he had and tried to forget what he had lost. He had never been good with loss, Belquis' death had been his first and it had taken him down deep. Now, Estelita was gone and he may never get her back. He thought of her daily, but every day with diminishing anguish. The heart, he was discovering, adjusts, it contracts or expands to accept what joy or pain life has to offer. Now, it only hurt when he let his sights linger over a man and his daughter he might see on the streets – and he would be reminded, like a prod to his soul, of a time when he also had a girl, a girl he had seen every single day of his life. A girl he had taken as a trophy and then let slip through his fingers.

He would console himself with the thought that one day she would return. It could be tomorrow, it could be much later. He sometimes imagined that he was eighty-years old and living a quiet life, his memory of his losses as dim as if it had happened to someone else, as if it was a story he had once overheard, when there would be a knock at the door and a sixty-year-old woman would be there with eyes that mirrored his. She might have dyed red hair and gold hoop earrings, or she could be completely gray haired and holding herself up with a cane. She might have the glowing complexion of a life lived in luxury, or dull and ravaged by poverty and hardship. The first five minutes would be awkward, two strangers stumbling around each other's feelings, and then, as if no time had passed, she would be his daughter once again. She would be there to bury him when his time came, to weep over his grave.

Or she could be the next face he saw.

42

Estelita steadied herself and stepped back into the crowd. She could see the parade of men and women float by, the trucks and tanks, the bearded rebels and rough-looking women smiling and waving. She watched them catch the flowers that were tossed to them, and joyfully toss them back to the crowd.

A flower landed at her feet but she didn't have the stamina to pick it up, let alone toss it back. She had spent the night huddled in a doorway, eyes peeled, shivering even in the balmy air. Her neck hurt, her back hurt, she couldn't remember her last meal but the thought of eating made her stomach turn. Having seen enough of what seemed like an endless parade, she moved further back, squeezing through the crush, which easily parted and then reassembled like river water does around a protruding boulder, surrounding her, drowning her. She wanted out, she wanted back to the solitude of her hotel room, just long enough to gather her thoughts, to make her next plan. She had nothing, all her belongings had been confiscated, her nice dresses, her pretty shoes, her handbags and jewels, all the makeup she'd bought in Mexico, the bottles of perfume. All gone, she had nothing or less than nothing. She had no prospects. She found herself at the end of the sidewalk, her back against a wall. She tried to edge to either side, but there was no give. All she could see before her were flexing backs and bobbing heads, children perched atop shoulders, arms, so many arms, waving, waving in the air.

Above it all, on the other side of the parade, she could see balconies overflowing with people. More hands waving flags and handkerchiefs with delirium, others picked up babies and swayed them high over their heads. Above and beyond the buildings that flanked the avenue could be seen a glittering trio of modern glass towers –the Havana Hilton, the Capri Hotel, and her beloved Riviera, loomed tall and silent. Their hundreds of windows casting a melancholy gaze upon the ecstatic spectacle. Much further up, she saw the sky was a tender, bashful blue. She fixed her sights on that, for it was completely impervious to the madness below.

The parade continued towards the wide plaza, the crowd went with it. Estelita stayed behind, leaning back against the wall, for it was the only thing holding her up. The crowd, so boisterous just a few minutes before, began to dwindle. Her burning eyes scanned the avenue now empty, scarred by the heavy treads of the tanks.

She felt small, and insignificant and mournfully alone. She saw intimate reunions taking place in the middle of the increasingly desolate stretch of highway. Those who lagged behind found one another, gleefully shouting the names of their loved ones, of sons and daughters, fathers and uncles, expressing their gratitude to the Virgin and the Saints.

"Panchito," one woman shouted at a bearded youth while she ran and frantically made the sign of the cross over and over again, tears streaming down her face. "Soy yo! Soy yo! – It's me, Panchito!"

As the last one of the trucks passed, so filled with soldiers that its engine wheezed and groaned and its tires wobbled from the weight, she placed her palms behind her, feeling the hot roughness of the cement wall and pushed, willing herself away. She stood on quivering legs that no longer felt like her own, legs too weak to keep her standing, in fact, all of her body felt foreign to her, a disobedient mass at odds with her desire. Like someone facing a trek up the tallest mountain imaginable, she summoned all her energy just to take the first step. But where to? Perhaps the hotel, certainly someone would know something by now. How long had she been on her own now? It seemed like forever, without her father, without Aspirrina, sustained only by the memory of Juan Carlos and illusions of what could be. She took one more step, and then another.

And then she saw them. The prisoners. Dozens of them. Mostly men. Walking in lines. Their clothes dirty and tattered. Their heads hanging in shame. Their haggard eyes downcast. Their hands tied in front of them. Alongside walked armed rebels, their olive green uniforms starched, their boots shiny. A palpable air of sadness traveled with them. An angry few walked alongside of them. White-hot anger distorting their faces.

"Traitors," they shouted at the silent prisoners. "Murderers!"

Neither the prisoners nor the guards showed any emotion nor looked at those who shouted. Intermittently, a prisoner would make a sudden, involuntary move to avoid being hit with a rock or a piece of rotten fruit.

They walked slowly, much too slowly, and the guards kept pace with them. No one here was in a hurry to meet his destiny. Estelita looked at each grimy, unshaven face with compassion. Their complexions were dark and gritty from walking for hours under the unforgiving sun. What pernicious twist of fate, she wondered, separated these men from the heroes that preceded them? Then she saw him. He blended in perfectly. He was disheveled and filthy. His white shirt dark with grime, his black pants torn and barely hanging from his emaciated frame. For a moment she allowed herself to believe her tired eyes were playing tricks on her; she had to peer intently to make sure. But it was he. There was a very particular way he always held his shoulders; the carriage of royalty, she'd often thought.

Her heart slowed down and sent a thick knot to her throat – then it started again, at an accelerated speed, beating much too fast. Too much blood. She felt herself spinning out of control.

"Juan Carlos, Juan Carlos, it's me!" she cried, sounding, for the moment, like all the other women.

He couldn't hear her. Or wouldn't. She took up their stride. She pushed forward to walk alongside him, yelling out over the guards who stood between them.

"Juan Carlos, Juan Carlos!" she wailed, tears blinding her. But he wouldn't acknowledge her. He looked away. Only away.

"Where are you taking them?" she begged of the guard, venturing closer. But the guard pushed her back roughly, without so much as a word. She stepped back and yelled, this time so loud that the words tore at her throat.

"Juan Carlos!"

Finally, he turned. His stare met hers briefly, and for an instant, her heart rejoiced. But his eyes made a quick, almost imperceptible movement – *you don't know me* they said. *Go away. Pretend we never met.*

"Don't come any closer," the guards warned her. Her mouth was paralyzed, locked into a soundless, mournful wail. She tried but couldn't utter another sound. Unable to scream, she moved forward, ready to knock down the guard if she had to, she had to get to him. He seemed so small, so helpless. Diminished by shame.

She could see where the rope was cutting into his wrists. She would get at those ropes and chew through them. She would drop to her knees and put her arms around his legs. She didn't care what happened after that. Wherever he was going, she would go too. They could shoot her. They could cut her into little pieces and feed her to the dogs. She was willing to risk everything.

The men started moving faster, and she had to pick up her pace to stay with them. Her legs felt leaden. She stumbled on the cobblestones. A shoe came off and still she kept up, limping along. She kicked off her other shoe. Her eyes so thick with tears she barely could see where she was going. But she could see the lines of prisoners moving relentlessly forward.

People bumped into her, pushed her aside. She didn't care. Her eyes were fixed on the narrow space between two guards. Waiting for an opportunity, *the* opportunity. When it came, she would break through. She would lock her arms around her lover, meld herself to him. Wherever he went, she would go. Whatever they did to him, they would have to do to her. She walked faster, filling herself with courage, a crazy, inexplicable kind of courage. She was ready. In an instant, Estelita lunged for him. But someone had taken hold of her arm. She was immobilized, and she could only watch enraged as Juan Carlos continued moving forward, walking away from her. For an instant, so quick as to be imperceptible, he turned his head and looked back. His eyes, full of love and sorrow, met hers one last time. She could feel it inside of her.

"Let me go," she screamed, thrashing desperately. "Let go of my arm," Estelita growled, baring teeth like fangs, turning quickly, a furious panther ready to kill, to claw with her bare hands whoever was holding her back. The hand did not let go but rather, with a tug she was too weak to resist, it spun her around causing her heels to buckle.

Hands were at her shoulder, shaking her.

"Eres tu?" the man said. Is it you?

That voice.

She found she could barely see past her tears. She wanted to answer, to shout a resounding yes, but her throat had constricted and she felt her heart pounding, expanding inside her chest, choking her. She kept her eyes closed, afraid that if she opened them he would vanish or someone else would be there instead. Fingers were on her eyes wiping away her tears and his touch made her tears all the more painful, made her all the more aware of the grim procession behind her, beginning to feel as if her bones were being torn from her, leaving her a senseless mess of blood and sinew.

Her head felt heavy and she felt it drop, but the gentle fingers that had been caressing her cheeks as if they were something precious, something velvet and good, took hold of her chin and lifted her face into light. She kept her eyes closed and hot tears dropped in thick, hot streams down her face and when she finally opened them her vision was clear and she was staring into her father's face. Thinner now and creased but the eyes were the same, perhaps deeper or kinder or it could have been her own eyes that were seeing him differently, reflecting back infinite, incalculable love.

"Papá," she managed to whisper before exhaustion, like a shadowy, leaching vine crept up her legs and drained what little strength was left in everything it touched, her ankles, her knees, her hips, her spine. Joyfully, she folded herself into his arms, feeling the familiar body against her own, feeling the safety of his embrace. With Esteban's arms around her she felt safe to let go but she did not fall, she

3333

felt herself being lifted and carried, weightless as a child and for just one blessed moment, she let herself sink into a dark, sweet oblivion.

EPILOGUE

AFTER MIDNIGHT

1969

Ten years into the new regime and she was still in demand, to perform after the Birth of José Martí Celebration, and after the day celebrating victory at the Bay of Pigs. On the sad days, set aside for mourning the assassination of Comandante Che Guevara in Bolivia, and the one commemorating the disappearance of Comandante Camilo Cienfuegos, she wore no regalia and sang a mournful ballad. Whether it was a joyful or mournful occasion, she was always there with her father at her side. She greeted every new year with a particularly extravagant show, something nuevo y espectacular.

January1st, for most countries New Year's Day, but here it was Liberation Day, when the whole country took to the streets to enjoy endless speeches and countless promises. Once the politics were done, she would take the stage and set it on fire.

They lived in a small house, granted to her by the government after its owners had departed for Miami. She did not like the town she had been assigned to, Palmagria was as far from Havana as a girl could get, but she loved her house and regretted how little she saw of it, but when she was home she felt complete.

Sometimes she touched the walls, felt their cool façade just to make sure it was there, it was real. She walked from room to room, the furniture left behind was in her taste, just the furniture she would have bought had the house come empty. It was just as she had dreamed, except it was not near the sea. But it was close enough, and most importantly, she had her father with her. Her father, and the mysterious Orquidea, the woman who stayed.

She wasn't the woman Estelita had envisioned. Orquidea was shy and quiet, and spoke very little of her past. She wasn't a mother, much too late for that now. But, in spite of her nervous silences, her inability to look anyone in the eye, Estelita could see that she loved Esteban, and he adored her. In so many ways it was just as she had always wanted, her father and his wife in a bedroom next to hers, her father in an armchair in the living room softly strumming a guitar, or reading a newspaper. The clanking of pots and pans in the kitchen where Orquidea cooked her awkward meals, some just plain inedible. Still, it smelled of home. After dinner a game of dominoes or barajas, a visit on the front porch with neighbors.

She had neighbors!

Yes, all her dreams had come true, in a most unexpected manner as dreams tend to do. She was grateful. If there had been no Revolución, if there had been no parade, if Juan Carlos had not been trotted down the streets for the traitor that he was, she never would have found her father.

She had the Revolución to thank for their reunion and for everything. They traveled in a much newer car now, also granted by the government, also left behind by a deported Cuban. Every weekend they filled it with her paraphernalia, feathered costumes, multicolored shoes, makeup, their whole ambulatory life stacked on top and hanging from the side. They went wherever they were told and every time she gave it her all. She had come too far, worked too hard to let even the hint of incompetence take it all away.

There had been men, but none of them lasted, they couldn't keep up with her and in her heart she knew that no one could ever replace Juan Carlos. At first she thought about him every day, but little by little she began to let go, to wish him well whenever he drifted into her thoughts. He had not been the man she thought he was, but everything had turned out so differently than she had anticipated back when she had been so young, so open. She kept the diamond earrings and never took them off. They became so much a part of her that she often forgot she had them on, until someone commented.

"Que precioso tus arêtes." What lovely earrings. And for a moment, when her fingers went to her earlobes she was back in that hotel room, with that man, in the dark. That world was gone but the new one gave her so much comfort. Comfort, she had decided, was more important than happiness, more important than passion, or love.

She had Esteban, who still pulled the car over and stopped at beaches whenever time allowed, and she'd jump into the clear blue water while he watched her from the shore remembering the days when he'd spend hours tinkering with the car's engine.

Look papá, I'm a dolphin, I'm a mermaid.

This car ran to perfection and her father could relax under an umbrella or walk the beach collecting shells and sand-polished rocks for his altar. She knew little of his practice and only requested that he do it in the privacy of his room, away from prying eyes. After a dip in the sea, they traveled on to places at once familiar and strange, all the places she'd seen in her childhood: Cierro Gordo, Palos Altos, Suspiros.

Her audiences, overjoyed by the enthusiastic clatter and fanfare of their arrival, the honking of horns, waving of arms, smiling of faces, lifting of dust off the road and the promise of something nuevo y espectacular – welcomed them with joyous applause and shouts of Viva la Revolución. Viva! She shouted back, Esteban did not.

Some of the farmers were familiar with Esteban de la Cruz, the rumbero who had once blazed so brightly then vanished. But, Esteban was not the man he once was, he no longer performed, gone were the rumba and the jokes, and the preening arrogance that once set hearts aflutter. At the moment, *she* was the main attraction, a young woman named Estelita de la Cruz who sang and danced while her father beamed with pride from the sidelines, who sang and danced as if the stiff military uniform she wore was made of silk and lace.

"Tiene algo," people whispered. She's got something.

"She was a big star in Havana, before everything changed."

"She's still lovely."

"At a distance..."

About The Author

Eduardo Santiago was born in Cuba and grew up in Los Angeles and Miami. He holds a BFA from the California Institute of the Arts and a Creative Writing MFA from Antioch University. He is also a two-time PEN Emerging Voices Fellow (2004 and 2010). His novel, *Tomorrow They Will Kiss* (Little, Brown and Co.), took best historical novel and best first book honors at the 2007 International Latino Book awards and was a finalist for the Edmund White Award for debut fiction. His shorter work of fiction and nonfiction have appeared in the Los Angeles Times, The Advocate, zyzzyva, Out Traveler, One For The Table, The Platte Valley Review and many other prominent publications. Mr. Santiago teaches creative writing for U.C.LA.'s extension program and is the founder and curator of the Idyllwild Authors Series.

ACKNOWLEDGEMENTS

The list is endless but I would be remiss if I didn't mention some of the friends and colleagues who helped me complete this novel either by reading early drafts or simply offering much needed support.
I am deeply indebted to Ann Parris, who proofread this novel when it was 800 pages long (while we sailed around the world aboard the Queen Elizabeth 2). My dear friend George Snyder helped me settle on a title and gave me great advise. B.J. Robbins read and critiqued countless drafts. More recent readers who contributed to the end product you hold in your hands, Diana Wagman, Carlos Portugal, Betty Anderson, Alan Carter and PEN Center U.S.A.
Huge thanks to my young and brilliant friend, Allison Strauss, who created the awesome cover and put up with my endless indecisions.
Finally, a sincere expression of gratitude to the men and women "in the rooms" who make it possible for me to finish what I start.

There are others, you know who you are, and how much I love you.

Eduardo Santiago

40658644R00256

Made in the USA
Charleston, SC
08 April 2015